BURN

DARK ISLAND SCOTS, #4

Jolie Vines

WWW.JOLIEVINES.COM

BLURB

I'd wreck his life. For mine, he'd burn down the world.

Jamieson was my penpal.

My first crush. My surf-crazy, impulsive, pyro boy, and the secret I kept from the world.

Until he broke us up before we ever met.

When I discover he's been imprisoned by an evil man, saving him becomes my only goal.

Except his enemy wants me too.

He was fire and water. With him, I'd either drown or burn.

Burn (Dark Island Scots, #4) brings this smexy and thrilling series to a breathtaking finish. This is Jamieson and Summer's romance, so expect fiercely passionate scenes between a plus-sized heroine and her fire-loving, reckless hero.

With nothing left to lose, our tribe of found family have to risk it all to end the war against them.

READER NOTE

Dear reader,

Thank you for picking up Burn. This is not a stand-alone, and you should start at the beginning of the Dark Island Scots series with Ruin.

Please be aware this series contains darker themes, including CNC (consensual non consent), predator-prey play, threats of violence to a child, death, and accounts of sexual assault. Plus all kinds of danger. A full list is on my website

https://www.jolievines.com

If you're an audio fan, you'll love to hear Zara Hampton-Brown and Zachary Webber conclude the story with their swoony narration.

Happy reading,

Jolie

1

Summer

It was strange, the object I fixated on in my weeks of being a prisoner.

Left alone for much of the time, it wasn't underwear or a shirt I wanted most, though that would've been nice. No, my obsession was for my lost pendant. A gift given to me on my fourteenth birthday.

Small, silver, with a little surfer in a circle.

My pen pal had sent it to me, and I'd worn it as a charm.

For all my lack of clothes, it was the thing I felt naked without.

Instinctively, my hand went to touch the space where it should've been, even as my focus was fixed on the woman in front of me. The one who'd removed my handcuffs and led me out of my locked cell and to a staffroom, halfway to rescuing me from this hellhole of a mansion.

Divine, who I guessed to be a sex worker from her long red wig and see-through négligée, was a friend of my sister's and had known I was missing. Her help was to repay a favour. She wanted me to make a break for a garden exit.

My impulsive mind had other ideas, because seconds ago, she'd told me news that had stopped me in my tracks.

I wasn't the only captive of police chief, Daniels.

In a station somewhere, he held a man accused of arson. Of burning down the house of another rich old pervert. His other prisoner was a vigilante, like me.

The chief intended to harm him.

It should be none of my business. I had to get out of this house, into the dark summer night and away across the remote Scottish countryside. I should be running for my life, not questioning my rescuer.

Except, impossibly, I knew the man she was talking about.

"Which police station?" I asked.

"Inverness." She narrowed her cat eyes, her voice low. "Hold up, sis. Why do you care?"

"I know him. Jamieson. He's a friend."

The pen pal.

My teenage crush.

We'd exchanged daily voice messages, and his energy matched mine but with a side of crazy I'd adored. He'd broken things off a year ago, and though that stung, I'd guessed there was more to the story than he'd told.

Seemed like I was right.

Divine darted an anxious look at the door. "So? Sorry to say, but that man's toast. He isn't going to last the night."

"You mean the chief will kill him?"

She folded her arms over her boobs. "Sure as shit, he

will. The cops who caught him at the scene of the fire are loyal. He's kept your arsonist friend hidden at the station, and the other pigs know better than to ask. All he needed was for McInver to wake and give him the go-ahead. That's where he's gone now—to the old man's hospital bed, so the clock is ticking. Do you think either of them will spare a guy who did what he did? Nope. He'll be disappeared into the same black hole as the last guy who crossed them. And the one before that. You see the pattern."

Panic clawed up my throat.

I had nothing. No money, no car, no working phone, as the one I'd found in the staffroom had powered down in front of my eyes, not even shoes. An old hunter's jacket I'd stolen covered my nudity. Weeks of being tied up had left me terrified and shaky. Even so, the flame of my impulsivity I'd thought dead flickered.

"He can't die. I need to do something."

Divine stepped over to the exit and poked her head out, subtly checking if the coast was clear. She jumped then darted back and flapped a hand. "Hide. People are coming."

I ducked behind the sofa, heart pounding.

Divine hid with me. My pulse thudded in my ears, much faster than the footsteps outside.

The voices passed us by.

Sitting on the cold floor with her knees bent elegantly to the side, Divine came back to me, her expression sympathetic but set. Her words were almost silent but deadly serious. "I don't care if this Jamieson is the King of England. I didn't rescue your ass for you to jump straight into a fight you can't win. You can't help him. Understand me? You're lucky to be alive yourself. Your sister has been turning the world upside down to find you. She even put herself up for auction to follow you."

I clapped my hands to my mouth, horrified that Breeze would've done that. I'd sold myself at a virginity auction to access the dark places where people traffickers operated. To gather information. I'd never intended to actually end up in the claws of one of the men. I'd been betrayed then abandoned, and I only had myself to blame for that.

The idea that my sister had followed was unbearable.

"Is she okay?" I asked, my voice wavering.

Divine pulled my hands down and held them. "She's fine. She needs you back with her and safe. But listen to me. The minute you get out of the mansion, you'll be on the security cameras. He'll know you've run, though he won't be sure who helped you or I'd be hung from the front gate as a warning to all others. You can't underestimate the power of that man. Not only does he own the law here, he has so many people in his pocket with bribes or blackmail. You can't win against him. You can't call other police forces in. No judge will order his arrest. His reach is everywhere. He's going to be angry, and he might chase you down." She flicked her gaze down my body and back up. "He never fucked you, did he?"

I shook my head in the negative and slumped against the back of the sofa, the dark, quiet room hiding my anguish. He'd threatened it, but for his own reasons had held off, tormenting me in other ways instead.

Too much time had passed for him simply to use me like he did other women and let me go.

It had broken me. Before, I'd lived in my impulses. Throwing myself into all kinds of shit I felt passionate about.

I'd thought that part of me gone, but that was until to-night.

I was free. Almost.

Divine clucked her tongue. "Better if he had, then you won't be the one who got away. Nothing we can do about that now. If you take my advice, don't go home. Don't go trying to rescue no Jamieson. Hide somewhere and stay hidden for as long as you can. He'll give up eventually. His interest in women doesn't last, and there will be some pretty new thing that he'll buy up to torture instead."

Everything she said was right. The police chief was a dangerous, vicious man. I had the chance to get away from him tonight and not look back. I'd find Breeze, and we could work out a way to live.

But that meant giving up on my pen pal.

It was my life for his. Or maybe my life versus both of us winding up dead.

If I went after him, the guy I'd thought of as my boy-friend for so long, I'd have to waltz straight into the police station where the chief worked. There would be cops by the dozen, cameras, locked doors. I had exactly no hope of free-ing a prisoner from his cell.

But the idea wouldn't quit.

It centred on the promise Jamieson and I had made to each other at the age of fourteen and repeated every year since.

Save me from myself if I go too far.

Always.

Well, he'd destroyed that commitment, so I had, too.

I squeezed Divine's hands then posed one last desperate question. "Come with me? I'm scared that you'll be in trouble for letting me go. I don't want you to stay."

Her scarlet-red lips thinned in an unhappy smile. "No, sis. This world isn't for you, but it's all I've got. I need the money, and there's other reasons for me to stay. I'll be fine. Promise. Say hi to Breeze when you find her. Tell her we're quits now."

Leaving her here felt wrong, but I had no choice. I released her, my target the staffroom door.

The garden exit was metres away down the corridor.

I only had one chance.

But as I stood from my hiding place, shock gutted me.

A man sat across the room on a sofa.

One leg resting on the other. Head cocked. His curious, knowing expression told me he'd been well aware that we were here. While we were hiding, he'd walked in and sat down, and neither of us had even heard him.

The chief's eyes stared right back at me.

2

Jamieson

Raised voices echoed outside my cell. I paced, glowering at the door.

I'd grown used to the rhythm of the police station, so something was off. Only two cops ever came to check on me or bring food. One I'd named Charmaine and the other Detective Dickhead. Whoever was shouting in the corridor wasn't them.

I moved to the door and listened, my blood still rushing from my brother's visit yesterday. I was furious. Ready to smack down.

Broken-fucking-hearted.

"…lock broke. It needs replacing," the stranger's voice said. "Not an easy repair. I can't do it now."

A maintenance guy, at a guess. What the hell did they need fixing in the middle of the night?

Charmaine grumbled something I couldn't make out before adding, "I need to talk to the detective in charge. Give me a minute."

A pause followed, then she spoke into her phone. She had to be directly outside my cell now as every word was clear.

"Hello? We have a problem. The exit door to the chief's personal wing is broken. The guy is saying it can't be fixed until morning."

After a beat, she gave a dark laugh. "Tonight? There was me thinking we'd have the pleasure of the little shit's company for a while longer. Can I watch?"

Had to be Detective Dickhead she was talking to.

What was happening tonight?

A chill ran down my spine.

Charmaine's voice returned louder, off the call now, I guessed. "We need access to these cells. Tonight. You have an hour."

The maintenance guy huffed. "That's insane. It means cutting through the metal. You need to move your inmates."

"There's only one person down here, and he'll be gone soon. If you hear any complaints, ignore it. You're here for one job. Just get it done."

The maintenance guy muttered something back, then the heavy interior door to the corridor whooshed—presumably Charmaine leaving—the clink of tools following.

Clenching my fists, I tried to force myself to think rather than just succumbing to the blind fury that had overtaken me.

When I'd been brought to my cell, we'd avoided the main front entrance, coming directly down a corridor and into this room. The only other part of the police station I'd seen was an interview room when my brother had managed to get in to see me.

This wing had its own exterior door.

A door which was busted on a night when I was apparently going to be taken from here.

My lips curved, and I gave up a silent laugh, resting against the unpainted concrete wall. My time was up. Detective Dickhead was coming for me, and Charmaine planned to watch. It couldn't be for anything good.

I'd lost interest in knowing my rights. They'd walked all over them from the minute I'd arrived. No phone call, no fingerprints taken, no record of me being here, only two cops keeping tabs on me. I went long stretches without even hearing another voice, and if I wasn't fucked in the head already, it could've driven me insane.

My brothers were pulling for me. Camden had got in here by calling himself McInver's son, which was a fucking joke, as although the old bastard had fathered all of us, none of us would take his name without very good reason.

Like trying to rescue me.

I swallowed back my regret that they wouldn't be successful.

It was better for them that I took the fall, and they had the chance of happier lives than the shitshow of our upbringings. Sin and Lottie would raise our little sister like she was their daughter. Struan and Thea would take on the world together. Camden...

I'd fallen on him in a hug designed to appear like a fight. A wave of unwanted grief hit me at that last contact.

Tonight I'd probably die. I hated that they'd hear it and mourn me.

Worse was the person who might never find out what happened. After spending a year trying to forget her, I'd had way too much time alone in my cell to think about Summer.

For so long, she'd been my endgame. The reason why I'd never even looked at another girl beyond spank bank material. Like me, Summer had spent time in foster care and had a mother who sold herself to men for money. We shared late nights talking about our hatred of the game.

I'd become obsessed.

Still was.

I'd saved myself for her. That last act would die with me.

She'd gone missing, and her sister and Camden were hunting her. Maybe she was dead, too. Maybe I'd finally meet her in some afterlife.

That thought brought my anger back with a vengeance.

Fuck the people who'd hurt her.

Fuck the cops who were right now making plans to deal with me.

For Summer's sake and mine, I was going out fighting. Bring it on, motherfuckers. I'd burn them all to the ground.

3

Summer

Divine slowly stood at my side, her arms out in panic. "Arran. Shit. I didn't hear you come in."

Arran. Son of the police chief. The eyes I'd focused in on were his, not his father's.

Even so, my hope broke apart.

I'd never met him but had heard the staff talk about him. His dad intended him to follow in his footsteps.

We were screwed.

Arran gazed at us, his neutral expression giving nothing away, the image of a cut-jawed, cruel rich boy. "I got that, otherwise you wouldn't have been telling her to run. Not in my earshot. My father's favourite releasing his plaything. What do you think will happen when he finds out?"

Divine opened her mouth but thought better about whatever she was going to say. The panic left her, and she turned a bolder stare on Arran.

I looked between them.

There was no chance of me getting away now. Arran

would march me back to my room and chain me up again. Worse—Divine had been seen helping me. She was in danger, too.

Except there was something strange about the energy in the room.

A tension between the two in their glaring contest.

I didn't get it. Divine wasn't jumping to defend or distance herself, or offer something to him in exchange for his blind eye. I couldn't let her get hurt for helping me. This was my doing, and I had to fix it.

I stepped in front of her but addressed Arran. "Divine hasn't done anything wrong. She needs to go back upstairs so she's there when your father returns."

"You're so much like your sister," she whispered.

Arran's attention leapt to me. "Does she now? Tell me, runaway, who's Jamieson?"

Dread crept into me. He'd overheard our conversation. "A friend."

"My father's prize catch," he stated. "How the hell would you know him? A call girl and an arsonist."

I pressed my lips together. The boy's cold mask slipped. Emotion boiled under his surface. I readied for a fight. For him to try to take a piece of me.

To get out of here, I'd risk my life.

After that, I could fall apart.

Cool fingers wrapped around my biceps, and Divine moved me aside. Calm authority exuded from her. "Summer isn't a call girl, so don't give her that judgemental shit. I know you don't like what your father does. Don't act like you're going to defend him."

Arran scowled at her.

He was maybe seventeen or eighteen, a little younger than me. Divine's dressing-down made him seem younger still.

"Don't act like you know anything about me," he retorted.

Divine continued. "Don't I, though? You're not like your dad. Never once have you been with any of the girls he brings in. You paid off Alisha to lie and tell him you fucked her. She comes here, sits in your room, and takes your money for doing nothing but playing video games with you."

He clenched his jaw. "Alisha should've kept her mouth shut."

"She did to anyone important, but you can't hide that kind of thing from a pro. And by that I mean professional."

Despite the fact that she was naked beyond the see-through nighty, inches shorter than him and half his weight, my new friend packed a punch with her words.

The authority in the room shifted her way.

She tucked her long red curls behind her ear and popped a hip. "I'm trained in working out exactly what a man likes and exploiting it. It's my job. I never instructed any of the girls to go after you because it was plain you weren't anything like your daddy. Then this evening, you helped McInver's son leave. The chief said to keep him here, but you drove him away in your fancy car. Wasn't that because you don't approve of the women he buys and the activity that goes on here? Camden agrees with you. The sons are not like the fathers."

"So what if I don't approve? I'm not the one in charge."

"Please, Arran. We're on the same side. You hate what I do but you can't hate this woman for wanting to escape. You dislike your father's choices so much you acted against him already once this evening. If you're regretting it, don't let us be the way you make up for it."

"Camden needed to go see his dad," Arran muttered back, but there was less venom in his words now. A confusion entering the mix.

My mind leapt to a conclusion, and I blurted out my thoughts. A fact I'd learned from reading my sister's emails before the phone I'd found died. "Camden? Jamieson's brother? He was here?"

Arran blinked at me. "Camden isn't…"

Realisation dawned in his expression, and he whirled away, giving up an outraged gasp. "Fucking hell. Right under my father's nose. That ballsy bastard."

There was another connection I hadn't voiced.

Camden was my sister's boyfriend. My sister was dating the brother of the man I'd spent years secretly talking to. Somehow, two worlds had collided in ways I could barely understand.

Divine watched him, calculation in her gaze. "They're brothers? When your father finds out you released him, he's going to lose his mind."

Arran dug his fingers into his dark-blond hair. "I didn't know. He didn't tell me. But why does it matter to you?"

I couldn't tell if this man was an ally or an enemy. Probably somewhere in between. But he had a car, and motivation to act against his father.

I snuck a look at Divine and tried to control my voice

so it didn't wobble. "You did the right thing for Camden. Where did you take him?"

"Not to his father's bedside, like I assumed he wanted. He asked to be returned to his car, then I watched him drive out of Inverness. He spoke to someone on the phone and had to rush off for some emergency."

If Camden had left Inverness, he wasn't around to help Jamieson. Maybe didn't even know about the current threat. I could be wrong, but I couldn't rely on that.

I worked faster to pull the pieces together, but it was like I was in the dark with a torch picking out tiny, individual bits of information. "Your father's going to kill Camden's brother tonight. He told Divine so. The servants were gossiping about it, too. We can't let him die."

Arran rolled his shoulders. "You don't know my father, what he's capable of and how far he'll go. He makes statements like that. He tells people so they cower, because if you make the mistake of assuming he's grandstanding, you're in for a shock. If he said he's going to walk into that police station and slit your friend's throat, no one will be able to stop him. He can paint the room red or he can fake a suicide. Whatever he chooses, you're already too late."

An echo of what Divine told me of the man's ruthlessness.

The woman moved closer to Arran and set her hand on his shoulder, tilting her head with a beseeching expression. "We might be, but you're not. Not if the chief hasn't left McInver's hospital room yet. You know him better than anyone, and you know your way around Inverness police station. You, Arran Daniels, heir to the Kendrick name and estate, are the only person who can stop this happening."

He worked his jaw, his expression troubled. "Tell me why I should. Tell me why I should care about saving this man."

She gifted him a soft smile. "Because this is who you're supposed to be. For the sake of your mother, you need to stand against your dad."

Outside the mansion, I sprinted for the sports car Arran had pointed out. From the staffroom cupboard, Divine had found me leggings and a pair of old All-stars. Not my size, but at least I had shoes now, along with the random lighter and rolling tobacco I'd discovered in my jacket pocket. I'd tucked my blonde hair under the hood of the hunter's coat but was under no illusion that the chief wouldn't know who I was on any security footage. With my thick thighs and curvy body, I was built different. Distinctive.

Keeping low, I crept to the car, popped the passenger door, and dove inside to conceal myself on the rear seats. After the longest five minutes ever, Arran sauntered out and climbed into the driver's seat, starting the engine with a roar. He peeled out of the car park and down the road without hesitation.

Our plan was of deniability. As things stood, there was no evidence of Divine helping me, and Arran was an innocent bystander, not realising I'd stowed away in his car.

Whatever else happened was on each of us as individuals.

Darkness eclipsed me in my hiding place. I cringed in on myself, balanced on the edge of insanity. I couldn't keep up with how quickly things had changed. I had expected to die, then been revived by the chance of escape, and skyrocketed by the need to help Jamieson.

Without that goal burning in me, I'd collapse.

As soon as I found my sister...

I took a rush of breath. "Arran, I need to make a call. Can I borrow your phone?"

He kept his gaze on the road but patted his pockets. "It's in the bag. You can sit up now."

I cautiously drew myself upright and peeked out of the windows, seeing only darkness, then reached for Arran's rucksack. In the low light, I rifled through the contents. A ribbon of material proved to be a lanyard with an identity pass on it. Beneath that was some items of clothing, a bottle of water, and packets of food.

"What's all this?"

He gave a strained laugh. "I grabbed a few things from my room. I've never done a prison break before but figured your dangerous friend will need a change of clothes from the jumpsuit they'll have put him in. Then I added one or two other things."

Until this moment, I wasn't sure if he was going to help free Jamieson. Emotion rushed in me, but I swallowed it down.

Couldn't break now.

I continued my hunt but came up empty for a phone. Instead, my knuckles brushed against a heavy metal object at the bottom of the bag. I withdrew my hand with a yelp. "Is that a gun?"

He gave a fast nod.

"Do you even know how to shoot it?" I shoved the bag

away from me.

"Of course I do. My father taught me."

My lip curled in horror. Guns like that were illegal. A small number of hunters or gamekeepers could have a rifle or maybe a shotgun. If we were even seen with a handgun, an armed response team would descend before we could blink. Then my brain caught up, and I spluttered a laugh.

"Arran, were you really planning on walking into a police station with a gun?"

"Shit. No. I don't know what I was thinking. Even I couldn't get away with that." He scrubbed his face, darting a look at me. "What are your ideas?"

That I was wildly out of control. That I couldn't see a way for this to work. That if it didn't, the worst would happen.

"I don't have any. I didn't know about any of this until thirty minutes ago." I massaged my wrists, lines indenting them from the handcuffs. "Tell me what you know about the station."

"Lots of people work there."

"Any idea how many?"

"No, I never counted."

I held back a sigh. "Is the building old or new?"

He raised a shoulder. "New, I guess. It's not a prison, but there's high walls and barbed wire."

Scenarios rose and fell behind my eyes. What I wouldn't give to remember any of the episodes of Prison Break I'd binge-watched once.

My frustration spilled over. "How the hell am I going to

enter a well-guarded police station and walk out with a man who's under lock and key?"

Arran clicked his fingers. "What if he was being transferred out? You could be a prison guard escorting him to jail."

"I'd need a uniform, a prison van, ID, some kind of paperwork."

Confidence and poise I didn't possess.

He *hmmed.* "No time for any of that. What if there was a riot in the city and all the officers had to leave to go control it? That might distract my dad for a while, too."

I opened and closed my mouth. That actually wasn't a bad idea for clearing some of the bodies from out of our way. "How do we cause a riot?"

He gave another shrug. "No clue. Got any gangster friends?"

"I don't know anyone in this city."

"As a plan, this is pretty weak."

The bright lights of Inverness appeared ahead, and we both went quiet as Arran navigated the streets. Soon, we were off the main road and down a slip road.

"The police station," he said.

I stared at the solid brick building. Plenty of cars were parked outside. Cameras scanned the vicinity. In the windows, office lights illuminated people moving around inside. It was three AM, but the place wasn't quiet.

Jamieson was in there.

My heart thumped unevenly. Would I even recognise him? We'd never met in person, except I'd memorised his face. Watched it change from a skinny boy to a too-handsome man.

I'd know him.

The reassurance came as fast as the fear.

Arran gazed up at the building. "My father's territory. He controls everyone here. Even the by-the-book cops are terrified of him. That building next door? It's the county court. Dad has at least one judge in his pocket, too."

"And Jamieson is locked in a cell. He might as well be a million miles away."

"It helps that he's in a room with no CCTV on the corridor."

My jaw dropped. "Why didn't you say that before?"

"I'm just working it out. My father has a set of rooms that aren't used by the rest of the station. One or two cells, a meeting room, no cameras in case he's processing someone like your friend. His private interrogation suite." A shiver ran over him. "I can't believe I'm even telling you this."

If he lost it now, I had no way of getting in. "You're doing the right thing," I said, but my voice trembled. "Where is this suite?"

Arran pulled away from our parking place and rounded the building. The front side was taller at three stories high, and to the right of that was an electronic gate, a couple of single buildings behind it.

"That's Dad's office." He pointed to the top of the main block to a darkened room, then dragged his finger down to indicate behind the gate. "And that's the interrogation suite."

A single-storey building. The gate was climbable, the

yard around it in shadows.

"That's where you think he's being held?"

"I know it."

My pulse sped a little faster, churning up blood that just wanted to freeze. After this, I'd shut down. Sleep for a week. Hide until I could start to process all I'd been through.

"If we can get Jamieson out of the building," I said, "jumping that gate and running to the car is the easy part. How are you at breaking and entering?"

As I spoke, headlights passed us, and a vehicle parked right outside the station. A tall man climbed out and lit a cigarette, lingering by his door.

Arran stiffened.

"Who's that?" I asked.

"Kenney. A detective and my father's right-hand man. If he sees my car, he'll come over. Shit."

Alarm added to my already thumping heart rate. The guy was fifty metres away but examining his phone rather than us.

"Can you drive away?"

"Fuck, I can't. He knows my car. He'll message my dad and say I'm here. I bet he already has." He shot me an apologetic look in the rearview mirror. "I'm going to need to talk to him. Explain why I'm here in the middle of the night."

From my dark hiding place, I watched the detective. "Isn't that going to bring your father here quicker?"

"I don't know. Not for my sake, but think about it. He's not here for a nightshift. Dad's called him in to help with your friend."

Icy fear slid through my veins. "Meaning our time is almost up."

Arran gave a single jerk of his chin. "I can't help you now. I wasn't joking when I said my father would kill me if I'm caught working against him. I need to go and talk to Kenney and play it out like I'm meant to be here. But I have no chance of walking through that building unspotted."

Which meant I had to do it.

I balanced for a second on absolute panic, every sense screaming at me to run. But my time as a captive had done more than break me. I'd lost my reason, too.

I couldn't walk away.

"Tell me exactly how to find the room," I whispered.

Arran snatched up the bag and thrust it to me. "Dad's pass is in there. Go to the gate, scan the ID, and enter the code into the keypad. It's six-six-six three-two-one. You'll be on camera, so if anyone is watching at that second, and they see you don't match the ID presented, you're on a fast countdown of being intercepted. Once you're in the yard, the station's side entrance is dead ahead."

"Can't I go straight into the interrogation suite?"

"I don't know the code for it. You have to use the staff door. The same pass will work there, but you'll have to dodge people in that corridor. Take the first right, then go through the coded door at the end. No one else goes in there apart from my dad and two of his closest team. Reverse the code for that one."

"Got it," I lied. My brain was so messed up, I didn't know if I could recall it all. "I need you to distract that detective."

"Exactly what I was going to say. I'll pretend I need to talk to him about something and get him indoors and away from this side of the building."

I took a second to let my total fear grip me then subside. Likewise, Arran stared dead forwards, keeping his attention on the detective who made a phone call.

"Don't go home after," I said in a rush. Like with Divine, he was in danger for helping me.

"Even if I had somewhere else to go, it would be pointless. I tried running when I was younger and I always got brought back. I can't escape him like you can."

My heart sank. My chances were slim to none but still better than his.

The detective pulled his phone from his ear and pressed the screen, presumably ending his call.

My stomach cramped from butterflies at what I had to do next. My fright all-encompassing.

Arran put his hand on the door handle, poised to leave on his half of the mission. "Give me a second to walk him inside, then go. If you get into the wing, open your friend's door, throw the bag into him, then run. If you're together, you've got no chance of getting out. If you clear the building, he might be able to do the same."

"Can you leave me the car keys?"

"And have every cop know exactly what you're driving? Don't talk crazy. Run, don't look back, and hide."

Arran climbed out and slammed the door, leaving it unlocked. He waved at the detective, but I missed the exchange as I hid my head, shaking from fear.

I couldn't breathe, but I always knew my loyalty came

above anything else. Safety. Common sense. Even air.

After a minute, I peeked again.

The coast was clear.

Reaching into the bag, I extracted the gun using my sleeve, carefully wiped it to smudge out any prints I'd left, and placed it under the seat. Then I opened the door and took my first step towards freeing my first and only love.

4

Jamieson

Fire had been my obsession since I'd watched a shed burn down when I was three or four years old. The flames took what they wanted. All they needed was an ignition point then they climbed, and licked, and ate.

The blackened remains they left were beautiful.

A rumour on the housing estate had been that the shed was the place where a kid had been taken to be abused. My impressionable mind had locked on to that method of cleansing. The sweetness of that revenge. I'd dealt my own vengeance in flames in the years after.

When other kids had perfected their skills in videogames, I'd learned how to start a fire. With or without matches or an accelerant, where to set it to give it the best chance of living, and how to hide my tracks.

The only real skill I'd ever learned aside from surfing waves or boosting cars.

Like I'd told Detective Dickhead when he'd taken me to the ground after I'd set fire to McInver's mansion, arson was hard to prove.

What was harder was how long I'd been in here without my Zippo.

I'd taken chunks out of my cell's concrete wall in an attempt to look for embedded stone. Flint and steel produced a spark. There was nothing here to catch alight—all materials plastic, all cloth polyester, but I needed that flare of life. It was the only way I'd ever felt in control.

No sound came from outside in the corridor. The repairs on the exit door had quietened.

I had this teasing image of it propped open, or even off the hinges. Freedom just metres away.

Something clicked outside—the corridor's interior door release. I knew the heavy thump of the usual cops' footsteps and the clink of the maintenance guy.

These were different.

Someone walking almost silently.

A slight intake of breath outside my cell. Fumbling fingers at my locked door.

No peeking through the little window or giving me orders to stand back. They were in a rush.

I held steady, squaring my shoulders.

This was it. They'd come. Tonight I was going to die, but I would take at least one of the bastards down with me.

The lock released. I balled my fists.

I rushed it as it swung open, colliding with a body and knocking them down.

From the floor, a terrified, wide-eyed woman stared at me. My world came to a staggering halt.

A fucking hallucination.

Almost the same pretty face as the lass I'd seen with Camden at McInver's mansion, but different. Perfect.

Mine.

Except she couldn't be Summer. Summer was missing. This was the sister my brother had helped escape McInver's mansion. The one he'd gone crazy over who I'd thought was Summer until he'd set me right. I was confused and making mistakes.

"Are ye Breeze?" I asked.

"No," she uttered in a voice that was so familiar.

But her eyes showed her pain at my error.

Summer. Could only be. I'd lost my fucking mind.

Summer's ghost jumped to her feet. A sound came from somewhere inside the police station, and she snapped her gaze down the corridor.

I stood there like I was frozen. Not helping her. Not *believing* in her.

"Take this." She shoved a rucksack at me. "You need to run."

Finally, my muscles released, and I unhinged my jaw. "How the fuck—?"

"There's no time to explain. We'll be safer if we split up."

She made for the entrance into the main police station building, but I lurched forward and snatched her around the waist.

The first time we'd touched apart from me knocking her down. It broke my mind. I'd vowed to myself that if ever we met, I'd never let her go.

Somehow, Summer was rescuing me. She'd been in trouble, but she'd made it here.

We needed to both get out alive.

"This way." I swung her in the other direction, passing the meeting room and another cell. Around the corner at the end of the corridor was the broken exit. If I couldn't open it, I'd wasted precious seconds.

But as we made the turn, a man stood ahead of us, and we screeched to a halt.

Blue uniform. Tool belt.

The maintenance guy stared at us, a heavy metal object in his hand and the door closed beside him.

Holy fuck. All he had to do was open his mouth and yell.

Instead, the man's stunned gaze sank down me and back up. Then deliberately, he left his position and quick-stepped past us, the swoosh of a door saying he'd gone into the main corridor. Thoughts flashed through my mind. He'd heard Charmaine's call to Detective Dickhead. The obvious threat she'd made.

Maybe not everyone liked bent cops.

No need to wait around to see if he was coming back.

I darted forward and grasped the handle, ready to twist or wrench or pull.

It swung open in my hand.

No lock. No alarm rang.

The night air rushed in, and I clamped Summer to my side, reeling but instantly going with the chance to get away. I took another moment to check our surroundings then crept out onto a short staircase. An overhead light sprang on. I ducked, but Summer made a sound of urgency.

"Don't stop." She tugged me across the yard.

On the far side was a tall black gate.

"We need to get you over that. Then run as fast as you can and don't look back."

"Not without ye."

"Don't worry about me."

I couldn't start to process that.

We ran to the gate.

Leaning into the railing, I pushed Summer in front of me and linked my fingers to give her a boost. She hesitated, but whatever she saw in my eyes changed her mind. I lifted her so she could swing herself over the top, then took a running leap myself. Spikes lined the top, cutting my fingers as they must have done Summer's, but I barely noticed the pain.

Neither of us cried out. Still no warning system activated.

I dropped down, landing softly.

We slunk down the alley, emerging at the front of the police station.

Vehicles waited in rows in the car park, but there were no more walls. No fences. Just a main road rising ahead of us with taxis and lorries flying past.

I wheeled around, barely believing the events of the last minute.

"I'm out. Fucking hell. How...?"

A police patrol car entered the slip road for the station.

Summer and I ducked at the same time, concealing ourselves behind some cop's flash car.

"I can't believe that worked," she whispered, her words drying up as she looked at me.

She took in every inch of my face as if I was about to disappear and she had to memorise me.

I did the same. At thick fair hair tucked under a hood like a girl in a fairy tale. Flushed cheeks, sparkling eyes. Everything about her was strange and new, but also entirely familiar.

I'd spent countless hours staring at her pictures while we swapped messages. Knew the turn of her cheek and the softness of her features.

What had I promised to myself?

I dove my fingers into her hair, cupped her head, and held her gaze. "I have no idea why you're here, how any of that just happened, but you're made of magic."

I kissed her. A short, hot press of my lips to hers.

Lightning struck me. I pulled away, stunned.

The car rumbled by, the shadow sliding past our hiding place.

"They were going to kill you," Summer choked, pressing trembling fingers to her mouth. "If they catch you, they still will."

"If I had a match, I'd burn the fucking place to the ground."

She reached into the pocket of her weird, old man's coat, and extracted an orange plastic lighter. "I remember your obsession. That you always needed to have a lighter or matches close to feel safe."

Holy fuck. I closed my fingers around it, holding her hand as well so my precious flames were clutched between us.

But she looked away, freeing herself from my grip.

Come to think of it, she hadn't kissed me back either.

I eased up to spy on the car parked at the end of the strip, indicating to Summer that we needed to move in case the driver walked our way.

At the back of the BMW, as I could now see it was, we kept low. The driver of the cruiser and their passenger laughed together, making some kind of police joke, probably at the expense of someone they'd beat up.

Their voices moved away, but my hatred for the corrupt bastards soared. We needed to get out of here, except I'd fixated on something right in front of me.

The petrol cap of the BMW.

Burning down the police station carried risks. There could be civilians inside. Innocents. But a small blaze outside would satisfy my demons for now.

I scanned the ground, spotting a sapling tree planted in the grass verge.

"Stay here," I ordered Summer.

She hissed a protest, but I slipped across the shadowy path and snapped off a thin green branch. Next, I needed cloth. Something flammable. I darted back and opened the rucksack by her feet. There were clothes. A shirt and joggers. I picked out a pair of cotton socks and held in my laugh.

"What are you doing? We're going to be caught."

"This will take two seconds. Trust me, the distraction

will be worth it."

The fuel panel of the older model beamer popped open without a lock. I twisted off the tank cap then stuck the sock inside, jamming it down with the thin stick before pulling it back so an inch of fuel-soaked material stuck out.

The rich scent of petrol filled the air.

"Step back," I muttered.

From the police station, a siren wailed. Summer squeaked in fear, and the cops down the road took off into the building.

I wanted to take my time over this. Revel in the first production of a spark in so long.

But I needed to get us away more.

With the flick of the lighter wheel, I fed a spark to the greedy material and let it catch.

Snatching Summer's hand, I ran with her, delight and fucking glee spiralling as the flame flickered and rushed, bright in the dark night.

It was dangerous to turn your back on a fire. It was more dangerous to cross a pyromaniac idiot like me.

We sprinted for the highway to the howl of the siren and the explosion of flames.

5

Summer

We raced across the main road. The station's alarm didn't quit. The burning car had imprinted in my vision.

Police car sirens wailed, adding to the mix. Lights sprang on in houses.

We were being hunted.

A few streets away, Jamieson slowed, darting into a car park to check the doors of a row of cars.

I couldn't run for long. After weeks locked up, I'd lost my strength. Not that I'd ever been much of a runner anyway.

None of the car doors opened, and Jamieson scowled.

"Fuck it. Keep going," he barked.

At the end of the road, he pointed across the junction. A huge trading estate spread out. Warehouses, loading areas, wide-open spaces.

I sucked in a breath, my fingers bracing my sides and a stitch panging. "You go. I'll be okay."

A scowl of disbelief was my answer, and he gripped my hand, guiding me to a dark lane instead, tall metal fences caging us in. The rutted lane circled another sprawling warehouse complex, only one small vehicle in sight.

Like he'd done with all the others, Jamieson checked the driver's-side door, tugging on the handle.

The ancient red Honda opened with a creak.

He huffed a surprised laugh and dove inside. I peeked back to watch the exit, spinning around to make sure no people were coming out of the building it backed onto.

In the distance, the sirens kept up their constant howl.

I couldn't slow my pulse. Not from the moment I realised I was going to be the one running into the station, and not now when we were about to be pinned down by every police car in the district.

"Fucking A," Jamieson crowed from the Honda.

He extracted something metal from the glove compartment. A screwdriver? I didn't get a chance to ask before he jammed it hard into the ignition of the car.

Then he jumped up from the seat and slammed his foot down on the screwdriver's handle, forcing it hard into the keyhole.

I clasped my hands to my mouth.

Jamieson's lips curved, and he sent a cocky glance my way. He twisted the screwdriver and the car's engine sprang to life with a rattle.

"Oh my God," I whispered.

"Get in," he ordered. "Drive us south out of the city, then I'll take over."

It made sense if he hid in the back. He knew I could drive, too, as he'd been there every virtual step of the way with my lessons the government had paid for.

Except something strange was happening to me. I was locking up. My muscles not wanting to obey.

It hurt to force myself, but I got into the driver's seat and closed myself in. Jamieson wedged his big body as low as he could in the back.

"We need to move," he urged. "If someone saw us, we'll have to ditch this ride and find another. The faster we clear the area, the safer we'll be."

The dark interior of the car helped hide my frozen state. With shaking fingers, I put the car into gear and trundled down the lane.

Before we reached the entrance to the trading estate, Jamieson tugged my hood back, revealing my blonde hair.

"More natural," he murmured. "Most people take their coats off to drive."

Most people weren't half naked under stolen jackets, or escorting wanted men from a jailbreak.

I couldn't answer.

Instead, I swung right and eased through the estate, taking the main road in the opposite direction to the police station.

We picked up speed, the old car sluggish to respond to the gear changes. I threw nervous glances to the street around, my fingers trembling.

Blue flashing lights appeared in the rearview.

I whimpered in panic. "They're behind us."

If they drove alongside and peered in, they'd catch sight of the man in the back. If they stopped us, how could they fail to see the screwdriver poking out of the ignition by my knee?

We'd be surrounded. Both of us hauled into a van. Cuffed to the seats.

Delivered back to the chief.

I'd waited so long to meet Jamieson, and it wasn't enough.

My chest rose and fell, my mouth open.

Jamieson's hand settled on my hip. He squeezed me gently, a silent signal to calm down. "They're going to be everywhere in the city. But they're not hunting this car. Or ye. Just keep out of their way like any other driver would. Don't speed up."

He was wrong. If that car contained the chief, I was done for. It took several tortuous seconds to fix my face, all while the patrol car closed in.

I'd slowed in my distress so accelerated a little to keep a steady pace.

The patrol car sped up until it was right behind me.

I squeezed the steering wheel so hard it could break.

"Please go past. Please," I begged under my breath.

The sirens blared—a warning for me to pull over.

I shuddered and indicated left. This was it. Finished. My worst impulsive action yet. Jamieson should've gone without me. He could've run further. Got away.

The patrol car eased around us and came alongside. The Honda was small, and the cops were higher up, so their view of the interior hid nothing. I sensed someone's hard gaze on me, and my skin prickled as if being scalded.

We were so busted.

"Sorry," I whispered on a sob and readied myself to stop.

But as I pulled the wheel, the police car swung out and overtook. It zipped off up the well-lit road.

I stared in astonishment and straightened. The noise and lights diminished, then the car went out of sight, swinging off into the city.

"Sh-sh-shit," I stammered.

They'd gone. Just *gone*.

"Good girl. Don't stop." Jamieson squeezed my hip again, but even his voice was tight.

I kept going, moving through the streets until I hit the exit heading south. We punched into the dark countryside, leaving Inverness behind.

As soon as it was safe, I came to a halt in a dark siding and half fell out of the driver's seat. I retched a couple of times then staggered around to get in the other side.

Jamieson climbed out, too, yanking down the zip on his jumpsuit. "Are ye okay? That was fucking amazing."

He stripped it, tossing it to the roadside before reaching into the rucksack for a shirt and joggers Arran had packed.

"Whose clothes are these? Doesn't matter. I'm changing in case I'm wearing a tracker," he explained.

I couldn't reply, or enjoy the show.

If I'd been messed up before, far worse was happening now. I slumped in the seat, curled away from him, unable to even accept Arran's water bottle he offered me.

"I have somewhere for us to go to hide out," he continued in gentle, calm tones, settling in behind the steering wheel. "We'll have to abandon the Honda and hike the last stretch to be sure we're not followed."

I couldn't answer.

I could barely breathe.

He got us back on the road, and I slipped further into misery.

*B*lack, velvety night surrounded the car. Jamieson threw glances at me as often as he peered behind, in both cases looking for danger.

It was oddly reminiscent of how I'd felt in his presence before. I'd hide in my bedroom with the lights off, listening to his voice messages with a picture of him on my screen, trying to ignore the noise from whichever asshole friends my mother's boyfriend had over that evening.

Back then, when I'd been fully in the grip of my crush, Jamieson had been a lifeline.

Fascinating at first, then addictive. I fell hard for him, anticipating every message like the hit of a drug. I'd never considered dating another boy.

I'd explored my body with only Jamieson on my mind.

One day, I'd fully expected to marry him.

Then a year ago, he went silent, leaving me bereft for

weeks until he sent that final, devastating message breaking things off.

In my hurt and anger, I'd taken an action I'd promised him I never would.

At school and college, I'd never been quiet about my hatred for men who controlled sex workers, and as a result had been invited to join a group of self-appointed vigilantes. A fuck-the-government club. I knew some of the members—mostly local troublemakers who wanted an excuse to get drunk and smash windows. Their ideas were pitiful.

Jamieson told me not to waste my energy.

But then he'd dumped me, and I'd joined their leagues. A few months in, and I was contacted by someone who had bigger plans than my useless vigilante colleagues. Convincing, compelling, system-breaking ones. Ideas that gave me a place to burn up my anguish.

I stared out of the car's windows and goggled at my own stupidity.

So quickly, I'd changed from valued equal to pawn.

How had I gone along with the plan and blindly waved away the red flags?

Jamieson and I had promised each other many things, but top of that list was words he'd made me say over and over. That for him, I'd be smart and not put myself in danger. If I did anything risky, he'd be the first to know so he could get me out of trouble.

We'd never met, but he'd been so serious.

Save me from myself if I go too far.

Always.

Until he broke my heart.

"Where have ye been?" he asked suddenly into the dark, startling me out of my memories. "I know you've been missing because my brother is with your sister, trying to find ye. How is it that you're here and they aren't? How did ye walk straight into a police station and unlock my door? How did ye come to me, Summer?"

The story was too long for my gummed-up brain to even attempt. The fear in which I'd crept through the station and entered the codes still gripped me. How I'd ducked into a room to hide from a man and how lucky I'd been not to be found. It was all words I couldn't voice. He was out. That was all that mattered. Next, Breeze needed to hear from me. I never had found Arran's phone in his bag.

"I need to call my sister," I said through a cotton-wool mouth.

"We'll make contact. I promise. But I need answers. It's killing me."

I peeked across at him, letting myself absorb the image. He didn't look like I'd expected. I mean, I'd known him the moment he'd burst out of the police station's cell room, could never mistake him. But the Jamieson I'd talked to for years was skinny and had a boyish face. This tall, muscular, savage man was a stranger with the same eyes as someone I once called a friend.

He'd hate me once he knew what I'd done.

Between his rejection and my actions, our relationship had been destroyed before it ever had a chance.

Twisted up, I melted back into my silent, broken state and let him drive me wherever it was he wanted to go.

6

Jamieson

We abandoned the car in a quarry lane deep in the Cairngorms, wiped it down for prints, then struck out on foot through the forest. There were a few places I'd try to find my family. This was my first guess—the log cabin on the McRae estate we'd first stayed in after escaping Torlum.

After that, shite got riskier.

I didn't have a phone, or the numbers for any of my brothers, so no way to get a message to them. Our pervert father's land was another place they might go, though I assumed the house was uninhabitable after my fire. Camden had faked a relationship enough to get to see me in jail, so who knew how far he'd taken that. Or if they were even still together as a group.

A chill skimmed over me despite the warm night.

The one thing that had got me through being locked up was the idea my family was safe. I'd missed them all. Had worried endlessly about Cassie. My solace had been that she would be well cared for by my brothers and their lasses. They were either here, or they weren't. I couldn't get my hopes up.

Behind me, Summer stumbled and fell to her knees in the thick pine needles.

Muttering apologies, I reached to help her stand, but she withdrew from my touch, dusting herself off and not meeting my eye.

Something was badly wrong. The Summer I knew would be leading this hike. Not terrified of every crash as a deer cleared our way. I was smart enough to know now wasn't the time to push her on it. I also didn't want to get her hopes up about finding her sister with my family. It was a guess on my part, but if things worked out, we'd walk straight into a warm welcome with all the people we loved in one place.

I'd have to run again, but at least they'd know I was free.

We kept walking until the edge of the woods appeared. I'd taken my time to memorise the glen and its slopes but played it cautious emerging from the tree line.

The cabin perched on the isolated hillside.

My heart fell.

Cars sat outside. Shiny, new models. Not the old Ford we'd stolen from our keeper or the blue Kia Theadora had borrowed. Someone else was staying here, not my family.

I hesitated. Needed to get closer to be sure.

"Keep with me," I told Summer then skirted the hill, climbing until we were adjacent to the cabin.

There were no lights on, but one small sign gave me pause. A reason not to head back to the quarry to retrieve the stolen car and get out of here.

On a bench outside the cabin, a T-shirt had been draped and perhaps left to dry. Camden's shirt, I was almost certain.

Reaching for Summer's canvas sleeve, I shot her a look. "I'm going to sneak over. Stay right here."

She didn't meet my gaze or react at all.

Across the grass, I got to the bench and picked up the shirt.

The logo read *Boys Get Blue Too.*

I released a hard breath.

It was his. They were still here. My fucking heart pounded. I couldn't believe Camden would discard it. We'd had so little on Torlum that every item was precious. I turned to go back to Summer, ready to explain why I was hyperventilating over a T-shirt.

A thudding noise reverberated overhead.

For the last stretch of the trip, there had been no sign of the cops. No car had chased us into the mountains. No blue lights or sirens broke the peace.

This was a helicopter.

It was coming in fast. We'd been found.

Spinning to face Summer, I gestured at the road and called out, "You have a choice. Go that way. Castle Braithar's not far along. The man who owns it is named Gordain, and he's a friend of my family. If ye tell him I've abandoned ye out here, he'll get ye home."

I didn't want to push her away. It grated against all I'd decided when it came to her.

The other option was she stayed with me.

If she made that choice, I'd never let her go again, no matter what.

The helicopter's rotor blades beat down, the roar louder and echoing across the glen. There was no doubt they were coming for me. We had seconds.

"Summer! Decide," I said, backing up. "Go to the castle or get ready to run again with me."

But she stepped from the tree line and stared at the craft, her hands rising to cover her mouth and the downdraft swirling her hair. I followed her gaze, squinting into the bright light and expecting to see uniforms. The blue-and-white colours of the police.

A fair-haired lass had her palm to the window, her shock clear.

I knew that face.

Had seen it at McInver's place. I'd mistaken Summer for her.

"Is that your sister?" I shouted against the noise.

Summer's gaze remained glued to the other woman.

With urgency, I scanned the windows, hoping beyond hope that she was with my brother. The wind from the aircraft whipped us, the pilot bringing it down on a flat piece of ground just beyond the house.

Another face appeared. Camden's. Others behind him.

Summer lurched past me, but I snatched her back and banded my arms around her from behind, keeping her from running straight into the path of the helicopter's descent.

Then it had touched down, and the doors opened.

Her sister half fell out and took a few steps before dropping to her knees on the grass. Despite the deafening noise of the rotor blades, I could make out her words.

"No. No! You were dead," she cried.

Summer shuddered, and I released her. She stumbled to the other woman and hugged her. Half a second later, Camden crashed into me, banding his arms around me in a hard hold. A second hit brought Struan to me, both men crushing me, asking questions I couldn't process.

They were here. I'd found them.

"We were coming for ye tonight." Camden released his grip and held me at arm's length, scanning me. "I've been out of my mind with worry, making up all these insane rescue missions."

"He isn't joking," Struan yelled over the still-beating rotor blades. "Honest to fuck, we were down for anything. Yet here ye are, a free man. How the hell did ye get out?"

I just stared at him. Last I'd seen, he was unconscious and being taken to hospital by his girlfriend. Now he was upright and walking around.

Thea slipped past him and gave me a tight hug before retreating to under Struan's arm.

I found my voice. "I barely know other than an hour ago, Summer showed up and unlocked my door."

All three switched their gazes to the two women.

Both were on their knees as if their strength had gone. Their embrace didn't stop. Breeze's shoulders shook while Summer had gone still. Numb, like she'd been in the car.

"Camden," another voice called. "What's going on?"

Two men approached from the helicopter. The red-headed guy calling my brother's name was Max, Struan's friend. I didn't know the other but guessed him to be the pilot.

"Family reunion," Camden replied.

Max stared between us then gave me a nod, his lip curving into a smirk. "Better that we saw nothing, aye? Seb and I will take the heli back unless you're going to need it again?"

Camden raised an eyebrow at me. We might not have grown up together, but I knew him well enough to understand his question. Did I need their help?

I had to run but couldn't be traceable. I didn't know the pilot. Couldn't trust him.

I shook my head, and my brother thanked the men for whatever the hell they'd been doing this evening, then they left, taking off again into the night.

The whir of blades moved away.

"Listen," I ordered my brothers. "I can't stick around. The police are chasing me."

Struan snorted. "No shite. Where did ye lose them?"

"At the station. They scrambled patrol cars, but we got out of Inverness unseen."

"Ye stole a ride?"

"I did. Ditched it an hour's walk away. I'll probably leave it there and take another. Wish I could hang around."

Camden gripped my shoulder. "Not so hasty. We need to talk and work out what we're doing."

"No, I'm leaving. I just broke out of fucking jail. There's heat on me, and I won't let that touch my family. I only came to let ye know and say goodbye."

My brothers swapped a glance, their expressions identical.

Our family characteristics were strong. Their look, and my intuition over their thinking.

Something else was going on.

Belatedly, I noted the absences from the party. "Where's Sin and Lottie? Where's Cassie?"

Camden's wince deepened my unease.

"Come inside and I'll explain," he said.

I could maybe relax for a minute, hear about what had happened to my family. I'd still need to go, but this way would get me a proper goodbye.

Camden collected a distraught Breeze and led her into the cabin, gesturing for the rest of us to follow while he muttered something low to her. Breeze clutched Summer's fingers like she couldn't bear to let go.

They weren't the same. Summer was taller. Her figure much more curvy. Like she'd been designed to drive me wild. I couldn't stop staring.

Instead of settling us in the lounge, Camden barked orders. "Grab the bags. Pack up and get ready to go. We're out of here and probably won't come back, so leave no trace."

I jogged upstairs with him. "Talk to me."

"You're not the only one in shite. There's a lot to catch ye up on, but here's the short version. After the fire, McInver fell into a coma. Wait, I need to go back further. The last time ye were properly with us was at the beach house when the cops raided."

We reached his bedroom. Summer and her sister were already inside, the latter stuffing clothes into the rucksack.

My brother paused in the hall. I braced myself, sensing something awful coming.

"They took Cassie."

I stared at him in horror.

He spoke through gritted teeth. "They knew who she was and had a social worker there. Ever since, we've been trying to get her back as well as ye. Tonight, Sin and Lottie found her."

"Thank fuck—"

He thumped the wall. "No, they didn't get her. She's with some foster family and not easy to reach."

My heart lurched, pain lancing me from fear for our little sister.

Then the pain turned to dread as I realised what I'd done.

"It's my fault," I said slowly. "I set that fire on the beach. That's why the police found us."

Camden forced me to look at him. "No. It was McInver. He had us followed."

I closed my eyes for a brief second, opening them to find my brother's gaze burning into mine.

"Please tell me he's moved on from his coma to dead," I said.

A rough, unfunny laugh was my answer, and Camden propelled me into the bunkroom I'd slept in before. "Close but no cigar. He's been unconscious the whole time ye were in the police station."

My bag waited on a dresser, and Camden brought my phone from his pocket and set it down next to it. He tapped the device. "Cassie called your number the single time we've heard from her, so keep that on loud."

I dipped my head, all kinds of churned up.

Camden continued. "I took a fucking DNA test to prove I was his son so I could get access to ye. That's how I got into the station. But also how I learned there's more going on than any of us realised." He paused, giving me a second to process the overload of information. "Forget that for now. McInver woke up this evening. The first thing he's going to do is disinherit me, and probably send the cops after me, too. Above that, we just returned from rescuing Breeze from her stepdad. He kidnapped her."

His voice broke, and anguish rippled over his features.

I'd barely paid attention to Breeze, other than her reaction to and differences from Summer, but I touched my brother's arm and tipped my head at the dividing wall to indicate the lasses next door. "Breeze is yours, aye?"

He gave a sharp nod before wrenching open my bag and tossing a long-sleeved shirt at me with a pointed indication at the tattoo on my arm.

So much had changed in the space of a couple of weeks.

"We're leaving, but were doing it together," Camden said, recovering himself. "Sin and Lottie were coming back here, because our next shot was to get ye before we returned for Cassie as a whole family. We'll meet them elsewhere instead and make a plan."

I couldn't imagine what they would have done to retrieve me. Camden's ace card had been pulled by our father waking up. Everyone was in pieces. Emotion rushed in me. I stuck my head down and got dressed in the shirt and my own jeans.

Whatever came next, I'd be the one to take the risks. I'd throw myself at the danger so they didn't have to.

Alongside that, I needed answers on what had happened to Summer, though I knew deep in my gut it couldn't be good.

And that I'd rain down my own brand of hellfire on whoever hurt her.

7

Summer

We exited the cabin, and I stared at the ground. Probably in shock, I guessed. Still not feeling safe.

Camden pulled my sister aside and said something low and urgent in her ear. She palmed his cheek then pushed up on her toes to kiss him, her cheeks wet and her anguish appearing to lessen at his touch.

A small ripple of surprise made it through my stunned bunny mind. I'd never seen her with a boyfriend.

I didn't trust him. Or any of them.

If I hadn't lost the ability to communicate, I'd persuade her to leave with me.

Then warm fingers curled around my elbow, and Jamieson guided me to the back of a big car. "Not letting you out of my sight, stranger," he said, then climbed in the front.

Breeze joined me in the back while Camden took the driver's seat, the other couple getting into a sports car.

I was stuck on Jamieson's *stranger* comment. He felt it, too, this weird situation between us. How we knew each other once but never like this.

My sister chafed my fingers, her features pinched with concern.

In the cabin, she'd stalled in her packing to ask me one question—whether I was okay. Still barely able to talk, I'd shaken my head to indicate that I wasn't, and fresh tears had spilled down her cheeks.

But my sister and I had been through bad times enough in the past. Our mother falling off the wagon and into a drug habit, her boyfriend on a rampage in our flat. We shared the instinct to save discussion for when we had time and space. Right now, there was neither.

In the front, Camden nudged Jamieson. "Call Sin. I sent a text to tell him not to come home but not why. He needs to know you're back."

Jamieson pulled out a phone and dialled a number.

"Guess again," he said to the other person on the line, then laughed at whatever they replied. "Nope. Escaped convict coming at ye live from inside a moving vehicle."

He listened again. "Too much to explain, but ye need to know we've left Gordain's place because of yours truly. I need to stay off the cops' radar, so we're heading your way."

Sin said something in reply, and Jamieson choked. "Then you've seen her. Is she okay?"

Breeze squeezed my fingers and whispered in my ear, "Their little sister was taken. We've been trying to get her back, find you, and get him out of jail. Just like that, you solved two of those problems."

I huddled deeper in the hunter's jacket. I'd caused more problems than I could ever solve.

Jamieson continued with his call. "Got it. See ye in a couple of hours." He immediately dialled another number, putting the call on loudspeaker.

"Thea, set the phone so Struan can hear me, too." He waited for a beat until his brother gave a quiet greeting from the other car. "I just spoke to Sin. He and Lottie are in Perth and said we should meet outside of there. Put some space between me and the Inverness cops. He's going to find somewhere for us to lie low for the night."

Struan and Thea's car was a pair of red taillights further on down the road. We'd passed a large body of water, though little else was visible in the dark night.

Struan's voice came on the line. "Straight down the A9, then. We need to get these cars off the road before morning, so he better find somewhere quick."

Jamieson looked across to Camden.

Breeze's boyfriend lifted his chin. "In case it isn't obvious, both belong to Daddy Dearest. One phone call from him to report them stolen, and we are no longer incognito. Our saving grace is the fact he's in a hospital bed and not home to see we've taken them, but that gives us a couple of days max. Less if his lawyer clues him in."

A muttered swear word came down the phone, and Struan spoke again. "A patrol car just passed us at the junction. I can either get in behind it or take a diversion."

"What diversion is there around the mountains? There's only one road south. We've already got a couple of hours' drive heading in a straight line. Dawn will be here before we know it. We slow down, keep on track, and fucking pray," Camden decided.

Seemed like that was the plan.

We merged onto the main road, everyone throwing glances around. Traffic was scarce, but we already knew the police were nearby.

I squeezed my eyes closed tight, grateful for the chance to try to get my head back in the game. To unlock my muscles without needing to immediately answer questions.

I'd walked straight into some unknown group dynamic with Jamieson's family and my sister. He'd never once told me he had brothers, I'd only found that out in my sister's message. Three of them in total, plus a sister, if I was hearing right. A small memory surfaced that contradicted me. Him telling me that he thought he might have a half-brother who also lived in Aberdeen. Was that one of these men or someone else?

Then again, I'd kept my own secrets.

The stranger comment was never more real.

"There's some things I need to tell you," my sister said quietly to me. "Jack kidnapped me because he thought he could get ransom money from Camden."

I blinked at her in astonishment. Jack was our mother's long-term boyfriend. He was a waste of space, but this was extreme, even for him.

She hastened on. "We just came back from there. He'd lured me to your flat by pretending you'd returned. Instead, he locked me in and waited for his payday. Luckily, Camden found me."

Her boyfriend stretched an arm back while keeping his gaze on the road. She took his hand and squeezed it before letting him go.

"Jack got knocked out, and Mum broke things off with

him," she continued. "She said she won't take him back. I'm worried about her, though."

I pressed my lips together, and Breeze heaved a sigh. The story of our childhoods had been Mum coping for a time then failing hard when things rattled her. It wasn't her fault. She'd had the worst life and no coping mechanisms for when things went wrong. She'd tried to put us first and fought to get us into foster care when she knew it was going to get bad. The image of her standing up to Jack was a welcome one, even if I couldn't smile about it.

Jamieson looked over at Camden. "That was ye, doing the knocking out?"

Camden returned a half-smile, his gaze on the road. "True. If I wasn't out of my mind with stress, I'd enjoy telling the story, but it can wait till later. The guy with Max is his cousin, Sebastian. He was our pilot tonight, but he'd come to the cabin with Max because he has an insider view of the kind of system we're up against."

In his lap, Jamieson idly flicked the wheel of the lighter I'd given him, sparks flaring and dying. "Bigger than McInver's murky world and the corrupt police chief he's friends with?"

"Much bigger," his brother replied.

Both sank into silence.

Tension grew that was greater than just me and my broken brain. My sister alternated between watching me and her boyfriend. Jamieson snuck glances at me in the side mirror, too.

I was drowning and couldn't surface. I couldn't laugh about the thrill of slinking into a police station and strolling out with a prisoner. Couldn't open my mouth to tell my tale.

Further down the road, Jamieson twisted to address Breeze. "Because my brother is too ignorant to do the job, I'll introduce myself. I'm Jamieson, though most people call me Burn. Sounds like you've been through an ordeal."

Burn. I didn't know the nickname, fitting as it was. I wondered who'd given it to him.

Breeze gave him a shaky smile. "Good to meet you. Your brothers have been trying every which way to reach you."

His gaze crept to me, and he tipped up his lips in a smile. "And your sister walked straight in and did the job single-handedly."

My heart thudded, panic tightening my insides.

I'd walked into a jail. He'd blown up a car. I'd been locked up for so long.

"You'll beg me for it," came the police chief's voice in my head, and I started.

As if she could sense my rushing fear, Breeze took my hand again. "She's amazing. Always has been. But I guess you know that already."

I met Jamieson's gaze, a zap of electricity startling me all the more.

"Police," Camden said suddenly.

Silence fell over us all.

"How many?" Jamieson asked.

Camden glanced in his rearview. "Just one. Not lit up. Coming in fast, though."

"I'll text Thea so they know," Breeze said then fast-typed a message with her phone held low.

The other car was way ahead, the brothers keeping a distance apart.

"Everyone slump or huddle," Camden said. "It's four AM. None of us want to be up at this time. Maybe we're heading to work."

We acted out his scenario, though I couldn't close my eyes. Instead, I twisted to watch the dark road.

Sure enough, the patrol car eased alongside.

Camden glanced over but kept his driving steady. They knew what Jamieson looked like. He'd changed clothes, but if they pulled us over, there was no way they couldn't identify him. His shorn hair showcased his angular face. A solid masculine jaw and expressive features that seemed to shift from wild amusement to savage fury in a flash. Even the shadowy interior of the car couldn't hide how distinctive he was.

An angel or a devil, depending on the moment.

At least he'd pocketed the lighter, no sparks flying now.

All the cops had to do was put the pieces of the puzzle together, assume we had allies, and guess we'd be making a break for it.

"Another one coming in," Jamieson said under his breath, his gaze on the mirror even in his slumped position.

Tension cramped my stomach. My sister shook.

Camden acknowledged him with a tiny jerk of his chin but kept his easy pose, not yet speeding up to lose the car still alongside us.

There was no off ramp here, no lights of any town. Only the outline of mountains against a now royal-blue sky.

My fear grew stronger, taking over every inch of me.

It had been terrifying when I'd been the one behind the wheel, but I didn't know Jamieson's brother. I couldn't tell if he was about to slam on the accelerator and speed off in a race to our deaths.

Both he and Jamieson had the same rigid muscles. Fists clenched out of sight of the windows.

The first police car hadn't budged from our right-hand side. With the second one approaching, they could box us in. Make it impossible to lose them.

"Dual carriageway is ending," Camden said quietly.

I peeked ahead. The two lanes merged into one. The police car would have to make a choice. Go on, or slide behind us with the other.

Suddenly, blue lights flashed.

The incoming car had lit up.

I gripped Breeze's hand, my breathing stalling in my lungs.

The car beside us floored it, sirens wailing a second later. The other followed, and both police cars shot off down the road, sliding into the single lane right as it merged. They sped on ahead, and I stared open-mouthed as they lit the glen and disappeared out of sight.

"What the fuck just happened?" Jamieson asked.

"Your brother," Breeze replied, holding up her phone. "Listen to this from Thea. I told her we had two cars on us, and she replied that Struan was going to create a distraction."

"What did he do?" Jamieson asked.

"I'll ask, but don't expect an answer if they're being chased."

Camden drew in a hard breath. "Tell them I'm getting us off the road. Dawn's almost here. We need shelter."

We might've been out of immediate danger, but who knew what was waiting ahead. Camden took the earliest possible exit and led us on a diversion through singletrack country lanes that wound around lochs and over bridges. Sin called to give us a location, and we skirted Perth with the sky now light and traffic building.

Hunger gnawed at my stomach. It was second to the intense worry I had about being caught.

Yet no further police cars dogged our tracks.

Our route delivered us away from town and up through a forest, finally down a rutted lane, fenced off at the end with warning signs not to enter.

"Sin said to open the gate and hide the car down the track," Breeze said.

Jamieson hopped out and yanked on the gate, the chain falling away, broken.

Camden drove us in, and Jamieson put the gate back in place behind us before climbing back in the car.

Further along, two vehicles parked at a track between the trees. Struan and Thea's sports car plus a chunky 4x4.

Jamieson huffed a laugh. "We're all here, then."

He exited and opened my door, stepping back so I could climb out. On shaky legs, I took in the unexpected sight. The location of our hideaway.

The ruins of a castle stood before us, trees concealing it on three sides. New stone and mortar showed repair work underway, and a cottage sat to one side. It was so remote that finally the tight ball inside me unravelled.

A dam of emotion broke so hard my head swam and darkness flickered at the edges of my vision.

Then Jamieson's arms were around me, and he was lifting me. Carrying me. I didn't know what was worse, the intense feeling of safety I had no right to claim or how good it felt for someone else to take the weight off my unsteady legs.

Or maybe secret option three—the fact that once he'd heard my story, Jamieson would never touch me the same way again.

8

Jamieson

Striding over the uneven ground, I carried Summer to the door of the cottage, Lottie swinging it open ahead of me.

The lass clasped her hands to her mouth, her eyes wide, but ushered me in. "Oh my God. This is Summer? Bring her through here."

Two of my brothers stood in the kitchen, the other members of our group coming in behind me, but my attention had been fully absorbed by the woman in my arms. Her eyes were closed, and her pulse fluttered at her neck.

She'd wobbled in front of me then passed out, and it scared the shite out of me.

In a small bedroom, Lottie patted the mattress of a cosy bed, and I placed Summer down, her fair hair spreading out, then reached for the fastening of her heavy coat, needing to make her comfortable.

Opening it, I revealed bare skin.

Her uncovered tits.

I dropped the jacket and stumbled back.

Breeze took my place at her bedside, Lottie with her.

"Why is she naked?" I gritted out.

Breeze stared wide-eyed at her sister and didn't answer.

"Can I take a look at her?" Lottie asked. At Breeze's nod, she placed her fingers on Summer's forehead then took her pulse. "I saw her faint. She doesn't have a fever, but her pulse is a little slow. Was she okay before that?"

"She's exhausted," Breeze replied. "She's been through an ordeal. At least I hope that's all it is."

An ordeal?

"What happened to her?" My temper reared for reasons unknown.

Her sister smoothed back her hair. "How much did she tell you?"

"Nothing."

Breeze met my gaze. "I hardly know myself, but it'll be better to let her tell the story in her own words. Can you give us the room? I want to get her settled so she can sleep more easily."

The last thing I wanted to do was walk away, but the picture building in my mind was worsening by the minute.

I'd been held in that police station illegally, police corruption a fucking joke at my expense. Before that, Camden had found Breeze in one of McInver's bedrooms. She'd been looking for her sister, which if I thought about it hard enough, told me some dirty old man had the lass. Why else would she be with McInver? Why else would any woman go near him if they didn't have to?

Then Summer walked straight into the station and extracted me, barely dressed as if she'd made a break for it herself.

She'd run from somewhere.

No wonder she'd collapsed.

I felt like doing the same, too.

I backed out of the room, Lottie squeezing my arm to welcome me back from the dead before she shut the door and closed me out.

A couple of steps took me into the kitchen, then Sin was in my face. The huge man gripped me by the shoulder and the side of my head.

"Fucking hell, you're here," he said. "Are ye hurt?"

"No—"

He bound me up in a bruising hug, cutting off any reply I could give.

In a cold rush, my adrenaline dropped. This was all I'd wanted for weeks. To be back with my family again. I didn't care that we were on the run. I'd never known peace and didn't want it now. Emotions roared.

"Where the fuck is Cassie?" I said on a breath.

"Not here."

"I know that. Is she safe?"

Sin released me. "She will be when we get her back. I'll explain everything in a minute. Are ye sure ye aren't injured?"

He was changing the subject from our sister. It pissed me off. "I'm invincible. Save your questions."

"Don't be a smart arse. Listen up, we're as safe here as we can be. The homeowners are away for at least a week, so we have this place for a while. The lass ye brought in is Breeze's sister, then?"

Camden had obviously told him so, but I inclined my head, oddly bothered by how everyone referred to her as someone else's. Belonging to Breeze, not me.

Sin directed me to the kitchen counter behind him, several bags piled along it. "Lottie and I brought food. Eat something and we'll talk."

"I don't want to fucking eat or talk. I want to go after Cassie," I snapped.

Even so, I fell on a brown paper bag, pulling out a breakfast roll. In seconds, I'd unwrapped it, chewed it down, and grabbed another. Struan handed me a bottle of water.

"How the fuck did ye get the cops off our arses?" I asked him.

My eldest brother twisted his lips in a smirk then directed me into a snug living room. "Drove like a maniac on the wrong side of the road, scared a few people enough to have them call nine-nine-nine, then scarpered before we could get caught. I know these roads. Used to steal cars and speed around them when I was a youngster."

I raised my eyebrows. Thea had once told me that Struan was a dangerous driver. Put him behind the wheel of a sports car, and no surprise that was the plan he came up with. I'd have done the same myself.

I threw myself into an armchair, eating my second roll. Until now, I'd paid no attention to our surroundings, trusting that Sin knew what he was doing. This was someone's home, or maybe a holiday rental like the beach house we'd stayed in.

Outside the window, I had a better view of the castle ruins. It looked like it was in the process of being rebuilt into some posh fucker's home while they were staying in this tiny cottage.

Sin settled onto the sofa, Camden and Thea taking seats next to him. Struan sat on the floor at his girlfriend's feet, his arm wrapping around her leg.

"How did ye find this place?" I asked.

"Luck. People post way too much about themselves online," Sin informed me. "I was after somewhere nearby that would be empty and found posts from some woman who bought the ruined tower with her partner. They're planning to document how they convert it into a home but then happily informed everyone they were taking a two-week break to some fucking paradise island. It was easy to find and scope the place while we were waiting for ye to drive down. Biggest risk is someone who knows them checking in or some contractor showing up. If that happens, we'll just drive away."

Everyone nodded agreement, the temporary state of staying anywhere second nature to us now.

Camden sat forward. "On that, we need a family protocol. After the fire, we got split up. If that happens again, I want a system in place to make sure we can find each other. Locations to go to first. Phone numbers memorised. Anything so we don't have the panic of not knowing."

His gaze settled on me, and his pain was right there in his eyes.

They'd missed me. Worried about me.

I swallowed hard. "Sorry that happened."

His gaze burned. "I didn't mean just ye, but fucking hell, man, we've been scared to death that we wouldn't see ye again."

I stared back, then swung my focus across the group to take them all in. "I didn't mean to get caught, but all I could see was how McInver's money has hurt my family. I needed the fire to consume it. Cleanse it away."

"Ye burned a whole wing of the building down," Camden told me, his tone softer. Forgiving.

I choked on a laugh, my chest tight. "Just one wing? I'll try harder next time to raze the whole fucking place to the ground."

None of them told me what I'd done was wrong. But Sin made a gesture, tilting his head where I was holding the little orange lighter, flicking the wheel absently. I hadn't even noticed I was doing it, but Summer had given me this, and it was a connection to her even if she wasn't awake.

"Just don't set fire to this place." He stretched out his arms, tiredness plain. "Besides Camden's protocol, we have a fuck ton to catch up on, then everyone needs to get some rest before tonight."

"What are we doing tonight?" I asked.

It was a stupid question. Everyone was here bar our sister. We'd driven down to this part of the country because she was nearby.

"Tell me we're busting out Cassie," I added before he could speak.

We all sat taller.

Sin's gaze darkened. "Fuck, yes. But I want to square out our information, because what we do next plays into everything else hanging over us. Burn, take the floor. Tell us all the shite that happened in that police station."

Any tiredness I'd felt evaporated at the reminder of the mission to get our sister. I launched into the very dull story of my incarceration. Of how Charmaine and Detective Dickhead were the only two officers I saw, but how they had my rap sheet up to early teenage years and seemed like they were trying to prove that was me but weren't sure.

"There were gaps in their information," I continued. "Like the fact I can't read. They didn't know that. What I don't get is why they didn't just charge me. Two weeks, I was in there. Any rights I had were walked over and ignored."

My brothers shared a grim expression, then Camden asked a question.

"Did ye ever meet the police chief?"

"Not had that pleasure."

He didn't smile. "And they never offered a deal or threatened ye with jail?"

I shook my head again. "Not so much. They wanted a confession but stopped short of beating it out of me. Got the feeling when ye came in to visit me, they would have let ye have that pleasure." My heart squeezed at what my brother had done. "Can't believe ye went through all of that for me. Put yourself forward as McInver's son."

Camden shoved his hair out of his eyes, revealing the whole of the scar down the side of his face. It was such a familiar gesture that my heart hurt even more.

"I got caught by his lawyer when I was searching his mansion for ye. I assumed he'd call me out for trespassing, but instead, he was desperate for someone to take over while McInver was unconscious. It was easy to prove that I was a blood relative, and because McInver had started the process of assigning his estate to his son, I stepped into those shoes."

"Which will be a problem now he's awake because he wanted Sin, not any of the rest of us," I caught up slowly.

Camden nodded. "I have a credit card the lawyer gave me, we're driving his cars. There's any number of things he could charge me with. I might not have the police chasing me, but I'd bet by tomorrow, there will be an arrest warrant with my name on it. Which brings me to the other thing ye don't know."

I tensed, anticipating the next hit.

Camden took a breath. "The police chief and McInver are part of a system that buys and sells women. We don't know to what extent they're involved, but considering the money and influence these men have, I'm going to guess they aren't casual in it."

He shot a look to the living room doorway, and to the bedroom the other side of the hall. "Breeze found out about something called the List. It's a group of men who have access to a regular sale of women. Or, more specifically, their bodies in virginity auctions. Breeze put herself into it to find Summer."

I recoiled, a picture building that I'd never anticipated. "How was Summer in a virginity auction?"

"That's something we'll find out when she wakes up. Breeze suspects her sister was trying to infiltrate them."

I leapt up and paced to the window, scoring my fingernails into my shorn hair. Why the hell had she done that? Why put herself in danger in that way?

Camden watched me, continuing his sordid summary. "Sit down. We've got a long way to go with this yet. The police chief took a liking to me as McInver's son and invited me to his mansion. He's landed gentry, with a title and everything. He had a sex party underway and expected me to partake. Almost like a baptism of fire to prove I could act in our father's place."

"And ye went along with it to have access to me," I concluded slowly, parking my arse back on the chair, though anger still licked me.

He curled his lip. "Of course I fucking didn't."

I blinked, realising what I'd said. My mind was still churning over what Summer had done. "I didn't mean that ye took part."

"I went there to ask for ownership of his prisoner and also to look for Summer. I didn't expect to find the group of women he'd assembled for my pleasure. I had no phone, no car because he'd driven me there, and barely got away because halfway through the evening, the news came that McInver was awake."

"How did ye escape?"

"His son, Arran, helped me. He hates the bullshit life his father leads, too."

Camden had risked his life for mine. I clamped down on my emotions to capture and hold his gaze. "Thank ye. I don't think I've ever had anyone in my life who would step up for me like that. Not until I met my brothers." Or until I'd met Summer.

Camden didn't look away. "Yeah, well, that's what family is for. The only other viable plan I had was to beat ye up so you'd need medical treatment, and then we'd somehow grab ye when they were transporting ye to hospital."

I managed a laugh, because I'd told Camden to hit me when he'd visited me in the station, and he hadn't been able to do it. Imagining him going all Tyson on me was a stretch. My brother could throw a punch, but he was a lover, not a fighter.

"I'd wear your bruises with pride," I replied with a grin.

He rolled his eyes. "My guess is the chief was holding ye because he and McInver are thick as thieves and used to running things between them. He didn't want to process ye as a normal criminal, because McInver would want his own personal revenge. So he held ye there for longer than expected, keeping ye out of sight of everyone apart from those two pet cops."

"Then with McInver awake, my number would've been up tonight," I summarised. "Because letting me go would be unacceptable to men like that."

My brothers and Thea all reacted, shifting uncomfortably or muttering angry swears.

Summer had saved me.

She'd risked her skin twice over with the vigilante shite and with me.

Sin moved the conversation on, derailing my thoughts. "In the meantime of all this happening, we were drawing a blank in finding Cassie. Then out of the blue, she rang your number and was able to give us enough information for us to track her down. Last night, Lottie and I staked out the place until her foster carers came home. We intended to bribe them with McInver's money to give her up, but they wouldn't let us get close and set the dogs on us to get us off the property. Cassie cried out for us, so at least we know she's all right."

I looked between each of them. "Why wouldn't she be all right?"

An awful feeling took hold of my gut. I'd been in foster care multiple times and had seen the worst things happen to the kids no one cared about.

It had kickstarted my obsession with protection and revenge.

Boosted my need for fire.

Sin balled his hands into fists. "We think the foster da could be violent."

I flashed through multiple stages of emotion in the space of seconds. For anyone to raise their hand to Cassie... They'd pay.

If anything, our situation now was simpler. We knew who we were and what we wanted—to be together and free. Step one was claiming back Cassie, then step two was the hard bit. Keeping our arses alive and out of jail.

"She doesn't stay there. We're taking her," I vowed.

Sin eased up from his seat and moved to the window. "It'll be better if ye don't come, for the sake of lying low."

"Is that a joke?" I snapped.

"No. If you're seen—"

"I dinna give a fuck. Our sister needs us. Don't even try to stop me."

A click came, a door closing in the hall, then Lottie appeared in the living room entryway. Her gaze shot straight to Sin. He exhaled, his whole body relaxing as if the sight of her somehow chilled him out. Last I'd seen of them, he was getting over his suspicions of her while making her sleep in his bed.

Now, both of them looked different. Like they wanted to melt into each other.

I'd already known he was obsessed with her, but seeing it was something else.

"How is she?" I asked Lottie, tilting my head at the door.

"Pretty sure it's just exhaustion affecting her," she replied. Her hand drifted to her stomach. "Breeze fell asleep next to her. She's so worried about her sister."

Camden sighed. "She'd just given up hope of ever seeing her again. It's fucked up that all that time, Summer was captive."

"Isn't it shocking? Both of them have suffered so much," Lottie said. "God knows what Summer's been through."

I glowered at the window, and my mind went to a different place. One where I had the right to curl around Summer and keep her safe. However unrealistic to a boy in and out of foster care homes, the lass had always been my end game, before Torlum, before lies, conspiracies, and money or power-hungry arseholes had broken into my nothing life and taken over. Summer was my teenage version of bliss, and now she was a single room away but further than ever.

Abruptly, Lottie retched, pulling me out of my reverie.

Sin leapt to his feet. "What's wrong?"

She pressed her hand to her mouth. "Nothing. Just a little nauseous."

She retched again, and my brother was at her side, Thea leaping up to follow them out of the room.

Struan gave a snort of laughter. "Fast work," he muttered.

"What do ye mean?" Camden asked.

"Sin wanted her pregnant. Bam, she's sick. No-brainer."

Lottie pregnant? That changed a whole load of things, too.

The world had moved on while I'd been locked up. So fast, I was dizzy.

Struan climbed up from his place on the floor. He'd been quiet in the discussion so far, but I knew better than to think he wasn't paying attention. He also moved without tightness, showing me he'd healed from the stab wound he'd carried. One tiny part of my worry eased.

"Quit staring at me every time I move," he griped.

"In my cell, I pictured ye dead in a hospital."

He stilled. "Yeah, well, I imagined worse about ye. Somehow, we both survived to make it here."

Neither of us said the natural conclusion—that luck couldn't hold out for long.

He stood next to Camden, both men watching me.

"So I have a question. Ye and Summer knew each other well," Struan said.

An intense feeling of protectiveness grew in me. "Not hearing a question, but yeah, we used to."

"Help me understand what happened last night. How did she get to ye? How did she even know ye were there?"

"No idea. She isn't talking."

"But she walked straight into a police station? Through locked doors? That requires access."

It did.

I'd tried and failed to make any sense of it.

"Ye mean someone on the inside," Camden added slowly.

Struan nodded. "The police chief, abuser of women, was keeping Burn in his police station while his son helped ye get away from his mansion. A son who'd have insider knowledge by the bucket-load."

"Ye think Arran helped her?" Camden asked. "I didn't see Summer in their house."

"Doesnae mean she wasn't there," he mused.

I struggled to keep up. "Are ye saying that the police chief had her?"

Struan raised his hands. "Just putting two and two together. Camden, didn't ye call me from Arran's phone?"

Camden swore and reached for the phone Struan held out.

He turned it over in his hands. "He might know the answers not only to this but also to what's happening with McInver. If our father actually set the cops on my trail yet.

But what if his dad tracks the call?"

I snapped out of my confusion, twisted up over all I'd heard and the thoughts that wouldn't stop. "Let him track us. We're driving cars that are probably blips on some system somewhere. Those two lasses in that bedroom suffered because of this. Breeze because she followed her sister into that system, Summer for God knows what. They're victims. Planning to ignore that?"

Camden scowled at me. "Of course I'm not."

"Then call this kid. What do we have to lose?"

Sin appeared back in the doorway and rested a shoulder on the frame. He lifted his chin. "Lottie's lying down. Make the call, then everyone needs to rest up. We can settle the details for Cassie's rescue after nightfall, but unless we have to, none of us are moving until dark. I'll take first watch."

Camden dialled a number. Put the call on loudspeaker in the living room.

It rang, a loud trill.

I'd never been the smartest. Never tried all that hard to learn. But I knew with increasing certainty that what I'd just escaped wasn't about to go away. The people my brothers were talking about had power and money. If they really wanted me killed, they wouldn't stop until I was a corpse.

Which meant that letting my family protect me would be a mistake.

I was a dead man walking. My name written on the bullets in a police-issue gun somewhere. If I had dodged death, that could only be temporary. I'd use the stolen time to set up my family and do everything I could to take the heat off of them.

Lottie was probably having a baby. Cassie needed stable parents who would love her and weren't in danger every minute.

The call rang out unanswered, but my mind was made up. My anger and impulses too much to control.

I was going down, but those I loved weren't going with me.

9

Breeze

Growing up, I thought I'd known how to control fear. All that the world could throw at me, I'd handled, no matter how bad it made me feel. Our father had been a waste of space who we'd never wanted to know, our mother caught in a cycle of suffering, spells in foster care, and not knowing what would happen next had sent us into turmoil.

Summer had been my constant.

She'd always been there, until she wasn't. Then I'd thrown everything I had into finding her. Accepting that she was dead had been the most exquisite pain.

I sat cross-legged on the quilt and stared at her, my fingers shaking.

Alive.

Breathing.

Not murdered and dumped somewhere like my brain had tried to fill in when faced with the question of what had happened to her.

My too-fast pulse slowed a degree. I hadn't let those thoughts in, not truly. At the same time of searching for her, I'd been falling in love with Camden, to some extent suspending one set of emotions as another took over.

I'd started the grieving process but never really committed. I hadn't reached the depths of despair, and I knew that to be true because I felt it now. How gut-wrenchingly awful it would've been to really know she'd died.

Under my gaze, her breathing remained steady. In and out. Her cheeks pink and her heart still beating.

How was it possible that I could have her and Camden? Surely that was too much.

Behind me, the door opened with a quiet whoosh. I peeked around at Lottie checking us over.

"You've been in here all day. I'll watch her for a minute. Go take a break. I won't leave her side," she promised.

I jerked my head and stood on wobbly legs, hugging Lottie as I left the room.

Still wide-eyed and emotional, I made my way to the kitchen. I entered from the hall to see Camden at the garden exit.

His mouth dropped open, and he was moving. In a heartbeat, he had me in his arms. His warmth enclosed me, everything instantly better.

"Are ye okay?"

"No," I choked, confusing things. "Nothing's wrong. I just need you."

I had to be sure that he was still mine. That I could have them both, in whatever way the world would allow. My sister, perfect on the outside, broken inside, my boyfriend with a deep scar down his face but the purest, most perfect heart.

Camden understood. Tucking my head against his, he carried me outside, cradling me to him.

In the helicopter, when we'd been flying away from Leith and on our way to find my sister waiting, Max McRae had used a phrase that had stuck with me. The kind of thing that happened alongside an adrenaline rush. High, horny, low.

I'd been elated at escaping with Camden, and now I was so down it felt like I was under the ground. I'd skipped the horny part completely, no time to linger over the stages.

It hit me now.

It soared higher when Camden carried me into the tower beside the cottage. He climbed a set of steps to a wooden platform, setting me on my feet at the top. I backed to the wall, unable to look at anything but him.

His gaze scalded. "Tell me what ye need from me."

"Make me feel that this isn't a dream. That I'm still in reality. That you're real and so is everything that just happened."

He paused for a beat then dipped his head. "Can I decide how to do that?"

I nodded, butterflies fluttering in my belly.

Camden's intelligent gaze took in the room then came back to me. "Go stand by the window."

I jumped to obey, taking my position next to the narrow sill, the view of a forest behind, a burst of excitement pulling me into that horny stage.

Camden and I shared a liking for him restraining me.

Tying up my arms or keeping my legs wide apart. Or both. But there was no bed in this space. No furniture at all.

I should have known that wouldn't cause a problem for my inventive boyfriend.

"Arms behind ye, hands clasped," he demanded.

I obeyed, and he stood in front of me, so close I could feel the warmth of him, though he didn't touch me in any way.

Not yet.

For a moment, he just breathed me in, then Camden slowly grazed his fingertips down my arms to the hem of my top, inching it up and off me. I re-tangled my fingers together, loving his intake of breath as his attention clung to my breasts.

"I'm going to strip ye, fuck ye until you're convinced of me, then I'll do it again until I have ye believing," he said with a kiss to my cheek.

Another kiss landed on the corner of my jaw, just below my ear, then he trailed down my throat. His clever fingers unclasped my bra, ridding me of it, then he paused to make sure my hands were where he'd ordered them.

Camden kissed first one breast, then the other, toying with my pebbled nipples. He sank to his knees. I didn't notice anything but that seductive action, until he pulled back to strip his own shirt. With his focus holding mine, he reached around me and bound my arms together with the T-shirt, knotting it quickly. I tested it, surprised with how firm the hold was.

He raised a bulky, bare shoulder. "I would have used yours, but I'd have felt bad if we tore it. Now for the rest of your clothes. You're not the only one needing reassurance. I need to see my name on your pussy."

He stripped me, guiding me back to lean beside the narrow window so he could bring my leg to his shoulder. Camden admired the tattoo he'd laid into my flesh, tracing the letters of his name with his tongue. He blew on me, making me shiver, then touched his lips to my core.

I moaned but resisted the urge to close my eyes. I needed him to give me the burst of feeling I'd got so many times from him. To take me out of my head then land me back on the planet.

He curled one hand around my hips to balance me, the other grasping one of my boobs, and he French kissed my lower lips. Camden worked me slowly, steadily building me up.

He licked and sucked, spending time on my clit and alternating sliding his tongue into me. I pressed my shoulders into the rough stonework, my breathing coming in fast little puffs. He knew exactly the speed to go. The pressure to apply. I almost longed to weave my hands in his hair, but this was perfect. I was so close, so fast.

"Give me this one while I'm on my knees for ye," he paused to say. "I'll take another when I'm fucking ye."

It was all I needed. The pressure of the past however many hours broke over me, eclipsed by a wave of pure, perfect feelings. My orgasm swept away every other thought, and I relaxed into a spiral of pleasure, almost sobbing with how good it felt.

Camden dropped me to my knees, wrestling with his jeans. I could only grin at how eagerly his cock sprang free. He sat against the wall with his legs wide and picked me up by my hips like I weighed nothing. I knelt over him, and he positioned his cock right where we needed him to be. I sank down with a moan that Camden cut off with his mouth against mine. Both of us breathing in the other until I was fully seated.

This. Just this. Only him.

He kissed me, taking most of the control of me riding him, his firm grasp on my hips guiding the speed and timing it with our dirty kiss. The slide of him inside me was matched by his tongue over mine.

I could do nothing but live right here in this moment. Enjoy him for everything he was and everything he did to me. I was so in love with him, and that was all I needed to keep me sane when the world tried to make me otherwise. I was a different person now, one held up by love. My smile returned.

Camden's hips jerked to meet my falls, his moves harder now. He thickened inside me, his muscles tightening, his gaze so intense. I loved watching him like this.

His fever kickstarted my second orgasm.

My breath hitched, and I held his gaze with mine, letting him see what he'd done to me.

Camden's lips parted. "I'm going to come."

I moaned and tumbled over the edge for a second time. Inside me, Camden thrust a few more times then stalled out, his cock pulsing. Coming in me hard.

He held me to him, his chest rising and falling like mine, but he made quick work of untying my hands, even if I was too dizzy to do anything but drape against him.

I hugged him, taking a long minute to come down from

my high.

Camden nudged my face with his, kissed my cheek. "Did that help?"

I let a relieved smile spread. "Yes."

"Because if it didn't, give me five and we'll try again."

I giggled, and he gazed at me like I was so special.

But it was him who was the special one. So beautiful. So *mine*.

"Everything's going to be okay," he promised. "I'll never let anything hurt ye again. I swear it."

I sagged against him. "I might need to borrow that strength again. She's alive, Camden. God, what has she been through? She can barely speak."

"I don't know, but whatever it is, she's safe now."

A sound downstairs interrupted us.

"Breeze? Lottie said your sister's waking up," Thea called.

A rush of fear returned, but I took a breath, climbing up with Camden to dress and return to my sister's side.

Summer

I woke to hushed voices, terror stealing my breath. Sleep was a safe place where no one could touch me. I'd done a lot of that when I'd been a prisoner—the only thing I'd had control over.

My brain tuned in to the danger. Except the voices were familiar.

I blinked at the room, remembering where I was.

Free.

I jerked up in the comfy bed.

In the doorway, Breeze gasped, another woman with her. The two moved quickly to my bedside.

"How long have I been out?" I asked.

"Most of the day." My sister sat on the mattress. She clutched my hand and squeezed it. "Do you know where you are?"

A cottage somewhere. We'd evaded the police. I'd... passed out?

"I think so," I said slowly. "With your boyfriend's family."

Jamieson's family.

"I fainted," I concluded.

The second woman looked me over. "How are ye feeling? Oh, excuse me. I'm Lottie. Wannabe nurse."

Breeze sent a small smile in her direction. "Lottie has helped me keep an eye on you."

"Thank you," I told them both.

Events rushed me.

Escaping the police chief's house.

The jailbreak.

Running from the cops.

I snapped my gaze to my sister. "How's Jamieson?"

I felt like I'd been operating through a veil, my senses clouded and the air thick around me. It still haunted me, my bad choices and the impact they had.

Like I couldn't make another decision safely again.

"He seems okay," Breeze said. "I'm more worried about you. I'd really like to know what happened."

She needed answers, but I was locked up.

"I'll explain, but..." I trailed off.

"How about we get ye up and feed ye?" Lottie suggested. "Come now, find your feet. You'll feel better once you're moving."

I'd needed the words to release me. Shakily, I swung out of the bed and stood. Voices came from outside the room, and someone passed by the partially open door.

I froze again. I couldn't have Jamieson hear my story. Not yet. I'd been so stupid, and I didn't want him to know just how badly I'd fucked up.

Lottie followed my gaze. "Why don't ye take this outside? It's a warm evening, and there's a ruined castle right next door. Sin and I checked it over while we kept an eye out for people. Go get some air, and I'll bring out some food in a minute."

Privacy sounded good. Mutely, I nodded.

There was a little bathroom off the bedroom, and my sister directed me in to freshen up. I wanted a shower, but it could wait. Or maybe I couldn't even do that without someone telling me I could do so safely.

I scrubbed cold water over my hands and face, dimly taking in the T-shirt Breeze must've put on me. Then I stepped into my stolen shoes and crept from the room. My sister escorted me down the hall and out of the front door.

I kept my focus down. If Jamieson saw me, he didn't say my name, even as I sensed people watching on.

Outside, the sweetly scented evening air surrounded me. I peeked at our surroundings, taking it in where I hadn't before. The cottage backed onto woodland with a rutted track leading to it. The cars were tucked out of sight, and the entranceway was fenced off, piles of rubble and stone indicating a construction site.

I stumbled on the uneven ground, my sister slipping her arm through mine.

"What even is this place?" I muttered.

"A refuge, for now."

To the left of the cottage were the ruins of a small castle. A round tower had repairs underway to the stonework, and the framework of a new roof rose over it like the skeleton of a boat. Breeze directed me in the door. A wooden staircase led up to an open floor, and I stepped onto the smooth planks, the orange-streaked evening sky above us through the roof beams.

My sister followed. "I still can't believe you're back. Just walking around in front of me like nothing happened." She folded her arms against what could only be miserable anticipation.

Unhappiness welled in me at the pain I'd caused her. "I'm so sorry. I made such a mess of it all. It's all my fault."

Disbelief and a willingness for me to be innocent were right there in her eyes. "You sold your body in an auction. You can't tell me that was on purpose. Not with our past. I know you better than that."

I retreated to the wall where I slid down and planted my backside on the floor. "I never intended to actually go through with it. It was a setup. Then a betrayal."

Breeze settled in front of me and schooled her features. "Give me every detail. Don't miss a thing."

I closed my eyes for a moment, going back a year in my mind. "It began with this group I joined."

"Small-time vigilantes who met at the church, I know," my sister said. "Camden and I tracked you down that far. What made you join them?"

Jamieson dumping me.

A sound came from outside the round tower. I ignored it and ploughed on.

"I had a thing going on with a guy, and he broke it off. It

doesn't matter. The group was a place I could go where my angst with the world was shared, and I wasn't the only one who felt like they were shouting into a void."

Breeze blinked a couple of times. "You had me. And why didn't you tell me about the guy who broke your heart? I didn't even know you were seeing anyone, yet it had to be a big deal to send you spiralling like that."

I didn't have a good answer for her. What had started as a casual chat became a long-term online friendship. Then all of a sudden, I'd been talking to Jamieson for so long and so intensely that there was no easy way to introduce him into conversations with my sister.

He'd become a lifeline.

An addictive secret.

Then my surf-hungry pyromaniac best friend was gone, and I'd drowned in his wake.

"Sorry." I hung my head. "I was so angry and hated him so much. All that hurt needed an outlet. The all-female group was pretty terrible anyway. Their idea of bringing down the establishment was smashing clothes shop windows after a skinful on a Friday night. I wanted more than that. One day, the organiser, Prudence, didn't turn up to the meeting. Instead, her brother came and told us she'd been arrested for shoplifting. The group basically disbanded then as no one else wanted to take over the running of it, but I was worried about Prue and talked to her brother for a while. You'll know him—Kayden. He owns the car repair garage down the road from the flats."

Breeze squinted. "I don't remember him."

She wouldn't forget him now. I never would either.

I waved my hand over my head. "Short blond hair with a close-cut fringe. A tattoo of a bird on his neck so he could pretend he'd been in jail. Anyway, we got to talking, and he shared the same ideas as me and his sister. Or so I thought. He asked to see me again, and I told him I wasn't interested in a date, but he confided that he had a plan to infiltrate a group of men involved in trafficking women."

My sister winced. "A lie, right?"

In a heartbeat, she'd picked up that he was the villain of my story. I'd missed the warning signs, so desperate to do something with my life.

The words didn't want to come, but I forced them out. "We met a few times, and he came up with a scheme to follow the money behind the trafficking ring. A sting operation. He had muscle but needed a honey trap." I thumbed at myself, the idiot who'd got sucked into the con. "He let me work out the details for myself, how he'd need someone to put herself up for auction, wear a tracker, and lead him and his friends right to the door of the buyer. It all felt so real, like what I was doing would make a difference. You know what it's like for women who get passed around by these men. They're always vulnerable and taken from poor countries, like Mum, or even just grabbed from the streets. I was smart and able. It couldn't hurt me."

A tear trickled down Breeze's cheek. "So you volunteered and walked right into danger. Oh, Summer. Why didn't you tell me?"

My hands shook. "I should have. But the plan came together fast, and at most, it should've been over within a couple of hours. I told Mum the first part so she'd know I'd gone to the club for the auction, just in case someone told her and blew my cover. Kayden delivered me there and promised he'd be right behind me every step of the way." My voice choked. "He had my bag of things. Spare clothes. My necklace."

My sister linked her fingers through mine, using our joined hands to swipe away her tears. "Your pendant?"

Jamieson's gift. The little silver surfer I'd pined over in the chief's mansion. Now it was gone forever.

For some reason, that broke me more than anything. "Yes. And I'll never get it back because I was the worst kind of idiot."

Breeze hugged me, and I shook against her shoulder.

"It was all fake, then?" she eventually asked through her tears.

Slowly, I nodded, shifting back to see her face. "All of it. I was sold. No one ever came. He took the money, and I bet he laughed."

A long moment passed until my sister could draw breath to speak again.

"It was the police chief who bought you?"

"Yes."

"And he kept you all this time?"

"Yes." My voice cracked.

"What a motherfucking bastard," Breeze bit out. "Both of them. They need to die."

The sound of splintering wood came from below us in the tower.

Moments later, footsteps stomped the gravel track, then a car door slammed. An engine roared. I climbed up to peer from the tower's narrow windows facing the road.

The sports car peeled away, lights off, and the tinted side windows making it impossible in the low light to see who was behind the wheel.

Except I knew.

"Hello?" Lottie's voice called.

Still staring into the gloom, I called down to her, "Come up."

She climbed the staircase, a steaming cup in her hand. "What happened with Burn?"

"Was that him in the car?" Breeze queried back.

I didn't need to ask. I felt the pull of him leaving my orbit.

"It was. Camden had been talking to him about Breeze's kidnap, then Burn disappeared. I figured he'd come out to see ye, but when I reached the door, he was breaking things then speeding off into the night."

"He overheard us talking," my sister guessed. She looked at me. "He was your online boyfriend, the one who broke up with you."

Not a question, but I nodded, miserable, everything wrong and getting worse. My suspicions grew over where he'd driven to in such a hurry.

"When he stomped back in and grabbed the car keys, he asked Camden about your address," Lottie added. "He wanted to know if you'd moved."

Which meant he knew exactly how to find the person who'd wronged me.

My sister made a sound of unhappiness. "He's gone after Kayden, hasn't he?"

I wanted revenge against the man, but if Jamieson really had gone there, he'd get caught by the police. There was next to no chance he could speed through the busy city of Edinburgh without getting picked up.

I'd been so angry at him, and now he was going to get hurt.

Yet again, I was the source of all bad things.

"Can you tell his brothers?" I asked Breeze.

"I'll go now. They're going to be beside themselves. They've only just got him back." She darted down the first few steps then turned back to me. "Don't vanish in the few minutes you're out of my sight."

I crossed my fingers and held them up to show her, like we'd done when we were little. "Promise I won't."

She left the tower. Lottie handed over the cup to me and gestured for me to sit on the floor. It was growing dark, but I welcomed the loss of light. It matched how I felt inside.

"Drink the tea," the Scottish woman said. "Thea's making ye a sandwich—I can't face food but I managed to make ye a drink. Before she and your sister come out, I wanted to ask ye about any injuries ye might have. I'm not trying to overstep, just to offer support when it might be easier to talk to a stranger than a loved one."

I drank the hot tea. "I'm not hurt."

Lottie's expression told me she didn't accept my words.

I held up my wrists. "This is the worst of it. The marks from handcuffs he put me in. Everything else is in my head."

Her careful gaze took me in. "Okay. Is there any chance ye could be pregnant?"

"None. I'm being truthful. He didn't rape me. He didn't do anything apart from calmly torture me with the things he said."

My throat constricted, and in a heartbeat, I was back in the scene, controlled by the whim of exactly the kind of man I despised and had wanted to bring down.

"I believe ye. I think your sister needs to know this."

I gazed at the stairway, wanting nothing but to slip into the darkness falling over the tower. "She really suffered from what I did, didn't she?"

Lottie pulled a grim smile. "It wasn't your fault, and I'm pretty sure as much suffering happened at your door."

For all my uncertainty about the people my sister had joined forces with, I liked Lottie. She seemed kind. Like she genuinely cared what happened to some strange woman who acted without the brains she'd been born with.

Another stupid, pointless tear dripped to the floorboards. "It was all my fault, though. I thought I was infiltrating a network like some kind of spy, but in reality I was being sold off."

I ran through the short version of what had happened, the words flowing more easily now.

"Do you think she'll be able to forgive me?" I finished.

"Course she will. She loves ye. I can hear her coming back. Tell her what ye just told me because I know that will be eating her up."

Breeze returned, Thea with her.

The dark-haired woman handed me a sandwich on a china plate. "I don't know what you like so it's just a basic cheese and ham job."

I smiled my thanks and stared at the food.

Breeze sat alongside me. "Burn didn't tell Camden where he was going, but Camden knows his brother and thinks our guess is spot on."

Another car door slammed, and an engine roared away.

"Struan's gone after him," Thea added. "The car he took is the one the police had joy riding reports about earlier, so he could get pulled over for that."

Lottie muttered something about hotheaded boys.

A small amount of relief pacified me that he had someone on his side, but I couldn't rest until he returned.

Lottie gave me a small nudge. "Eat up. It'll do ye good. But don't mind me if I leave ye to it. See ye back in the cottage when you're done."

Her words released me to tuck into my first meal in a day, and I devoured the sandwich as her and Thea's footsteps disappeared from the tower.

Leaving Breeze and me alone again.

Lottie's words guided me, and I swallowed my mouthful then gave the explanation my sister needed.

"Jamieson isn't the only one the police are after. Divine, your friend who helped me get out of the mansion, said the police chief won't give me up easily." I stared at my sister to convey the message. "He kept me locked up but didn't touch me. At all."

Confusion clouded her eyes. "He didn't…?"

"No. He wanted…" My words dried up, and I tried again. "He just didn't."

"God, Summer." She closed her eyes and set her forehead on my shoulder, steadying herself against that piece of news.

I didn't feel the same relief. His threats had done a different kind of damage.

"Walk me through what happened after your auction," Breeze asked.

"There were about ten women there. We were led inside the mansion and had to wait around for a while, then a butler guy told me what I'd be expected to do. I think he was running the show. By that point, I'd realised no one was coming to rescue me. Kayden was supposed to be right behind my car, so I knew it was bullshit. I told the man I wasn't for sale. That the deal was off and it had all been a mistake. I repeated it to the chief when I saw him and said he needed to let me go and get a refund."

"But he didn't."

He hadn't. Not for a month. He'd handcuffed me to a pipe, and I'd just sat in a room, slowly going mad with the realisation I'd never be released. And with his specific words of torture.

I shook my head as an answer. "Divine thinks he'll come after me. She saved my life."

"I need to speak to her to thank her. Did she take you to Inverness?"

"No, that was Arran, the chief's son."

"Arran's the man who helped Camden, too," Breeze said. "He got him out of that house and away from his dad. If he hadn't, Camden would be a prisoner still now."

I shuddered. "He took me to the police station but couldn't help anymore."

"He just left you there?"

"One of the detectives saw his car. He had no reason for being there so had to make something up, which meant I was the only one who could take any action. Still, I couldn't have done it without him."

"Do you know if he got away?" she asked. "Camden tried calling him but got no answer."

"No, which I feel guilty about. He was nice. Nothing like his dad. I'm worried about Divine, too. Both of them put their asses on the line for me."

"You're worth that. You're worth everything," my sister said softly.

We both went quiet. I could fill the silence and tell her what the police chief had done, on top of what he hadn't. The torment he'd inflicted in the weeks I'd been his. But those words had become stuck, too.

Then shock unlocked my jaw. "God, Mum. Does she know I'm okay?"

"She does. I called her earlier, and she cried. She wants to see you."

"I'll go to her."

I'd visit our mother, pack a bag, then go on the run. Breeze had to go with me, if she'd leave her new boyfriend. So far, I couldn't judge how deeply she was in with these people. They were dangerous for sure. I couldn't frame that question yet.

Instead, I picked another topic. "When I was imprisoned, I had this recurring nightmare of Mum ODing. All because of me."

Our mother had more demons than she could ever

handle. A result of far worse circumstances than I'd ever been through. Her go-to method for tackling the worst of it was a long-standing drug addiction. I had no doubt that my disappearance would have sent her spiralling. Guilt drowned me.

"Actually, I think she's trying to quit again. Along with her kicking Jack out, she might even have a chance."

"Tell me again what happened that night. Don't leave out any details," I asked, glad for the focus to be off me.

Not for a second did I forget that Jamieson was out there somewhere. My heart was in tatters at the thought he might not come back.

Voice messages from the past

Fucksurfing: Why nothing from ye this morning? Waiting.

SumOne: Mum was out working last night, but some guy hit her. He broke her nose, so I went with her to A&E in the middle of the night to get it set. I missed school, and Mum didn't call them, so I'm in the shit.

Fucksurfing: Fuck that guy.

SumOne: Fuck all the guys who do this.

Jamieson

My phone buzzed, charging on the centre console of the fancy car. Camden had returned it to me, but it was my oldest brother's name on the screen.

I swiped to answer, keeping the car's path steady on the dark road as I set the phone to loudspeaker. "What's up?"

"Where the fuck are ye going?" Struan barked down the line.

No point in hiding anything. "Summer was tricked into selling herself. I'm going to find the lowlife responsible."

Silence met my words, then, "Tricked?"

"Tricked."

I took the ramp onto the M90 motorway and slid the dark-purple sports car into fifth. It was late, but traffic flowed steadily around me. I weaved through and shot across to the fast lane, putting my foot down.

We were an hour outside of Edinburgh and the Leith district where Summer lived.

And where Kayden worked.

I'd been down her road any number of times on street maps, first searching for the girl I was chatting to, then because I had an obsessive need to be familiar with her life.

I knew the location of the garage she'd told her sister about.

I also knew exactly how to get to Kayden to come and meet me, if he wasn't there. Nothing brought people running like an alarm blaring and pretty orange-red flames crawling the walls.

"Don't worry," I told Struan. "I'll be back in time for our Cassie mission. This is a side quest."

In my rearview, a chunky, matte-black Range Rover merged in to hang on to my tail.

I swore and chuckled, my heart thumping. "Just ye back there?"

"Just me. Camden and Sin wanted to come, but that meant splitting our resources too much, and we didn't know how quickly you'd be back. Pretty sure they'd insist on ye abandoning this revenge plan."

I peered back, though I couldn't see his face. "Meaning ye won't?"

"For fucking weeks, I've been on light duties. Sin started work for Gordain. I had a chat with Max about becoming a mechanic, but until I was healed, no one let me do shite. Know what I was doing instead?"

"What?"

"Building my strength up, aka, waiting. And what else but for this? I need in on the action."

A thrill flashed through me. "For real? I don't intend to go easy on this fucker."

"Deadly fucking serious. Now listen, the minute we're off the motorway, stop. We need to lose that car you're in— the one that half the cops in Scotland would've heard about. Heading into the city in it's a fucking stupid idea."

Light dawned on my thick head. Struan was right. I stamped on the accelerator and made fast work of the remaining miles.

In our procession of two, we crossed the Queensbury Bridge, my brother never leaving my wake.

The second I was over the water, I sped down the off ramp to the closest housing estate and screeched to a halt.

He followed and pulled over ahead of me. I wiped the car for prints, grabbed my phone, then jogged to climb in beside him.

"If this is a trick to get me home, we're going to fall out." I buckled in.

Struan snorted and wasted no time in getting us away. "Consider it brotherly bonding. Now before I lose my mind about ditching that fucking gorgeous Bentley, catch me up with everything ye know."

With my anger simmering, I outlined what I'd overheard Summer tell her sister.

It was hard to control the urgency in me. The exacting, powerful need to fuck up Kayden. Summer deserved nothing less. She was open-hearted and passionate, and this guy had seen her as nothing more than a commodity.

Beyond that, my guilt ate me up. I'd hurt her so badly, she'd felt the need to use up that pain in the first opportunity that came her way.

I'd die to avenge her.

Kayden would suffer worse.

Struan listened, taking it all in. "Does Summer know you're doing this?"

"I didn't tell her, but I'll fill her in after we're back. I eavesdropped on her so didn't get a chance."

He raised a dark eyebrow.

"Don't tell me ye wouldn't do the same for Thea," I snapped out. I wasn't ashamed of listening in. She wouldn't have told me it all herself, and no action would have been taken. Good manners could go fuck themselves.

"I'm a possessive arsehole, so of course I would. Just wasn't sure that Summer was your Thea until this second. I've got your back. Let's bring this wee shite to his knees."

We cruised into Edinburgh. A police car eased past us, going in the opposite direction. It didn't stop. I paid it no attention. Made no attempt to hide.

If this was my last act, it was a worthy one.

The fact the cop car didn't stop was a sign this was right.

The streets of Leith were familiar, though I'd never been here in real life before. Struan had in the rescue of

Breeze, he told me. We passed the tower block where Summer had a bedsit then kept going, down the street to a rundown building on the corner.

The white sign read *K. Jobs Automotive.*

Kayden's garage.

The roller doors were closed, but a narrow window at the side of the building was lit.

Someone was home.

"This it?" Struan idled the engine.

"Yup."

"We'll hide the car then circle back."

Pulling away felt wrong, but we tucked the car in an alley two streets along, then I was out in the fresh air, my brother jogging to keep up.

"Gameplan?" He fell in alongside me.

"None, except for fucking him up."

We marched down the street. Struan grabbed my wrist and lifted it, pointing at the lighter I was flicking.

"Really?"

I gave him a happier grin. Of course arson was on the table. "Goes without saying, doesn't it?"

He uttered a dark laugh and, side by side, we made short work of the distance to the garage.

I scanned it on our approach. It stood alone, a pub next door but divided by a big garden. Otherwise, the surrounding houses and flats were across a wide street. None close enough to be in danger of a little blaze. No CCTV in sight either.

Ignoring the shutters, I rounded to the side door and

thumped on it. "Kayden!"

For a moment, nothing happened. I smacked it again.

"Who's there?" a challenge came.

"Got an award for a ye, big man."

Silence followed.

I booted the door, testing the lock. "Oh, come on. It's shiny and it says first prize, fucker."

Under my skin, beneath the psycho clown front Kayden would see, I was seething. A mess. He'd led her into a trap then left her to be raped. Maybe even murdered.

Simply fucking him up wasn't nearly enough.

"Let me," Struan muttered.

He grabbed my shoulder for leverage, reared back, and kicked the door.

It splintered and gave, revealing a man inside.

Short blond hair, tattoo of a bird on his neck.

I grinned maniacally. "Hello, Kayden."

Our target switched his gaze to Struan then back to me.

From the room behind him, another person peeped out. A small, fair-haired girl of maybe sixteen.

I jerked my chin at her. "Go home, sweetheart. I need a word with your boyfriend."

She shouldered a rucksack, scuttling around Kayden. "He's not my boyfriend. I only came around because he said he had work for me."

She passed us and jogged across the road to the block of flats where Summer and her mum lived.

I turned back to Kayden, advancing on him in the wide

workshop. Unable to get around us, he retreated deeper into the garage.

"Isn't it a bit late for ye to be assaulting schoolgirls? Or was she another recruit to be sold at auction?" I queried.

Struan propped the door shut at my back and followed me in.

Kayden narrowed his gaze and slipped behind a blue VW, using the car to separate us. The scent of fuel filled the air, the concrete floor streaked with black grease.

"Which bitch are ye here to threaten me about?"

Which? My blood boiled.

In a move from *The* fucking *Matrix,* I sprang onto the car's bonnet and launched at him. Kayden grappled me, but I was stronger. Several inches taller at six-two. The time I'd spent on Torlum working the cold land had built muscle, and even in my cell at the police station, I'd maintained it.

In a heartbeat, I had his arms behind his back and his face pushed down on the VW's dented paintwork.

"I'm here for Summer. Say her name, motherfucker."

"Summer," he said without hesitation. "I don't know what she told ye, but this isn't my problem. She knew what she was getting into. It pays well. I'm only the driver. I drop girls off at the club. There's nothing in it for me."

I slammed my fist into the back of his head, bouncing his face off the metal while restraining his wrists in my vice-like grip. "Liar."

A picture formed in my mind.

Summer's experience wasn't a one-off. Kayden had done this before. We might even have interrupted him doing it again tonight.

The very first thing that'd bonded Summer and me was a hatred for the men in this game. The ones who profited off women's misery. Women like my mother. Like Summer's mother. They were victims of men like this.

Any restraint I had lifted.

Kayden deserved no mercy.

"Confession time, and I might be lenient. How much did ye get for Summer's auction?"

He groaned under my hold. "Honestly, I just drove—"

I smacked his head again, and blood trickled from his nose. He wrestled one arm free and braced himself against the car, but I pulled the other one higher on his back, close to breaking point.

He screamed. "Okay, okay. Five hundred quid. She can have the money. I've got more than that in my jacket. Take it."

His eyes were wild, whites showing. His gaze leapt to Struan as if my brother would help him.

Struan left his lean on the wall and collected Kayden's leather jacket from a hook. He rifled through the pockets and extracted a box of matches and a clip of notes.

"Mine," I demanded.

Without question, my brother pocketed the cash and tossed me the matches.

I released Kayden's head to catch them in midair, the pack rattling. I still needed to get my Zippo back, but it had been left in the woods outside McInver's on the night of the fire. I'd used matches that day, too.

They were more elegant solution to needing a flame. No fingerprints. No evidence. All disappearing into ash.

"Don't touch anything in here," I told my brother, a plan coming together quickly.

Struan resumed his lean, flicking his fingers at me to get on with it.

"What about her things?" I asked Kayden.

"Don't know what you're talking about."

"She had clothes. A bag. Her pendant."

"Chucked it all."

My rage spiked. "Ye did what?"

He squealed again, his cheek copping my next hit. "I have the pendant. If I give that over, will ye let me go?"

"Try."

He eyed Struan again. "Inside that little cupboard."

Struan pushed off the wall and pointed to a small key cupboard on the wall above the messy, tool-and-litter-strewn workbench. He opened it, revealing hooks. A couple had car keys on, but the bottom row contained different items, draped with care.

"What's that?" I said, unease building.

I knew the answer.

Jewellery. Silver necklaces, wrapped twice around the hooks, or sparkly bead bracelets, and some cheaper plastic trinkets.

"Fucking hell," my brother spat. "A trophy cupboard."

Struan took a handful of jewellery, brows furrowed as he extracted a slender silver chain with a surfer pendant from the lot.

He knew Summer's property.

We all wore a version of her pendant on our skin.

He stepped over, and I reached out, taking the precious object with care.

My heart beat faster.

Once or twice upon a time, I'd been in the situation where I held power over a man's life. The first was a convicted paedophile who'd been released from jail to live in the Aberdeen community. The fucker changed his name and went on to hurt more kids.

One of them was a girl in the same foster home as me. I'd heard her confiding in an older girl.

I'd burned his house down with him in it. Killed the bastard.

Then on Torlum, I'd done the same to Jenkins. He'd wanted to buy me or Cassie from our keeper. People like that didn't deserve to live.

Men like him broke my limits.

If I'd come here with any restraint, it fled.

Except I had no chance to process the strength of my emotion because Kayden burst up in a rush of power.

He yelled in outrage and shoved me away, half falling where he rounded the car. My brother intercepted him, and Kayden threw a punch.

He missed and danced back to the doors, pulling down a stack of cardboard boxes like they could protect him.

The whole place was a fire hazard. He really needed to tidy up.

"Arseholes like ye think you'll get more pussy by being the hero," Kayden ranted, caught in the corner between the two of us. "You're looking at it wrong. Girls like Summer will eventually be on their backs, spreading their legs whether ye take a cut or not. It's not my problem that you're whipped. Get the fuck out of my business and leave the real men to run the show."

I laughed, because this was going to be a pleasure.

"Or what?" I queried, tilting my head at him, curious to see where he thought this might go. "Hey bro," I said to Struan. "What do ye rate Kayden here's chances of getting past us?"

Struan glowered from in the front of the VW, clearly unhappy about having to dodge a punch. "Slim to fucking none."

He was right. Kayden had done too much for us to let him go. Not just to Summer, but other lasses as well. There had to have been eight or more trophies on his hooks. Eight lives ruined by him.

We could break bones and take him out of the game for a while, but he was scum. He'd do it again.

Kayden had activated my destruct button, and I couldn't back down.

"Yeah? What the fuck are ye going to do? People are on their way here. I called the cops, so back the fuck off," he bleated.

I ignored him and scanned the garage until I found what I wanted.

The place was too small to have a petrol pump, but a plastic container sat on the floor under the counter. I kicked it, and a dull, heavy liquid slosh resounded.

Full. Exactly what I wanted.

Hefting it up, I twisted the cap and talked to Kayden. "So here's how I see it. Ye and the cops are not the best of friends. They wouldn't lift a finger to help a miserable waste of space like ye, so there's no one coming to help."

I upended the canister, petrol splashing at my feet.

In the corner of my vision, Struan backed up.

"Ye probably don't have friends either as you'll fuck anyone over for pay. The only thing I can do now is pass on a message from all the women who suffered at your hands." I kept pouring in a line, across the floor and closer to him. "Hey, Kayden, we don't forgive ye. Now catch."

I tossed the container.

Palmed the matches.

One strike, and I dropped the flame to my feet. The petrol caught with a whoosh of inhaled breath as it woke.

"What the fuck?" Kayden yelped. Like an idiot, he'd caught the petrol tank in midair. Soaked himself. He scrambled back and chucked it aside. It bounced off the counter, scattering metal tools and spilling on the worktop.

Too late.

Fire on fuel sometimes started almost invisible, feeding off the accelerant then whatever else it could find. That applied to alcohol and to some forms of putty or gum mixtures. I was never that interested in getting technical. This wasn't a career choice. No one was going to make me take an exam. I was happy with the simplicity of a match and something flammable.

The flames on Kayden's dirty fuel didn't hide or sneak in low.

They moved fast.

They rushed to him, climbing where the fuel had splashed his body and setting light to his hands. His shirt. Reaching up from his shoulders and singeing his hair.

He screamed. Under him, the dirty floor burned. The cardboard took next, flaring bright. An occupational hazard if ever I saw one.

The fire surrounded me.

I stood perfectly still, unable to take my gaze off the burning man.

"For Christ's sake, move," Struan urged. He grabbed my shoulder and pulled me to the door.

This had been my problem at McInver's mansion.

After going to all the effort of giving life to a fire, I wanted to watch it eat. Witness the evil turn to cinders.

But more, I needed Summer to know I'd avenged her.

With a final glance at a shrieking, clawing, twisted Kayden, I let my brother drag me into the night.

12

Voice messages from the past

Fucksurfing: I got ye something.

SumOne: For my birthday?

Fucksurfing: It'll arrive today at some point. I saw it and wanted ye to wear it.

Fucksurfing: Summmmmmer.

Fucksurfing: Waiting...

SumOne: I just checked the post. I love it. I'll never take it off. I can't believe you stole that just for me.

Fucksurfing: Hey, who said I stole it?

Fucksurfing: Heh. I did. Happy birthday, my everyone.

Summer

Perched on the bed in the dark room, I waited. Unable to move. Unable to think of anything apart from Jamieson.

I'd told my sister I wanted to rest, allowing her to leave my side so she could be with her boyfriend. But relaxing was impossible. I couldn't until I heard what had happened to Jamieson. I couldn't even heave myself to the bathroom to wash, so locked up I'd become.

A light tap came at my door.

"Come in," I called.

Thea appeared in the doorframe, backlit by yellow light, bright against my dark pit of gloom. "Struan called. They're on their way back."

My shoulders sank. "Thank God. Did he say what happened?"

She shook her head. "We're going to have to wait to hear. At least we know they're okay."

She gave me a moment to reply, but I'd tensed up again.

A quiet snick of the door closing informed me she'd gone.

Darkness consumed me once more.

I hated it. Might as well have still been at the Chief's mansion for all the freedom I'd regained. Kayden could've taken a beating tonight, but that didn't make me feel better. What was to stop him doing it again? Hurting someone else as desperate as I'd been?

He needed to be stopped, but I had no power. I couldn't even get off the bed.

At long last, the sounds of an engine reached me. Voices.

Footsteps in the house.

Then, my door opening.

I closed my eyes, shaking. My pulse skipping along too fast.

Whoever was there shut us in and crossed the floor, kneeling at my feet. Jamieson. I knew him by the scent of petrol and smoke.

"What did you do?" I asked, my voice scratchy. Then I corrected myself. "What did you do for me?"

"Look at me," he uttered.

I cracked open my eyes, and he sat back on the rug, his attention fixed on me.

His muscles tensed. "I heard what ye said about Kayden. I paid a visit."

My breathing stuttered. "Did you hurt him?"

He paused for a moment then slowly nodded. "Could say that. Pretty sure I killed him."

Kayden was dead. It was so odd how this unapologetic admission didn't faze me.

"Ye weren't the only one he'd hurt," Jamieson continued. "But you're the most important. The world's a better place without men like him in it."

He'd risked so much to avenge me.

My breathing came faster. For the first time since I'd lost my hope in the police chief's mansion, emotions other than fear woke.

Jamieson settled on the rug in a sprawl, his focus still laser-fixed, but his body language relaxing. I was still a mess. Still broken. But more now, too.

Attracted.

I didn't want it. Hate and pain still swarmed me.

But it was like I hadn't truly *seen* him until this second. At the masculine contours of his face. The stubble on his jaw. How his close-cropped hair hid nothing of his handsome features. Then there was his long body. Thick thighs in his jeans. Powerful arms with a black tattoo on the upper part of his forearm.

That was new. He'd never had ink that he'd told me about.

His broad chest stretched his T-shirt, and there was something languid in his pose. If I'd met him without all our history, before everything went to shit, I'd have wanted to crawl up his body.

His gaze held mine when I finally settled on his too-handsome face.

"Are ye scared of me?" His voice came out dark.

I shook my head *no*.

"Ye don't hate me for what I did?"

"Not for that. Not for tonight."

For a long time, he was my whole world. Secret and safe because he lived in my phone. I didn't know what we were now.

"I hate myself for hurting ye," he continued. "I'm not apologising for eavesdropping either. It did me good to hear the consequences of my actions. Fuelled me into righting some tiny part of that wrong. I fucked ye up, and that sent ye willingly into Kayden's scheme. Now he's dead and can't hurt anyone again. I still need to pay more back for the damage ye took, but trust me, I will."

I'd gone mute again, too many thoughts colliding. My actions were not his responsibility. He owed me nothing, maybe aside from an explanation over what broke us in the first place.

"He's really dead?" I finally managed.

"Set him and his workshop on fire, so if he doesn't croak, he'll wish he did." Jamieson stared at me, his expression pleading like he needed me to understand. "Soon, I'm heading out again with my brothers to retrieve Cassie. I hate leaving, but her safety is at stake, and we'll have a better chance of getting her with all four of us there. We'll talk properly when I'm back. You'll be with the lasses. I promise you'll be safe."

His gaze drifted over me. "I know ye slept, but have ye eaten? Taken a shower?"

I forced myself to reply. "I need a shower but I can't do anything without being told. I think I'm broken."

"After what you've been through, I'm not surprised."

"Make me?" I asked.

He watched me for a moment then leapt up in a single flex of strong muscles. Jamieson paced into the bathroom, the light springing on and the fan whirring. Then he pressed the shower button, and water rained down in the stall, steam swirling.

"Strip and get in," he ordered.

It was exactly the release I needed.

Still shaky, I climbed up and crept to the bathroom.

I tested the water then turned. Jamieson leaned against the wall.

"I'll be back in a few hours," he said slowly.

I didn't want him to walk out. He was going again, and I was scared for him.

"Wait," I asked.

He held his ground. "Waiting."

My breath caught. He'd used that phrase on his voice messages when I took too long to respond. A cheeky, cherished tease to get my answer faster.

In rapid succession, my mind shot from my happy place of his regular messages to the day of our breakup. Him standing right there and staring at me was all I'd wanted. To yell at him. To demand an explanation.

But there were pieces of me missing or scattered.

My dignity was part of that. I'd been stripped at the chief's mansion. Every staff member or random person who'd brought me food there had seen me naked. What started as humiliating became normal.

Facing my fear, I reached for my hem and pulled the T-shirt my sister had given me over my head.

Jamieson's gaze shot to my boobs. He swore and slammed his eyes closed.

"Open your eyes," I ordered.

He obeyed, then stared at my face with his jaw tight. Like his impulsiveness was screaming at him to take all of me in.

Something in his avid attention emboldened me. I stripped the leggings next, leaving me completely naked. In doing this, I was replacing the unwanted ogling of all the strangers who'd played a part in my confinement with the heat pouring off this man.

"Get under the water," Jamieson gritted out.

I did, leaving the shower door open and gasping at the hot water sluicing over me.

"Wash yourself, Summer," came my next instruction.

"Eyes on me," I snapped back.

He held my gaze then let his focus go lower.

Turning my back on him, I picked up the shower gel and squeezed a blob into my palm. Lathered it up. Rubbed the suds into my skin. Over my breasts, my nipples hard. Between my legs.

Warmth eked into me where until now, I'd felt only cold.

I peeked over my shoulder.

Across the bathroom, Jamieson adjusted his stance, a thick bulge in his jeans.

"Shampoo your hair," he demanded, gripping the towel rail at his back.

I obeyed, collecting a little bottle of expensive-looking shampoo. The floral scent surrounded me as I scrubbed it into my long, blonde hair.

At every peek behind me, the man watching me breathed hard, his chest rising and falling in the steamy air.

I had no idea what I was doing. Only that it was possible. That my arms and legs worked.

That his avid stare gifted me life where I'd felt empty.

"Rinse," he said.

I closed my eyes and tipped my head back under the water.

"The other bottle," Jamieson spoke again.

"Conditioner," I informed him.

He rolled his shoulders back. "Knew ye needed it, no idea what it's for."

He didn't need a lesson. I rubbed it into the ends of my

hair then washed that away, too.

Although Jamieson hadn't released his hands, or stroked his very obvious erection, his gaze soaked me in. After my order for him to ogle me, he didn't hide his interest in my body. Just like he hadn't hidden his spying, admitting all.

Sharp need grabbed me. For what, I wasn't sure. Definitely for him to stay interested. It made me feel safe. That I had him on my side, even if that was impossible.

God, I needed to get out of here.

Jamieson broke his hold and collected a towel in his arms. Slowly, he approached me and shut off the water.

"Arms up," he said into the now-quiet room.

I did as he asked, and he wrapped the towel around me. Without pause, he swept his arms around my back and behind my knees, collecting me to his chest.

I wasn't small. Inches taller than Breeze. Two stone heavier. Even a month of captivity hadn't made a dent on my curves. Jamieson carried me to the bedroom as if I weighed nothing, my wet hair dripping on him. He set me down on the bed, so close it made me dizzy. Then he released me, pressing his hands down into the quilt either side of me so he loomed over me, his head next to mine.

I liked him in my space. Would obey any order he gave right now.

He reached into his jeans pocket and brought out an item.

A shining pendant on a fine chain.

A little surfer.

My lost treasure.

My heart constricted with a rush of happy pain.

"You're fucking beautiful, Summer. Put this around your throat where it belongs. Then dry up and get dressed," he muttered.

"Why?" I whispered.

"Because I have the worst feeling if I take my eyes off ye, you'll disappear."

He pressed a single, fast kiss to my forehead, dropped the pendant on my chest, and stalked out of the room.

13

Jamieson

One of the things that bonded me and my brothers, beyond being kidnapped, was a set of instincts we shared. We all had similarities. Could pick up on each other's moods. We didn't always agree, but we heard each other out.

In the front seat of the Range Rover, Sin slid me filthy looks.

He was pissed off and not trying to hide it.

I ignored him. My brain had fixated on better thoughts.

Summer's curvy body.

It was the first time I'd ever seen a woman naked in real life. At least a woman I wanted to see naked. Years ago, Summer used to complain to me about her weight, comparing her figure to her shorter, skinnier sister's. I'd told her then that she was perfect, knowing that whatever her body shape, she'd be it for me.

Now I'd seen the swoop of her waist down to a highly grabbable arse, and the weight of her round tits. I was done.

for.

Which was why my mind was with her, in the other car the lasses had taken out. Originally, Thea and Breeze had said they'd alternate taking watches at the castle ruins and, if anyone came, all four of them would leave.

None of us liked that plan.

We were all more comfortable with the women being along for the ride. At least in part. They'd stopped in a pub car park a few miles back and would wait there for us to return. It was remote enough to not expect any passing police cars, and close enough for us to be with them quickly if anything happened.

I settled in my seat, my body warm from memories that wouldn't quit.

Summer had turned her back on me in the shower, and I'd got fixated on the top of her thighs, the curve that would guide my dick to the centre of her. This perfect gap…

I'd never learned to read, but I could hold that mental image to perfection.

A darker thought occurred. Her lack of bruises. Fuck. Despite the physical evidence, there was no chance she hadn't been attacked. I shouldn't have ogled her. Shouldn't have—

"Are ye even fucking listening?" Sin snapped.

I blinked, coming back to the present. "No."

He growled in exasperation. "I was saying that ye can't take any more risks. If there's a chance of ye being spotted tonight, walk away."

I huffed. "Fuck that."

"I'm not joking. After the stunt ye pulled tonight—"

"Stunt?"

"Aye, a badly thought through chaotic attack."

I waggled my head, trying to retreat back into my cocky skin. "Sounds like me all over."

"Seriously? Is that the attitude you're going with?"

My temper rippled. I looked up to Sin almost as a father. Struan was my dangerous big brother, Camden my smarter, coolheaded one, but Sin was everything I wished I could be. Strong and powerful and a threat to his enemies while being exactly what the rest of us needed. He was our leader, and I'd follow him anywhere, trusting that his judgement was good.

But I had a new agenda.

I wanted my family to thrive, which meant I had to split from them. When the time was right, or when being around me put them at risk, I'd walk away. Maybe it was better to bring that on sooner rather than later.

I offered him an eyeroll, risking enraging him further. "Don't tell me ye wouldn't have done the same for Lottie."

He scowled at me in the rearview, not buying the same argument I'd used with Struan.

"Of course I fucking would, but with a decent plan. Backup. Forethought. Ye took off without a word and put yourself in danger."

I sighed and leaned forward, bracing against the seat backs. "Don't know if ye noticed, but I'm in danger no matter what."

"Hold the wheel," Sin snapped at Struan in the passenger seat.

Struan did as he asked, and Sin twisted to face me in

the back.

His glower pinned me down. "Drop the kamikaze shite. Do something like that again, and I will fucking handcuff ye to my arm, which will get really fucking awkward fast. Don't test me on this. I'm one person short of reuniting my family, and nothing and no one is going to break that, including ye. Got it?"

My bravado slipped.

The bleak expression in his eyes showed me how he'd felt about me being missing. This wasn't about control, it was about the bond between us.

Eventually, I'd have to break it. Him.

My backchat dried up.

"Adulting sucks," I grouched.

Sin's expression softened a tiny bit, and he righted himself to face the road. "No it doesn't," he finally said. "Being a kid was a thousand times worse for all of us. At least now, we have a chance to change our fate."

Ten minutes later, and with our lights off, he slid the big car into a pitch-black country road, no signs of life for a while.

The car bumped into a rutted lay-by and stopped.

"The house is half a mile down this road, set back in a wide plot of land and with a single neighbour," Sin said. "There's a stream that runs behind it, adjacent to the road. We're going to cross this field and approach the house from the wee river. It's our best bet for staying out of sight and avoiding the dogs guarding the house."

"How many dogs?" Struan asked.

"At least two," Sin replied. "Coming in via the waterway is my only strategy for them not hearing or smelling us right off. It should be shallow this time of year, but does anyone have a problem getting wet?"

We all made sounds in the negative.

Camden took over the plan, clearly talked through while I was out with Struan on our merry burning mission.

"We stake out the house first and look for an entry point where none of us will get savaged. If we can identify exactly where Cassie is, our best bet is to rush the place and use the element of surprise. There's four of us and probably only the husband of the family to worry about. Sin will take him on, I'll hold off the wife, Struan, ye will take any other people there, and Burn, your job is to grab Cassie and run to the car, stopping for nothing." He swept a fierce gaze over everyone, landing on me. "She's our only objective, but we should aim not to hurt anyone unnecessarily either."

Sin snorted. "Reckon a stray punch might help out the da."

I stared at him. "Oh, look at ye being all calm and reasonable."

"I wasn't saying ye can't be angry or take action."

"Just without your say-so first?"

"Stop arguing," Camden ordered. "Everyone ready? All know what we're doing?"

Each of us gave a low whoop, and we climbed from the car, shutting the doors with a gentler touch than four amped-up men should be capable of. Energy crackled between us.

That was another brotherly thing we shared—trigger-happy adrenaline and a desire to fuck shite up.

We climbed the field gate and crossed the tall grass in single file. At whatever-the-fuck o'clock, there was little moon to see by, but my eyes adjusted fast, and we found the stream, following it along the field edge in the direction of the house. A couple of hundred yards along, the riverbank ended in thick undergrowth, so we took to the ankle-deep water. The water rushed over my boots, the riverbed thankfully rocky instead of sludge. It stank, though. A rich odour of decaying leaves and whatever shite ran off the fields and hills.

We picked our way along, trying to minimise sloshing, until ahead, a glimmer of light pierced the trees.

Sin stopped us. "That's the neighbour's security light. When Lottie and I staked it out, that light sprang on whenever one of the dogs ran near the boundary."

"The dogs are loose, then," I replied.

They were a risk, not that I imagined any of us cared about getting bitten, but more that they'd do away with our element of surprise. Dealing with a locked door would eat into our time.

My brother grunted and continued on. The closer we got, the better I could make out the hulking shape of the house and shadowy gardens. No children's play equipment cluttered the grass. Cassie had told our family there was another child here, the foster carer's older daughter. How did anyone who owned one let alone two kids not have a swing, or slide, or anything for them to play on outdoors? Even the estate I grew up on had rusted trampolines in half the gardens.

We finally reached the end of the trees. The riverbank had been cleared where it edged the garden, giving us a straight view up to the house.

Tension and excitement held us all taut.

"Low and quiet, eyes open," Sin ordered.

Whispers of agreement returned.

We spread out, Struan and Camden crouching to below the level of the bank to sneak around the property.

Sin and I took up our positions as watchers. I surveyed the two-storey family home, going from window to window and searching the shadows.

Something felt off.

"She isn't here," I muttered.

Sin glanced at me. "What makes ye say that?"

"No idea. Gut instinct?" I whispered back. "What happened when ye came here before?"

"We parked up on the track and waited for the family to return. A car pulled up and drove straight past us, a woman climbing out to open the gate. Lottie hailed her, and she glanced at us, definitely hearing, but secured the gate and got back in the car then drove to the house. There, the two adults opened the back doors. Cassie hopped down, and an older girl got out the other side. I yelled out. Not her name, just *hey,* and she saw us."

I pictured the scene, the little six-year-old with her long, unruly dark curls and big blue eyes.

Sin continued, forcing out the words into the night air like they hurt him. "She's so smart. She didn't call our names either, just hollered."

"What did she say?"

"*Hello, hey, over here.*"

I nodded, emotion choking me. Not long before the police raid that saw me run from our holiday home and Cassie captured, she'd had a breakdown of sorts. The poor wee lass to that point had been calm and sweet, funny and sometimes showing a bossy little attitude that we all loved. Even after being kidnapped and arriving on Torlum, she didn't cry. But that one afternoon, she'd flipped out and begged to be allowed to stay with Lottie as her mother and Sin as her da, with us as her three brothers and a sister in Thea. We'd promised her that. Then she'd been ripped away from us.

I took a steadying breath. "She knows we're looking for her, at least. That we care and we haven't given her up."

"I'll never do that," Sin vowed.

"None of us will. But where the fuck are they? Think they got spooked?"

He clenched his fists, half turning away, then something made him snatch at his pocket. "Message," he reported, then crouched to peer at his phone. Even with the screen mostly hidden, it was shockingly bright, highlighting the hard angles of his face.

"No cars out front, according to Camden," he read. "Fuck's sake. You're right—they're not here. They've taken her somewhere else."

My breathing came harder. If Cassie wasn't in the house, we had no other clues. No way of tracing her.

Fresh fury broke over me. "Give me one reason why I don't storm that fucking place now and hunt for evidence. Speak, Sin. I'm giving ye a chance to add your input, like ye asked."

His eyes gleamed. "Will ye wait for our brothers?"

"No. Go get the car. Tell them to be ready if I need help."

He didn't stop me. I gave him half a second then scaled the shallow bank, dripping river water. Patchy grass led the way to the house, and I sprinted.

A dog barked, the sound coming from ahead.

"No ye fucking don't," I growled at the shadows.

The kitchen door was twenty metres in front of me. I sucked in air and flat out ran for it, ready to shoulder barge the fucker in.

A massive black dog rounded the house, panting hard. Its claws clacked on the patio stones, and it sighted me and howled. A second animal pursued it, letting out a deep bark.

Storming the ground, I had metres to go.

I couldn't make it in time.

I'd expected to die sometime soon, but not at the jaws of drooling guard dogs.

"Fuck off," I yelled at them.

I reached the door right as the first dog leapt. Its body collided with mine, and it snapped at my face, missing my jaw by millimetres.

The animal fell to the ground and swung around.

I lost no momentum. Crashing into the door, I lucked out. The wood splintered and gave, the lock breaking out of the rotten setting.

I dropped to the kitchen floor then rolled up fast, pain radiating from the hit.

The second of the dogs scampered after me, crossing the threshold. It sped past, and I slammed the door in the other's face, sliding an unbroken top bolt and locking the bigger animal outside.

I took a breath, palm flat to the glass.

A menacing growl came from behind me.

Slowly, I turned.

The other dog faced off with me across the kitchen floor. No other sounds came from in the house. No lights sprang on at the crash. No cars outside, no one coming to investigate the fuss. Aye, no one was home. That didn't save my neck if Mr Bones decided to take a piece of me.

I swung my gaze around, then snapped on a light from the switch by the door.

The dog blinked at me. A Doberman, I guessed. Not that I knew shite about dog breeds. But this animal was a pointy-eared, black-and-tan, smart-looking beast.

And also not budging from his spot.

Not attacking was good.

"You're actually pretty cute," I told my housemate. "Are ye hungry? Got to be some doggy kibble in here some-where."

I took a step.

Mr Bones commenced his low growl again, and I stopped dead.

"Okay. I'll stand right here. Ye know, ye remind me of my brother, Sin. He looks at me like that, too."

Mr Bones held his ground, neither leaping at my face nor letting me be.

I scanned our surroundings. The kitchen was a mess. I hadn't lived in the lap of luxury, but even the flat where I grew up when Ma was alive had never been this bad. Dirt stained the black-and-white-checked lino, with a sticky patch under my feet and mud tracked through. Several of the cabinet doors were swinging at angles, which told me someone had a temper and had slammed them too hard. Plates were crammed into the sink, and open packets had been left on the counter.

It stank of piss and rotten food.

On the fridge across the room, notepaper with squiggles of writing were held to the metal by fridge magnets.

I needed those pieces of paper. Might not be able to read them, but my brothers would, and it could be the only clue we'd get.

Mr Bones took his beady-eyed gaze off me for a moment, raising his nose to sniff the air.

"What is it, pretty boy? Did they leave ye without any grub?" Slowly, I inched towards the counter, reaching down to flip open the small cupboard.

Pots and pans waited inside.

I grimaced at them then leaned to reach further.

Mr Bones commenced his low, rolling growl again.

"It's okay, everything's fine," I coached him. "I'm an excellent doggy babysitter. I'd never leave ye hungry."

The next cabinet was below the manky sink. I swung the door out, striking gold with an open bag of little brown pellets of dogfood.

"Your lucky day," I told Mr Bones.

He jerked forward, claws clacking, and I snatched up the bag, grabbing a handful to toss it across the kitchen. The Doberman leapt after the food.

Outside, the other animal howled a mournful sound. I wasn't all that tender-hearted, but I paused to ram open the kitchen window and toss a handful of food out for him, too.

At the fridge, I snatched the pieces of paper, some handwritten, some printed, and shoved them into my pocket. Another handful of food kept Mr Bones occupied, the little pellets rolling in front of his nose across the lino. I searched the drawers, coming up empty for anything else useful.

Needed to hunt around the rest of the house.

The hallway door beckoned me.

In the back of my mind, a countdown ticked. For all I knew, despite the place's shitty state, there could be a silent alarm wailing. The neighbour could have heard the dogs and called the cops. Without Cassie being here, we couldn't afford to linger.

A happier bark brought my attention back to Mr Bones.

He sat nicely beside me, eyes much brighter now.

"Okay, friend. I'm going to do something now, and you're going to tell your doggy pal the rules. I'll open the kitchen door, chuck the bag of food out the back, and ye two are going to eat to your hearts' content. The deal is ye leave me alone after, got it?"

The dog gave a happy *wuff,* wagging its little stump of a tail.

Muttering to myself, I held up the green bag of dog food, leading Mr Bones to the garden door. Another handful of food went out the window to occupy the savage one, then I yanked open the back door and tossed the bag.

Both dogs chased it to the grass.

I didn't wait to watch them destroy it. Instead, I bolted the door again, turned, and sprinted to the hall. A fast hunt around the living room revealed only DVDs in a drawer under a crappy TV and not much else. Upstairs, I entered the big bedroom, yanking open drawers with my sleeve over my hand to avoid prints.

A couple of crime novels got searched before I tore the last pages out of each just for fun, then a pair of reading glasses got stood on and ground into the carpet.

On the other side of the bed, I searched more drawers. This time, a small notebook bounced once and landed right between my boots.

I grinned at the handwritten entries, no clue what they meant, but this was what I'd been hunting.

Back on the landing, I took a second to peer in the other bedroom.

Throughout the house, there had been few indications that kids lived here. Still no toys, no general kid junk.

But this room had two single beds. An overstuffed wardrobe.

And a red coat hanging on a hook.

I knew that coat. Lottie had brought it for Cassie on Torlum. Our sister had been delivered to the hostel and left. Like us, she had nothing, apart from the DNA that tormented us all. Lottie had risked coming to see us to bring a bag of clothes, a hairbrush, and an old red jacket of hers. It was too big for the little girl, but she'd adored it.

I wasn't fucking leaving it here.

Barging in, I snatched the coat, pulling the wardrobe door open with it. One side had bigger clothes, but three or four hangers crammed in a corner held items I knew were our sister's. A quick hunt of a chest of drawers gave me a few more items, then I whipped back the duvet.

The soft toy bought for her on the first shopping trip after our escape snuggled next to her pillow. I snatched it, squidging the middle. The phone my brother told me he'd hidden inside it wasn't there, but I added the toy to my collection, reaching a conclusion as I turned to leave the room.

All her things were here. The family's possessions were, too. If they'd left, it was in a hurry.

My phone buzzed in my jeans pocket. I extracted it, Sin's picture on the screen.

Calling me was a last-ditch action. I couldn't read a text, so any message had to be a voice recording.

An actual phone call meant nothing good.

I swiped to answer and held the phone up to my ear.

My brother uttered three words that chilled my blood. "Get out. Now."

14

Summer

A sob came down the phone, my call to my mother finally being returned. Leaning on a fence post at the edge of a dark field, I listened with my free hand clutched to my pendant, right over my heart.

"I blame myself," Mum said. "I tried so hard to keep my life separate to yours. I failed. Both of my babies were in danger because of me."

"No, Mum. I made my choices. I'm a grown woman."

"You're eighteen."

I didn't feel that age. Adult themes had been foisted on me and my sister from when we'd been far too young. We'd both matured earlier than we should've. Then again, at my age, Mum had two children, our father a man who'd taken her in when she was barely a teenager then discarded her when she started to fall apart.

"I should've done more to protect you," Mum continued. "My life is not yours. You don't need to avenge me for what I went through. I need you to know that I'm making changes. Jack's gone. I'm back on a programme with the doctor. I went today, and they offered therapy again, alongside getting me clean. I even had my first group session this evening. Can you believe, there were three other women there who'd been through similar shit as me?"

I clutched the phone. This was all I'd wanted. "I'm so proud of you."

"It won't be easy. I can't sleep for shit, but I know I need to do it for good this time. Will you come home soon?"

"I will, I promise." I had money for her, too. When we'd left the house, Struan had appeared beside me and handed over a clip of notes. Hundreds of pounds. He'd muttered that Kayden paid up, and I only had one place I wanted the money to go.

"Bring your sister and her boyfriend. Do you know he flew into Edinburgh in a helicopter to save her? Everyone was talking about it around here." She gave a small laugh. "And something else happened tonight. Remember the garage along the road? It burned down tonight. They think the owner was inside."

My muscles seized. "That's terrible."

"No, it isn't. Jessica upstairs said her daughter, Pacey, was being groomed by that man. Her daughter's keeping her lips shut, but everyone's glad he's dead."

The Leith community was tight. If no one regretted Kayden's death, Jamieson might get away with it.

Mum took a breath. "You've been gone a whole month, and I was out of it for most of that time. When you come back, we'll have a happier life. I swear it to you."

With a few more minutes of reassurance to my mother

that I was safe and sound, I told her I loved her and hung up.

Any trip back to visit would need to be brief. My home address was the first place the chief would look for me.

Realisation dismayed me.

How long until I could go home for good? For how long would he hunt me down, and what would he do to catch me?

I quickly wrote a text to Mum, just to be on the safe side.

Summer: If anyone comes looking for me, don't let them in. Say you haven't heard from me.

She penned a fast reply.

Mum: Well, duh. As if I'd ever give you up.

I laughed, but then a brief glimmer of my old spark returned, shaped like indignation.

My aim had been to bring down men like the chief. Not to run like a scared child.

But how would I do that now? How would I evade capture and still be able to stop him and others who behaved the same way?

My resentment warmed me, and I glared out at the dark. After my chat with Mum, her story was fresh in my mind. The abuse she suffered. How many people needed to be hurt before someone took down the kingpins?

Footsteps crunched dried twigs behind me, and I spun around. Thea approached.

Earlier, I'd asked my sister about the people we were with. She said they were good and that she trusted them.

Trust was a harder commodity for me to give.

"Just me," the dark-haired beauty said, the love child lookalike of Ariana Grande and Olivia Rodrigo.

"Lottie and your sister are both exhausted so are dozing. I've been checking my phone every ten seconds so got out of the car so I don't disturb them. I'm so worried."

She was with Struan, the most dangerous of the brothers, based on my initial assessment. We'd heard nothing from the men on their rescue mission, and I'd tried to block the fear out of my mind. Jamieson's stay in my life would be temporary.

I gave a short nod. "I wish I could do more."

She sipped from a water bottle. "Same. I can't handle just standing around. I went with Struan and Camden to rescue Breeze. I mean, all I did was wait at the fucking helicopter for them to return. I was a liability, or worse, a distraction. I hated that. The knowledge that I couldn't really help."

I shifted my position, her helplessness echoing how I felt. My sister had told me about her rescue, and I hated that I wasn't there for her. "I'm not a fan of feeling weak either."

Her gaze locked on to mine. Around us, the isolated car park gave way to sprawling fields. The country pub was dark aside from a light over the back door, and the last of the staff had left, giving our car only a cursory glance. They didn't give a damn who'd parked up here in their hurry to get home for the night.

"It's the one thing I hate about being a woman," Thea said slowly. "The fact that I'm physically weaker."

"That men exploit that position of power," I added.

"Exactly. And not just occasionally. Regularly."

I held the eye contact. I didn't know anything about this woman, but I recognised her anger. It mapped to mine.

She blinked, something dawning in her gaze. "Shit, that was insensitive of me, considering what you've just been through."

I shook my head. "Actually, it helps to know others have the same ideas. It feeds my anger and my drive to do something about it."

"Then you're in good company here. The fact that the brothers exist and that their sister is lost to them is all due to one abusive man."

"Who?"

"Their father. They only found each other because others wanted his money and tried to get them out of the way. Ask Burn about it. His story, not mine."

A small piece of the puzzle slid into place. Jamieson never told me about his siblings because he didn't know.

Thea snorted. "Well, apart from the fact my dad was one of the people who kidnapped them. Hence how I'm involved."

I stared at her.

If Jamieson had been kidnapped, perhaps that was the reason he broke us apart.

Doors opened at the car, and low voices followed. Lottie appeared with Breeze behind her.

My sister rubbed her eyes. "Nothing yet?"

"I haven't heard anything," Thea replied. "I messaged Struan. His phone will be on silent, but I know he'll be checking in on me."

Lottie sighed. "They all will. We can only assume they're still trying to get Cassie. God, this is so frustrating. Just waiting it out. I want to do something."

Thea gestured to me. "Summer and I were just having the same conversation. If I could design some kind of shock collar that could debilitate a man, I'd wear that bad boy every day."

Lottie let out a giggle of amusement. "How many times would ye have shocked Struan with that if it existed?"

Thea laughed, too, and for a moment, the two women looked so similar.

I tilted my head. "Are you two related?"

Lottie nodded. "We're sisters. We share the same father but only found out recently."

I widened my eyes. "The kidnapper dad? Did he fess up?"

Thea made jazz hands. "Nope. And he's dead now, so we can't tell him off about it. Yet another man fucking women over."

"Sounds like a fun topic of conversation I missed," Lottie quipped.

Thea smiled at me. "Summer's coming up with a plan."

I hesitated. Was I? I didn't feel like I could do much by myself, but then again, I wasn't by myself.

Then I sensed the weight of my sister's gaze on me.

"Can I talk to you for a moment?" she said, her voice tight.

Lottie and Thea exchanged a glance and returned to

the big car.

"What plan?" my sister asked.

"I don't have one. I'm just coming through my shock and reeling in anger at what happened to me, and to you. I get the impression Thea and Lottie aren't strangers to our shitty world either."

She held her gaze on me, and I continued.

"I spoke to Mum. She's detoxing, and it's messing with her sleep. She asked me to come home."

Breeze's stare remained steady. "If that's what you want, I'll go with you. Is that with a plan for you to stay?"

I gave a slow shake of my head. Words that had frozen inside me came easier now. "I don't think I can. Divine's parting words were that the chief wouldn't leave me alone. She thinks he'll hunt me down."

My sister held still, some thoughts processing behind her eyes. "I wondered if he'd come after you. Camden told me something the chief said when he was at the mansion. McInver bought me at the first auction, and Camden at my second. The chief was angry because I was his type. He'd wanted me as a swap." Breeze gestured between us. "We're so similar. Blonde hair, big boobs, same age pretty much. If I'm his type, you are as well."

I shivered. "Yesterday, the thought of him hunting me filled me with dread. He terrorised me. He might not have touched me, but his threats messed with my head. Now, I'm angry. I don't want to live in fear. I don't want to spend my days worrying about what'll happen if he catches me again. It hit home when I spoke to Mum because of what she went through. Nothing has changed since her abduction and sale. A generation on, and it's all still happening. No one's challenging these men at the top."

"Your vigilante phase isn't over, is it?" Resignation filled my sister's tone.

"I thought that part of me dead, but it isn't. That indignation is still there. I swear to you that I won't do anything without talking to you again."

The first time in weeks, my blood was rushing, and brightness a small bud inside me. It wasn't strong. I was pretty sure I was in some way permanently damaged.

Could I even make the decision to walk out into the night or say boo to a goose?

"I don't want you defeated, I just want you alive," Breeze said softly. "More than I want the men who hurt you dead."

I squeezed my eyes tight shut for a minute, hearing my words from her point of view. No matter what, I'd never disappear on her again. I wouldn't do that to her. "Sorry. I don't want to worry you. I'm just relieved to feel something after being numb."

"It's okay. I get it. Anything you want to do, just involve me. We'll do it together and smarter."

On the road, headlights preceded the rumble of a car. Breeze and I tucked in our dark corner by the field entrance and watched it sail past, not slowing. On the drive here, Lottie had told me how Struan had gone over the cars, looking for a tracking device. He'd found nothing, but that didn't make anyone feel safer. We were all just waiting for the next attack.

I asked my sister something else that was on my mind. "I'm also worried about Divine. You two are friends, aren't you? Can you call her?"

"She's a dancer at Baby Girl. I spoke to her there once before, and it's three AM now so she'd be coming off her shift. Unless she's still with the chief."

A ripple of something unpleasant ran down my spine. "Pretty sure that after he found me gone, his party would be over and he'd be on the warpath."

Breeze huffed a small, unfunny laugh and took out her phone, putting it on loudspeaker after she dialled a number.

"Baby Girl. Mikey speaking."

"Oh hey, Mikey. It's Chantelle, Divine's cousin. Can I have a quick word?"

Whoever Mikey was paused for a moment. "Who did you say it was?"

"Chantelle. I was there for a dancer interview the other day when Neville got fired."

She widened her eyes at me, and I smiled at her acting skills.

"Uh, sure! I remember. One sec, I'll get her."

She muted the call while Mikey walked through the club, the sound of conversation meeting us.

"Neville was one of the bouncers. Vanessa wanted me to give him a blow job to prove my skills. Luckily, I got away with that one."

My jaw dropped. "You are full of surprises."

More murmuring sounded from the club, then Divine came on the line.

"Hi, Chantelle?"

"Hey, cuz. It's me. I'm just ringing to thank you for the

package you tracked down for me," Breeze replied.

"Holy shit. It arrived, then." The line crackled like she was gripping the phone. "Good to know, but you really shouldn't be calling me at work."

"I need to have a chat with you."

"Honey, not now. I'm still working. Heading straight out with a client."

"I lost your number, can you give it to me again?"

"Oh, double seven ask me that. For two, two, three it'll get me in the shit with the boss," the exotic dancer replied with a laugh.

Breeze widened her eyes at me and rummaged in her bag, grabbing out an eyebrow pencil.

I stuck out my arm, and she scrawled on it with the pencil. 0-7-7-4-2-2-3.

Divine was giving her phone number in code. I grinned at my sister.

"I don't want to get you in trouble," my sister said.

"You won't. I'm forty-five years old."

4-5 my sister scrawled on my skin.

"Don't talk rubbish. You're younger than that."

"What's in a number? Three, two, one, it's all the same. Got to go. Great news about your parcel. Don't call me, I'll call you. Love ya."

The call disconnected, and Breeze scrawled the last of the phone number on my arm. Then she keyed it into her phone and saved it under Saviour.

"I'll drop call her, then she'll have my number. Hopefully she'll call back soon. Which reminds me, I have your phone. I found it in your cardigan which I borrowed one evening. Sorry."

I gave an incredulous smile. "You can have anything of mine. You never have to ask. It'll be good to have my phone back, though. It's a new one as I broke my old one. Well, secondhand but the same model. Kayden warned me not to take it so I left it in my bedsit."

Breeze let out a sigh. "That explains why there was nothing on it. No clues to help me search for you."

The only thing I'd done was to add my contacts and log in to the chat function where I used to talk to Jamieson. My stupid heart never gave him up.

For a long moment, I got lost in memories.

How we'd started talking, how I'd found him so funny and sweet.

It had been his bravery when we'd first met that inspired my need for justice. He'd done things I could only dream of. His presence in my life had been hot and bright like the fire he loved.

Until it burned out.

And now he was fighting to pull his life back together again.

I was battling different demons and with worse odds. I had a dangerous, influential man chasing me down. If Divine was right, he wouldn't stop until he claimed me.

Then this suggestion of revenge swirled and built as storm clouds in the back of my mind. I didn't know how, but I had to do something to get my own back. To help others.

I'd failed in my first attempt at anything real, but that didn't mean I would again.

Jamieson had wanted to talk, but if he succeeded in rescuing his sister, I was the chink in their armour.

I had to leave. I also had to pay him back for Kayden. Energy zipped through me, readying me to take action, something, anything.

At the same second, Thea revved the car's engine and hollered out the window, "The men are in trouble. Get in. They need our help."

15

Jamieson

I slunk down the stairs, ears trained on the raised voices coming from the front of the building. Through the window beside the front door, Struan and Camden stood under bright light in the middle of the yard, both with their hands out and talking to someone over the fence. Beyond them, at the gate, Sin had returned with the Range Rover. He didn't climb from the car, and I held my ground, trying to work out what the fuck was going on.

"Give me one reason why I don't call the police," a woman's voice came.

Camden nodded, gaze fixed on who I guessed must be the neighbour. "You'd be within your rights, but I swear we aren't burglars."

In my arms, I carried a bundle of Cassie's clothes plus the notebook I'd found in the parents' bedroom, wrapped up in her red coat.

If I wasn't a burglar, I was fucking Santa Claus.

"Why else would ye be here in the middle of the night?"

the woman scoffed. "All I've had from that family is endless trouble and last-minute orders to feed their damn dogs. Then I'm woken in the early hours to strange men creeping across the lawn."

I eased closer to the window until I could spot the woman. In her hand, she held a phone with screen lit, probably poised to ring 999.

At his back, Struan held his phone, the screen activated and the red End Call dot at the bottom showing me he was on a live call. To Thea, I imagined, so she'd know to drive away and not expect us to follow.

Camden held up his hands. "All we want is our girl back. They have her, and we've reason to think they aren't treating her well."

"The child staying with them?"

"Aye, her name's Cassie."

The woman's mouth twisted in disgust. "What would three men want with a wee lassie? What are ye, some kind of perverts?"

"Fuck, no. She's our sister. Please listen to me."

Camden took a step towards her, but the woman bristled, holding up her phone.

"Don't ye dare come any closer. That wean has been through enough."

What could I do? If I went out there, she'd feel even more threatened. If the police came, it was all over.

Ah shite. Any second, the dogs would probably come running once they'd scoffed all the food.

Another car pulled up alongside Sin's.

My heart fucking hammered.

Lottie climbed out, and Summer emerged after her. They opened the gate to the front garden and approached, Lottie speaking quieter than I could hear.

The neighbour lowered the phone she brandished, staring at the lasses.

They were in danger. I needed to literally call off the dogs so they could handle this without getting savaged. I turned on my heel and jogged down the hall to the kitchen. There, I rifled through cupboards.

I'd already given up the dry dog food. I needed another lure.

As quietly as I could, I opened and closed doors until finally I found what I was looking for. A tin of steak pieces in gravy. A quick peek outside the back showed me the animals snuffling around the lawn as they chased down the last of the pellets.

Just had to hope they were still hungry.

I yanked back the can's ring pull and grabbed a dish, shaking out the jellied contents onto it, and mashing it down with the side of the can. Then as quietly as I could, I opened the back door.

"Hey, Mr Bones. Looky here."

Both animals lifted their heads. The evil one growled, white teeth bared and hackles rising. I swung the door open wide, placing the bowl of rich-smelling meat on the kitchen floor.

"Main course is served. Come on," I encouraged, stepping aside so they could see my offer.

Mr Bones sniffed the air then trotted past, stumpy tail

waggling.

He lowered his head to the bowl and took an enthusiastic bite.

The second animal didn't budge.

He gave me the evil eye, though his gaze darted to his buddy. Drool slid from his mouth.

I took a risk. I couldn't hear any more shouting from the front of the house, but my family would have to leave sharpish, regardless of whether the neighbour called the police. I moved outside, clearing the way for the evil pooch.

If he leapt at me and savaged my throat, at least I'd done as much as I could.

The beast stared at me, head lowered and shoulders up. He took a step, then another, then crept past to join Mr Bones.

I breathed a sigh of relief and reached in to pull the door to, closing them in the house.

Jamieson two, rabid dogs nil.

I still had Cassie's things bundled against my side so sprinted around the house to the front corner.

"...never hurt her," Lottie's voice came. "Cassie is my little girl. We love her and only want her away from these people."

"Then why is she in care in the first place?"

Lottie stumbled over an answer, and to my surprise, Summer piped up.

I couldn't get over her voice in real life. Clear and real. Music to my ears.

"I was in and out of care as a child," she said. "Not because my mother was a bad person but because shit happens and her priority was keeping us safe. You said it yourself that your neighbours are bad people. All I know is that when Cassie's family get her back, no harm will ever come to her again."

The neighbour's answer was low and hesitant. I couldn't make out her words, but her tone had changed.

Summer pushed her advantage. "We're sorry for disturbing your evening. We're going to leave now, but if there's anything you can tell us about the little girl's disappearance, it really will be in her interests."

For some reason, her help caught me in the throat.

There were four of us brothers, and two pairs of sisters. Except everyone apart from Summer and me were matched up. It wasn't fair. We'd known each other the longest.

Sheer want rushed in me for all the wrongs between us to be righted.

She was here, fixing things.

I was also pretty certain that if I strode out with stolen goods in my arms, I'd blow the tentative peace she'd created with the neighbour. I sprinted through the dark garden to the hedgerow. A high fence lay beyond it. Muttering swear words, I scrambled over it one-handed, landing hard on the other side.

From the front of the house, engines purred.

Shite. They were done. They were leaving without me. I took off down the fence line, half falling on the uneven ground and rocks.

Ahead, lights climbed the drive.

My family's two cars eased away.

I sucked in air and put my head down, pounding over the ground until I met the road, a burst of speed taking me out of sight of the neighbour if she still watched on. But the cars were ahead of me now.

Halfway up the hill, they slowed, the red brake lights bright.

I bolted, finally reaching the rear car. I yanked the door open. Lottie gazed at me from the passenger seat.

"Next car," Sin told me from the other side of her.

But Lottie grabbed my arm, her gaze glued to the bundle I carried. "Are these Cassie's?"

I nodded and handed them over, slamming the door on her as she brought them to her face with her eyes welling up.

A door popped open on the car ahead, and I trudged to it and climbed in, landing beside Summer in the back seat.

In the front, Struan gave me a quick once-over and put his foot down, taking us away from our failed mission.

We'd missed our sister by a day or two, but it wasn't over.

"Thea," I said. "Call Lottie and tell her there's a book in the things I stole. We need to take this rescue up a level, and if it fucking kills me, our next attempt will bring her home."

16

Summer

The journey back to the castle ruins was a slow and cautious one. We took side roads, waiting for gaps in traffic before cutting across anything more major. In the forest surrounding the castle, Jamieson went ahead to check the lie of the land before the rest of us approached.

Meanwhile, the family was making a plan.

The last thing the neighbour told me was that she believed the foster carers had taken Cassie to a sister-in-law's house, though she didn't know where. In the other car, Lottie scoured the diary that Jamieson had found for clues.

We parked up, and Jamieson came around to my side. Mud spattered his dark jeans, and his T-shirt was torn.

A flash of heat zipped through me.

I blinked at the reaction.

Sin gestured to the cottage. "At most, we'll be here a few more hours while we prep to leave."

"Where will we go?" Lottie asked.

He sighed heavily. "Fuck knows. Give me time, and I'll work out something. But staying in one place for too long feels risky."

Thea raised a hand. "I have an idea. I've had the first rent payment come in from Torlum. You know we stayed in the beach house a couple of weeks ago? I could book us a holiday house like that for a couple of weeks. That way, we'd have a legitimate place to stay with no fear of a home-owner kicking us out."

Sin jabbed a finger in her direction. "Perfect. Find somewhere isolated and big enough for all of us. Use a fake name, and we'll arrive separately."

"Choose somewhere by the water," Jamieson asked, tension in his tone.

My fingers went to my surfer pendant, hidden beneath my shirt.

Thea and Lottie went inside, my sister following with a quizzical glance back at me.

I sent her a look to say that I wasn't about to vanish.

"There's something else I wanted to suggest," Jamieson continued to those of us remaining outside. "Tonight was a fucking bust, but it's only made me angrier and more determined. We were pulled from Torlum by a rescue crew. Why don't we talk to Gordain? Or at least Max? They know more than we do about extracting people."

Sin and Struan exchanged a glance, then Sin answered.

"We could. Do we trust them? There's a risk that Gordain decides Cassie is better off without us."

"Or," Struan cut in, "we just fucking ask. They offered help in the first place. Max brought Sebastian to meet us because he knows both sides of this. He is a rich boy who got jailed unfairly, and Max said that since then, he's made a point of getting to know the judges and the way the system works."

They debated between them, and my mind went back to being in the car with Arran, when he mentioned the local judge.

"I think the police chief pays off at least one local judge," I found myself saying.

The attention of all four men fell on me.

Heat flooded my cheeks. I'd never been shy, but a month of imprisonment had changed a lot. "His son told me that when we reached the station. Before I used his father's pass to walk in and free Jamieson."

"Good to know," Sin replied. "It adds yet more people to our list of enemies."

I shivered.

Jamieson watched me. "Can I talk to ye?"

At my nod, he turned back to his brothers, muttering

something and handing over scrunched-up pieces of paper from his pocket. The men went into the house, and Jamieson came back to me.

My heart thundered.

Despite days of being in each other's vicinity, and after years of living in each other's phones, somehow this felt like our first meeting.

"Hi," he said.

How was it he felt everything I did? Like we shared a wavelength.

I took a step backwards.

Jamieson held his ground. "I've got a thousand questions for ye, but most of them have escaped my brain."

"You want to know what happened to me."

"Kayden sold ye to the police chief. One dead, one to go."

How could he talk like that? He couldn't take on the head of the police service.

I swallowed and changed the subject. "Sorry you didn't find your sister tonight."

"I am, too. I heard ye talking with the neighbour."

I'd leapt from the car with Lottie with no real idea about what I was doing, only the drive to help. That payback I needed to give, at least in one minor way. Lottie had been tearful as Thea drove us through the night. I'd taken her hand, and she'd said she was glad I was there.

It had given me the release to climb from the car.

Idiotic, really. If they were packing up and leaving today, I'd ask to be dropped off somewhere on the way, hopefully taking my sister with me.

I inched backwards more.

Behind, the forest spread out, the night giving way to a silver dawn. Light enough now to see the wood for the trees.

"Let me start with an apology," Jamieson said. "Your friendship was the most important of my life and the one thing that kept me going. I owe ye an explanation and more."

Friendship.

I'd been so hooked on him that the word burned.

He swore and raked his fingernails through his short hair. "I don't even know where to start."

"It's okay," I said, my voice smaller than I'd intended.

"No isn't. I pushed ye away."

He had. And his rejection had cut me in two. A flurry of thoughts hit me. The knowledge from Thea that he'd been kidnapped. The fact that he'd overheard me talk to my sister about him, and how I blamed him. Emotion choked me, and I took another step into the tree line now.

He didn't owe me anything. He'd been my teenage crush and now he wasn't.

If I stayed near him, I'd hurt him and his family. I was a danger to them, particularly if he got it into his head that he needed to take more revenge on my behalf.

"It's fine. Doesn't matter. You had a lot going on, according to what I heard from Thea," I spoke, suddenly clearly.

"Understatement."

"We weren't real friends," I bit out the words I didn't believe. "You didn't owe me anything. We were just random online acquaintances. Nothing more."

Jamieson furrowed his brow. "That wasn't true for me."

It had to be. For both our sakes. I forced out the thing I had to say. "You should know I'm leaving. When you go, I want to be dropped off on the way."

"Fuck that."

"I'm not staying. I can't."

"I want ye to."

"That doesn't matter to me," I lied.

Though I'd steeled myself, his expression broke something in me. I wanted him. Wanted to close the distance and wrap my arms around his broad shoulders. I'd imagined far too many times what it would be like to touch him, and he was so close yet an immeasurable distance away.

Pain sliced into me as fast as the lust had.

I couldn't take it. I was broken, and his twisted appearance of heartbreak cut too deep.

I turned and skittered away.

Blindly, I fast-walked, dodging trees and crashing through the undergrowth. Footsteps at my back told me Jamieson was in pursuit.

"Summer, wait," he ordered.

I couldn't handle a conversation with him where we chatted and filled each other in on our lives despite knowing we'd have to separate. It already hurt too much. I couldn't be casual about him.

I put my head down and ran.

His voice followed. "Stop. Now."

I drove my limbs into the ground, speeding up.

His pounding footsteps didn't slow.

"Summer," he snapped. "Fucking stop."

"No," I yelled back, my voice cracking and my breathing coming hard.

He swore again, closing in on me, so much I could sense him right at my back.

Electricity licked up my spine, the shock of it breaking me out of my panic, better emotion replacing it.

Excitement. A thrill at him chasing me.

A hand grasped my shoulder.

I squealed and jerked, falling to the bed of pine needles and leaves.

Jamieson tumbled with me, his arm hooking under me so I landed on my side and pinned to his body. My back to his front, his hard form over mine and my cheek pressed to the dirt.

The silence of the dark woods settled around us.

With him on top of me, I breathed hard, too aware of every place we touched.

Jamieson didn't let go. His grip on me tightened, and his mouth came to my ear, his breath tickling my hair. "Don't run from me. It makes me want to hunt ye down."

His chest rose and fell against my shoulder blades.

That same zap of heat ignited in me again, concentrating between my legs.

All my fears and panics evaporated, replaced by complete focus on the predator who'd captured me. My mind quietened.

Nothing but this very moment filled my thoughts.

Subtly, I flexed, pressing my ass back into his groin.

The hard ridge of his cock met my move, and my breath hitched.

Jamieson gave up a low, animalistic sound and thrust his hips, driving his erection against me. "Don't unless ye want this."

I needed to know what he'd do. Urgency fuelled my brimming need.

But my hunter seemed to come to an awareness. Abruptly, he dislodged his hold on me and rolled away. "Fuck. I shouldn't have done that."

Slowly, I shifted to sit up, brushing dried leaves from my hair. I couldn't meet his gaze. "I did it first."

He didn't answer, though I sensed the weight of his focus solely on me. He stood, and I did, too.

After a beat, Jamieson raised his hand and slid it to the back of my neck. Then he guided me ahead of him and started walking us back towards the ruins.

I went willingly, liking his dominance and how he'd taken control.

Neither of us spoke again, not even as we entered the cottage. In the kitchen, Camden and Breeze prepared food. Jamieson refused the offer of a meal, and I shook my head at my sister, conscious that I probably had pine needles stuck to my skin somewhere. Her gaze took in the connection between me and the man at my back, but she kept her mouth shut.

Jamieson drove me into the living room, his grip on me more casual, probably because I was less likely to sprint away now. Thea and Struan talked in the corner, studying her phone. Lottie had a notebook open in front of her and the scraps of paper Jamieson had handed over earlier.

Sin spotted us and tilted his head. "Burn, go get some sleep while ye can. I'll wake ye when we're ready to go."

I'd rested a lot in the past day, but Jamieson had first gone after Kayden and then on the rescue mission. He had to be exhausted. I peeked up to see him jerk his head at his brother.

He didn't let me go. "You're staying with me," he muttered in my ear.

I didn't fight him. He'd chased me and caught me. That told my brain I was his, and the effect settled me more than anything else had done since my escape.

The chief's words that haunted me had become completely quiet. Kept at bay.

We entered the bedroom, Jamieson closing the door behind us. He drew the curtains then grabbed the back of his shirt, hauling it over his head.

I held my ground, a little dizzy at the reveal of his flesh.

Rounded biceps with that tattoo, though I couldn't make out the detail. Ridges above his belly from his six-pack. A dusting of dark hair that led down beneath his jeans.

As if reading my mind, his fingers went to his button, and he undid it and pulled the jeans off, sitting on the bed to kick off his shoes and strip his socks.

I didn't look away.

In just a pair of tight, black boxers, he took my hand, towing me into the bathroom.

"What are you doing?" I stammered.

"Told ye, I'm not letting ye out of my sight, which means it's your turn to sit and watch me get wet."

He pushed the button for the shower, then positioned me by the counter. With both hands on my hips, he lifted me and set me on the ledge, for a second standing between my thighs.

His proximity dizzied me.

But Jamieson didn't linger. He shucked off his boxers and stepped under the spray without closing the stall door.

I let my eyes take their fill. He was beyond strong and good-looking. Taller than my imagination had gifted me. His tight backside stealing my attention fully.

The sensation of need and excitement he'd given me in the woods hadn't gone away. I didn't know how to explore it, though. How to ask.

I wanted him to turn around, but he remained facing away, lathering up with the same body wash I'd used to cleanse my skin. His hands slid efficiently over his long body but lingered over the point at the top of his legs I couldn't see. Only for a moment, as he muttered a swear word and moved on.

Finally, he was done, and shut the water off. "Pass me a towel," he asked.

I hopped down and grabbed one from the rail, holding it out so he needed to swivel to see it. He'd seen me completely naked, after all.

"Put it in my hand."

"Come and take it," I replied.

He peered back at me. "I don't want to scare ye."

Why would the sight of his dick scare me? The answer

came fast. He thought me traumatised by the chief.

"You won't."

Slowly, Jamieson turned.

My gaze snapped involuntarily to his jutting length, hard, and pointing right at me. God. That was bigger than any I'd seen before, though my experience was limited to pictures on my phone.

I couldn't stop staring.

For a moment, he let me, then finally accepted the towel from my hands and covered himself up, fastening it around his waist. He then reached past me and took a second towel from the rail and scrubbed over his damp skin.

Overheated, I inched to the wall, giving him space while he stole toothpaste to brush his teeth with his finger.

Now he was mostly covered up, my attention came back to his inkwork. It was a surfer against a rocky island, a circle banding around it.

My pendant but on his skin.

I squinted at it in confusion.

"When did you get that?" I asked.

Jamieson followed my gaze in the mirror then shut off the tap and took my hand in his again, guiding me back to the bedroom. "Story for another time when I'm not about to pass out."

It was only now I recognised the exhaustion hanging over him.

On the bed, he laid out in just the towel. "Need me to get dressed?"

I shook my head, then spoke because he'd closed his

eyes. "No."

Jamieson tugged me down next to him, and I curled on the duvet, leaving a few inches of space between us.

For a long moment, I thought he'd drifted to sleep, and I soaked in his features in the low light.

I'd imagined this far too often when I listened to his voice lying on my own bed at home.

When I'd first explored my body, it was with his voice playing out around me.

Still, I couldn't breach that feeling of intimacy with this physical reality. They didn't map to each other.

Suddenly Jamieson spoke, his voice thick and drowsy with the need for sleep. "Waiting," he said.

That so-familiar phrase.

"For what?"

"Ye to fucking touch me, Summer. For years, I had to imagine this moment because it could never happen. Now you're inches away, and it's blowing my mind. So move closer and take my hand. Let me die happy."

Slowly, tentatively, I eased over. Then I slid my fingers into his waiting hand. Still, I was rigid. Not wanting to feel.

He gripped me, his touch warm.

Our fingers interlaced, and I got a sudden rush of feeling I didn't recognise.

Jamieson went silent. Somehow, this felt momentous.

"Tell me something. Anything," he finally spoke into the dark.

I held my breath. I should start with the rescue. The chief.

You'll beg me for it.

But I took too long.

Jamieson rolled to face me, not letting go. "I forgot my-self. You need as many answers as I'm demanding. So here goes. That message I sent you…"

My flush of warmth cooled.

He swallowed and started again. "I broke things off with you because I was kidnapped and I thought I was go-ing to die. You deserved better than to wait around for a boy who wasn't coming back."

I'd so badly needed this explanation. The implosion of my secret crush had torn me to shreds. Thea's words came back to me. "You and your brothers were kidnapped and hidden away?"

"You've heard this already, then."

"Only that. Thea said it was your tale to tell."

His thumb stroked mine, then Jamieson blew out a breath and rolled over, facing the other way.

"What are you doing?" I asked.

"It's really fucking hard seeing ye when I talk. I'm so used to being alone and recording messages for ye. Now you're here, so fucking pretty it hurts, and my dick won't behave. I'll face away until he calms down. Okay, do ye re-member what happened at McCaffrey's house?"

I forced my mind off Jamieson's dick. *McCaffrey.* I knew the name. Jamieson had found out his foster sister had been abused by a man who lived near them, and vowed to set fire to his house. He'd done it, and the man died in his bed.

In the days after, his messages to me had become rushed and urgent. The police knew it was him and had issued a warrant for his arrest, despite his age. He'd been on the run, and then he'd gone silent.

"Of course I do."

"A day after the fire, I was picked up by two men in an unmarked van."

"I thought the police caught you," I replied.

"I assumed the same, but the men delivered me to Torlum, an island way out to the west. Middle of nowhere. That's where I met my brothers as we were delivered one by one, though we didn't know we were related until the day Cassie arrived. Sin worked it out."

"Why were you taken there?"

"To hide us away. Turns out we all share a rich daddy. Surprise."

I opened my mouth, but no words came out. One of my and Jamieson's favourite conversations had been what we'd do if we had money. Our dreams had been basic. Food in the fridge. Nice clothes. A train ticket from Edinburgh to Aberdeen.

He gave a big yawn, his fingers still holding mine at the small of his back. "I didn't know that then, or anything about what was happening, only that I'd fucked up and had no future. Ages later, we eventually managed to get a phone which is how I sent that final message to ye. Believe me, Summer, the last thing I wanted was for us to lose contact. I thought I was going to be murdered there. Everything had spiralled out of control."

So he'd let me go.

I understood, my mind filling in the gaps in my knowledge. I'd gone from frantic, wondering what happened to him, to devastated, knowing that he didn't want me anymore.

Except that wasn't how I worked. I burned hot, and my commitment to the things I cared about never wavered.

It still hurt an unreasonable amount.

"I get it. You wanted to give me a clean break," I managed, forcing away the bitterness in my voice.

"No, I didn't want that. I just had to do it," he contradicted. Jamieson dislodged my hold and rolled to face me again, his gaze on fire. "I remember every word I said. *Summer, this thing between us has gone on too long. It isn't working for me anymore. I can't keep stopping and starting to listen to messages all day. Grow the fuck up, stop sending them to me, and this is the last I'll send to ye. Have a great life. Forget about me.*"

I winced, the wound fresh and deep.

He'd severed our connection so brutally, and I'd had no way of understanding it. This glimmer of what his life had been at that time was a bandage over the gaping hole in my heart.

"You didn't want to," I repeated.

"No! It was the biggest fuck-up of my life. The worst I could've possibly made while I was living a fucking nightmare. It's no excuse. Believe me, I regret every word I said, and it's even more cutting now we've met because I know what it did to ye."

Hesitantly, I brought my hand to his face and traced down the side. His blame game had to stop, which meant I needed to start talking. "You know, the problem with listening in on conversations that aren't meant for you is that you hear things you won't like. I told my sister why I did something incredibly stupid. It was nothing to do with you and all about a flawed part of me that acts without thinking."

"I hurt ye. Ye went out and looked for a way to use up that pain."

"Yes! *I* did. It was all on me." Tears welled, and I blinked them away.

By degrees, I was coming back to life. I'd lost my voice for a couple of days, but that was returning.

"I walked into danger and only have myself to blame. I'm wholly responsible. Breakups happen. Heartbreak isn't an excuse."

Jamieson watched me, and his lips curved almost into a smile. "Outside, ye said we were nothing. That was a lie."

It had been. I stalled in my explanations. "It was a lie. In part. We became nothing, and that's how we need to stay."

His hint of amusement fled. "Why?"

"Because I still need to get away from you. I'm a danger to your family. You broke us up, but it was the right thing to do."

As I spoke, my voice took on urgency. Emotion rolled and built.

I'd needed to have this conversation, even if we hadn't got to my part yet, but it didn't change anything.

In contrast, Jamieson stilled and took on an air of complete control. "If ye run again, expect me to hunt ye down."

Heat chased my fear. "Is that a warning or a promise?"

But instead of answering, he closed the gap between us, cupped the back of my head, and kissed me.

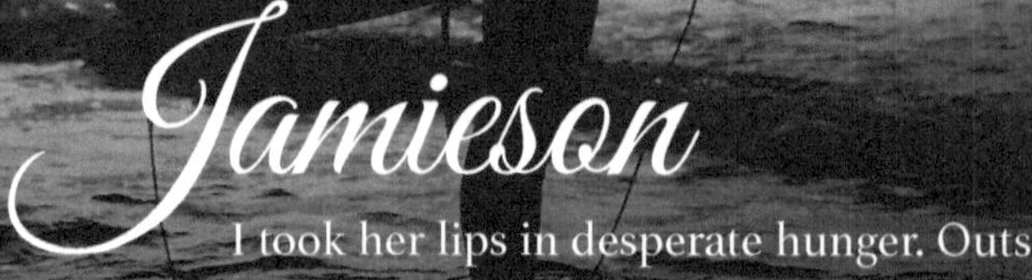

17

Jamieson

I took her lips in desperate hunger. Outside the police station, I'd kissed her, but it had been all too brief. Right now, if I didn't get more of her, I'd stop breathing.

Crawling over her, I braced myself on the mattress to get closer. Summer whimpered under my mouth, and my need shot to blazing heat. I had no experience and could only follow the urgency in my blood. But my instincts were twisted.

I wanted to hold her by the throat.

Punish her for trying to run.

I wanted to have her a little bit afraid so she'd never pull stunts like that again.

The darker edge of me that set fire to things wanted ownership now.

Summer set a hand on my chest. "Stop."

I snapped out of my state and backed up, searching her expression.

My too-slow mind caught up with what I'd done. The

past month, she'd been terrorised by an abuser. Assaulted. And I'd just forced her to kiss me.

Horror shrank my lust, and I scrambled away, breathing hard. "Shite. Sorry. I can't believe I did that."

She pressed her hand to her mouth. "Don't apologise."

"After everything you've been through—"

"You don't know what I went through."

"It doesn't matter."

Her gaze sank down my body. The towel I'd fastened around my waist had fallen away. My dick pointed at her, thick and hard.

"Make me," she whispered, still staring at my junk.

My dick pulsed for her, but I locked my muscles. "What?"

"Force me."

This was fucked up. Her words, and the fact that they only made me harder.

Summer sat up. "I mean it. I'm giving you permission. Hunt me down like in the woods. Like you threatened to do again. I... I can't do this myself. I freeze up and lock down. I don't want to stay like this. I need you to just take it."

Because she'd been hurt.

Because she wanted me to be the last if I couldn't be the first.

I groaned and rolled away, staggering across the room to where my bag had been dropped. Rifling inside, I snatched out a pair of boxers and dragged them on. It had always been Summer for me, but nothing about our lives had ever been straightforward. Now she wanted me to attack her, and even if my words said the right thing, my brain wasn't along for the ride. Nor my body.

Hunting her down… The idea churned inside me. I breathed harder. But even so, I managed a denial.

"No," I forced from my lips, still facing away.

"Why not?"

"I won't make it worse for ye than it already is."

She sighed. "You think I was raped. You didn't stick around to hear the second half of what I told my sister. The chief didn't touch me. No one did. Not like that."

Slowly, I turned.

Summer sat on the bed with her toes pointed and touching the rug, her cautious gaze on me. "Will you listen now without rushing off on a murderous rampage?"

I nodded once.

"You heard how I got taken to the chief's house. Once I was there, I was delivered to a room with a group of women. A butler guy came in and told us the chief would be with us soon and to take our places in the drawing room. He looked at me and told me to go lie on a white sofa. We'd been there an hour already, and I started to get scared that nobody was coming to take me away. It was supposed to be instant. Kayden's gang following the car using the tracker in my shirt. The other women seemed to know the drill, and they filed into the room, chattering amongst themselves. I stayed behind and told the butler there had been a mistake. I wasn't for sale and I wanted to go home."

Camden had given me a visual of the police chief's sex parties. Picturing Summer in the middle of that scene sickened my stomach. "What did he say?"

"He went red and told me if I wanted more money, I'd have to take that up with the agency when I went back. I explained that I was never meant to be there and it wasn't about the money. He got angry. Then he shouted that I just had to lie on my back with my legs open, how hard could that be?"

Anger built steadily in me, a flickering flame rising. "He tried to make ye do it?"

Her long hair fell forward over her shoulder. "He really did. He ranted at me and told me I'd regret it if I continued in the game I was playing. Eventually, one of the other women called for him and said there was a problem with the music or something like that. He shoved me into a corner and told me to stay, then went into the main room. I caught a glimpse through the doors." She cringed in on herself. "The women had mostly stripped and were posing with sex toys, or in groups, but bored-looking, like they were clocking in for a day job."

Summer's attention fixed on me. "Remember the stage we went through where we sent each other porn videos?"

I gave a short nod, lost in the scene she was describing, desperate for the outcome to be different and for her to have made an escape.

"I thought that was so sexy, but it was only because we were sharing in it. These women were putting on a performance, and it was fucked up that the chief could find that attractive. All these beautiful, smart women were acting for him, and great for them because they got paid. What the hell's wrong with a man who gets off on that?"

"It's a power game," I muttered. "And he might be a lonely old scrote, but that doesn't change how dangerous he is. What happened next?"

"The butler came back. I'd tried to leave the holding room, but all the doors were locked. He yanked at the long T-shirt I wore that barely covered my underwear. It was how I'd been presented at auction, like an innocent schoolgirl just out of bed. I got upset and pushed him away and yelled that I wouldn't go through with it. Then the double doors flung open. The chief walked in. It was the first time I saw him, though I knew from the women's conversations who he was. The model of a shrewd businessman, all power-ful in a suit and with his fair hair swept to the side." She hunched her shoulders. "He had this aura that I must obey him or face a world of pain. I couldn't, though. My fucking stubbornness. I slowly worked out I'd been tricked, and I had this insane idea that I could just walk out if I explained the mistake. So I did exactly that. I said I'd been taken to the auction by a man who lied to me, and I never agreed to this. I asked him to let me go."

Even after that, she'd been there a month. The anger in me seared and scalded. "Ye told him the truth and he locked ye up?"

Summer gave a short gasp of emotion. "Of course he did. Are you surprised? My mother was kidnapped from the streets, or maybe sold by a relative, and taken unwillingly to another country to be forced into prostitution. Even know-ing that, I had this notion that the same couldn't happen to me. The chief looked me up and down then spoke qui-etly to his butler, ignoring me. The man snatched me by the arm and towed me upstairs to a small bedroom. It had a little bathroom but no windows, and other than the times the chief ordered me to be brought out, I was kept in there."

I grasped the chest of drawers at my back, dimly noting a rattling of the mirror and the other objects on the top.

"He ripped off my clothes. The heavy weight in the shirt fell free. It was a coin, not a tracker. I was such an idiot." Summer's chest rose and fell. "Every day for the first week, the chief would come to my room. At first, I was angry, and I'd scream at him to let me go."

"Others must have heard."

"They did! Every person who brought me food knew. I told them all."

Which meant they weren't surprised. Just like Kayden, he'd done it before.

The sourness in my mouth worsened.

Summer continued. "At first, he simply asked me if I'd changed my mind and was ready to go through with the contract. I'd yell my answer and he'd leave. By the second week, he changed his tune, and so did I. My reality had set in, and I knew he wasn't about to let me go. He opened the door and just watched me. Then he told me I'd beg him for it or I'd stay in that room until I was too spoiled for him to want it anymore. And do you know what? At no point did he get angry. He enjoyed it. I had made it into a challenge for him, and he intended to break me. Another week on, and he'd send the butler to handcuff me and take me downstairs. I didn't fight it. He'd lead me into the big room with a new party of women and told me to watch. The chief came in and fucked them in front of me."

"To show ye what he wanted," I bit out.

"Like I'd suddenly give up my resistance and fall in."

Kayden had delivered her into this hell and paid for

his sins. The butler had tried to force her, and along with the chief, he needed to burn, too. I had no problem adding more names to my mental list.

"Some of the women there must have recognised you. They knew you were a prisoner and chose to ignore it," I spluttered.

"I wasn't allowed to talk to them. He had the butler gag me once when I yelled. I don't think they knew why I was there, not like the other staff did. The chief would have them act out all kinds of fantasies. They'd have to fuck each other, or pretend one was unwilling and drag her onto a platform. He liked a show. A group of them writhing in front of him. He used toys on them, or they would do it to themselves if they weren't part of the main action."

"In the middle of that was ye, ignoring his training," I managed.

"I guess it was training. In my mind, he'd put me there to break down my resistance so I'd willingly give in to him. I don't think he's above rape, but breaking me had become his game." She gripped her elbows, horror stark in her features. "When I escaped, it was because Divine, one of the working women, knew I was missing. She persuaded the chief's son to help, and that's how I got to Inverness and through the doors of the police station. He gave me the access and worked out where you'd be. But Divine told me without a shadow of a doubt that the chief would come after me."

My mind roiled with all she'd been through. My eyes were wet. "For a month, ye suffered that, but ye still came after me."

"You were a prisoner, too. He was going to kill you."

I bit down on my urge to tell her to never protect me.

She was precious. I wasn't worth the risk.

Summer continued. "But you were a prisoner for over a year on the island, from what I've worked out. Was your prison keeper kind?"

"No, but Keep's dead, and so are the men who imprisoned us there. Believe me, that goes a long way to making me feel better. If the chief wants ye, he'll have to go through me, and seeing as I'm in his sights, too, that gives me even more reason."

"We can't beat him."

"Then I'll die trying."

Summer exhaled and stared at me. "No, you won't. But that isn't the point of this. I want you to understand me. I was never raped, but I was shown the value of my virginity as a weapon to be used against me. If I don't have that, he can never claim it, no matter what else he does to me. I want you to take it from me. By force. You broke my heart so easily, and I want you to break my body, too."

"Summer, no."

"You say we're friends? Prove it. I need to get rid of my virginity and I can't just lie here on my back without panicking. I don't have time to work through this...whatever's wrong with me. Chase me down and do what I ask, because after a month of refusing to give it up to save myself, it's the only way I can do this now."

I opened my mouth to refuse her, but the words got stuck. She was supposed to be my first and only. I could never hurt her. And it was fucked up that I wanted the image she painted. To pursue her like we had in the forest then dominate her.

Force myself on her.

My dick was rock-hard again, and I palmed it through my boxers, needing any kind of relief. Summer dropped her gaze to my hand, and her breath hitched.

"I have your permission to just grab ye and take ye?"

"Yes," she breathed. "Fast and with words to tell me you mean it. You'll have me and I get no choice."

"And the only reason is so I can take the virginity ye don't want?"

She hesitated then nodded.

A lie.

A shout came from outside the room.

Summer jumped, and I took a stupidly long second to move.

At the door, I peered out.

Down the hall, Camden moved our way. "A car has just turned up. Grab your shite. We need to go."

18

Jamieson

I dressed fast, my heart racing. Summer darted around the room, snatching up items of our and my family's possessions. Hushed voices called through the cottage, and footsteps drummed. In the hall, I took Summer's hand and kept her close behind me, alert for whoever had found us.

We'd always known that our stay at the castle ruins would be short, and leaving at a minute's notice wasn't unexpected. It was the *who* that scared the shite out of me.

At the front door, Sin stared out the peephole. "They're approaching. Is everyone ready?"

We all gave quiet agreement, my family emerging from the kitchen and living room, bags over shoulders, Lottie hastily tidying up behind her before she dashed over to join Sin.

Most of our things were still in the cars. Cassie's, too. We'd intended to leave no trace.

"Who's out there?" I demanded.

"Unknown." Sin flicked his gaze at me. "Not cops. Two men and a woman. They arrived in a family car."

"What are we going to do?" Camden asked.

"Walk straight out, go past them, and get into our cars and leave. Same seating configuration as earlier. No one speak, no lingering." He eyed his girlfriend. "Definitely no apologising for the mess we've left."

"It isn't a mess. We've been good housekeepers," Lottie commented.

Sin grunted. "Doubt they'll see it that way. Keep your heads down in case they take pictures or video. The worst-case scenario is they chase us. I'll intervene then."

"Or they call the police," Summer whispered.

Sin raised a shoulder. "If it was the homeowners, they would have marched straight up or hung back and called the cops already. These people have been talking amongst themselves. No one's used their phone. My guess is they are here to check in on the house. We were unlucky in that we hadn't left sooner. Opening the door now. Heads down, let's go."

All eight of us filed out of the house. The group auto-matically clustered around Summer and me, sheltering us from the three people across the track.

"Who the hell are you?" one of the men called out. "That's private property."

"Keep moving," Sin urged.

Our cars were further down the lane, under the cover of trees. That meant we had to march straight past the in-comers. I didn't like hiding. Not knowing my enemy. I raised my head to look their way.

A dark-haired woman stood in front of a man in glasses, both glowering at Sin. The second man scanned us all, his phone raised.

For a second, I saw the lens, and the lens saw me.

"Down, idiot," Struan snapped and slung an arm over my shoulders, forcing my head lower.

"If you've stolen anything, or there is damage," the man shouted after us.

He didn't finish his threat, presumably assessing the numbers or maybe the size of us men and not liking his odds.

I didn't take a second look.

At the cars, we threw ourselves inside. Sin and Struan drove us away, gravel spitting from our tyres.

We left the castle ruins behind like we did every other place we stayed in.

For a long while, nobody spoke, though we all darted glances out of the back window at the winding woodland road.

Thea's phone buzzed, and she answered it, putting Sin on loudspeaker. Their car was behind ours.

"I don't think they've pursued us. We'll keep driving. Thea, do ye have an address for us?"

She tapped something on her screen. "Yep. Just confirmed. We're taking a risk in going there early."

"Worth taking," my brother concluded.

Thea gave him a postcode, then hung up.

"Where are we headed?" I asked.

Thea twisted around and held her phone out. Onscreen

was a picture of a weatherbeaten house. Sandy ground and stiff coastal sea grass edged it, and my heart leapt.

I needed the water, even if I couldn't surf.

"I started looking for holiday rentals we could book and stay in without fear of someone kicking us out," Thea said. "The place we were all happiest was the beach house. Funnily enough, that's vacant right now, but it would be foolish going back to somewhere we could be traced. Particularly with the two of you on the run. I searched way further up the coastline, far beyond Aberdeen, and found this house. It's remote enough that no neighbour overlooks us, but on the sea. I doubt they'll have surfboards or wetsuits, but—"

"You can get in the water," Summer said. She gave a small smile to Thea. "Sorry to interrupt. Is Struan like Jamieson? Needs to get out on the waves?"

Thea's lips curved. "Pretty sure yours is worse than mine in that respect, but it was high on my list of things we needed. There's enough bedrooms for all of us, and Lottie thinks the foster carers took Cassie north, so we'll be in the right part of the country."

"I have money," Summer added. "I was going to give it to my mother so she won't have to walk the street, but I can split it."

Thea blinked at her. "You're such a sweetheart. Keep the cash. Get your mum set up. I've got more than enough to take care of us for a few weeks. Beyond that, and we need to find work or do something, but that's a bridge to cross when we come to it. Who knows where we'll be by then."

She continued with a description of the house, but I'd got stuck on the easy way she'd given ownership of me to Summer at the start of the conversation. Yours. I wished it could be that way. I regretted everything about the way I'd broken us up, and the fact I still couldn't give her safety. She'd never be mine, but I'd always be hers.

I tuned back in when Struan spoke directly to me.

"Get down in the seat and close your eyes for an hour or two," he commanded. "There's a long drive ahead, and it's better to keep your ugly mug out of the sight of traffic."

Yet again, we were dicing with danger, driving stolen cars in broad daylight to a holiday house we weren't meant to get to until late afternoon. But we had no choice. For once, I was glad not to be in control of this. I hadn't slept in days, and my need to be ever vigilant for Summer and her staggering request hadn't dimmed. Right now, there was nothing I could do but rest. I settled on the back seat and put my head in her lap.

"Stroke my hair," I asked.

Instantly, Summer's hands went to my short lengths, her fingertips making soothing circles on my scalp and grazing down my neck.

Then I was falling asleep in exactly the position I'd always wanted to be in.

Several years earlier

I couldn't remember the exact website or app where I'd met Summer. It was some kind of shite in school where we talked with pupils from other schools. Or maybe something organised by social workers. Either way, we were encouraged to connect with kids living in challenging circumstances.

She didn't even use a real picture, or her name, as we were allowed to be anonymous. It was her words that won me over. The project was designed for us to talk in voice messages about our experiences growing up but in a positive way, like how we were going to make the world a better place.

I remember word for word Summer's first entry.

SumOne: I'm going to bring it to mankind.

The chat was moderated, so she'd picked her words to get past that check.

I'd replied, despite hating the whole point of this exercise. I was supposed to be encouraging other kids in making plans for the future, or perhaps the idea was that I could see I wasn't special and therefore had no right to be angry at the shitshow of my life.

FSurfing: Same. Meet you at ten. I have tools.

She'd liked my comment but hadn't responded.

Her answers to other people were smartarsed and cute, though. Rebellious in a way that spoke to me.

A week later, I was back on the website, using my headphones and a tablet in the school library. It was that or a session with the school counsellor, and I'd rather have burned my skin from my bones before suffering yet another therapy session with a grown-up boring on and using words I didn't understand.

Alone and intensely interested, I listened to another comment SumOne had made under the prompt *Which historical figure do you want to be like?*

SumOne: Alix of Hesse. I just learned about her this week

and am in love. She was a granddaughter of Queen Victoria and wildly dangerous. At age six, her mother died. At twelve, she met the heir to the Russian throne and eventually married him. During World War I, she became regent when the Tsar left for the front. She did such a bad job, sacking ministers and fekking up the country so much that her husband had to abdicate. She was then murdered by the Bolsheviks, and if she isn't the poster girl for living out childhood trauma, I don't know who is.

Short answer, became queen, fekked up everything, didn't pass on her trauma by way of earning a spectacular death.

She'd got that past the censor by the banal start, I guessed, but I was hooked.

Thirteen-year-old me caught a fast fixation.

In a week, I'd got her to accept a friend request. In a month, I had her contact in my phone. A phone I'd stolen that only worked on WiFi, but whatever.

We took our conversations over to private chat with my new @Fucksurfing and her @SumOne accounts becoming the centre of my world.

I always knew the day we met would change everything. Just like I knew my life was going to be a short one.

19

Summer

We journeyed north. On my lap, Jamieson slept hard, giving me free rein to touch him. If I removed my fingers or stopped gently stroking him, he'd grumble in his sleep and shift. So I kept up the lulling movement.

I didn't know where I stood with him. We weren't a couple, and could never be. Maybe we were friends now, but a friend wouldn't make the request that I'd blurted out in the cottage bedroom.

I wished things could be simpler and that other people hadn't screwed us over.

"Hey, are you okay?" Thea's voice interrupted my thoughts.

I blinked at her in the front seat, twisted round to look at me.

"Was I grinding my teeth or something?" I asked.

"No, I was just worrying about you. You haven't had a minute to settle since you arrived, and then we had to take off at no notice again. That must've been alarming."

Did I trust her? I found myself wanting to.

"I'm angry," I confessed, sparing a glance for her boyfriend who kept his gaze on the road. "The more I think about what other people have done to me and the people I care about, the more frustrated I get. They're out there getting away with the worst kind of actions, and I have no way of stopping them."

Wow. The words just flowed, like a dam had burst.

"It makes me angry, too," she agreed against the rumble of the tyres on the road. "And isn't enough to wish them dead. The system needs to change so more people don't jump into the space they left and do the same things."

We both went quiet for a while.

She meant Kayden, I guessed. Her boyfriend had been there with Jamieson. But she was right in a more general sense, too. Abusers exploited positions of power but also systems that allowed them to get away with their crimes. In some cases, like the police chief, they literally wrote the rules.

It meant that the only way to prevent that would be to change the system.

I didn't like feeling hopeless, but that was a steep ask.

Into the silence of the car, Struan suddenly spoke. "My mother got repeatedly fucked over by people in positions of authority. And actually fucked by them, too. Like a landlord arsehole who worked for the council. He'd threaten her with eviction if she didn't suck his dick. She even tried to report him and got nowhere, but instead, her benefits got screwed up. Debts racked up against her which meant she ended up doing shady shite to get by. I'm pretty sure that's why she ended up in jail."

"Is she still in jail now?" I asked.

He inclined his head, gripping the steering wheel hard enough that his knuckles stood out. Thea slipped her fingers into his free hand, and his shoulders went down a little at the touch.

I blew out a breath. "Isn't that fucked up? Of course no one believed her. They never do. My mother has similar stories. She was a normal girl who got abducted and sold into the sex trade. She told me and Breeze that she'd gone into detail over what had happened to her years later when she had to make a claim for housing. It gained her the support she needed, which shows her story was accepted, but no one followed up on her accusations. They're not interested. That tells me that no one's going to believe me if I report the chief of police for locking me up. Or probably even care if he buys women."

Thea wrinkled her nose. "They should. It's one thing a woman choosing to sell her body, but something very different when she's forced or manipulated into doing it."

Under my fingertips, Jamieson nudged me with his head. I'd frozen up, my mind drifting off to some dark place.

I'd never felt so powerless.

At the same point, at least I was free, however temporary. I'd fight to make it permanent.

"Sleep," I whispered to him and drew my thumb over his temple.

I focused on soothing him, but an entirely different plan sparked in my mind.

A long while later, we skirted Aberdeen.

I considered waking Jamieson, as it was his home town,

but I let him sleep. Happy memories probably were few and far between. Instead, I let myself remember all the times I'd pictured him there. He'd rarely left the place. I wondered if he ever wanted to go back.

Further up the coast, the roads grew quieter and the homes fewer. Mostly farms or small holdings. We passed signs for Peterhead, a gas terminal, then rolled down a single-lane track under the cover of a canopy of trees.

Eventually, we arrived at a house.

Struan idled the car, and we all peered at the building. It sat on its own in the landscape, no vehicle outside. No signs of life at all.

"Home sweet home," Thea said. "We're allowed to check in from four. It's midday now, but I bet the place is ready. It was empty last week according to the online calendar, so surely the cleaning staff have been and gone whenever the previous guests left. That's the only risk—that we get seen by any staff who might be out here, because obviously I didn't book in all of us. Just a single family."

"Is someone meant to be meeting you?" I asked.

"Nope. The management company emailed the code to get the key out of the safe on the wall outside. I'm going to check it out."

She hopped out of the car, and her boyfriend followed her.

They crossed the front garden and approached the house, opening the front door and disappearing inside. I eased up to check the road. Our other car hadn't approached yet, Sin deciding to hold back until we knew we could all enter the house unseen.

As it was, the large house surrounded by open space seemed perfect. To the right, the ocean spread out, bracketed by a long, windswept beach with wide dunes and tufted grass. A coastguard lookout clung to a hillside, and in the far distance, industrial buildings rose from the horizon. Out to sea, tall wind farms spun their sails.

It wasn't a picture postcard, but there was beauty in the isolation.

The other side of the road, fields led inland with stands of fir trees providing windbreaks. I squinted at what looked like the ruins of a church, the weatherbeaten stones rising in two large archways, the roof and walls gone.

If I ran from here, I'd get nowhere.

Except to a place more isolated where anything could happen unseen. In a flash, I was in my imagination and racing down the dark road, Jamieson hard at my heels.

"What's wrong?" the man in question suddenly asked.

He sat up and scanned our surroundings.

"Nothing." Flustered, I put the back of my hand to my hot cheek.

"Your breathing sped up." He brought his gaze back to me and furrowed his brow.

Slowly, he took my hand and pressed it to my chest, his fingers fitting between mine.

"Your heart's pounding."

I closed my eyes for a second. "I was thinking about what I asked you earlier."

"Were ye now?" He eased closer.

Even with my eyes closed, I sensed his every movement.

"As it happens, I was dreaming about the same thing."

I gave a shaky laugh. "Dream or nightmare?"

But before he could answer, a tap came at the window. I quickly opened my eyes.

Thea waved at us. "Coast is clear. Sin's bringing everyone else down. Come and claim a bedroom before they get here."

She opened the boot and took out a bag, ending our ability to speak privately. But as we entered the house, Jamieson slid his arm over my shoulders, bringing his mouth to my ear.

"Dream," he whispered.

His brother hollered for him from the front of the house, and he swatted my backside.

"Now go choose us a bedroom where we can cuddle after."

*S*itting cross-legged on the bed, Breeze twisted her phone in her hands. Throughout the journey here, we'd kept in text contact. She hadn't liked me being in the other car.

"How are you feeling?" she asked.

I shrugged, peering out of the big window that overlooked the sea. It was hard to imagine Jamieson and I lying in bed together enjoying the view. It was hard to imagine anywhere so peaceful and calm.

"I'm worried about Mum."

My sister made a sound of agreement. "In a day or two, we'll go to her. We'll pick up your clothes and things, too."

I *hmmed* agreement, lost in my thoughts. Outside, Struan said something to Jamieson then climbed into the Range Rover and took off alone. Then Jamieson faced the water and just stared.

This was the third place I'd been to with him and his family in a few short days. How long could we hide out here? How much time did I have left to do the things I wanted to do?

"I've been thinking," I said to Breeze.

"Uh-oh. Let me guess, more vigilante plans?"

I turned to her, forcing a smile. "Kind of, but within the boundary I promised you I'd stay. I just can't take this. Our whole lives feel like they've been leading to this moment. From the way we came into existence after Mum's abuse to the way I messed everything up in trying to right a wrong. I want... No, I need to do something to put even the smallest part of this right."

My sister paled but didn't seem surprised. "I know. I would never expect you to walk away from a fight."

I sat beside her, taking one of her hands. "I'm so sorry for everything you suffered in trying to find me. If you tell me to do nothing ever again, I'll do that. I love you."

Breeze held my fingers. "In some ways, I wish I could, but all the way here, I was thinking about how brave you are. How you were made to do something different to me. Even when we were little, I knew I'd be content with a quiet life but you wouldn't."

I gave a slow, sad shake of my head. "It eats at me. The indignation. The anger. I think I'll go insane if I can't at least tell people what happened to me."

I trailed off and sat back, my idea forming more.

Struan's mother had tried telling her story but had been ignored. Our mother's accusations had been accepted, but no consequence came from it.

It was because the information didn't go further than people who wanted it suppressed.

I didn't want to jump forward a decade or twenty years and be telling the same story.

"What if I went public with what happened to me?" I said slowly. "I could record a statement giving all the facts and naming names then upload it everywhere."

Breeze watched me for a long moment. "You'd become a bigger target."

I raised a shoulder. "I already am. Why shouldn't I get to tell the world what happened? I know without a doubt that anyone in a position of authority won't believe me, or even if they do, they won't do anything. Not against the chief of police. On the way here, Struan told me something about his mum where she was ignored."

Footsteps came in the hall, and Thea passed my open bedroom door.

She tapped on the doorframe. "Sin's making a run to the shops. Do you want anything?"

I had no mind for food. "Do they sell courage? I'm thinking of doing something crazy, and my hands are shaking."

The dark-haired woman advanced, looking between

me and Breeze. "I'm here for the crazy. God knows we've all been there."

I swallowed my rising excitement. "I'm going to expose the police chief and his system."

"Hell yes." She perched on a white chair that sat in front of the dressing table. "How are you going to do that?"

I stood and paced the room, nervous energy infecting me.

"I don't know, but I can't get the idea out of my mind. There are so many women I know who have stories to tell about the abuse of men. Me, Struan's mother, my mother, Breeze, Divine. It's compelling, isn't it?"

"It could be to a journalist," Thea said, interest sparking in her gaze.

Breeze angled her head. "How will we get a journalist to take us seriously?"

Us. My sister had included herself. My excitement grew.

Thea smiled. "I happen to know a journalism student who owes me a very big favour. His name is Henry, and his father ran the prison on Torlum where our men were kept. Not only that, but his sister, Esme, stabbed my boyfriend. A few days ago, Henry had the audacity to send me a message, so desperate to be my friend again now I've inherited the island. I might not be able to have Esme arrested, but they owe us, and I am more than ready to find ways to make them pay. Let me make a call, and I'll get him on board."

20

Summer

The afternoon eased by. After Struan left, Lottie had instructed everyone to rest up—they wouldn't be going after their sister until tomorrow at the earliest, and she'd explain more later.

Jamieson crossed the beach by himself, stripped, and entered the water. No hesitation for the chill. Like the sea welcomed him back then absorbed him. I watched from the window, unable to look away. Fearful that at any second, his head could disappear beneath the waves and he'd vanish.

He didn't, though.

After a while of messing around in the surf and then just floating under the cool summer sun, he got out, using a T-shirt to scrub the seawater from his tall frame. Back in the house, he joined me in the bedroom, stripped his wet underwear, and collapsed naked on the bed, sinking into a heavy sleep again.

Even in his dreams, his fingers clutched mine.

The scent of seawater clung to him, adding to my catalogue of all that made up real-life Jamieson.

I still hadn't gotten over how strange it was seeing him after so many years. Of how much I loved his presence. His voice. How he looked at me.

Most of all, his touch.

Everything was better for him being near, and I let that awareness sink into me as I carefully pulled the quilt over him then just watched him sleep.

When he broke up with me, he'd deleted every single message we'd ever sent in our private chat. At the time, I hadn't cared, never wanting to listen to his words or see his face again. Now, I wished I could use the time lying here to remember all the things we'd ever said. Or find when he'd first sent a picture of himself.

For a long time, I'd been too shy to send my own, not trusting him, but the pictures kept coming; Jamieson in school uniform in the hallway outside his classroom, barred for some reason. Jamieson in a stolen car, being driven by bigger, badder kids from his neighbourhood. Jamieson in his bed, his dark hair messy and his blue-eyed gaze so open.

He'd been sweet, funny, and had hooked me in.

After that, we'd sent daily pictures of what we were doing. I'd relied so much on the burst of happiness his presence gave me.

Nothing had changed, and my crush reared up harder and faster than ever.

I was in such trouble with him.

By early evening, happy voices chattered downstairs, and the smell of food drifted through the house. My stomach rumbled. I'd never been one to miss a meal, but I couldn't remember the last time I'd eaten.

At a low roll of laughter from one of his brothers, Jamieson made a soft sound, blinking his eyes open. Instantly, his gaze clung to me.

He brought our joined hands to his mouth and kissed my knuckles. "Hey."

"Hey," I repeated.

He threw a heavy arm over me and hugged me to him.

Warmth bloomed in me, and I was the young teenager again, staring at her phone screen and taking in the cute face of her first infatuation.

I might have wanted him rough, but once, I'd craved this gentle side, too. Except that was dangerous thinking.

But then the same icy rush followed. I tried not to stiffen.

I needed to tell him about my interview plan. That would cure him of wanting to hug me.

My belly rumbled, and Jamieson's lips curved into a smile.

"Lottie," he bellowed, at the same point reaching to cover my ears with his hands. "What's cooking?"

"Burgers. Get yourselves down here," she called back with a smile in her tone.

"Oh my God. I love ye, Ma," he hollered back.

Still naked, he leapt up and pulled me with him. His pile of clothes scattered sand where he pulled them on, but it didn't seem to trouble him.

In the meantime, I was trying not to stare at his body. At his big, swinging, half-hard dick. He had no worries about being naked in front of me, and for that, I was very grateful.

Downstairs, most of the family were gathered in the large kitchen-diner. The overhead spotlights produced a bright glow, and Camden and Sin handed out plates piled with burgers in buns.

Lottie sighted us from her position at the stove. "Great, you're just in time. It's basic fare tonight. We managed to pick up a decent shop, but comfort food was called for today. I'll take my time and make a proper meal tomorrow."

"This is amazing," I said. "Thank you."

She gave a happy smile. "I live for this, so it's my pleasure."

Jamieson extended an arm to take a plate, at the same time, giving my hip a possessive squeeze. A jolt of lust struck me.

He slid me a glance like he knew how I felt, then handed me food.

For several minutes, chatter ceased and everyone ate, mostly not moving from the spot where they'd received their plate like we were all half-starved. Lottie had called this basic, but she'd managed to find sauces and fry onions.

"A goddamned feast," Sin muttered, his gaze lighting up when Lottie handed him another burger.

Jamieson finished his third and looked around the room. "Where's Struan?"

Thea grinned. "Secret mission. We're hunkering down for the night, so he decided to make it more interesting. He'll be back soon."

On cue, a motor rumbled outside. Despite the expectation, we all quietened. Safety couldn't be assumed.

Jamieson set his plate down and stomped up the hall.

"It's him," he called back. After a beat, his voice returned. "Holy shite. He didn't." The door creaked open. "What the hell, bro," he called out.

Struan replied, but I couldn't make out his words. No matter. I was already hurrying down the hall.

Outside in the dusk, Struan and Jamieson stood by the Range Rover, laughing together. Instantly, I saw why. On the roof, surfboards had been secured, and the men slid them down with a rush of the lightweight fibreglass or foam, whatever they were made of.

"Where did ye get them?" Jamieson asked his brother.

"Raided the last holiday home. I took wetsuits, too. Thea said no one was staying there, and the arsehole guy who owned the place pissed me off by the way he treated all of ye after I was taken to hospital. If anyone gives a shite, I can deliver this back when we're done, but fuck that guy."

"Fuck that guy," his brothers muttered back, all grinning at each other.

Struan pulled the last board from the roof rack and set it on the ground. "I have no fucking clue how safe we are here, but it feels better than anywhere else we've been in a while. I vote we try to enjoy it before everything goes to shite again. We'll eat well, surf, find Cassie, and relax."

Jamieson slung his arm around his neck. "Sounds like a plan. Who wants to hit the water?"

I darted my gaze at the waves rolling onto the beach. Throughout the whole afternoon, I'd only seen a single dog walker further down the coast. But it wasn't fear of getting spotted that had me retreating into the house. "I don't like the cold."

Jamieson pursued me. "Then wear a wetsuit."

I padded backwards. He kept on coming, capturing me at the bottom of the stairs.

A thrill shot through me.

"It happens to be a dream of mine to have ye sitting astride my board."

"Oh yeah?" I was flirting with him, and worse, I liked it. "If I go into the sea with you, what do I get out of the bargain?"

"I'll consider what ye asked."

My breath caught.

His gaze held mine. Searched it. Then he continued. "But on one condition."

"Which is?" I whispered.

He threw a glance over his shoulder, making sure none of his family were in hearing distance. They weren't—all had stayed outside in the warm evening.

Even so, he lowered his head to speak in my ear. "Let me love on ye in all the other ways. I want to get ye used to my kiss. To hugging me in bed. Little touches alongside the big ones. Do we have a deal?"

It was no hardship to give him the smallest nod.

Yes.

Even if it hurt, I'd let him try.

Half an hour later, and I was trying on a wetsuit in my bedroom. These things were not designed to go on easy, and I didn't even want to glance in the mirror to see how it displayed my sausage thighs.

Another point yelled louder in my mind.

The suit was so tight, there was no easy access. I wanted Jamieson to do...things to me, and it would be in the way. I stripped it off and dressed again in my borrowed clothes.

Breeze knocked on the door and giggled. "Who would've guessed it, two girls from Leith heading out to surf."

She entered, perfectly proportioned in her wetsuit.

I'd always tried not to compare myself to her. Petite, better shaped than me. But it wasn't easy.

"Oh, you aren't surfing?" she said, taking me in.

"Maybe later. I felt like an overstuffed sofa in the wetsuit."

"Are you kidding? I'd kill for your height and curves. Jamieson would fall off his board when he saw you."

Still, she accepted my answer. Together, we trotted downstairs.

"You seem happier," I told her.

"I am. I have you back, and you have a non-lethal plan to move ahead with. But it isn't just me. Everyone's feeling it. There's an air across the whole family of lightness. Can you feel it?"

We passed the living room where Sin sat with Lottie on his lap. Despite the remoteness of the house, he hadn't felt entirely comfortable with leaving the place empty while we all took to the beach so had opted to take the first watch.

By the way Lottie leaned in and took his mouth in a blistering kiss, he wouldn't be lonely while he did it.

I swapped an amused glance with my sister. Even so,

I regretted that I couldn't be so relaxed like that myself. Jamieson wanted the smooth to go with the rough, and for his sake, I'd try.

Barefoot, we crossed the cool sands, a gentle evening breeze dancing the salty ocean smell over us. It was summer, but the day had been blustery. Night had brought calmer weather, perfect for playing outside.

Two people stood on the beach, while two others carved up the waves. I knew Jamieson from his brother in the water immediately.

He stood alert on his board, sighting me. Then he jerked and fell, crashing into the waves. I shot my hand to my mouth, and my sister laughed, elbowing me.

"Ohmigod. Didn't I say? Even without the wetsuit. That boy is hooked on you." Her smile reduced, and she slowed. "I think I'm starting to understand why you didn't tell me about him. I'm hooked on Camden in the same way, and if I couldn't have him, if I felt like this but had the doubt of separation..." She trailed off.

She was in love. The realisation came quickly.

I didn't dislike Camden now either. I'd been wary at first, but he seemed gentle and he made her smile. Looked for her when she wasn't around.

"Add to that the fact I was so young and he was the first boy I ever liked." I chewed my lip. "He's still the only boy I ever liked. Except now he's a huge man, and that's something else to get used to."

She linked her arm through mine. "If you want tips, feel free to ask."

My cheeks heated. I was eleven months younger than

her, but right now, the gulf felt so much wider. "You had sex?"

I was scared to ask. Terrified to understand the detail of what she'd been through to find me. I'd hid from the subject but I wasn't a coward.

"With Camden?" I added.

"Yes, with Camden, and only him. He bought me at my second auction. I'll fill you in."

She walked me through her experience, the way Camden had helped her and how sweet he'd been. How they'd shared in their hunt for their siblings, his search for Jamieson, hers for me.

We reached the water's edge, and Camden splashed out, snatching Breeze up into his arms. She shrieked, and he carried her until he was waist height then dropped down, submerging them both.

Thea laughed at them and called out encouragement. Breeze had joined this family, I realised. In the time I'd been gone, she'd forged bonds.

Jamieson sat on his board, watching me.

His gaze slid down me, but if he was disappointed that I'd ditched the wetsuit, it didn't show.

He beckoned.

I tested the surf with my toe then shook my head.

Something about the way he observed me had me stalling.

Electricity crackled between us. It was always this way when I thought about him. His combination of fire and water was a dangerous thing.

To my right, my sister and her boyfriend play fought in the shallows, splashing each other. Beyond them, Struan and Thea entered the water, joining in the fun.

Slowly, and with my gaze on Jamieson, I walked the other way. Heel to toe, following the waterline.

Out on the break, he tracked me. First paddling, then catching a roller and mirroring my movement away from the group. Not advancing, not coming in. Rising and falling on the dark waves.

I kept going down the beach.

From the water, he hunted me.

Ahead was nothing but open space, the pale sand broadening out so the road and fields got further and further away. It wasn't so late that we had complete darkness, and the horizon had an orange-grey tint which gave me just enough light to see where I was going.

Into the looming isolation.

My pulse picked up.

I could run.

Sprint across the sand until nobody could see me, though one would definitely chase after me

My senses heightened with small bursts of adrenaline.

I glanced in the direction I'd come, still able to pick out the rough shapes of the rest of our party. I checked again for Jamieson's progress, knowing he'd be close.

Nothing but the black sea looked back at me.

I stopped and scanned the water, searching for his shape or the white length of the board.

He wasn't there.

"Jamieson," I called softly.

Mild panic set in.

It had only been a matter of seconds that I'd stopped watching him. He couldn't have gone under, surely. No, the surfboard would still be floating.

Where the hell...?

Muted footsteps drummed, the sand deadening the sound. I gasped and spun around. From metres away, Jamieson sprinted at me, his expression fierce and his deadly determined aim locked on me. I barely had time to brace myself when he skidded to a halt, taking out my feet.

I fell.

But I didn't hit the ground, instead, landing on his hard body.

I stifled an automatic squeal of shock, fright and excitement mixing together.

"On your feet," he snapped out.

I stumbled, Jamieson grappling me to get in front of him. Then he was marching me along by the scruff of my neck. His board bobbed at the water's edge. He must've paddled hard to get the jump on me.

Not that I cared. Rising desperation clawed inside me. I needed him to manage this. To force me into doing whatever he had in mind.

I could only hope he delivered what I asked. Still, that scared me. I wanted it and I didn't in equal measures. The only thing I knew for sure is that I felt safe with him.

Jamieson drove me on until we reached the board, then without pause, he pushed me down onto it. "I said I wanted ye on my board. Straddle it."

A wave rushed the beach, rippling over my fingers where I was palms-down on the surfboard. I knelt slowly and turned, seawater dampening my knees and shins. Jamieson stared down at me, his features almost invisible in the dark.

Abruptly, he sank down in front of me, cupped the back of my head, and tipped me back to lie on his board beneath him, my upper body on the board but my legs either side in the sand.

Another wave flooded around us.

"What are you, argh," I yelped.

Seawater splashed me again, wetting my hair. Salt danced on my tongue.

"I like ye this way," he rasped in my ear. "All laid out and ready for me."

I shivered both from the cold and from the effect he had on me. How he made his every word sound so filthy.

In this position, I had my head to the ocean. A big wave could drench me easily. But I didn't move, held in place by Jamieson kneeling between my legs, his wetsuit damp on my thighs.

I closed my eyes, at war with competing emotions.

There was something romantic about this, and I needed him to be harder on me.

Then his hand was in my ponytail again. He pulled my head to the side and dropped a hard kiss to my throat.

"Don't scream. Don't make a sound, or everyone will know."

I nodded, not getting far with his restraint.

With his other hand, he yanked up my shirt. My mouth dropped open, but I kept my silence, breathing hard, my body alive with the thrill.

He didn't hesitate, slipping his big hands into my bra top to take hold of my breasts in a harsh grab. My already rigid nipples pebbled more against his palms as he felt me up.

I stiffened. Alarmed by my instant flood of liquid heat.

Then Jamieson gave a low sound of need that did something to my brain.

He kept going, yanking up my skirt so he could cup me between my legs, spread over the board.

A wave jolted us. He forced his finger inside me.

I cried out in shock.

Jamieson swore and reached to cram his other hand over my mouth, stifling me.

It didn't stop him moving his fingers. He slid another into me, starting up a rhythm that sent shockwaves through my system. I hadn't done this to myself in forever, and never had let anyone else touch me.

I kept my eyes closed. It helped not to see him. He'd taken what I'd asked and made it into something different than I'd expected, but it was…good.

Also strange. But if he stopped, I was pretty sure I was going to die.

Lucky for me, he didn't. He quickly worked out how to play me, leaving my mouth to play with my clit. The actions were perfect. Better than I could ever do.

"This tight little pussy is mine," he gritted out. "If I wanted to, I could rip these clothes away and fuck ye right here on my surfboard. My big dick would take your pristine sweet virginity, and I'd mix my cum with your blood. Would ye let me, or would ye fight me off? You're so fucking wet, I think I have my answer."

I couldn't reply, even if he hadn't commanded me to silence.

The rhythmic motion he kept up with his fingers in my slick heat got harder. He pressed down on my clit in perfect circles.

"Your pussy spasmed around my hand from that threat. Is that what ye need?"

I mumbled some kind of depraved sound behind his hand. I should check that no one could see us, but my vision had gone.

An orgasm built, faster than I'd ever managed. Another wave washed up to us, a baptism of seawater, showing me the power Jamieson held. I cared about nothing other than what he was doing to me.

"Fight me, Summer," he added, low and angry. "See how far ye get. From now on, I'm taking what I want whether ye like it or not."

Exactly what I needed.

Pure pleasure spilled through me.

My legs shook, and I arched on the board, my heels in the sand. Then I lost my muscle tone and collapsed.

Jamieson groaned, though the sound was distant to my checked-out mind. Still, he worked me through it. His fierce grip not easing.

He'd rocked me to my bones.

I only wanted more.

21

Jamieson

Firelight flickered over me, the orange light warming the cheeks of my family where we lounged in a circle around the fire pit.

Sparks flew from the crackling wood, matching the energy rising in my blood.

Further down the coast, a couple of small blazes lit the beach, groups of teenagers messing around them, presumably from a local village. I'd watched them for a while then decided we could take the small risk. It helped that the holiday home had a purpose-built area with a surround to block out the wind. And conceal us from any onlookers.

The door of the house opened, and Summer emerged, returning from taking a shower, her fair hair damp and re-tied in a ponytail.

I sat taller, watching her every move.

At the water's edge, I'd been rough with her. Maybe even scared her.

But if she wanted more, however I protested, I was

a fucking liar. If she wanted me to chase her, I was there. Blood up. Dick hard. Ready to charge her into the ground.

I could give her what she wanted. The only problem? Reining myself in once I'd started.

She moved to the edge of the group, hesitating for a moment.

Fuck that.

I lurched to my feet and snatched her wrist, pulling her down with me to land in my lap. Summer gave up a small *oof* of breath but huddled in, curling her arms around mine.

I'd barely left her side in days, but my move was designed to make my intentions towards her public. Each of my brothers sat with their woman. Sin encased Lottie, his huge body surrounding hers like she needed protection from the world. Struan lay on his side with Thea resting against him. Camden had his arm around Breeze's shoulders.

Just like with their lasses, Summer was mine and under my protection.

I wanted a conversation with my family, but I got caught on the scent of Summer's hair and nuzzled into her neck. She let me, her fingertips light on my biceps.

"Good time for a family meeting," Lottie said. "While we're all together and no one's trying to chase us for a minute, I have an update for ye. And an announcement."

Across the fire, Struan caught my gaze, and I raised an eyebrow at him.

We knew what was coming.

She took a breath, but it was Sin who spoke.

"Lottie's pregnant."

Breeze gasped, and Summer clapped her hands to her mouth. Thea smiled but didn't look surprised, presumably already knowing or guessing the news.

Two things struck me at once. The way my brother had switched out using her full name of Violet for the nickname everyone else used, and my sharp stab of jealousy.

That was unexpected.

To the tune of everyone congratulating the couple, I extended my fingers across Summer's belly, giving in to the fleeting fantasy of knocking her up.

I'd been a walking hard-on for her already, but this stunned me into silence.

She caught my hand with hers. Holding me but not pushing me away.

"Fast work, brother," Struan was saying when I tuned back in.

Sin raised a shoulder. "I'm not saying this is good timing or that we know what we're doing, but we're really fucking happy."

"I can't imagine anyone being a better mother than you," Thea told her sister. "You're already the mum of our group. Ooh, I get to knit baby booties now."

"I'll take him or her for drives if they keep ye awake in the night," Camden vowed.

"I'll teach the bairn to surf," I promised. "Or steal cars. Ye can choose." Both skills were useful.

Lottie's cheeks reddened, and she swallowed plain emotion. "I can't imagine better aunties and uncles for our baby. Or a big sister in Cassie when we get her back. Which brings me onto the update. Ye all know I've been searching through the paperwork Burn found in the foster carer's home. It was a diary, of sorts, with calendar dates and events noted. Things like their daughter's dentist appointments. But also she recorded that they were away in the spring at her sister's house. It says Aviemore."

My heart sped a little faster. "The neighbour said they'd gone to her sister's. We know where she is."

Lottie nodded. "Aviemore's a relatively small town, and it narrows down our search from the rest of the Highlands, but it's August. The place will be filled with tourists. One of the other things ye grabbed was a receipt from a shop with an Aviemore address."

"Why would they keep that?" Summer asked.

"Exactly what I wondered," Lottie replied.

Summer hunched her shoulders. "Can't imagine it would be a souvenir. Did you search for the address of the shop?"

"I did," Lottie agreed. "It's a farm shop on a big estate where there's cabins for holiday rentals."

"Then they went on a family holiday with the sister and kept the receipt to try to claim back Cassie's expenses," I rumbled.

Everyone looked at me.

"Prison made ye smarter," Struan quipped.

I pulled a daft face at him, and Lottie continued.

"That makes sense. If this time they're visiting in a hurry, maybe they'll stay in the same place. It gives us somewhere to start, at least."

"What are we waiting for?" Struan demanded.

Lottie took a heavy breath. "An opportunity. The estate has a summer fair happening tomorrow. If we go in and raid the place when it's rammed with people, it could help us. Enough general noise and fuss could disguise us getting away."

Her words sank in, and all of us had to be picturing the same deal. Spying Cassie. Causing a distraction. Getting caught up in a crowd.

"Or the opposite," I said. "We'd have to be sneaky as fuck."

Lottie brushed her hand over her belly and nodded. "I want to drive over to subtly scope it out. Just me and Sin so we don't raise suspicions and can report back. Sound good?"

"No chance," Struan said at the same time as the rest of us protested. "I'll go. Better as they'll know your faces but not mine."

He squeezed Thea. "Want to come with me?"

"As if I'd let you go alone," she replied softly.

"Suits me to keep ye hidden away and safe from now on," Sin said low to Lottie. "I need to call Gordain like Burn prompted so it'll give me space to get hold of him."

Lottie pursed her lips but nodded. She gave a big yawn.

"Want to go to bed?" Sin asked her.

"In a minute. It's so cosy here. Does anyone else have anything to share?"

Summer threw a quick peek at me. "Actually, I do."

My whole family gave her their attention.

"You all know what happened to me," she started. "Getting locked up for a month would probably floor some people, and it did for me for a couple of days. I'm grateful you let me stay with you while I came out of that. I've been a ghost creeping around the edge of your family."

Ripples of sympathy passed over the faces watching her. But no one interrupted. It was obvious she had more to say.

My gut tightened. Whatever she was about to do, I'd do it with her.

Walk away from my brothers. Their lasses. Cassie and the new bairn.

Two days ago, I was gunning to leave. I didn't want that now, but I'd do it for her.

"I promised my sister I wouldn't leap into anything physically dangerous," Summer continued slowly. "But I can't live in fear and do nothing. That isn't who I am. When something scares me, it shows me it's worth my attention, and the world I just witnessed where women are commodities scares the shit out of me. I'm so angry. At myself and how I let myself be used, but more at the system that's in place to use women who didn't make the choices I did. Who were forced or manipulated into it with no escape route. I'm going to record a video and tell the world exactly what happened to me, naming police chief, Daniels."

"Holy shite," I muttered. "There's the Summer I know."

She didn't falter. "But beyond that, I know that I'm far from alone in shitty experiences. I want to ask my mother if she'll tell her story, too. She was sold off when she was a teenager and never really recovered from it, no matter how much she tried."

"I'll make one describing the virginity auctions and what I know about the list in detail," Breeze added.

Summer's mouth dropped open, a smile forming quickly for her sister.

Struan lifted his chin. "Thea talked to me about this earlier. She wants to go to the prison to ask my ma if she'll describe her worst experiences, then record the video in her place. Now ye have four. That makes a series, aye?"

Summer stared, her grip on me tightening. "You're serious? And you're okay with that?"

My dangerous older brother summoned a grim smile. "I used to think that would be the worst thing ever, that kind of public show and tell, but the more I think about what happened to Ma, the angrier I get. Fuck yeah do I want her story heard."

In my arms, Summer sat taller, boosted up by everyone being onside. "Okay, God, I'm piecing this together, and it's becoming even more compelling. If we can get in touch with Divine, the dancer who helped set me free, I want her story, too. And anyone else she knows who wants to talk. They can even be anonymous, but I won't."

She hugged my arms around her, as if needing the reassurance I was still there.

Or maybe as a warning.

I loved her idea. Fuck the implications. Blowing shite up was my jam.

"What do ye plan to do with the videos?" I asked low.

"Post them everywhere. Thea might even have a journalist contact who can bring some ideas to the party."

Thea shifted and waggled her phone. "He wants me to call him, but I'll go inside and do that in a minute. We've got your back in this, trust me."

Summer took a shuddering breath. "I don't know why you're all being so nice. I'm the outsider and a dangerous one at that. I'll only make things more difficult for everyone. Particularly with your little sister still to be found and a new baby on their way."

"We've all been outsiders," Lottie added in fast. "To be honest, ye feel like the missing piece. Out of any of us, ye and Burn formed the start of this group a long time ago. I think I speak for everyone when I say how glad I am that you're here."

I hugged Summer, and she whispered a quiet thanks to my family.

There was a general movement in the group, the lasses readying to go inside.

But where Thea adjusted her position against my brother, she revealed the tattoo on his arm.

I knew the second Summer spotted it.

She stilled, her gaze on his inkwork. "You have the same tattoo as Jamieson. The little surfer against rocks."

Struan cocked his head. "We all have it, why?"

He gestured to Thea who tugged aside her shirt to reveal the brand on the back of her shoulder. Sin pulled up his shirt sleeve to reveal his, while in front of him, Lottie did the same with hers. Finally, Camden placed his finger on the same artwork on his arm.

"It's my handiwork. I designed that not long after we were freed from Torlum. Burn gave me the idea."

With her fingers covering her mouth, Summer jumped her gaze from tattoo to tattoo. Her attention came to her sister. "Do you have it as well?"

Breeze shook her head. "Not yet, but I have something else of his handiwork. That's a story for another time. I'll get this one, too. I can't believe I didn't make the connection until now. It was right there in front of my eyes."

"What connection?" Camden asked.

Slowly, Summer drew her pendant out from under her shirt. The pendant I'd given her years ago then reclaimed for her by way of fire.

The metal gleamed in the light from the flames.

As one, my family leaned in to look at the little surfer that was almost identical to the ink we all wore.

"Jamieson gave this to me when we were pen pals. It was supposed to remind me of him," she whispered.

"See?" Lottie spluttered, her eyes bright with emotion. "I said ye were the core of our family. Welcome home."

22

Jamieson

The women left the fire pit to head inside the house, talking about the videos they wanted to make. Summer shot me a glance which I returned, conveying to her that I wouldn't be far behind.

Yet my brothers and I all lingered around the fire.

Back on Torlum, we used to do this. Find kindling to burn and warm ourselves after surfing the icy seas.

No one had ever disturbed us, the locals steering clear of the young offenders they'd heard were being rehabilitated on their island.

When I'd been held in the police station, I'd thought a lot about the island. Mostly my regrets that I hadn't burned down our youth hostel prison before we'd left. It felt like a loose end. Something that needed to be righted.

"Did ye say you'd been back to Torlum?" I asked Sin.

My brother watched the waves. He gestured to the water with his head. "Surf with me? There's something I need to tell ye regarding that."

We padded down the beach, Camden and Struan falling in alongside. A line of fucked-up men, brothers with a fierce bond that was still being forged.

Each of us slipped into the water on our boards. One after the other.

Surfing had always been my thing, an obsession I'd developed after getting taster sessions at a school holiday scheme organised by social workers. Somewhere for me to pass my time that didn't involve stealing or getting stoned. The first time I went, I'd hated how much I loved it, hence the fuck-surfing name I'd used to talk to Summer, but it was ironic. The waves and the water gave me life. I'd passed the love on to my brothers on the island. The youth hostel had ancient boards we'd been able to use, and the freedom it gave us couldn't be beat.

Nothing cleared your head like floating on the sea. The only thing to do was wait for a wave to ride.

Though the night was calm, there was enough of a break to pop up and surf for a while. In the middle of it all, Sin filled me in on how he and Lottie returned to Torlum in order to move her mother into another house.

"I didn't hide." He cruised over to me and pushed up onto his board, slicking seawater from his short hair. "At first, I was cautious because I was with my lass. But then I couldn't handle it. Those people had been in on our imprisonment. Why the fuck should I be the one to avoid them?"

"What did ye do?"

"Challenged them. Gathered a group of the arseholes to tell them exactly what I thought of them. And to threaten them in case anyone came asking questions. Funnily enough, none of them wanted to take me on."

"Ballsy bastard," Struan cackled.

I blew out a breath, impressed but not surprised. "Did ye return to the hostel?"

"We did, and that's something else ye need to know. Keep's grave was empty."

"Empty? Like a hole in the ground?"

At my horrified expression, he grimaced. "Exactly that. A pile of dirt and no body."

"Jesus fuck. How? No one knew she was dead. We covered our tracks."

"The more I think about it, the more I'm convinced that someone who knew her took her for an honest burial. There's been no alert about it. I've searched on the island and on the local news sources. No one's saying shite. And none of those islanders said a word to me when I faced off to them."

It didn't stop the curl of unease inside me. "Three people died on Torlum," I said into the briny air. "First Keep, then Charterman, then Jenkins when I set his house on fire. Do we think they were all carted off to a graveyard like good Christian souls?"

Sin shook his head. "Charterman was handled by Thea's dad. Fuck knows what went down with Jenkins, but no one's seen him since the fire. His house is ashes, so if he survived it, he's long gone."

My unease didn't shift. Surely the evil pervert hadn't survived.

If he did, I'd failed. He was another loose end.

Something Summer said had stuck in my mind. She felt like she was a hazard to my family, same as I did. Tonight, Sin and Lottie had announced they were going to be parents. Let alone the fact that we had to find Cassie and bring her back to a safe home.

How could we do that when we'd left so many open doors behind us?

I had to handle the dangers to my family.

"Is it fucking weird," Struan's voice broke my concentration, "that the fact that Sin got Lottie pregnant has become a massive challenge to me?"

I huffed a laugh, glad for the distraction. "Do ye want to knock up Thea?"

"More than I've ever wanted anything in my life," he confessed. "Which is messed up because she doesn't want it yet. She's talking about going back to university to study social work when our lives aren't in danger every ten minutes. I want that for her. I want her to be happy."

"But you're driven to wanting to make her pregnant as well," Sin concluded for him.

He sighed. "All the day long."

Camden paddled closer until the four of us had made a kind of circle. All sitting on our boards in a patch of calm sea.

"Want to hear something weirder?" he said. "I'm the same. Breeze and I haven't been careful, and that's on me. I can't help it. Just the thought of the risk." He gazed between us, his eyes bright. "By the look of ye, everyone knows what I'm talking about. But my point is if she doesn't want it, I'll control it."

Struan sent a swipe of water my way. "Ye, too, Burn?"

I shrugged, somewhere between alarmed and uncomfortably turned on. "I don't know about the mechanics of it, but the thought alone is driving me nuts. And I'm a virgin. What the hell does it do when you're, ye know, trying not to blow your load right where it's going to do the damage?"

All three of them pulled the same expression. A little guilty.

Sin spoke first. "No good asking me, considering what I did. But if Lottie hadn't wanted to be a ma, I'd have worked it out with her. Wrapped it up or whatever. That's what contraception exists for."

Struan looked away into the dark horizon, the waves washing gently over the front of his white surfboard. "Yeah, can't be like our fuck-up of a da."

We all did the same kind of uncomfortable shoulder roll.

McInver had done that. Knocked up all of our mothers within a short timeframe then Cassie's later on. His spunk spree era.

"For fuck's sake, how am I like him when he had no part in my life?" I complained. "He's twisted and a pervert."

"Can't help what's in our blood," Sin rumbled. "Scar, remember the conversation we had in the sea at the beach house? What did I tell ye?"

Camden braced himself on his board. "Anything consensual is fine. If ye want to tie up your partner or knock her up, it's okay if she's down for that." He squinted at me, his features just visible. "Come to think of it, ye weren't near enough to hear all of that chat. The point Sin made was about communication and consent. And that you're not messed up or wrong if ye like something...out there. It's just a kink."

There was a moment of pause where that sank in.

I'd hunted Summer down this evening. Confused my-self with how turned on it had made me. Somehow, I'd got it right for her, which was a minor miracle considering all my experience was fictional.

"Really regretting missing that conversation," I quipped.

Sin and Struan shared a glance before Sin turned to me.

"Talk to us. As brothers, we need to trust and rely on each other if we're going to survive. So I'll start. My kink, if ye like, is knocking Lottie up. She worked it out before I did and called me on it. It's more than just the risk, though. I want her to be pregnant then for us to have lots of bairns to provide a good life for. Kids who will get to sleep in a bed every night."

"Aye, not on a cold floor," Struan cut in.

"Or in the back of a car," Camden added.

I had my own version of that. Ma moved us between places often, never holding on to a home for long. I'd des-perately wanted a bed of my own.

I'd got it after she'd overdosed and I was thrown into foster care and a house with four kids in bunk beds.

Thanks for listening, universe.

Sin waited for my contribution but continued on when I kept my trap shut. "That's a deep-seated need we all have because of the way we were raised. My kids will never won-der where their next meal is coming from or that their ma won't come home from work because some client got too rough with her. Unlike me, they'll have a da who gives a shite and provides for them. I want all that, even if I have to go to extremes to deliver it, and it speaks to a deep need in me, but right now the bit that's talking loudest is the first part. Fucking...breeding. It's taken over my thoughts. It's okay if ye have something like that going on, too."

I swallowed, glad for the darkness and the background noise of the rushing water.

Camden spluttered his confession. "Restraining Breeze. Tying her up with whatever I have to hand. Also the pregnancy thing, to more or less extent."

A sense of amusement and brotherly bonding grew. This was ridiculous, and I needed the conversation so much.

It helped to know Summer and I weren't doing anything wrong.

"What about ye?" Sin asked Struan.

Our oldest brother swore and stretched out his arms, not answering for a minute. Sharing was harder for him, but he opened his mouth anyway. "Don't judge."

"Never," we all swore.

"Scaring Thea. At least at the start. It's turned into needing to dominate her and have her obey me, but for a while, I wanted her afraid. It gave me a real buzz. I'm trying to control the pregnancy side and use that energy up in other ways."

All three of them watched me.

I tipped my head back and stared at the pinpricks of light above us, the stars out in full force and listening to our entertaining conversation.

I liked how small the universe made me feel. I was in my place and just a speck in the grand scheme. Nothing of interest to those giant, burning suns.

I forced out my words.

"Aside from the pregnancy thing, which is really messing with me that we share that, chasing Summer down and forcing myself on her," I spoke to the heavens. Not looking at my brothers for fear of judgement.

After a beat, Sin spoke. "With her agreement, aye?"

"Of course with her fucking agreement," I retorted. "Ye all know where she's been for the last month. I'm not an animal."

He held up his hands. "Didn't say ye were, and I see nothing wrong in that either. All of these things are okay. None of us are like McInver, and we never will be. As a minimum, we respect our women. He never loved anything but his money."

Love. There was a word I didn't want to think about. Sin loved Lottie. Of course he did. Struan and Thea. Camden and Breeze.

Then there was me.

Summer was mine. My obsession. My everything. She always had been.

After breaking her so badly, I needed her to love me back.

Sin gave a dark chuckle, and his lips quirked into a knowing smile. "In a few years, we're going to have one hell of a problem."

"What?" I asked.

"A fuck ton of kids between us."

23

Summer

In the dark bedroom, I stared out the windows, piecing over the script I'd sat with Breeze and written. It had been good laying out the facts, but I couldn't imagine reading from a page. It felt wooden when I tried.

Thea had spoken to Henry, her journalist student friend, though it sounded like he wasn't really a friend at all, and the man had agreed to help. He'd suggested talking to his professor, Tricia Thomas, who had written pieces on criminal cases for TV news and had an interest in women's stories.

We needed someone with her skills. External validation to what we were doing.

Henry promised a conversation in the next couple of days, which would give me time to warm up to making my video.

Also to work out all the other things I needed to think about, like how to run and hide from a man who refused to let me. And from who I didn't want to stray far.

The bedroom door clicked, and Jamieson strolled in, locking it behind him. He must've stripped his wetsuit downstairs as he wore only his jeans and a wry smile.

He crawled across the bed and ran his arms around me, rolling us so he was on his back and I was on his bare chest.

"Hi." He kissed my forehead.

My heart thumped, the competing sensations of wanting more and needing to freeze up all too present.

"Are ye okay?" he asked.

I nodded against him.

"About earlier. That was as far as I could take it."

He meant grabbing me on the beach. His hands all over me.

"Will you try again?" I asked. Getting rid of my virginity was vital.

"If ye want me to. But I plan to exploit our deal first." He placed me back on the bed and sat up, taking my hand in his. With his gaze holding mine, he kissed my knuckles, each in turn.

"What are you doing?" I whispered.

"I want to get ye used to my touch. So I'm going to love on ye a little now, but this isn't about sex. Completely unrelated and leading to nowhere apart from us getting close. Sound good?"

I shivered, liking the separation. It took away a layer of pressure around the bigger issues. "Very."

He gave a cocky grin. With slow moves, he turned my hand and extended my fingers, then placed a kiss in the centre of my palm. Another to my wrist.

"I want to map every part of ye. Memorise each soft square of skin. For the longest time, I've imagined doing this."

He drew his lips over my forearm to the inside of my elbow, kissing it almost like he had with my mouth. My biceps, my shoulders, up my throat to a sensitive spot under my ear.

I closed my eyes, my breathing coming in small hitches.

He didn't stop.

His lips skimmed my hairline then down my nose, stopping briefly to press against my closed, fluttering eyelids. Too briefly, they ghosted over my lips then carried on.

He stopped, and I opened my eyes, missing his touch immediately.

Jamieson reached into his back pocket and brought something out. A pen, I realised.

With his finger, he pointed at the branding tattoo on his arm, then placed the same finger on my wrist.

Breeze had told me that Camden would tattoo her tonight. I nodded for Jamieson to ink me in a temporary way.

I expected him to uncap the pen and just start, but instead, he rested back against the pillows and tapped his lap.

I stared at him for a second then slowly rolled up.

"Straddle me like I wanted on my surfboard," he commanded.

His instructions were easy to follow, not even the tiniest of panics spiralling through me. I clambered on, knees in the quilt, and settled down firmly, his thick bulge right at the apex of my thighs.

He was hard. I flushed warmer.

Jamieson grunted like he was in pain. "Ignore that. Completely involuntary. Cross your arms in front of ye, wrists outwards."

In the narrow space between us, I did, and he took hold of my wrists then pulled them up and behind my head. Then he sat forward so we were chest to chest, folding his legs under me.

We were so close.

He brought the pen to my wrist at the side of my head, a nudge guiding me to turn my face away. Drawing on me at this angle wouldn't be easy.

"Making things harder on yourself," I muttered.

The double meaning of my words hit me after, and I gave a soft laugh.

Jamieson kissed my cheek. "Always."

In short dashes, he sketched the tattoo on my wrist. He didn't take long, but I measured every breath. How mine matched the rise and falls of his broad, bare chest. How each line drawn calmed me down.

When he was done, he kissed my throat softly and handed me the pen. "Draw something on me."

I took it and withdrew my hands to see his work. He'd made the circle smaller than his but still perfect. I gazed at it.

"Like it?"

I loved it. Realising the whole family had it did something to my heart I barely understood.

"It's perfect. What should I draw on you?"

"Whatever ye want. But I have another condition. A demand, actually."

"Which is?"

"We do it naked."

Those twin competing emotions roared. Needy heat and icy fear.

"Remember, this won't lead to sex. No matter how it feels," he vowed.

I needed to break through my barriers, in more ways than one. Climbing off him, I held my breath and stripped the T-shirt and then the crop top. Without looking at anything other than the floor, I removed my leggings, leaving myself entirely naked.

On the bed, Jamieson swore then removed his jeans in a fast swoosh of clothing. He patted the mattress. "Get back up here."

"Like we were?" I said, hesitating for more than one reason.

"Exactly like we were."

My heart pounded, but I took the challenge, kneeling on the bed then gingerly taking my position on his lap. I could do this. It was no different than five minutes ago, just minus a little bit of material.

Holding my breath, I settled on his lap with his ultra-hard dick under me, this time, the length of it pressed against my wet core. It pulsed, and I gave a squeak of breath.

Jamieson ran his arms around me and tucked his head

down on my neck. His muscles shook. His skin was hot to the touch.

For a long moment, we just breathed against each other.

I trusted him, I realised. Right now, I was at my most vulnerable, but so was he. Neither of us shied from it.

"Do the drawing," he ordered through a tight voice.

Carefully, I pushed up on my knees to gain height. The position left me with access only to his bulky shoulder.

He'd be lucky to get a stick drawing with how dizzy he made me.

Somehow, I laid down the first swoop of the pen on the back of his shoulder then remembered how to breathe.

In my imagination, he'd always been tall but skinny. In touching his muscular form, I was rewriting that old view.

I let the purpose of making a sketch distract me.

"How did you get so strong?"

Jamieson shivered. In this pose, my boobs were right in front of his face, nothing dividing us. He stayed good to his word, not turning this into anything more.

"Long days working on Torlum. I bulked up."

I continued my drawing, laying down the pattern of a wave around the letter S. The water hugged my initial in the same way he hugged my curves. I was naturally laying down on his smooth skin how I felt inside.

At sea. Choppy. Surrounded.

"Tell me what you're drawing," he asked.

His mouth pressed to my breastbone, his hands gripped my waist. Now I'd raised up, his dick stood tall, pressing against my leg. I could so easily slide down onto it, but I knew that would kill off every inch of the tentative peace I'd found.

I'd panic and ruin this.

"Wait until I'm done," I breathed.

He grumbled but let me continue.

I added detail to the crest of the wave. The letter it swept around was big, three inches deep. Probably skewed from the angle I had to work with.

"Why do you smell so good?" Jamieson asked.

"Stop trying to distract me or this is going to be terrible."

"It won't."

He lasted thirty seconds.

"Why are you so goddamned beautiful?"

My stomach tightened. "Why did you delete our chats?"

I stopped drawing, no clue why I'd blurted that. The empty space in our private chat where thousands of messages had lived haunted me. "Forget it. If you hadn't, I would've."

"Ye went back and checked, then?"

He tipped down my chin, making me look at him for an answer.

I didn't want to. The hurt was mine, and so highly personal I didn't want him to see it. But one glance in my eyes, and his expression told me he saw it all.

Jamieson swore softly and brushed his thumb over my cheek.

Then he lifted me off him and stretched for his phone on the bedside table.

In a couple of taps, he located our private conversation thread, holding the screen so I could see it.

"I already explained why I tried to stop ye thinking about me. For the first and only time in my life, I'd wanted to be noble so it didn't hurt so much when ye heard about my death. Or worse, heard nothing from me again. But at no point did I let go."

He thumbed through the settings, making sure I could see what he was doing. Then he selected the archive function.

"Want me to undo it?" he asked quietly.

I stared at the number beside that innocuous setting I'd never found. The count of our messages sent, higher than I ever imagined.

They'd been there all along.

"You mean this whole time…"

"Pandora's box, right here. All the messages right back to the very first. I could never forget ye, but I could hide these away so ye could forget me."

If this was a choice, I could only see one option.

With my heart aching, I pressed his finger on the button.

Instantly it started to work, our years of conversations returning.

We stared in silence until his phone went dark.

"Want to listen to us?" he asked.

"No," I replied, too fast.

If I heard the voices of our younger selves, filled with hope, or curiosity, or the first tendrils of love, I'd probably cry for everything that had been lost.

And right now, I needed to live for what we still had.

Jamieson stowed away the phone, no argument, probably feeling the same things I was. We'd always been in tune.

He stood from the bed and entered the bathroom, switching on the light to check the drawing on his back. Somehow, it wasn't skewed. The S of my name sat perfectly straight on his shoulder.

He gazed at it, angling to see it better.

Then with a smirk at me, he yanked on his jeans, marched to the bedroom door, and stuck his head out into the hall. "Yo, Scar?"

I snatched the quilt over my naked body.

From elsewhere in the house, a faint buzzing ceased. Then Camden's voice followed. "What's up?"

"When you're finished, can ye come up and lay some new ink on me?"

My mouth dropped open. "Don't joke."

He listened to Camden's reply then practically bounced back to the bed. "I never would. When Camden's done tattooing your sister with the brand ye inspired, I'm getting your design on my shoulder. Ye claimed me. I want the world to see it."

There were any number of things I could've said. I could have laughed and said the S stood for surfing or savage, but I only nodded.

A short while later, and after I'd dressed again, Camden joined us. He muttered something about initials being tattooed into skin, and I made a note to ask my sister what he meant. Then he got busy carving my artwork onto Jamieson.

When he was finished, and he asked me if I wanted anything done as well, I didn't hesitate to hold out my wrist with the surfer brand.

And let loose my desire to make the temporary permanent.

24

Arran

Bound by the wrists and chained to the wall, I adjusted my position, jagged pain zapping across my body. This time, probably only a couple of bones had been broken—I couldn't move my little finger, the digit swollen and pulsing with a deep ache, and it hurt when I breathed, suggesting he'd fucked up my ribs—but that was no big deal.

I'd known so much worse.

Previous beatings had left me unconscious. Once with a broken arm.

Being locked away for days was far more standard.

A noise came from the hall of my father's mansion, and I lifted my head, peering through bruised, swollen eyes.

The lock turned, and the door opened. Campbell, my father's top henchman, or butler as he called himself, entered.

He sneered, looking me over. "Your father will see ye now."

I kept in a laugh. He'd see me now? Like I'd been sitting in a waiting room, early for an appointment.

I didn't answer, and Campbell leaned over to remove my handcuffs.

The second he released me, I rose in a rush and knocked the elderly man to the floor. Then I planted my bare foot on his throat.

Always my tormentor. As bad as my father for abuse.

Maybe worse on a personal level.

Campbell stared at me in outrage, gripping my ankle. I didn't budge. I was seventeen now and strong, despite the fact I hadn't eaten in the time I'd been held in this room, the same room they'd kept Summer in. I didn't regret helping her. I'd suffered worse for lesser transgressions.

Campbell had taken pleasure in hunting me on more than one occasion. A couple of years ago, I'd run. He'd returned me barely able to walk.

In the eyes of my father's employee, I witnessed the exact second he realised I wasn't his bitch anymore.

His panic drove me higher. I pressed down, transferring more of my weight to the spindly, saggy throat.

Something popped.

Campbell choked, spluttering and writhing. I pinned him to the floor, not allowing myself to live in the moment but letting the recent past control me.

He was going to die here.

The edges of a flashback burst in my mind.

My memory had been ruined at some point during my childhood and a lot of it lost, so I swam in the glimpsed images, absorbing every detail. Taking a beating from Campbell wasn't a surprise revelation. But the thick belt he used to punish me had a metal buckle. It flashed in the sun ahead of it, landing on my back.

"Arran," my father snapped from the doorway.

Faltering, I lost my balance and crashed to the floor.

Campbell sucked in air with heaving moans, turning onto his side with his hands at his neck.

He vomited, straining to draw weak breaths.

Slowly, I dragged my gaze to my father.

Dad considered his employee with a neutral, unconcerned expression, then brought his focus to me. "I ordered you brought to my office. Get up."

He turned and marched away, and I pushed up from the floor and staggered after him. It was a distance from the grimy bedroom to his opulent office suite. On the way, through the pale, early dawn light in the corridors, I passed one of the maids. If she thought it unusual that I was naked and bruised, she didn't show it.

At my father's door, I knocked.

"Enter and stand ready," his voice returned.

I obeyed, closing the door behind me and advancing to wait in front of his desk. I stood at the position of attention, though, with my arms crossed in front of my body, shielding my junk from his view.

As a younger man, Dad had been in the army. His training ground for leading the police force. He intended the same for me, hence his regular sessions of toughening me up.

Dad steepled his fingers. "You distracted Kenney on purpose to let that slut into the station."

I remained silent. I wasn't above lying but I knew my father. This was a test.

He waited several long seconds before continuing. "You colluded with a whore against your own father then used privileged information and access to help a prisoner escape."

All true, apart from the whore part.

I didn't share my father's view of women. I might never have known my mother, but at some point, I'd had one. She deserved better. All women did.

"You embarrassed me in front of my staff who now believe I can't control my own son. All acts of extreme insubordination."

He rose to his full height, an inch below mine, and rounded his desk, coming to stand at my shoulder, his gaze scalding.

I kept up my stare at the spot on the wall behind his desk.

His intimidation was immaculate. I'd seen him use the tactic many times, and not just on his son.

He watched me. Tracking every movement.

I breathed through my nose, fixed on the single truth that could save me. If he wanted me dead, he would've ordered it done days ago.

It was a small, tiny strand of hope, but I clung to it.

"Or," my father breathed, "you really did intend to join me and Kenney, as I'd previously asked. The whore in the trunk was a stowaway. Which makes you an ignorant child."

Dad had made it known that he intended to kill his prisoner. He'd wanted me there, probably to pull the trigger and be blooded, like he'd done with me when teaching me to shoot, hunting rabbits then deer. He'd daubed my forehead with their blood. I could easily imagine him doing the same with his prisoner. My alibi, in a nutshell, was his intention to make me a killer and my sudden decision to want to please him.

The moment stretched out with infinite tension. A knife's edge of life or death. I wished that I didn't care, and that death didn't scare me so much. But I was only human.

Maybe I had more in me of my mother than my father.

After the longest, coldest moment of time, Dad turned and crossed the room, returning with something that he thrust into my arms.

I dropped my gaze. A jumpsuit.

My pulse skipped and raced, but I understood the implication, and yanked on the item of clothing, zipping it up. My fingers trembled, but I managed my task.

Dad dropped back into his chair with a huff of breath. "You would never betray me," he decided out loud. "My only son. My single investment in the future and my heir. Not like McInver's legacy. His pack of wild boys."

I merely waited.

My father sighed and pointed at the seat opposite him. "Sit down, for Christ's sake. I need information and you're going to give it to me. Tell me, do you talk when you fuck?"

I opened and closed my mouth. I'd never slept with one of the women Dad brought in. Divine had been right. We'd play videogames.

My father smashed his fist on his desk. "Answer me. There's a rat in my household, and I need to know who it is. Are you inadvertently telling the whores things they shouldn't know?" The pretence of a smile graced his thin lips. "I do it. I don't blame you."

"No, sir," I replied.

There was no way I'd pass the blame on to any of the women.

Dad glowered. "Fine. We're leaving in an hour. Go and prepare."

"Permission to speak, sir," I ventured.

He tipped his head. "Granted."

"In what way would you like me to prepare?"

"Shower. You smell disgusting. Eat something. We're going back to make another attempt at talking to McInver."

I could ask more, but I knew my father. He preferred the sound of his own voice.

"Since the old bastard woke from his coma, I've been unable to get through to him," Dad continued. "We'd been ready to extend our operation, but I can't progress it without his agreement. His signature on the dotted line, so to speak. For twenty years, we've worked together. Do you know how much time and effort it took me to go from a lowly lieutenant, stationed in piss-poor towns throughout Europe, to owning an empire?"

Dad had never been lowly. His father had left him this mansion and a fortune hidden away in Swiss banks.

Until now, I hadn't been sure how much he'd been involved in the trading of the flesh that he so loved to sample. I'd guessed it to be significant, but I had no evidence.

"No, sir," I answered.

He smiled, pleased that I was neither broken nor whole, but somewhere in between. Malleable, exactly as he wanted me. Just as I'd always needed to be to survive.

But then his smile dropped.

"This time, you'll be with me," he explained. "McInver will see what it is to have a true, obedient heir. He still has a soft spot for the boys he sired. Misplaced, of course. At first, I envied him having a son with a backbone. Then I realised what that meant and what it's done to him. That's the reason why I know you'd never work against me, Arran. You know what would happen if you did. Whose life would be forfeit."

"Mine, sir."

He smiled, and anger revealed itself in the tightness of his features. Fast and deadly, the real man.

Fear screamed through me.

"If I suspect you again, in even the smallest way, your mother will pay with her blood."

It was a bluff. There was no way my mother was still alive. Dad would have used her against me before now if she had been.

The realisation came fast, and confusion filtered through my fear.

What kind of man did that? What kind of man did any of the things my father did? I'd met and helped McInver's son. Helped another of them be rescued rather than executed. They'd risen up against their sire.

On the other hand, they weren't alone like I was.

All I'd ever had was my father.

"The whore and the prisoner," I started. "Do you need

my help going after them?"

Dad gave an approving nod. "Your thoughtfulness does you credit, but don't worry about that. I know exactly how to find them. They won't get away."

25

Summer

I woke to the trickle of running water and the pounding of my heart.

Danger, my senses screamed.

I sat up slowly, taking in the bedroom, pale in the early morning light. Not the mansion I'd been locked up in.

The bed beside me was empty, the door to the bathroom closed. Jamieson had to be in the shower.

The rest of the house lay in silence.

I held my breath, my hand over my thudding heart, listening intently for any other sound.

Nothing. My wrist stung from the small tattoo, but that was all my senses picked up.

I'd had a nightmare. The chief standing in my doorway, his beady eyes on me. *You'll beg me for it.*

Me crawling on my knees to him.

Just a dream. It was nothing more. He wasn't here.

Even so, I needed to be sure it wasn't something else

that had alerted me. With stealth, I clambered from the bed and padded silently to the window, easing to peer out so if anyone was there, I'd see them before they saw me.

On the road below, only our two cars waited, no other vehicles in sight. Likewise, the beach was empty. No dog walkers or runners passing by.

My panic didn't cease.

I backed away and moved to the bedroom door, the gentle splashes of the shower continuing. In the hall, all the other bedroom doors were closed. I passed them and, at the top of the stairs, peeked down.

Nothing. The front door was closed with the lock engaged, and the big living room to the left of the entryway empty of people.

Careful to avoid any creaks, I tiptoed down the edge of the staircase, glancing down the hall at the bottom into the kitchen and dining room.

Nothing.

Still, my senses whirred.

Was it all just a bad dream? I'd never been this jumpy before, and there were multiple other people in the house who would have woken at a noise. Everyone seemed to be on high alert.

Moving on, I checked out the dining room and then the wide kitchen. All was as we'd left it. The counters cleared, the faint smell of the food Lottie had prepared last night the only real sign we'd been here.

Another door waited at the far end of the kitchen, a separate laundry room, or maybe a boot room, I wasn't sure.

The last place I had to check.

My breathing came faster. My pulse sped. To get to the room, I had to cross the kitchen. I'd be unable to avoid walking in front of the huge window that overlooked the beach and the sea.

Slinking around the centre of the house had been one thing, but here, I was completely exposed.

I took a step.

A man loomed up the other side of the glass.

A big, shadowed figure staring right at me.

I squealed in fright. My whole body took a screenshot of shock. Scrambling backwards, I landed on the cold stone floor and backed up against the kitchen island.

I'd been found.

We were in the middle of nowhere, and the police chief had tracked us down. He'd grab me then hunt down Jamieson, unawares upstairs.

The intruder didn't pause.

With urgency, he darted to the kitchen door, his prey sighted.

At least that door was locked. I needed to alert the house.

But as I opened my mouth to scream my warning, the kitchen door flew open. My throat closed over, and I couldn't make a sound.

Had to get away. I unfroze my muscles.

Sprinting into the hallway, I sensed a hand at my back.

But only a dark laugh followed.

I paused. Spun around.

In the doorway, Jamieson cracked up, leaning on the

handle.

My mouth dropped open. Nothing came out.

"What the hell just happened?" He entered, scrubbing his bare, sand-covered feet off on the kitchen mat that read a cheery *Welcome.*

I closed my eyes for a long second. "You were upstairs in the shower."

"Nope. I hit the surf early. Probably one of my brothers. Struan and Thea's bathroom backs onto ours."

Emotion rolled over me in a fast hit. I advanced on him, taking in his T-shirt and boxers. A surfboard rested against the garden fence.

"No, I woke up and you weren't there and I heard the water running. I had this terrible feeling someone was in the house."

His smile disappeared. His gaze flitted over my features. "Ye were scared."

I drew closer, my words piling over themselves. "If someone finds us here, it's game over. They'd capture me and then arrest you."

Jamieson kicked the door closed and twisted the key in the lock. He moved in on me and took hold of my waist, then without pause, boosted me to sit on the kitchen counter. Now, we were eye to eye, him bracing himself with his hands either side of my hips.

"I'm sorry to have frightened ye," he said with total seriousness. "When I got up, I kissed your cheek and told ye I'd be back soon, but I should have woken ye. My problem was I couldn't sleep next to ye. Want to know why?"

I nodded miserably.

He tipped his head to indicate down his body. "I spent the night desperate for ye. So insanely hard I couldn't ignore it anymore. After everything ye went through with the fucking chief of police performing in front of ye, I wasn't about to let ye walk in on me taking care of myself. So I headed out for a surf where I could handle myself."

Astonishment chased away most of my alarm. "Are you telling me...?"

He nodded once and fast. "Jacked myself off in the sea. It was fucking cold, and my shoulder stung. Not my finest hour."

I leaned in and kissed him. An unexpected impulse, pressing my lips to his icy ones.

I'd been terrified, but maybe it was simply because he hadn't been there. He was being so careful with me. Caring for me enough to separate out every one of his desires. I needed him to know how grateful I was.

But just as fast, panic froze me. I stalled.

I couldn't do it. I couldn't make any demands of him. It hit my wall of trauma and bounced me off.

As if he'd read my mind, Jamieson uttered a growl. He cupped the back of my head and pushed my shoulder until I was laid out on the counter. Then he fitted his mouth to mine again and took it in a blistering, bruising kiss.

Spread out on my back with him over me, I could only take. *Harder,* I urged him in my head. Somehow, he obeyed, his fingers twisting into my hair to tug on the roots.

It worked.

Instead of wanting to scream and run, I could accept it. Live in it.

He took harsh swoops of my lips, parting them to thrust his tongue into my mouth, slicking it over mine. I closed my eyes in amazement, all senses trained to the sheer pleasure that bloomed where we touched. Lower. My nipples beaded, and a pulse beat between my legs.

A familiar ache followed.

One I'd felt when I was alone and listening to his messages. Utter need. Back then, it had been honest and perfectly formed. Now it was tainted by the knowledge that if I was controlling this, or if he wasn't so savage, the pleasure would vanish.

I blocked that from my mind and let him hold me down, take what he wanted from my willing lips.

Finally, he eased up, pulling back to swipe over my lower lip with his thumb.

He tasted of seawater. And something more coppery. Blood, I realised.

"Cut your lip," he grumbled, giving me room to sit up.

I pressed my fingertips to my plump, swollen flesh. They came away with spots of bright-red blood.

I smiled.

Jamieson watched me then swore softly to himself. He spun away and grabbed a glass, filling it from the tap over the sink. He downed half, tipped the rest over his head, refilled it, and offered it to me.

I took it and sipped the cold water.

"I've been thinking," Jamieson said. He dripped water everywhere. "After I got out of jail, I thought it better for me not to be around my family. The same way ye feel half the time, too."

"If I was a walking target before, that's only going to get worse."

He inclined his head. "Yet ye can't walk away from your sister, right? I can't leave my brothers and our kin. How about this. We create a distraction to draw the chief away."

I couldn't walk away from him either. "Like a decoy?"

"Exactly. Appear somewhere that will get his attention but is far enough away to waste his time. If we do that before Cassie's rescue, he'll be out of the way. We can be long gone by the time he realises."

"I like the idea."

"It keeps us together and our families safer."

He held my gaze, and the moment played out. I'd run from him, and now he was asking me to stay at his side. I slowly nodded.

The swift relief in his eyes caught me in the throat.

Footsteps descended the stairs. I hopped down from the counter and straightened my clothes. Jamieson turned away and cupped himself over his tight boxer shorts, muttering swear words.

Smiling brightly, Camden entered the kitchen. "Morning, Summer. Oh, shite, you've cut your lip. Sea air will do that. Dries them right out."

I hid a smile at the tiny injury from my secret tryst, then pressed the cool glass to the cut to staunch it.

Jamieson's brother passed me and opened cupboards, searching for something. Finally, he brandished a jar of coffee. "Score. Hey, does Breeze prefer coffee or tea? She's still asleep, and I want to surprise her."

"Coffee," I answered, my cheeks warm. "No sugar, lots

of milk."

He saluted and moved to put the kettle on. "Got a lot to learn about each other, but we're having fun working it out."

While it boiled, he cocked his head at Jamieson. "What's up with ye?"

Still with his back to the room, Jamieson slid him a look but didn't answer.

"Morning wood." Struan strolled in with Sin right behind him. "Am I right?"

I burst out laughing, slapping my hand to my mouth.

All four of them stared at me with eyebrows raised like I'd never laughed in front of them before. Maybe I hadn't.

"Hold your breath and flex a muscle," Camden instructed, going back to his brother. "It directs the blood flow elsewhere."

"And jump up and down on the spot. That'll see ye good," Struan added with a sly grin.

Jamieson balled up his fists then did exactly that, hopping a couple of times.

His brothers cracked up.

He spun around, scowling. "Idiots."

I couldn't help peeking at his shorts.

"Yeah, but it worked, and we're all safe from being poked in the eye." Struan grinned.

Jamieson grumbled and came to my side. "We've had an idea."

Briefly, he filled them in on our distraction plan.

"It's risky leaving here," Sin observed.

"Fucking breathing is risky," Jamieson replied. "If he is looking for us across the country, he isn't hunting us here. If we're smart about it, it'll work."

"The moment I upload a naming-and-shaming video, we want him searching somewhere else," I added. "We don't have to be dangerous about it. Just get on CCTV somewhere he can access after the fact."

All of them pondered that.

Jamieson took a steadying breath. "There's another thing. If we do that, we need to take a car. Struan and Thea will have the other one as they go to find Cassie, leaving the rest of ye here with no transport."

Sin grimaced. "So long as you're all back the same day, it won't matter. Not ideal, though."

It left them as sitting ducks. Though they weren't the ones being hunted by the police, that we knew of.

But before anyone else could speak, my sister hollered down the stairs, urgency in her tone. "Summer!"

I was running.

Halfway down the steps, she held up her phone.

"Divine," Breeze uttered. She swiped to answer the call. "Hello?"

"Sis, I'm finally outta there. Are you somewhere private?" the exotic dancer said.

"I'm with my sister. She can hear you."

"Thank the baby Jesus for that. Hey, Summer, how are you doing?"

People kept asking that, and I had no good answer. "It's great to hear your voice. Where did you say you were?"

"Just walked in my front door. I've been at the mansion since we spoke last. I don't take my phone when I go there."

She was safe. I sagged against the wall. "Catch us up with what happened after I left."

"Girl, it went off. I was supposed to stay the night, so I was there when the chief returned, long after all the other ladies had left. I didn't see him come in, but he had a blood spatter on his shirt."

My breath caught. Jamieson curled an arm around me, and I clung to it. "Whose blood?"

"You think I asked? Someone copped a beating, but he wasn't about to tell me. I just got on my back as ordered. But midway through him getting down to business, he decided to switch things up and marched me downstairs to where you were supposed to be. The drama that followed once he opened the door and found you missing. His butler took a clout to the head. Knocked the guy sideways. He questioned everyone, including me. Never seen anger like it."

My knees trembled. Fear rose in a fierce crest.

"He searched the camera footage and saw that you'd snuck away in his son's car. Honestly, I thought my number was up. I was sure he'd call me out, but this lady lived to see another day."

"I owe you danger money," I managed, though my voice trembled.

"You owe nothing but to keep your ass safe."

"Do you know if Arran got away?" I said.

She went quiet. "I don't know. I haven't seen him. Listen, because this is important. I was with the chief overnight, and he is gunning for you. Do you remember all my warnings? Double down on those. Don't go home. Don't go anywhere the address might be linked to your name. Got any relatives you care about besides your sister?"

All the worry I'd felt this morning returned in a rush. "Our mother. I told her not to answer the door to anyone."

Divine made an unhappy sound. "Think that will stop him? Tell that bitch to take a holiday. I'm serious. He's coming for you. If he wants to use her to get to you, he will. A locked door can't stop him."

My wretched sense of hopelessness returned.

The plan I'd had was falling apart. I had to go to Mum. Jamieson's family had to go to get Cassie. There were only two cars, and I had to choose.

Jamieson backed away and spoke urgently with his brothers.

I watched them, a new hope forming. Maybe for the first time, I could rely on someone else.

"Divine, I need to ask you something," I said.

"Oh Lord. Spill it."

"I'm going to expose him. Make a video naming him and saying what happened to me."

The dancer went silent.

"I know what you're going to say already. I won't live in fear. What I want is a series of videos. My sister is going to make one, exposing Vanessa and the List. Our mother will be a third, if she wants to be part of it. A friend's mother is another victim who we hope will tell her tale. Will you?"

I held my breath.

"Ye don't know what you're asking. If I told all the

things I knew," Divine said slowly, "I'd be snitching on a judge, barristers, CEOs in fancy offices. It isn't just the chief I'd have to worry about, and sis, he's the worst of them all."

On the other end of the line, a little squeal came with the patter of feet, the babble of a child following. Divine muffled the phone and replied in a caring, maternal voice to the child.

In a heartbeat, I knew we'd lost her.

Then she hung up without giving her reply.

26

Jamieson

"Then it's decided." I looked between my brothers, getting nods in reply.

Camden passed me and climbed the staircase to join Breeze who was examining her sister's new inkwork. Her permanent bond to our family.

"We'll go to your ma's," Camden said. "Text her now. Get her to pack a bag so we can collect her and get moving."

Summer clutched Breeze's hand. "I wanted to go to her. I have that money to give her."

"We'll take it and get her to safety," Breeze vowed.

Camden's phone buzzed. As one, we all swung to face it. Somehow, our phones had become the greatest source of danger.

His eyebrows furrowed. "It's Golding."

"Who?" I asked.

"Our father's lawyer. He found me snooping around McInver's mansion, and I pretended to be the son McInver actually wanted to get to ye." My brother answered. "Mr

Golding. I'm with my family and I'm putting ye on loud-speaker."

He pressed something onscreen, and the man's voice came through. English.

"Wonderful, wonderful, in fact, that's remarkably perfect," the lawyer gushed down the line. "It suits me for you all to hear this. First, please accept my apologies for the limited contact over the past few days. Following the wondrous event of your father's awakening from his coma, I've been at his bedside and busy with his requests. You'll be glad to hear he's alert and aware. All his marbles are intact. It's a miracle. My wishes came true. Such a—"

"Get to the point," Camden intoned.

I already knew how this would go down. McInver waking up meant only bad things. He'd report us to the police. Maybe even charge Camden with the actions he took in order to get to me. The cars we'd travelled in were his, and no way would the old man look kindly on us using them.

"At once, at once. So, to my point. Your father would like to see you."

I stiffened. My brothers did, too.

"Who does he want to see?" Camden asked.

"All four of you," the lawyer advised.

"Be specific," Sin added.

The lawyer cleared his throat. "Struan Gallagher, Sinclair Stone, Camden Marshall, and Jamieson Buchanan."

"How does he know my name?" I barked at the phone.

Summer widened her eyes at me. I was pretty sure I'd never told her my surname, only that it started with a B. I'd signed myself off as JB the single time I'd posted her anything.

Her pendant. A scrawl of a note with it that simply read:

Happy birthday.

Your JB.

"I'm afraid you have me at a disadvantage, sir," the lawyer replied. "To whom am I speaking?"

"Jamieson Buchanan. I've never even met the miserable old fucker."

The lawyer sighed. "A regret Mr McInver expresses keenly. Since becoming aware of the existence of his children, your father has become highly solicitous to bring you into the fold. Not solely Mr Stone, whose fire he so admires, but all of you. He is fully aware of the inheritance proceedings commenced with Mr Marshall and ecstatic at the prospect of two of his sons wishing to become closer to him. Mr Marshall's cunning and prowess impressed him ever so much. To have all four of you at his bedside is his dearest wish."

There was a long, concerned silence among us all.

Slowly, Camden spoke. "Then the fact we're driving his cars is okay with him?"

"Completely. He's glad for it. Like I said, he's fully aware of all that happened while he was sleeping. Even yesterday, I was contacted by the police who'd found one of the vehicles on the outskirts of Edinburgh. Local residents had reported it as abandoned and with keys left inside. I arranged for it to be returned to the Great House, and your father chuckled about it."

Struan had me abandon that sports car after he'd come

with me to manage the problem of Kayden.

"You need not worry about the police," Golding added. "Only that your father awaits you with open arms."

Camden shook his head. "I know there's a catch. He isnae that generous. Give us the condition."

The lawyer paused. "You have three days to present yourselves at his bedside."

"There it is. Let me guess, after which he'll press the destruct button on our freedom?"

"Well, I'm sure, that is to say—" the lawyer spluttered.

Camden cut him off. "Got ye loud and clear, Golding. We'll be in touch."

He tapped the screen to kill the call and blew out a breath. "What the fuck does he want with all of us? And how does he know your name, Burn? Ye weren't even in his house."

Struan huffed a laugh. "Apart from when he burned it down. McInver knows exactly who we all are, including Cassie. It was his doing that she got taken by the cops. The question is, what does he want from us?"

"Could it be a trap?" Summer asked.

My brother shrugged, but I just watched her.

She was scared again. I'd burn down the world to keep her safe.

Summer took a fast breath. "Isn't your father part of the same world as the police chief? McInver bought Breeze. The chief bought me from the same place. They have to know each other."

Camden nodded. "They do. They're business partners."

"Then he's trying to reel you in so he can capture Jamieson," she spluttered.

I caught and held her trembling fingers. "I'm not going to walk into his hospital room and offer myself up for the slaughter. Dinna fret."

Sin had been mostly quiet but now gave up his thoughts. "That isn't McInver's style. He plays games but he's desperate for an heir. The language the lawyer used to compliment me and Scar sounded like McInver all over. He liked my fire but told me I lacked cunning. Now he's all over the fact that one of the other of his sons manipulated the lawyer while he was unconscious. By now, he knows we act as one and his money means nothing to us. My guess is he's for real. If he wants one of us, he'll have to take us all, and his brush with death has shown him that. His having Golding recite our names is his message to us."

I shrugged. "We can't ignore Summer's point that his business partner made him a better offer and he's given us up. I say we test him."

Everyone looked at me.

"I need to collect something from his house anyway. I'm going to steal another of his cars. Let's see how the wrinkly old ballsack likes that."

<h1 style="text-align:center">27</h1>

Summer

At the door to our safe house, my sister threw her arms around me, holding on tight. "I wish you weren't going anywhere."

We'd just gotten off the phone to our mother and were ready to leave.

Mum had agreed to pack a bag and leave the block of flats for a friend's house outside of Edinburgh. Breeze and her boyfriend were driving down to pick her up and take her on the trip, the only way we could feel sure she'd be safe.

Also to get her video evidence, if she was willing to give it.

It was a big ask of a woman who was trying to recover and stay sober. A raking over of ashes. Perhaps healing, too. She'd opened up in her counselling groups. Either way, the choice was hers alone.

I squeezed my sister back. "We'll be careful. Promise you will as well."

"Always. When do you think you'll be back?"

The drive into the Cairngorms would take a couple of hours at least. I wasn't sure where else Jamieson had in mind for us to cause a scene and distract the chief, but it had to be a good distance away to be effective.

"Late this evening. I'll keep in touch. Love you."

"I love you, too."

She released me and crossed the scrubby garden to reach their car. In the driver's seat, Camden raised a hand, and they drove away.

The worst feeling came over me.

A sickening dread that I wouldn't see my sister again.

The police would pick them up and take them into custody so the chief could use them against me. Or Mum would already be missing. Or I'd be the one in trouble and unable to get back to them.

Strong arms curled around my shoulders, and Jamieson pulled me against his body.

Instantly, my spiralling thoughts ceased, and I tuned in to him instead. His presence calming and exciting in different ways.

"They'll be okay," he promised with a soft kiss to my neck. "Camden might seem chill, but he's a thousand times smarter than me. And he can throw a punch. He's fierce as fuck when protecting those he loves. Your sister is safe with him."

"He loves her?" I asked.

It was a pointless question. Jamieson's brother gravitated around Breeze. It was obvious that he was devoted. It made me like him all the more. I just needed to hear Jamieson say it.

His voice came back deeper. Tighter. His mouth next to my ear. "Yes, he loves her. Can ye doubt it?"

My heart thumped, and I was glad to keep my focus on the distant car and not to be looking at him.

The door banged again, and Struan strode past us to the big Range Rover. "Ye fit?"

Jamieson sighed, his breath tickling my ear. He released me but took my hand to guide me to the car. "Let's do this thing."

With Struan and Theadora in the front, Jamieson and I climbed into the back.

The problem of not having enough vehicles between us would be solved this morning with Jamieson's plan to steal another of McInver's cars. We'd be dropped off outside of the old man's estate, then would sneak in.

I had to admit deep curiosity about the man who'd fathered Jamieson and his brothers. When we were kids, I'd asked him who his daddy was, and he'd shrugged off the answer until eventually, one day he told me it was some rich old guy. That's all his mum had ever said.

I wished I had time to sit and listen through the messages retrieved from Jamieson's archive. To remember who we used to be. To hear how we used to talk to each other.

Struan curved the car expertly round the narrow country lanes, though his body language was tight.

"I'm going to speak to Struan's mother on the phone this morning," Thea said. "At least I hope so. I looked for online appointments at the jail, but the earliest is days away. She's allowed phone calls, I just have to time it right, and obviously she needs to be willing. It helps that I've met her before. Also, I think she'd like to speak to her son."

She reached out and took her boyfriend's hand. From that touch alone, I understood that it would be a tough conversation. And they were doing it because of me.

"Thank you," I told them both.

Struan shrugged. "This needs to be done." He switched his gaze to Jamieson. "I'll go with ye to the house."

Jamieson shook his head, his hand still clutching mine. "We'll be okay. Ye have your task, we have ours. If it looks dodgy, I'll get us out without anyone seeing us. I can steal a car from somewhere else. It's better for all of us if ye can locate Cassie."

His brother glowered but didn't protest.

"If ye have the chance," Jamieson added, "will ye grab

her?"

"Fuck yeah."

"Good."

We drove on, everyone lapsing into a tense silence.

A couple of hours later, we were deep in the Cairngorms. Struan navigated off the main road and onto a rutted lane which seemed to go on for miles.

Finally, he pulled over under the shade of thick trees.

"We waited here for as long as we could," he told Jamieson. "Nobody wanted to leave ye behind."

It took a long second for me to realise he meant after the fire Jamieson set.

Jamieson shrugged and popped the door. "Getting caught was my own fault. I willnae make the mistake again."

I climbed out, too, murmuring a quiet goodbye to Thea. If all went well today, she'd find Cassie and get to talk to Struan's mother. The more I thought about all the things we were doing, the more it made a big picture. A broken-up jigsaw puzzle of which I'd found just a few pieces.

All we could do was push on and try to make the picture on the box our own.

Our ride rolled away, leaving me and Jamieson to our fate.

We hadn't been completely alone together since I'd saved him from the police station. Aside from our time on that beach when others were in earshot. All of a sudden, my heart pumped faster, my body stirring.

He flicked his gaze up and down me, a smirk playing with his lips. "Don't look at me like that or we'll never get anything done."

"How was I looking at you?" I jogged along beside him as he plunged us into the thick woods.

Sunlight filtered through, the day warm and birds chirping.

He didn't answer, and I peeked at him, needing to know his mind.

"Tell me," I tried again.

Jamieson stopped abruptly and crowded me against the nearest tree. The bark crackled at my back, the scratches barely registering.

"Like you're dying for me to prowl after ye and throw ye down on the ground. Tear away those tight black leggings and fuck ye into the dirt. I'm down for it, Summer. If you're ready for me, I'll give ye what ye need and I won't be gentle."

He held my gaze, and I wavered, straddling the edge of a desperate yes and a fearful no.

But I took too long over my decision, and he pushed away from the tree with a huff of breath.

"As I thought."

His gaze drifted down me, then Jamieson's eyes narrowed. He stooped and picked up something from beside my feet. Held it up.

My mouth dropped open. It was his Zippo. My brain caught up. The silver metal lighter he'd left behind after the fire.

My gift to him years ago.

"Here? This is where you left it?"

With a flick of his thumb, he opened the lighter and

spun the little wheel. An orange flame flickered, and Jamieson laughed.

"I left it by a tree on this path in the dark, knowing I was about to commit a crime and not needing the evidence on me when matches would burn and vanish. More, I couldn't stand the thought of losing it permanently to an evidence room. What are the odds that it was right by your fucking feet?"

He leaned in and sank his lips onto mine, my head softly thumping onto the tree.

"A good omen," he said against my mouth. "Everything about ye is. Now let's go steal us our new ride."

On the other side of the woodland, a vast park opened out. At the bottom was a stately home, one part in ruins but with construction work underway. A forklift truck busied across the wide car park, carrying pallets of something over to a small team of builders.

For a long while, we watched the place, scoping it out.

Walking straight up to the construction crew was out of the question, even if we did want to test his father. On the other hand, they weren't security. They'd have no idea whether we were entitled to be there or not.

"Camden spent more time here than any of us," Jamieson told me. "He and your sister explored the place and even spent the night here. He thinks there's something to be found in a basement or cellar."

"What does that mean? Some kind of evidence?"

He shrugged. "Last night, when ye were listing all the videos to be recorded, it made me think of the systems in place. Lasses taken from the streets or wherever, coerced by people like Kayden or forced into selling their bodies. Rich men buying them doesn't feel accidental. Someone like Mc-Inver or the police chief would want guarantees. Not only for their safety but for keeping the pussy supply coming."

I'd thought the same. "You're thinking we could prove they're behind it?"

He shrugged. "Once ye post your video, some other police bigwig would surely need to investigate Chief Daniels. He'd get away with it if he's got them in his pocket. But if there was something concrete that they couldn't ignore." He trailed off. "I've no idea what that looks like, but if there's a chance to deepen our case, I want to take it."

I held my excitement at bay. I didn't expect to change the world by making the videos. Only to tell the truth and expose the people who needed to be exposed in a way that was permanently on record. In the grand scheme of things, I didn't matter enough for a big deal investigation.

I knew that instinctively, but hope was a dangerous thing.

Down at the house, the construction crew's activity stopped. They stood together in a group, chatting, then climbed into their vans. In a line, they drove off down the main estate road, kicking up dust.

Jamieson checked the time with his phone reading it out in a friendly voice. "Mid-morning food break?"

"I don't know, but this might be the only chance we get."

He brought his gaze to me, and his eyes twinkled. "Ready to run?"

My adrenaline surged, and I caught his hand and took

off.

Down the field of dense summer grass and wild flowers we tore, first making it to an outcrop of trees, then to a low boundary wall to the car park.

We ducked down, and Jamieson took a breath.

"That building over there is the garage. Camden gave me the code. We either go there right now and try it, or we make an attempt at the house. Ye choose."

I gazed between the looming, pale stone mansion and the separate, much smaller outbuilding. The safe choice was to get a car and go. We had another objective. To lead the chief of police on a merry dance. To get seen somewhere far away from our safe house. Delaying here wasn't good enough, not far enough, but I wanted the picture Jamieson had painted. Having evidence to hand over along with my exposé.

"The house," I whispered, closer to my old impulsive self than I'd been in forever.

Jamieson grinned and half stood.

At the same second, a man appeared next to the ruined part of the house and sat on the front steps. I yanked Jamieson down behind the wall. My heart sped.

"What?" he mouthed.

"A guy," I whispered back almost silently.

We waited for a minute, but no shouts came. Slowly, Jamieson peeked over the wall. He dropped back down. "He's pretty young. Maybe some apprentice they didn't take with them. Fuck."

I took my own glance, watching the stranger enjoy his sunny rest. His gaze was on his phone and not our hiding place.

If he saw us, surely he'd call his boss.

"We won't make it past him into the house easily," I suggested. "The rest of the crew can't be far away. If he summons them back, they could stop us leaving. Look, we can get around to the garage by staying low behind this wall. We're just going to have to grab the car. We won't be able to avoid driving past this guy, but he won't be able to stop us."

For a beat, Jamieson considered the plan, then gave a short nod. Holding my hand, he walked at a stoop around the perimeter of the wall. At the edge nearest the garage, he turned me and tipped his head at our target.

I nodded, and together, we hopped the wall and jogged over the gravel to the car park entrance.

Here, we were in plain sight of the house, the construction site, and anyone looking on. We had to be fast.

At the keypad, Jamieson hesitated. "Camden told me the code. I memorised it."

My brain caught up. He might know the code, but tapping it into the keypad took concentration to overcome his word and number blindness.

"Let me." I slipped in front of him.

"Four-five-six-one-two-three," he recited.

I tapped the digits in.

With a rattle, the big doors rolled, opening.

I threw an anxious glance over my shoulder. I couldn't see the apprentice, but he could surely hear the noise.

"Come on," Jamieson urged and ducked under the opening door.

I followed. Inside the garage, two vehicles waited. The first was the dark-purple sports car Struan had driven, the one the lawyer said had been returned, but next to that was a chunky SUV.

Jamieson circled it. "What type of car is it? I've never seen one like this."

I'd gone straight to a key box on the wall, taking out the set of keys with a fob the same gunmetal grey as the flashy car.

I skipped over to the back of the car. "It's an Aston Martin DBX707. Brand-new by the looks of it."

He held his hand out for the keys.

I kept them, that stirring of impulse not quitting. "Mind if I drive your daddy's prized car?"

Jamieson's smile grew. "Be my guest."

28

Jamieson

Summer started the engine with a meaty rev, sliding me a glance that was pure sex. She didn't hesitate, though, putting a foot down to speed out of the garage.

If the apprentice saw us, it would be through a cloud of dust.

We took the gravel lane out of the estate, onto a wider road. The isolation of McInver's place meant there were few other vehicles here as well, and I directed Summer to get us onto the A9 and heading towards Inverness.

We wouldn't go into the city, though, instead taking a route south, skirting the edge of Loch Ness and out into the Western Highlands.

She didn't ask our eventual destination, but a sense of rightness burned in me.

I had my Zippo back, I'd shown her the house my pervert father owned, and now I was taking her to the place where everything had gone wrong for us.

Torlum.

The prison island.

My family knew we were coming here—I'd needed information from Thea on her family's boat—but Summer hadn't heard.

It was the perfect place. So far away from our beach hideout, and a less obvious place for me to return to.

The missing element was getting the chief's attention, but I had a plan for that, too.

"Do ye think less of me now ye know about my da?" I asked Summer.

Across the car, she sat easy in her seat, open hillside and farmland speeding by. "Of course not. Did you think any less of me when I told you about mine?"

Summer's father had never been a mystery to her, even if she didn't have any contact with the man. He was a deadbeat who'd been happy to impregnate and abandon her teenaged mother. If the man had any good in him, it had all gone to his daughters.

"Never. It's just new information for me."

She chewed on that. "Are you struggling to process it?"

"Maybe. I hadn't thought about it until ye were there with me at his place. I'm seeing it through your eyes. If I'm right and he's a trafficker, that's some pretty shitty genes to carry."

Summer stretched out and took my fingers.

She didn't take her eyes off the road, but that touch fucking sank me.

There had only been a handful of times where she'd voluntarily reached out for me. I'd touched her. Brought her arms around me. Told her what to do.

She'd been broken but she was coming back stronger. My woman was a queen, and she was rising.

We drove on, talking of all things, while I tried not to let out how much I wanted to serve her.

The trip up through the Isle of Skye dulled my mood a little.

"After I got taken to the island, I escaped several times, stole cars, anything to get away."

"Then it is Torlum we're going to," she replied quietly.

"Felt like a good idea. Not so sure now." I tried to ease the tension in my muscles, but the end of the trip was drawing near, and I needed to turn this apprehension into better energy.

At Uig, we parked away from the main ferry port, and I directed Summer down the lesser-used slipway to where private boats were kept. There were cameras on the main passenger ferry ramp. I didn't want to be seen yet.

Thea's boat was easy to find, and with Summer's help to unlock it, I got us out on the water with no hanging around. The one good thing about my time on the islands, besides meeting my brothers and sister, had been how much I knew about the ocean.

Despite the season, it was still chilly away from the coast, but there was nothing for it but to settle in for the trip.

At last, Torlum appeared through the haze of the Atlantic, or whatever the fuck the sea around the Hebrides was called.

I stared at the cliffs rising to the lighthouse. The stretch of beach.

Summer checked her phone. "I've got no signal."

Mine was the same. I rolled my shoulders. "It goes that way sometimes. We'll only be here an hour, tops."

Again, she didn't ask for details, trusting I had this.

I took us further to the east and docked away from the main jetty onto the island, no one looking on to identify me yet. After tying up the boat, I helped Summer jump to the deck, and we strode onto dry land.

I'd expected to feel some strength of...something. Probably not fear. Maybe more of the dread that had caught me on Skye. Instead, my emotions flattened.

Torlum's village stood in the distance, Jenkins' house at the edge of it, a shell with blackened walls.

We'd been poised to escape, but he'd snatched hold of me, taking me by surprise. With his dirty hand over my mouth, he'd dragged me into the house.

I'd broken free and slammed my fist into his face, smacking him to the floor. Took a flame to the curtains, letting it burn.

But I hadn't seen him die. Even staring at his wasteland of a home didn't give me the sense of cleansing it should've.

"Come on," I muttered and stomped across the moor to where it all started.

A warmer wind accompanied us across the open ground to the youth hostel. Here, I'd been brought, fighting all the way. The run-down, white, L-shaped building hadn't changed.

"Sin and Camden had already arrived when they brought me in," I uttered. "Apart from Struan, we were captured in age order. I was scared shitless, but I didn't show that to my brothers."

She tucked her hands into her armpits, waiting for me to go on.

We joined the rutted track that led to the building. The youth hostel sign had fallen, kissing the dirt.

"I was fitted with a tracker and put to work. There was no explanation, no paperwork, no reason given to why I'd been taken there. I was scared of Sin, didn't want to like Camden, and I fought to get away. I failed. They always brought me back no matter how far I got. One day, I confronted our keeper, this dour-faced bitch who'd electrocute us with a Taser whenever she felt we got out of line. She was the one who gave us the nicknames you might've heard us use. Ruin for Struan, Sin for Sinclair, Scar for Camden, and Burn for me. None were for good reasons, even if accurate for me. I'd screamed blue murder at her before, but it didn't bother her. This time, I demanded to know when I'd be set free. She laughed and told me I'd earned my place in Hell and I'd never see the mainland again."

As I spoke, we circled the building. I had no intention of going back inside again. I had all I needed in the backpack I carried.

Summer followed. "That's when you recorded that message for me. It's so desolate here."

"And I thought I'd die with no way of ye ever knowing."

"I understand."

She didn't hide the hurt in her voice. Finally, I felt something. An echo of the pain at letting her go.

I took a few steps on, coming to the rear of the building. There, as my brother had described, was the hole in the ground.

Summer's eyes rounded. "Is that a grave?"

"It was. Someone moved the body."

"Whose body?"

"Keep. The woman I mentioned. She fell on her own Taser with a little help from Camden."

The horror of Keep's gross corpse being dragged from her not-so-final resting place wasn't going to distract me from my plan. Whoever took her deserved that shite. Not me.

I set down the backpack and rummaged inside, taking out the two cans of lighter fluid I'd found in the utility room at our hideaway. I'd already filled my Zippo so handed a canister to Summer, keeping the other for myself.

With my back to the moor, I regarded her. "The one regret I have beyond losing ye to this place is the fact the fucking building's still standing. Help me make it better. Cleanse it from my history and yours."

Summer dragged her gaze from the hostel to me, her shock clear. "We're going to burn it?"

I let my crazy show. "To the ground."

29

Sin

Violet crossed the kitchen, collecting the last of the ingredients to go into her creation. Slow-roasted pork rubbed with a mix of spices, salt, and brown sugar, ready to be shredded for tacos. Mediterranean vegetables to go with it and cool dips on the side.

Violet. I'd tried switching to *Lottie,* like everyone else called her. But no, it didn't stick. She was my Violet and would always be.

She'd promised our family a feast and was delivering. Whatever time they started rolling back home, there would be a warm welcome.

I glared at my phone on the counter next to me. So far, I'd heard from Struan and Thea that they'd found the holiday park and were staking it out. Camden and Breeze had picked up the lasses' ma and got her safely out of Leith.

From Burn and Summer, we'd heard nothing.

I disliked my family being so spread out. I couldn't protect them all when everyone had gone in a different direction.

Still, I had to trust that they were in control. We were all survivors and every one of us scrappy as fuck.

Violet opened the oven door and returned to the weighed-down roast tray that would go on for a slow cook.

I jumped up. "I've got that."

She rolled her eyes but stepped back, letting me do the heavy lifting. I'd peeled and chopped and obeyed her chef orders, but she'd told me to butt out when it came to the finishing touches.

With the food safely in, I ushered her to a stool so she could wait me out while I finished clearing up. I had a lot to learn when it came to keeping my woman happy. Her standards were higher than mine and the lads'. We'd taken care of ourselves at the hostel, but no one gave a fuck if the floor hadn't been cleaned.

Violet gave a fuck, though, so I was watching and learning.

"Ye don't have to wait on me like this," she said from her perch, chin resting on her hand.

"I do. You're already busy over there making my bairn. I'll finish this then carry ye upstairs so I can gently fuck your brains out while we still have an empty house."

Her eyes widened, and she sat taller.

The tension in the room flashed to hot and heavy.

I rinsed my hands, dried them, and prowled back to her, not hiding how I was ogling her tits that strained the apron she'd tied on over her clothes. "Show me again."

Violet's cheeks flushed pink, and she removed her apron, reached into her dress pocket, and brought out the little capped pregnancy test. Held it up.

Pregnant the wee screen read.

Deep satisfaction mixed with excitement in my blood. "You're so fucking clever," I told her.

Violet shook her head, never looking away from me. "That's all on nature, not me."

I wasn't having that. "Naw. Look at what ye did. Ye took the smallest part of me and part of yourself and brought them together. You're making our baby. Put your arms around my shoulders."

Her lips parted, but Violet obeyed. I lifted her from the stool and did as I'd threatened. Carried her up the stairs to our bedroom. I could have laid her out on the kitchen counter and made her the feast, but anyone could turn up, and I wasn't in the mood to be interrupted.

Booting the door shut behind us, I set my lass down on the bed.

The doors were locked, the food had hours on the timer. We were good to go.

With no waiting around, I reached under her tunic dress and stripped her underwear in one go, baring her pretty pink cunt.

Violet's breath came in a rushed inhale, and she fixed her gaze on me.

"Tell me what it feels like to have my bairn inside your body." I raised her leg and planted her foot on my shoulder. Kissed her ankle while staring down at heaven.

"Incredible. A miracle. I can't wait until I can feel them moving around. Until I can put your hand on my belly so ye can feel them kick." She withdrew her foot from my grasp and wriggled to strip her dress and bra, revealing her weighty, round tits.

I'd swear they were already bigger if that was even possible.

"Get naked," she demanded.

I tore my clothes from my body and knelt back between her legs. Violet tried to pull me into a hug, but I grazed her nipple with my tongue as I passed, and she groaned, her fingers going into my hair to hold me right where I was.

No complaints from me.

I could spend days worshipping at the altar of her tits.

I settled and drove my fingers over her soft skin, toying with her.

There was nothing I liked better than to have her body as my plaything. But also my comfort. I'd learned that the ultimate way to relax was spread out at her side, her nipple in my mouth and her plump flesh in my palms. Kneading her. Getting horny as fuck but doing nothing more until the stress left me.

Luckily, she shared my obsession.

I rolled her nipple with my tongue before sucking hard, cupping her, my hand going to the other side so it wasn't neglected. I pinched and tugged on her nipple, loving how her flesh rippled when I released it. My curvy lass was built for my pleasure.

With her mouth open, Violet arched into my touch. One hand stayed in my hair, and the other rounded my shoulder, and she felt up my hard biceps.

While I kept up a rhythmic tug with my mouth, echoing it with my finger and thumb on her other nipple, Violet

let me just play. Giving up the noises I loved. Responsive in every way. Something deep inside me needed this. The fulfilment of having my woman taken care of and well fucked, as she would be by the end of it.

She travelled her fingers down her body to the wet centre of her. Under my gaze, she glanced over her clit and hissed.

I needed in there, too.

I gave her a long lick and swapped to the other nipple, sucking hard, then pulling away to link our gazes. "Take care of these."

I kissed her belly and lower, rumbling approval as she began the same action at her tits, thumbing herself in tandem.

At her pussy, I spread her lips and gave her a long lick from entrance to clit. Her taste flooded my mouth, and against the bed, my heavy dick got even harder.

Another long suck at her clit, and she groaned louder, her heels driving into the bed.

"Wait a sec."

I sat up. "What's wrong?"

Violet breathed hard and rolled up, a hand to my chest pressing me to lie down. She straddled me, her face flushed and her lips parted. Without a word, she took my hands and brought them to her tits, then lifted to get my dick into position.

Lust kicked through me hard. Normally, she wanted me to lead. She liked me ordering her around, but I was down for her taking the reins whenever she wanted.

She nudged me to her entrance and impaled herself

on me.

I closed my eyes at the sheer pleasure of her tight heat enclosing my rigid length. Nothing felt as good as this. But I had to see every second of it. Violet hadn't fully seated, taking a moment to adjust to the size of me, her knees spread wide.

"Love seeing my dick stretching your cunt," I gritted out.

Violet whimpered and sank down the remaining inches, bracing herself with a tight grip on my shoulders. I took more pulls at her nipples, obsessed with this. With her.

"If I hadn't already put a baby in ye," I said with an upwards thrust of my hips, "I'd make it happen sooner or later. Fill ye full of my cum every chance I have. Make ye come over and over so ye take me deep inside."

Violet heaved in a breath, her gaze hazy.

"I'm serious. I want this rounded with my bairn." I set a hand on her belly then cupped her tits. "These swollen even more. Ripe to my touch. Desperate for relief."

If she'd planned to ride me, I'd derailed that. I abandoned her tits and scooted up the bed, taking her with me so I had the cushions at my back. Then I gripped her hips and slammed her down onto me.

Violet moaned, loud and long.

I grinned at her losing control and leaned in to steal a kiss.

She kissed me back but gasped against my lips while I drove into her again from beneath. Again and again, sliding into her. Then all my dirty words fled as she clamped down on me. Violet hugged me, burying her face in my neck—a tell that she was close. I kept the pace exact, hitting the same spot over and over again until her orgasm hit. She went over the edge and sank on me.

I flipped us so I was over her once more, then I withdrew from inside her, crawled up her body, and pushed her tits together over my dick. I was slick from her so glided into the gap easily, the valley of her making a fucking gorgeous sight where I fucked her tits.

Violet took over plumping herself for me, and I braced myself on the bedstead and mattress and kept going until my balls tightened.

I came, jerking and spilling cum on her chest.

Jesus fuck.

Moving off her, I drove my fingers in the mess then pressed it into her still-hard nipples, scooping up the rest to rub over her pussy, pushing it inside. With my fingers still inside her, I rubbed her clit, at the same time leaning in to kiss her.

I'd learned her body to perfection, or at least I was getting there. Violet came again, this time with my cum in and on her. Then I collapsed down and hauled her onto me for a very satisfied hug.

Smug fucking man.

A while later, we emerged from the shower, where I'd bent her over again and used the showerhead on her, and we dried ourselves, dressing slowly.

At the earliest, I expected my family home in the evening, and it was after six now. Our alone time would be coming to an end.

My phone rang in my jeans pocket.

At the same moment, the rumble of an engine came from outside. I snatched my phone, and Violet darted to the window.

"Camden and Breeze," she said with a relieved smile.

"Gordain." I held up the screen to show her then swiped to answer.

I'd messaged the man earlier and asked him to call when he had a chance. He'd shot back a reply saying he'd hole up in his office with Sebastian in a couple of hours' time.

Jogging downstairs, I made up my mind about this man at last. I didn't trust easily, but Gordain McRae had proven himself time and again to be on the side of fucking decent humanity and not for what he could get out of the deal. He'd given us a place to stay, guidance, and more than one offer of help.

"One second, my brother and his lass just got home. I'll let them in."

"Good to know ye have somewhere to stay," Gordain replied. "Take your time in settling. I'm here with Sebastian."

I unlocked the front door, pointing at the phone and mouthing who was on the line.

Camden swapped a look with me, and the four of us ushered into the lounge. It had a big picture window that faced north where the beach curved into the far distance. We were a short while off sunset, but clouds had rolled in, the day darkening.

I settled into my seat with a momentary panic of a storm and two of our family being a boat ride away from the mainland.

"Everyone good?" I asked.

Serious nods followed.

I set the phone on the table and put it on loudspeaker. "Gordain, I'm here with Violet, Camden, Breeze, and we can all hear ye. Thanks for taking the time to call."

"I've been out of my mind with worry," the older man chastised me. "I get that ye have your secrets, but no one can do everything on their own. Sometimes ye just have to let others fucking help."

I wanted to resent him telling me off, but more, I craved a father figure to guide me. I'd never had it, and I'd paid that price for too long.

"I know. I'm sorry we ran again without talking to ye. I don't know why you're being so helpful."

Gordain gave a short laugh. "Me neither. But there it is."

Another voice came on the line, younger and English. "He's like this with everyone," Sebastian commented, warmth in his tone. "Gordain's a fixer. He can't bear it if he can see something going wrong when there's a chance he can make it right. I'm a prime example of that. If you stop disappearing on us, you'll work that out as well."

I knew little of Sebastian except that he was a helicopter pilot, that he'd once been in prison, and he was somehow related to the McRaes. Beyond that, his story was a mystery.

"We've had good reason to keep moving," I retorted. It was weak, though. I wanted their help now. Had asked for it.

"Aye, I'm sure of that," Gordain shot back. "It's naw a bad thing. Ye come across as more of a stand-and-fight guy, but there are times when it's better to retreat. Listen up. Don't tell me where ye are. I'm calling on a secure line, but I guess yours isn't. I want your trust, so we're going to keep this safe. I've got my suspicions on what's going on with ye, but I don't like assumptions. I deal better with facts."

I exhaled, knowing what he was asking.

One by one, I went from Violet to Camden to Breeze, earning agreement from each of them. The rest of our family weren't here to approve what I was going to do, but I knew they trusted me to lead where I saw fit.

I opened my mouth and spilled the story as it had unfolded. Our kidnappings, Struan's friendship with Gordain's nephew, Max, which led to our rescue. How the islanders had pursued us, who our father was, and the reason behind it all. The inheritance at stake. Next came the harder part.

"There's another person who's after us now. A business partner of McInver's. He's a powerful man, and rich. Possibly a woman trafficker. Definitely an abusive fucker. He threatened to kill one of my brothers and is hunting us. He's the reason we ran."

Silence met my declaration. Gordain and Sebastian had let me speak, my family giving me the floor.

"Sounds like a great guy. How did he make his threat?" Gordain returned.

"He caught one of my brothers after the fire at McInver's and told others he intended to end his life in order to send a message. Separately, he had one of our lasses, and she escaped him. He wants them both and he presumably intends to defend his partnership with our father, whatever the fuck that looks like."

Gordain pieced through my words. The spilling of

truths. "What degree of power are we talking about?"

"Significant."

"We might be able to help. Over to Sebastian to talk about what he and I have discovered in recent years."

The Englishman came on the line, his deep voice confident but also sombre, like the subject matter had been the source of heartache. "Several years ago, I was a regular contender in a fight club. Call it my misspent youth. One night, I left the club, and in the car park, witnessed an assault in progress. A man, a lot older than me, was beating up a girl. She appeared maybe fifteen and was obviously terrified. The fucker had a knife. I stepped in, and there was a scuffle. I knocked the man to the ground to protect the girl. Then the police turned up."

"Did they arrest him?" Violet asked.

Sebastian gave an unfunny laugh. "No. He claimed I was the aggressor and the knife was mine. The girl had run, and there were no witnesses. On the other hand, I had my winnings from the fight club and a police record for being caught before. The man went to hospital, claimed I'd caused permanent damage, and the police prosecuted me."

"That's so unfair," Violet gasped.

I took her hand, not liking where this was going.

Sebastian continued. "It gets worse, and what I have to tell you next is confidential. I was found guilty and sentenced to five years in prison. The judge liked having someone to carry the can for violence in the city streets, and we made the mistake of believing justice would prevail. I was innocent, and it didn't matter. I served three of those years and came out determined to own the system if it ever came to facing off with it again. At least eventually, I did. I was in a dark place for a while. My uncle played a big part in helping me see a way through it."

The older man muttered something about wishing he'd done more at the time.

"All for stopping a fight. Did ye ever find out what happened to the girl?" Violet breathed.

Gordain laughed, and Sebastian spoke with amusement in his voice.

"You could say that. Years later, I married her." The pilot continued on. "Gordain and I set out to understand the positions of power, particularly in Scotland as that's where I served my time. There's a relatively small network of men, and it is all men, who rule the roost. The few women in top positions aren't part of the power struggle. There might be political reasons that they're open to changing their minds, but none of them work in the same way as the old boys," Sebastian intoned. "There are private clubs, secret meetings, places where business decisions happen, and money changes hands. We didn't hold any political power as a family, but one carefully placed bribe or favour, and the judge would have dismissed my case."

I recoiled from the phone, though nothing of what Sebastian said surprised me. The only reason people sought power that I could fathom was so they could use it for themselves. Not to make society better, but to further their own aims.

"And these people are all powerful?" Camden asked, his expression grim.

"They are. The systems of government they serve are a sham, or at best, govern everyone else apart from them. Newspapers can be silenced. Politicians can be paid off, if they aren't part of the network."

Silence followed while the implications of our situation sank in.

If the chief of police was against us, we stood no chance.

"So, onto the million-pound question. What is it ye want?" Gordain asked into the quiet room.

At least that was easy. "Freedom from prosecution for things we did as self-defence, or crimes that could be blamed on us but are fictional. Separately, I want custody of our sister."

"That'll mean two separate approaches. One to the chief of police in Scotland, a smarmy son of a bitch called Daniels, who's also a local earl and landowner, and the other to a family court judge. There's upwards of fifteen of those but three who are known to us as corrupted and who hold sway over the rest. Fisher, Haroldson, and Villin. A bribe would work best for any of the latter."

Camden groaned, pinching the bridge of his nose.

Violet's shoulders sagged, Breeze's, too.

I tried to see a path through it. "If we can't bribe them, what about threats?"

"Can't help you there," Sebastian said. "I had to learn how not to use my fists."

Gordain came back on the line, his voice tense now. "I take it this isn't a solution for ye. Then listen up. Until we can work out a way forward, lie low and collect evidence. Witnesses who are trustworthy and will back ye up. If the worst comes to the worst, ye need people to call on as a minimum to make it look like ye have a case and won't be walked over. Count me as one."

"I appreciate that," I said, grateful for all he'd done, and for Sebastian filling us in on how the chief's world worked, even if they didn't know he was our aggressor. Not least for the offer of future help implied.

It was a relief to have shared the bulk of our story, even if lying low couldn't happen, not with our plans for Cassie and the lasses poised to expose their stories.

At least his advice on finding witnesses set my mind into action. Gave me a path to follow.

But the second we ended the call with a promise to come to him the minute we needed help, another engine roared outside.

Everyone lurched to the window, the sense of danger unending.

"Struan and Thea," Camden announced.

My hackles lowered, but as I jogged to the door, I knew something was wrong.

They closed in on the house, Struan dropping a kiss on Thea's hair. The lass's expression cut me in two.

Violet pushed under my arm. "What happened?"

"We saw her," Struan said. "We were fifty yards away, and she ran to get to us and got caught. Now we've fucking lost her."

Violet guided them inside while I stood back.

It kept getting worse. Whenever we had a win, some twist of fate shoved us two steps back.

In the living room, they fell onto the sofas, exhaustion clear. Violet muttered about food, but we needed the story first.

Just before I could demand it, a video call from Burn landed on my, Struan's, and Camden's phones simultaneously.

I answered it, peering at my screen.

Flames rose behind him. His maniacal grin appeared.

Our brother had started a fire.

30

Jamieson

Smoke billowed from the hostel's reception, the rising wind swirling it high above us. Inside the decrepit space, the plastic blinds dripped, melting, and the cheap wooden furniture caught.

Flames climbed the walls.

I hadn't even had to set foot inside. The door lay open where we'd left it that way after our escape, so I'd picked an incendiary point, doused it with lighter fluid, and set my blaze.

Then I'd remembered a fact about the place that had been hidden to us the whole time we'd lived here. Keep had Wi-Fi. I even knew the code.

While it lasted, I'd dialled my brothers, Summer's hand clutched in mine.

Onscreen, my brothers and their lasses stared at me, mouths open in shock but something else there, too. A need for this to happen. I'd felt it for a long time, and deep satisfaction grew in my belly.

The smaller picture displayed the white building cloaked with black smoke and orange flames shooting through the windows. My fire spread, loving the chance to destroy and consume the place of our abuse.

"It's done," I told them, embers landing on my hair. "I'm going to film this, tag the chief when I upload it, then get the fuck out of here. I needed ye all to see it burn. Look at it. All the misery of this hole turning to ash."

"Fucking hell," Camden said with a tight laugh. "Got to say I love that sight."

"Isn't it pretty?" My grin turned lunatic.

Sin leaned in, no doubt about to be the voice of reason, though his fixed expression told me how this affected him, too. "Get the video then leave. We need ye both home safe."

"I told ye I was going to."

"I mean it, Jamieson. Don't dick around. Summer? Your boy has form for lingering around fires. That's why he ended up in a jail cell. People will see the smoke and investigate. Ye have a few minutes at best to get your footage then run. Get to it now."

I saluted him sarcastically then ended the call.

Summer grabbed my phone and activated the video. "We're not putting your face in this."

"Fine, but I want the fucker to hear my voice."

I backed up until the heat licked my neck. I'd never feared it. I craved the warmth of Summer in all ways.

My lass gave me a nod, and I spread out my arms.

"Police Chief Daniels. This is for ye, so don't ye dare look away. You're a corrupt, abusive arsehole whose reign of hurting people is over. I'm coming for ye. Mark my words, because I won't repeat them. Just wait to see what we've got in store for ye."

Summer panned the camera to the right to take in the burning building, then she knelt to bring the name sign of Torlum Youth Hostel into shot. Her gaze raised to me, worry and excitement combined. "Done. What was all that about you're coming for him?"

I prowled over and collected my phone from her, stowing it in my pocket. Sin's warning played in the back of my mind, but I silenced it, too hooked on all I could see in front of me.

My beautiful woman, her fair hair loose and blowing in the wind and backlit by flames.

Something crashed in the hostel, but I didn't flinch.

"I challenged him because I mean to go through with my threat. He hurt ye."

Her gaze trained on me like I was dangerous.

She wanted it, too. Revenge.

But there was something else there. Heat from lust, not fire.

Instantly, my mind leapt from the blaze and to darker thoughts. My ever-high adrenaline and testosterone peaked. "Get on your knees."

Summer's cheeks flushed pink. She backed away from me, but the challenge remained in her eyes. Then she turned and sprinted around the building.

I gave her a second then sprinted after her, rounding the corner to grasp her by the shoulder. She gave a cut-off gasp and tumbled into the soft heather.

I landed astride her and flipped her over, loving the

flare of lust in her gaze. "What happens when ye run from me, Summer? It means I get to take what I want."

God knows I needed it.

Needed her in every way.

Not just in those she'd begged me for.

My jeans button opened at a flick of my wrist, I dragged down my fly and took out my already hard cock. Kneeling over her, I paused for a second for any sign of fear. She couldn't demand this of me, but I'd still deliver and take the control she wanted.

Almost shaking with need, I ran the end of my dick over her pink lips.

"Open."

Summer obeyed, slamming her eyes closed when I thrust into her mouth. Fucking hell. My mind dizzied at my length parting her lips. How her mouth enclosed me in her heat.

Her tongue slid over the thick vein.

I braced myself over her head, hands in the dirt, resisting the urge to blow my load.

"Suck," I managed to add.

Sin had told us to run, but this wouldn't take long. I was too high from the fire. Too turned on by the heat of Summer.

The lass breathed through her nose and sucked me down.

Of all the ways I'd pictured her when we were younger, this had often topped my list. I'd bet the fantasy had featured for her, too. In fact, I knew it as she'd told me. The pyromaniac boy she wanted. Jumping to extremes no one else dared.

Mouth open, I jacked my hips, fucking her mouth. Nothing had ever felt like this, nothing could have prepared me. Only having my dick in her could beat it. Chasing her down then fucking into her tight pussy was endgame. Coming in her.

Summer sucked harder, and my balls tightened, every other thought vanishing. I gave up a grunt of pure pleasure.

Then I made the awful, fucking terrible mistake of raising my head.

A shape lurched around the corner of the hostel. A man in a heavy coat shuffled towards us. He groaned out a weird, fucked-up sound, one half of his face red and tight with scars.

With burns.

Holy fucking shite. Withdrawing from Summer's perfect mouth, I leapt up and stuffed my dick back in my jeans. My erection faded from the horrifying sight of the man who'd tried to buy me and Cassie from our keeper.

A man who should be dead.

"Jenkins," I bit out.

Summer squealed and clambered to her feet, both hands clapping to her mouth. I shoved her behind me, never taking my eyes off my enemy. Before, I'd been afraid of him, but I wasn't now. Not of this broken shell of human.

I curved my lip in a sneer. "Last I saw of ye, I'd locked ye in your burning house. Didn't have the decency to die then, ye miserable old bastard."

He let out another low moan, some kind of white

bandage at his throat. I did a double-take at it. He couldn't speak? How fucking delightful. That suited me, as I had a lot to say to him.

"Did ye follow us here, or are ye haunting this site like a ghost? God," I spluttered, realisation flooding me.

He stood directly at the edge of Keep's grave.

"What the fuck have ye done with that body?"

My anger and the memories of childish fear wound tight inside me, along with all the other emotions of the day.

My hands clenched into fists.

For a long time, he'd been top of my list of people who needed payback. Well, his time was now.

Disdain dripped from my voice. "Maybe you've come to me so I can end your pitiful life."

"Jamieson," Summer whispered.

I shot her a look, my attention always hers first above anything.

She pointed in the other direction. Across the moor, through the clouds of black smoke, people were coming.

Two groups. No, three.

My heart beat faster. We couldn't afford to be caught.

But that meant walking away from the revenge I'd needed.

I sucked in a breath, but my answer was easy. Summer came first. I caught her fingers and tugged. Then we were running.

Across the moor, we sprinted. Not slowing despite a shout coming from behind. I drove my feet into the uneven ground, half pulling Summer with me.

Too many times, I'd done this. Run from the island. The paid-off islanders had always brought me back. This time, they'd fail.

We hit the beach, the sand dragging at our steps. The boat was where we'd left it, tied off on the pontoon.

The wind whipped the sea into choppy peaks, the waves much higher than when we'd first made the crossing.

I dropped into the deck, bracing my knees to steady myself against the pitch. With a hand out to Summer, I urged her on. "They're coming."

Two people had already made it to the sand. One waved, calling something that was lost to the rising storm.

Wide-eyed, Summer sucked in a breath and dove in alongside me. I cast off, shoved the dock to give us a head start, then primed the engine. For a heart-stopping minute, the ignition failed. I jabbed the button, but nothing.

At last, it sputtered then roared to life with the stench of diesel.

We sailed away from Torlum with the fire and angry islanders left far behind.

31

Jamieson

Tension gripped us for the trip back to the mainland. The choppy seas lapped the boat, tossing us around, but we kept moving. So long as the motor stayed alive, we'd make it.

But the skies darkened further.

Rain fell in the distance, blurring the line of ocean and sky.

The tarp roof on Thea's boat flapped in the rising gale, slowing us all the more. The engine whined, straining in its fight against the elements.

Something cracked at the front of the boat.

"What the hell was that?" Summer asked.

"Hold this," I asked her, gesturing to the stick that controlled the boat's direction. No fucking idea what it was called.

She grasped it and held our course while I knelt on the bench at the front and leaned over.

Something had hit our hull. Driftwood, maybe.

A crack yawned.

Only an inch wide, but water rushed into the shell of the boat.

Shite. Fucking why?

I scanned the horizon. Land appeared in our direction of travel. The Isle of Skye with a coastline of cliffs and inlets I knew well.

We were at least fifteen minutes out.

Summer sighted it and shot a relieved smile at me.

My answering expression dented her happiness.

"What is it?"

"We're taking on water. The boat's damaged."

Her eyes widened. "Ohmigod. I need to see."

Behind her, the engine gave a guttural cough.

And stopped.

Summer turned her frightened gaze from it to me. "The engine's dead. Can you swim that far? I don't know if I can. Oh God."

"It won't come to that." I stormed over to the failed engine, cranking on it once again.

Nothing. The fucking thing refused to turn over.

I'd stolen cars in the past, so many times. Boats on occasion, too. But I knew fuck all about engines. I'd never been trained in anything. That lack of skill killed me now.

"You are not going to die on us," I yelled at it.

Summer retreated, staring from the water to the land. "Are you kidding me?" she yelled at the sky. "All this and you're going to drown us in the sea? Fuck you, universe."

"We won't," I answered. "I promise. Even if I have to swim with ye on my back, I swear to ye now that I'll bring us in."

My frustration soared, and I raised a fist and smacked down on the engine casing. "Ye piece of shite. Fifteen minutes. That's all we're asking of ye. Your sole reason for existence is to take people from point A to B. But no. Today ye woke up and chose violence."

I thumped it again, harder.

"I'm naw taking this from one more person or thing in my life. I'll take ye apart piece by motherfucking piece so each dies a watery death. Is that working for ye? Start or die."

Even in the midst of her panic, Summer cracked up.

I grinned and watched her for a second.

Around us, the sea had risen. Or more, we'd lowered as the insides of the boat filled with water.

The time to make a decision was here. The wind blustered around us, the sea doing its level best to take us into its watery embrace.

We couldn't make it to Skye without a soaking.

Rain pattered down, instantly drenching.

Something in Summer's expression cracked.

"Fuck you, Boaty McFuckFace," she howled and smacked down on the start button.

The engine purred.

The boat lurched back to life.

Unprepared, we both stumbled to the floor. She burst out in a laugh, and I scrabbled to get back on the steering stick, my jaw wired open in astonishment.

"Your tantrum worked." I shook with laughter.

She bent over double, her laugh musical.

Living in her joy, I focused on bringing us in, this time at a different bay than the one we set out from, not slowing the boat until the last second. We hit the dock with a thud, and I leapt out.

Summer held my hand and sprang free, then we both dropped to the wooden boards, and I enclosed her in my arms.

Not for a second would I have admitted to myself that I felt out of control. Just like fire, the water loved me. But that had been fucking close.

Summer breathed with me, then pushed off me to stand. "We need to get to the mainland then upload that video."

She was right. Skye only had one road on and off. To do anything more here was dangerous.

"From now on, I'm only listening to ye," I replied.

I untied the boat from the mooring and kicked it back out to sea.

Another bridge burned, but it felt good doing it.

We climbed the hill and skirted through fields to return to the car park. If the police had been summoned for the fire, they weren't here yet. Maybe they'd take their own boat out to the island. We weren't going to sit around to find out.

Back in the Aston Martin, I got behind the wheel.

The car was built for speed, but I obeyed every traffic law, getting us to safety slow and steady. Once we were over the Skye Bridge, we plunged through the darkening countryside, and I took the right to Fort Augustus, guessing any cops would be coming from the opposite direction and Inverness. It meant a longer trip home, but we were in no rush now.

I parked up in Fort Augustus' town centre, readying the video on my phone.

"Oh my God. Food," Summer sighed.

I followed her gaze to a fish and chip shop. Thea had given me money this morning. I'd tried to push it back into her hands, but she'd insisted. The cash came from Torlum's rents, as the island belonged to her now, and she claimed the islanders owed us for all they'd done.

Hard to argue with that.

I fished a handful of notes from out of my pocket. "Go buy us a feast. We're celebrating."

She glanced up and down the street. People milled around, checking out the lock gates on the canal, no one paying us any attention.

"Okay, it looks safe enough. What do you want?"

"Ye."

"To eat, I mean."

"Same answer."

Summer groaned and hid her face.

To save her blushes, I raised an easy shoulder. "It's been so long since I had a choice, it's lost all meaning. Anything ye choose will be perfect."

She dipped her head. "This is kind of feeling like our

official first date. A drive followed by food."

"Do I get a kiss?"

Her smile lit me up.

"Ask me after I've been fed."

She hopped out of the car, and I finished with the video upload. A new social media account, tagging the regional police headquarters. There was no way the chief wouldn't get to see it. No way he'd fail to send units out to the far Western Highlands.

In the meantime, we'd be merrily back in the northeast.

Summer returned with a bag of food. For several minutes of our first date, we stuffed our faces with fried fish, chicken, and chips. Curry sauce. Sweet and sour. Washed down with Coke.

When we were done and the rubbish binned, I leaned across the car and kissed her.

Summer let me.

After the blow job interruption, I only needed her more. I palmed her cheek and poured all my urgency for her into that kiss.

My phone blared, and I groaned. "Go away, we're busy."

"It could be important."

I heaved a sigh and snatched it up.

Sin's name was onscreen.

I answered with a twinge of guilt that I hadn't texted him already.

"When I tell ye to report in, report the fuck in," my brother snarled.

"Sorry, lost track of time. Job done. We're fine but a few hours away. It'll be late by the time we get back."

Sin grumbled. "There's been some updates. Things ye need to know." He launched into an explanation of a conversation he'd had with Gordain and Sebastian.

I got us back on the road, driving out of town while listening to him speak.

"He suggests we either bribe our enemies or collect evidence? Fuck. Did I destroy that chance in burning down the hostel?"

"No. We have the paperwork and laptop from Keep's office. That's pretty much the only evidence we've got, though." A pause followed. "There's something else. At the end of the call, Struan and Thea arrived home. They saw Cassie."

"They did? Is she okay?"

"She was, but I fucked it up." Struan's voice came on the line.

My heart sank. "Tell us."

"We found the holiday park and staked it out from woodland on the opposite slope. There's twenty or so chalets and a clubhouse building with a shop. For ages, we saw nothing but strangers roaming around. I said we needed to get closer."

"What happened?"

"We'd descended the hill and were walking parallel to the first line of chalets. Thea grabbed my arm and pointed. Cassie had just walked out of the clubhouse, her fucking foster da with his hand gripping her wrist."

Anger poisoned me.

"Somehow, she looked our way and saw us. She yelled, just like she did with Sin and Lottie, but this time, she wrenched away from him and ran."

Pain stabbed me. "She couldn't reach ye?"

"No. We were the wrong side of a fence. Too tall to get over. The entrance was around the other side of the park. I called her name and started running, ready to take on the foster da. If it was just me and him, I could take the fucker down, no problem. He picked her up and bundled her inside a chalet, all while she screamed for help. When we got to the entranceway of the park, a police car rolled in."

"Holy shite," I bit out.

"Exactly. We had to fucking hide. We got back to the woods and watched on as the cops went to the clubhouse then the chalet. A woman and older girl returned soon after, and they went inside, too. Another police car arrived then a third, and two cops started a patrol. We hid and had to watch as the family packed up and drove her away. Again. We couldn't move from the spot. She knows we're trying to reach her, and now we made things harder. It's all gone wrong."

My mind raced over what they could've done, but I came up blank. The police would never give her up to us. Never listen if we claimed she'd been hurt. All of us knew foster care and how easily kids could be ignored or not believed if they made any claims over how they were treated.

"It wasnae your fault. We'll get her back another way," I vowed.

"How? We've no fucking clue where she is now. They know we followed them. I fucked everything up."

Sin growled something, but Struan's voice receded.

"He's stormed off," Sin said on a hard breath. "We need a new plan for our sister, but fuck knows what that looks like."

It was fully night now, and at the Spean Bridge junction, our headlights picked up a road sign for the Cairngorms.

An idea formed in my mind.

"What ye said about Gordain's advice," I slowly said. "Bribing a judge requires cash. McInver has bundles of money."

"Like we'd go to him with our caps in hand," Sin retorted.

"I'm not done," I snapped back. "We don't have to beg. Camden thinks there's something in McInver's house that will implicate him. We were there earlier, and the only people on site were a construction crew. Even if they've left a guard, we could bypass them."

"What do ye mean bypass them? You're not going back," my brother spat.

"Why not? By morning, the police will be actively searching for me. The chief can't hide me from the rest of the force anymore. I've made his involvement with me public, even if he doesn't reveal my name. I'll need to lie low. We're about an hour away from McInver's place and will pass a few miles from his door. We need to know what he's hiding. We need that leverage over the old fucker if we're ever going to get Cassie back." I reached for Summer's fingers. "Fancy a raid?"

Her lips curved in a way I was utterly obsessed with. Her sense of adventure, her impulse for fucking shite up. No one matched me like this lass.

"There are other ways we can do this. Come home. We'll talk it out," Sin insisted.

"What other ways? Even if Struan and Thea had miraculously returned with Cassie, how are we going to keep her? How are ye and Lottie going to raise a bairn without a permanent home? Remember what ye told me in the sea? Your child will never sleep on the floor. I won't let that happen to my niece or nephew or my little sister. McInver brought us into this world, and he has to be our solution to being able to live in it without being constantly on the run. If there's a chance, I'm taking it."

"I don't like this."

"Noted. See ye on the other side."

Hanging up on my brother, I set our direction for my father's half-ruined mansion.

The dark night swallowed us whole.

In silence, we exited the main road and into the mountains. We weaved through country lanes that I knew by memory, finding the lane where we'd hid the car this morning.

It felt like a lifetime ago.

From this morning where I'd scared Summer in the kitchen, to stealing the car, to taking the boat out to Torlum. The fire. Jenkins. Our fucking first date outside a Fort Augustus chip shop.

My time with Summer had been a whirlwind, and I had the worst feeling that I was spiralling towards something that I couldn't avoid.

Every second counted.

We left the car under the cover of trees and stole

through the woods. There was little moonlight tonight, the weather blustery from the storm on the coast, clouds darkening the land even more. But unlike our first trek through the woods following my jailbreak, this time, Summer led the way.

At the edge of the park, we watched the house, spotting no signs of life. Our advance was slow, but confidence grew with each step. By stages, we neared the mansion until we'd reached the car park.

Summer glanced my way. "Run for it?"

With a huff of a laugh, I caught her hand in mine, and we jogged across the gravel on light feet, speeding to the shadowy steps. Camden had described the place as having police tape across the entrance. I hadn't seen it behind the apprentice lad, and it wasn't there now.

The heavy door wouldn't budge under my hand.

I retreated a few steps, centred myself, and shoulder barged it. The door gave, spilling me onto the marble floor beyond. I leapt up and spun around.

No alarm.

No lights.

Summer skittered to my side, and we breathed in stale air, hints of stone dust and burned wood still lingering.

I put my mouth next to her ear, enjoying her shiver. "Lead me."

She held my eye, a smile forming. "Breeze messaged me. Other than demanding we be quick, she said Camden already explored the cellar down the corridor to the left."

We both peered into the dark.

Summer circled me, considering the dark house

around us. Her low voice returned. "Which means either he missed something there, or—"

"There's another cellar," I concluded for her.

She pursed her lips, her features silvered in the barely there light. "What if it was under the part of the building that burned down?"

From what we'd seen of it this morning, it was still a building site, covered in rubble and debris. We'd never find it under that.

Something in my gut told me that thinking was off.

"Then we'd be screwed, but I just have this idea… McInver isn't a subtle man, from what I know. Like the chief, he regularly ships in women to fuck. He doesn't hide it. He gave them nothing when they took their pregnancy news to him. He lives in a place like this, and he's richer than the Pope. He's brazen and does what the fuck he wants. If he's got dark secrets, my guess is he won't have liked hiding them."

Summer nodded, following where my mind was going. Which was grand because I didn't have a clue beyond my instinct for the man.

"Huh. Then he'd want them in plain sight. What's through here?" she asked.

I turned to the huge double doors. "The great hall. I burst in there after I'd set fire to the kitchens. I had to get my family out."

She paced over. "Sounds impressive, which matches your grandstanding concept."

I went with her, and we entered the cavernous room. McInver's great hall had been the centre of his mansion, but everything to the right had been burned, and part of the hall's ceiling was missing.

Summer activated the torch on her phone. Where the entrance had been cleared, presumably by the workmen, this space was still littered with fallen rock and plasterwork that crunched under our feet.

We drifted through it, taking in the dark shadowy corners, searching for anything out of the ordinary.

Dead in the centre at the top of the room, a large wooden chair sat by itself. Our torchlight picked up the glint of gold from decoration on its cushion.

Summer's eyebrows pinched together. "His throne?"

I drew closer, taking in the elaborately decorated seat. It appeared heavy and was probably old. Maybe McInver liked to lord it up from a throne, but that didn't explain the metal links on the front two legs and at the top of the seat.

A memory hit me. Camden had described how Breeze had been chained naked to a chair. He'd had to release her so they could run. McInver had put her on display, and I'd bet any money this was the seat.

But as I stared at it, a new detail emerged. Something that wouldn't be apparent if the house lights were on and the shadows not so deep. There was a line in the wooden block flooring around the base.

My heart beat faster. I grabbed Summer's hand and towed her around the back of the seat.

"Look."

"At what?"

The line continued in a square around the base.

I booted it.

The heavy piece of furniture tipped forwards, landing with a crash that echoed through the great hall.

It took the square of flooring with it. Beneath, a hole gaped.

Summer squeaked and gripped my arm. "Fuck."

She knelt and held her torch in the gap, revealing a steep set of stairs. Before I could speak, she was descending.

I hustled to follow, overly aware of the noise I'd made. Right now, there could be guards on their way. Perhaps they already were from motion sensors and silent alarms.

But this felt too important to run from without reason.

At the bottom of the steps, a room spread around us, the walls painted white. Narrower than the great hall, it hosted a corner with a small amount of furniture, three blank walls, and one covered in pictures.

Sickness wound through me.

Even from a distance, I knew they were of women.

"Film this," Summer spoke through her teeth.

She drew closer, but I held her back so I could capture the room without her in the shot. I advanced on the pictures, my gaze on the screen.

I couldn't help but see the faces.

On the left-hand side, the pictures started as faded, brownish prints. Then Polaroids, the colours bolder and the faces clearer still. To the right, the images became glossier, the photograph quality better.

Every single one held a different woman. Some young, some older, some scared-looking, cringing away from the photographer. Others directing a bold glare at the camera.

All were bare-arse naked.

"His...conquests?" Summer asked. "Or something worse?"

I panned the camera from left to right, capturing every face. Then I lowered my phone. "Got to be the second option. See how they're pictured. What the photographer has focused on." I gestured at one of a dark-haired lass. "Her face is out of focus, but her tits are dead centre on the shot. It's a fucking catalogue."

Summer recoiled. "No," she whispered.

At the same second, a creak came from the floor above us.

Dread slammed into me.

Someone was there.

We couldn't be caught down here.

I reached for Summer, but she darted forward to the wall of horror. One by one, she removed the photos, collecting them in a stack.

I shot a glance to the steps, any second expecting a light to shine down. Or worse, for someone to heft up the throne and shut us in.

No further sound came, so I took a risk. This felt too important. Evidence of something, even if we weren't sure what. From a side table, I grabbed a cardboard box. Something light shifted in the bottom, but I ignored it, carrying it to Summer to hold the pictures.

Side by side, I helped her with the task, snatching McInver's trophies from his wall and stowing them safely away. When we were done, I gestured for Summer to kill her light and stay behind me. I extinguished my own, and we crept towards the patch of grey that marked the exit to our hiding place.

I ascended the steps, wincing as one creaked, and peered out. The hall beyond was silent, the shadows still lurking, no torches, no voices.

But someone was here, I was certain of it.

Anyone in the mansion would have heard the crash of the throne falling. It was too heavy to have toppled by itself.

I sensed the weight of someone's gaze on us, though nothing moved. Either way, we needed to get out of here. I finished my climb and crouched to guide Summer out.

I lifted the chair to cover our tracks.

Summer hunched her shoulders like her skin crawled as much as mine, and with my arm around her, we quick-stepped through the hall then out of the front door.

No one followed.

A short laugh came from my lips. "I can't believe we got away with that. I was sure somebody was there."

Summer held the box to her chest. "Why? It's as empty as the grave."

"Didn't ye hear that noise?"

"I didn't hear anything."

I blinked at her. Had I imagined that? Maybe my senses were working overtime, and I'd made up the creaking noise.

"Fucking hell." I gave another laugh, my relief sharp.

It had all been in my head. All I knew of this place was danger and destruction. We'd just waltzed in and out with my father's treasure—the evidence we needed—and were going to walk away scot-free.

Joy replaced my panic, and I nudged Summer in the direction of the garage.

"Where are we going?"

"We're going to get Struan his car back and take two home with us. Give McInver every chance to show his true colours before we show ours."

She took off running, tossing a smirk back at me.

Instantly, my blood was up.

"Don't run from me unless ye mean it," I warned.

Summer sped up, her laugh the best thing I'd ever heard. She bypassed the garage, sprinting around the edge.

I let her have her lead, torn between making good on my threat that I'd always chase her and the need to get the fuck out of here.

Except what was the rush? Summer was right, there was nobody here. It was an empty building in the middle of nowhere, and we were completely alone. Once we got home, there would be conversations to be had, serious shite to talk about.

It'd be hours before we were alone in bed together.

I pursued her hard, easily catching up with her at the rear of the building. We were completely hidden here, the car park wall on one side and the garage on the other. No Jenkins to interrupt us. No one here but us and the ghosts of my dead ancestors.

Like before, I tumbled Summer to the grass, dropping the box to one side so it didn't spill.

I stole a kiss, taking deep pulls of her lips. Then I collected her hands and pinned her arms above her head.

"Thought I told ye not to run from me," I gritted out, trying to hide my smile. "I'm having ye whether ye like it or not. Hear me?"

She turned her head, biting her lip.

A greater turn-on than if she'd held me closer. Earlier, she'd sucked my dick so nicely, but I needed more. A reminder that life mattered when I'd been staring at the evidence of my father's evils.

Still holding her wrists, and astride her legs so she couldn't move, I gripped the front of her shirt and tore it down the middle. The flimsy material gave easily, revealing a tight bra top. With my gaze on hers, I tugged aside the cups and exposed her tits, pawing at her.

"Fight me off. See if ye can. I'll take worse from your body."

Summer squirmed, but I grabbed a handful then ducked to suck on her. Her nipple in my mouth gave me an insane burst of need.

I was so hard.

Wound up and unable to stop.

Summer had started this by running. I'd never deny her anything, and that included taking this as far as it could go.

And yet...

For the first time ever, something stilled my forward drive. This wasn't safe.

I wasn't the impulsive kid anymore.

I had to grow the fuck up.

32

Summer

Jamieson lifted off me, his brows deep slashes of consternation.

I jerked up, listening out for someone approaching. A car. The police.

Without explaining, he collected me from the ground in a dead lift and threw me over his shoulder, stomping around the side of the building.

"You're not safe. I was about to fuck ye into the ground in a place that's so far from where we should be. I think I lost my mind."

I struggled to understand, all while I burned over him wanting to claim me.

Except he hadn't.

"You don't want me?" I whispered.

"No." He stormed on. "I want ye more than air. I owe ye better than to endanger your life any more than I already have."

I gave a surprised laugh.

At the doors, he set me down, tapped in the garage code.

I clutched the sides of my ruined top. "You just matured in front of my eyes. Like you did when I first saw you in real life. You'd changed from a boy to a man. Now the change is complete."

He slid me a look. "Does it affect how ye see me?"

"You just keep on getting better."

His gaze scalded in response.

Inside the building, he snatched the last set of keys and let me into the dark-purple Bentley sports car. We sped from the estate with the lights off and returned to the car we'd stolen earlier.

Under the cover of the thick, dark trees, Jamieson climbed out. "Which do ye want to drive home?"

I loved the sound of home. "This one."

He beckoned me, and I skipped around, meeting him by the driver's-side door.

I wanted him so much, my body was alive with need. "Is here safer?"

Jamieson dove his hand into my hair and brought my mouth to his for a deep kiss. Then he swatted my backside. "Don't even consider it. Get in the car."

I obeyed.

In convoy, we set out into the night once again.

A couple of hours later, we arrived back at the safe house. Jamieson had pulled us over into a side road for a short wait to be sure we hadn't been followed and to check for trackers. But it was past midnight and dark. The roads were silent. No one followed us.

If there were any patrols out in northern Scotland, they were heading west. Drawn by the fire. By the video taken on Torlum.

We'd done it.

We'd carried out our plan and made our attack, but there was so much more to do. The other videos to compile. The journalist to talk to. All of that paled to the bigger matter right at the forefront of my thoughts.

With a sense of staggering relief, we parked up, and I flew from the car, arriving in front of Jamieson. I wanted to grab on to him, but I stopped short. Linked our gazes.

He held my stare, and I took a step backwards, my heart pounding.

The front door flew open. "Oh, thank God, at last," my sister uttered. "I've been so worried about you. It seemed to take forever for you to get back."

I trotted back to the car and collected the box of photos. "Here, these were hidden in McInver's basement. A real wall of horrors."

Breeze accepted the box. "Jamieson called to tell us what you'd found. Holy shit." Then she squinted at me. "What happened to your shirt?"

Jamieson's arm curved around me. It tightened.

I owed my sister all the time and explanations in the world, but there was something that needed to happen first. Tension climbing higher than the storm clouds on the coast.

It crept over me. Scared me. Excited me.

I gave her a half-smile, but I was already moving, slipping out of Jamieson's hold. "Go inside. We'll be a minute."

She angled her head with an inquisitive look but retreated into the house.

"Are ye running again, Summer?" Jamieson said, low and dark.

I didn't answer. Instead, I spun around and flew down the path. The rain from the islands hadn't reached the east coast, and I pelted through the warm summer evening, skirting the beach and heading out towards the fields.

Jamieson chased me.

He could easily have caught up, but he let me fly, never more than a few metres behind. I needed this. The closer he got, and the deeper the ache in my lungs, the more my heart pounded. The more my fear built.

Whatever I'd wanted, asked for, it still frightened me. That final act, him claiming me... My heart thundered.

Fingers grasped my shoulder. I shrieked and yanked away.

"Fucking stop," he snarled.

I only ran harder.

A low wall edged the path, marking the field boundary. Beyond, the stone outline of an old building rose, stark against the night sky. Two tall arches that had been either end of the structure stood tall, but with no roof. Mostly no walls.

A ruined chapel.

A place of rebirth.

I dove over the boundary wall to the short grass and scrambled to the shell of a building. But Jamieson was right behind me. Collided with me. Took us to the ground in a tumble of limbs.

My breath knocked from my lungs, and every thought fled.

"Don't try to escape," he growled, "it only fuels me up. Do ye understand that? Do ye know what I'm going to do now?"

Without waiting for any frantic reply, Jamieson gripped the front of my shirt and my bra in his fist, using it to pull me to him to take my mouth in a hard kiss.

Nothing gentle. No tender care from him.

I'd been so desperate to rid myself of my virginity, but it hadn't happened. Since then, the urgency had built up too much. Got confused with closeness and care.

That was absent here.

Only desperation drove on the actions playing out.

Jamieson's tongue dove into my mouth, slicking over mine. He nipped my lip then sat back, his features completely hidden. But I sensed how he burned. Hid my face by turning it to the dry, cool grass.

In harsh moves, Jamieson stripped my lower half then abruptly flipped me over so I was facedown. I braced myself on the ground, my insides tightening at the telling sound of his zip lowering. Then he was there, pressed to my back, his mouth next to my ear and his solid dick sliding between my legs.

He glided over the centre of me, his blunt end lodged against my core.

"I dreamed of this."

I shivered, unable to answer.

"Every fantasy, every time I fucked my fist, it was over ye. You're mine. Your cunt is mine to take, and ye get no choice in this."

There was no waiting. No opportunity for me to say a word. He surged his hips and thrust inside.

I keened silently, my fists gripping the grass, every sense trained on the feeling of him inside my body. The jab of pain and strange weight of him right *there.*

Jamieson withdrew and then worked his hips again, keeping up the motion until he was fully seated. He breathed hard against my neck, his arm shaking in my narrow slice of vision. Rough kisses landed on my shoulder and the side of my face, then he rested his forehead against my hair.

All the while, his body moved, a slow, steady motion that started easy but was building.

I pictured how someone else would see us. A big man seizing a girl and tearing away her clothes, using her body. Fucking her on the ground where he'd caught her.

An attack. A crime.

All arranged by me.

Jamieson gave up a low growl of pleasure.

I hadn't forgotten that this was his first time, too. His virginity being lost to my depraved ask.

Not that it showed. He was leading this and owning me. I'd wanted it, but he'd delivered his own part of this, too.

His rhythm continued, charging me up until the pain changed to something other.

A bright, new sensation.

A blooming ache of pleasure spread inside me. Addictive and more like he'd made me feel when he'd touched me before. But better. Deeper. Promising something incredible.

My fear and sense of danger throbbed.

A small sound burst from my lips.

Jamieson slowed and pushed up, still connected to me as he changed position. He grazed over the swell of my hips and ass, and I pictured his fascination with what he could see in the faint light.

He pushed my knee up and my legs wider, giving him access to feel up what he was doing to me. A hand curved under my thigh and to my clit.

"Ye should see what I'm doing to ye. You're taking every inch of me in your tight pussy, and fucking hell, this feels incredible. Now I need ye to be a good little captive and come on my dick. I want ye clamping down on me before I mark ye as mine with my cum."

I moaned now, unable to resist, unable to hide my sounds.

Jamieson stroked me with his fingers, working my clit in steady circles while he fucked me. The spiralling, twisting heat inside me caught. I took short breaths, only able to concentrate on that one thing. The promise of something big coming.

"Come for me, Summer. I can't hold on. Ye feel too good."

Like his words had released me, a heart-pounding, body shock of an orgasm exploded. A dizzying minute passed where all I could feel were the waves of utter pleasure that rinsed me. It felt so different with him there. A thousand times better. Unbelievably good.

Jamieson gave up a masculine growl and stilled, his

dick pulsing deep inside me. Marking me by filling me with his cum like he'd promised. Somehow that made it even hotter. The thought and feeling extending my heady rush.

Dimly, I came down from my heights, becoming aware of the sounds of the night. Of Jamieson breathing hard over me. He withdrew from me but kept his hand at my core, inserting two fingers where his dick had just been.

I gasped, and he gave a short laugh and pulled away, kneeling with a hand at my elbow to haul me into the same position. Then his mouth was on mine once more in a kiss that was more tender than any we'd shared.

"I just caught ye, fucked ye, and came in ye," he said against my lips. "Had to feel it. Am I going to get ye pregnant?"

But as I opened my mouth to reply, to tell him I'd been getting the contraceptive shot for over a year so I didn't need to handle periods, he kissed me again to silence me.

"Actually, I don't want to know. I want there to be the chance that I can because that is so fucking hot it's making me lose my mind."

I raised a shoulder, drifting a hand up to cup his face. Then I leaned in and kissed him this time.

Jamieson froze in shock, but then took over, ravishing my mouth.

I had no clue who I was anymore. Myself again, maybe. Or something new. After a minute, Jamieson leapt up, grabbing my clothes from where he'd discarded them.

"Arms up," he ordered.

Like a child, I lifted my arms in the air for him to tug away my shredded T-shirt. He dragged off his own and planted it over my head. It swamped me, but at least I was decent to go back into the house, even if he was bare-chested. Then he used the ruined shirt to swipe between my legs.

"Luckily I don't think ye bled. That would be hard to disguise. We need showers, and rounds two and three, but I'm pretty certain there's an audience waiting for us."

I nodded and pulled on my underwear and leggings. The real world was never far away. Even if we'd just stolen a slice of Heaven.

In contented silence, we strolled back to the house, Jamieson's arm over my shoulder. I wondered if I should feel different now I was no longer a virgin.

The overriding sense was of a deeper connection to Jamieson. Not even a shadow of the relief I expected now that the chief or any other bringer of pain couldn't take my first time.

I was so deep in my happy place that only something truly shocking could pull me out.

At the house, we entered the front door to find the family around the kitchen table.

Grim faces looked back at us.

My sister sat with the box of McInver's photos in front of her, her eyes wet like she'd been crying.

In her hands, she clasped a Polaroid, the naked figure in the picture hidden by her palm, and she uttered words that chilled me to the core.

"It's Mum."

33

Summer

I advanced into the kitchen, my gaze fixed on the photo in my sister's hands.

"She's so young," Breeze continued. "But it's definitely her. The earliest picture I ever saw of her was taken by a midwife in her second pregnancy, and her face is exactly the same. She looks so much like us. You more than me. Here."

My gut twisted into knots. I didn't want to see.

At the same point, I had to.

Shaking, I extended a hand to take the picture. Jamieson hugged me from behind but hid his face, giving me the support I needed without making this worse. The rest of the family drifted out of the room, leaving only the three of us.

I raised the photo.

The figure on the image was a girl, as tall as an adult, but definitely several years off being a woman. Too childlike in every other way to mistake the fact. Like the others, she was naked.

Her defiant face glared back at me. So obviously Mum. So like me as a girl.

I covered her naked body like my sister had done and just gazed at her face. We'd known for years that she'd been trafficked. The authorities were aware and had done nothing. Her life had been ruined by whoever took this picture.

"What does this mean?" I forced my lips to move. "How did McInver have this photo? Was she sold to him? Or was he the trafficker?"

Breeze heaved a heavy sigh. "I don't think we can find that out. Not from Mum. She was too traumatised to remember the faces of the men who abducted her."

I nodded mutely. When Mum told us her story, she'd talked about an interview with the police and the reasons they gave for not investigating her case.

"There's something else you need to know," Breeze said. "A few minutes ago, Mum sent through her video. Camden and I picked her up and drove her to her friend's place without any issue. The woman she's staying with used to walk the streets but got clean a couple of years ago and moved away, though they kept in touch. She was so happy to be able to help Mum and had a lovely spare bedroom. Mum and I sat on the bed, and I told her what you planned to do. I told her exactly what had happened to me when I tried to find you. She asked questions about your experience, and I gave her the story. I hope you don't mind. It felt necessary."

"Of course I don't," I managed.

"It gave her the motivation to make the video. She said she didn't think she'd have been able without it. Right now, she has all the support in place to live a better life, and she only wanted to help us with ours."

I could only look at Mum's face. When I was younger, I went through periods of hating the fact I existed. I couldn't bring myself to think the same about Breeze, but my life was proof of the destruction of my mother's.

Was my request for an exposé help or the opposite?

My sister tapped her phone. "She sent it to me to check it was good enough for you. She doesn't want either of us to feel bad for her. Only that she wants to help us make the impact we're trying to make. I'll forward it now. She said to call her tomorrow."

"Do we tell her about the photo?" I asked.

"Not yet. Tonight was so exposing for her. I can't imagine what this will do. We need more information first."

My phone vibrated with the incoming message. Then twice more.

"You've also got mine and the one Thea recorded for Struan's mum. We've heard nothing from Divine, so I think we have to assume she's out. Go watch them. They're powerful. You need to make yours, then we'll talk to the journalist and upload them all in the morning."

I nodded and went to leave the kitchen. Jamieson stayed with me, my rock.

"Oh," Breeze called after me. "A last disaster. I took a risk and ran up to your bedsit. I grabbed as much stuff as I could, but it had been ransacked. To be expected, I imagine? We were lucky."

My heart thumped, cracking some of the ice that had formed around me from the horrible realisation. I darted back to the kitchen and enclosed my sister in a tight hug.

Then I made for the stairs again.

Jamieson stood in the door of the living room, and I paused, waiting for him. In the room beyond, Lottie and Sin sat on the sofa, but Struan stood glaring back at Jamieson.

Swift tension rose, hanging in the air.

"Fucking drop it," Struan bit out.

I had no idea what had been said, but Jamieson's jaw tightened. He broke position and stormed into the room, pulling a fist back. Then he swung, connecting with Struan's face.

I gasped, and Struan staggered back, his hand coming up to cup his injury. He rounded on Jamieson.

I anticipated a fight, but Struan only snapped a single word.

"Again."

Jamieson shoved him this time, knocking his brother to the floor. He followed him down and knelt on his chest, gripping Struan by the neckline of his shirt. Then he grumbled in his face, "It wasn't your fault, ye fucking idiot. Drop the hangdog look and get your head back in the fucking game. We need ye with it. Cassie needs us all for our next attempt. Got it?"

He lifted off him and extended a hand to Struan.

Struan closed his eyes and banged his head on the floor but then gripped his brother's hand and let Jamieson pull him up.

"Thanks," the older brother muttered.

"Don't mention it." Jamieson hugged him.

The men embraced, each slapping the other's back.

I kept going up the stairs.

When I reach the top, Jamieson called my name from the bottom.

"Do ye want to be alone?"

I took a breath. "No."

I didn't at all. I needed him with me. Jamieson was a dynamo. Nothing stopped him. Nothing held him down or beat him. I needed that strength now. Craved his touch and the way he held me.

But I had to watch Mum's video. Despite the fact the she'd made it to go public on my request, I felt the need to do it alone. To honour what she'd done for me.

"Yes," I followed up, my voice weak.

His gaze soaked me in. "Wait there."

He disappeared back into the lounge then returned, holding something.

Headphones.

"I'll stay with ye, but have these on. Listen to music with my eyes closed so ye have the privacy but a hug, too. If that's what ye need."

My heart fluttered with emotion so strong. He knew me so well. He'd found a solution to a problem I hadn't even voiced.

"Please."

He jogged up to join me, and we holed up in our bedroom, curtains drawn, a couple of lamps on low. As he'd promised, Jamieson slid the headphones over his ears then curled around me, his eyes closed and listening to something that made him smile.

I huddled in, held my breath to calm my speeding heart, then played Mum's video.

On the screen, she smiled. "My name is Myrilla Andrews, but most people call me Myr. It's the only part of my identity I kept after I was kidnapped and trafficked to England at the age of thirteen."

A tear slid down my cheek for my beautiful mother, so put together and looking healthier than I'd seen her in a long time. She'd borrowed a blazer, presumably from her friend, and her hair was shiny, subtle makeup hiding the damage drugs had done to her.

With careful wording and exacting details, Mum told the story of being bought by a stranger, raped and used as a toy for six months, then discarded. She was taken in from the streets by another man who got her pregnant almost immediately. Nine months later, she had a daughter. Not even a year later, she'd had a second. No matter how much she loved her children, her mental health deteriorated rapidly. She didn't love our father and didn't regret it when he kicked her out. This time, she knew enough to go to the local authority, who put her into emergency housing with her babies. Social care had already been aware of her, but she'd previously run from them. Now, she welcomed it. There was a police interview, but she remembered nothing of her kidnapping experience and couldn't give them any details of faces. Her trauma had blocked it all out. She told them she'd been raised by a relative but couldn't recall their name or address, or even the country of her origin.

"That was a lie," my mother said. "I didn't want to be deported. My childhood in a border town between Belarus and Russia had been almost as bad as the experience of my teenage years. I'd never known a happy home, and I didn't want to go back. I wanted my girls to be safe in England and have better lives than mine. I forgot the language I'd grown up with almost overnight. I can't recall any of it now. Likewise, police dropped my case from the lack of evidence, and I was given a council flat, regular visits from a social worker, and a small amount to live on. After everything else I'd been through, it was bliss."

This was new information.

The region she'd come from, her memories.

My heart ached for all she'd suffered and how brave she'd been. Breeze and I never blamed her for her addictions and the times she couldn't care for us. She always tried so hard to put us first. But the moment we were old enough to take care of ourselves, part of her stopped trying. She moved in with Jack, walked the streets, and sank into a drug habit.

"You might find my story shocking," Mum went on. "But I can guarantee this is still happening today. Up until recently, I earned money as a prostitute, and new girls appear on that scene all the time. Practically children. Given no option but to sell their bodies, and all because of the uncaring men who run this as a business, or ones who buy trafficked women for themselves. Or maybe both. How do you fight back? The only power I have is in my words. Thank you for listening."

The video ended. I wanted to burst into tears. But it didn't come. I skipped forward to the next, hearing Struan's mother's account, as told by Thea. Davina was her name. She'd been abused by a relative in Scotland then not believed by her family. She'd found herself on the streets, had been grabbed by a man, and found herself sold to a brothel. Her first client was a man named McInver who'd told her he'd paid well for her virginity. After that, she worked on her back in the brothel. At the time, she'd considered herself lucky for getting paid. McInver bought her again, and this time, she got pregnant.

She lost her job.

McInver didn't want to know.

Her life after had been one of desperation, trying to raise a child in the worst situation. Her greatest threat had been for her boy to be taken into foster care, so she often evaded the services and was now in prison for benefit fraud that she had no idea how she'd committed.

Breeze's video socked me in the gut as well. She named the nightclub, Vanessa, the owner, and McInver as well.

When I was done with them, I shut down my phone and stared inwardly, trying to focus on my thoughts. They'd done incredibly. When I could speak, I'd thank them all.

I had my own recording to make first.

The picture painted was compelling. It pointed to McInver as the villain, which he undoubtedly was, but he was far from alone.

Would anyone care about a decrepit old rich man? They might read a headline and tut, but it probably wouldn't shock anyone.

Naming the chief of police was essential.

But I couldn't open my mouth. The same shock that had smothered me following my imprisonment had sunk over me again. I had too much buzzing around my mind. No idea how to start with it.

Warm arms squeezed me, and I shot my attention to Jamieson. At no point had I forgotten he was there. The comfort of being with him held me up.

He watched me in return, his headphones still in place. I reached and pulled them from his ears.

"I can't do it. There's been so much suffering, mine is nothing in comparison. I can't even think how I'm going to start this."

I expected him to reassure me, but he held his careful gaze on me. "Then don't."

"What?"

"How long have ye got?"

"Until morning."

He lifted from the bed and moved to the bathroom, yanking the cord for the light. Then he switched the shower on. "You've been through an insane day. Don't force it. Baby steps. Take a shower, take a nap, and I'll wake ye in plenty of time to get it done."

Slowly, I nodded.

Baby steps. I could do that.

I entered the bathroom and shed my clothes. At the shower door, I peered back at Jamieson. "Are you coming?"

He was naked and stepping in with me in a flash. Under the hot water, Jamieson kissed me, then set about washing every inch of me. He shampooed my hair and conditioned it. Poured shower gel on the flannel and scrubbed my skin, taking care to be tender between my legs.

I ached from where we'd had sex, but it wasn't a bad thing.

I needed more. Like he understood, Jamieson fitted his mouth to mine to deliver a blistering kiss. He sank down my body, lavishing attention on my nipples then lower, until he pulled my leg onto his shoulder and kissed my lower lips.

I braced myself against the wall and just felt, shutting out all the other clamouring thoughts from my brain.

He slid two fingers inside me and crooked them to rub over my G-spot while he sucked on my clit. In rhythmic moves, he brought me quickly to the edge and over until I draped onto him.

His trick had worked.

I was empty-headed the whole time he finished rinsing us off, wrapped me in towels, and ushered me back to bed. Once we'd dried off, he covered us up and extinguished the lamps.

He curled around me, protecting me with his body from all the attacks of the world.

His dick pulsed against my thigh, rigid and neglected.

"Ignore that," he muttered, his voice thick.

Something had changed in me. I'd transformed from an impulsive child to a broken adult and now to something else. Like Jamieson, I'd endured, learned, and matured.

I faced him and curved a leg over his hip, bringing him to my core. Then before I could overthink it, I reached for his hard length and sank onto it in one swift move.

He made a sound of shock and need, so impossibly hot.

But he didn't move. Instead, he clamped hold of me, encouraging my legs around his waist as he rolled to his back.

"If I could, I'd fucking live like this. Buried in ye."

It was on me to take it further. I pressed my hands to his chest and rose just enough to keep him inside me then slid down again to the thickest part. He gripped my hips, his muscles tensed and jaw gritted.

God, I loved the sight.

By degrees, I worked out how to ride him. What speed he liked. What movements made him tip his head back in pleasure.

The orgasm creeping up on me took me by surprise, but I chased it, gasping at the rush of warmth, and love, and deep satisfaction.

Jamieson took over where I drooped. He held me tight and jacked his hips, working himself into a frenzy until he stilled, coming inside me.

We fell asleep in each other's arms.

Happiness. That's what Jamieson was. Exciting, scarily impulsive, pure sunshine happiness.

And I was still so deep in love with him.

At dawn, he kissed me awake and went to leave the bed. I pulled him back onto me, bringing him to me so his dick slid straight into my body.

"Just live in me for a minute," I begged.

He didn't move, just staying put, clutching on, hard inside me.

At last, I released him, and he stood, dressed, kissed me once more, and left the room.

It was my time to get this done.

I collected my phone from the bedside table, nudging his in the process. The screen lit, showing me what he'd been listening to last night. I stared, recognising the familiar app.

The whole time I'd been wallowing in the videos, he'd been listening to the recordings we'd made. The archive of messages between us that stretched back years.

This last burst of Jamieson-shaped happiness gave me the energy to get up and get on with what I had to do.

34

Summer

Tricia Thomas, Thea's journalist contact, took my call at eight AM.

Earlier, I'd searched for her online and liked what I saw. She'd worked at leading universities for twenty years, and before that had been an investigative journalist and a prominent name in her field. She was close to retirement but still put out pieces here and there. Many of them were women-centric. Focusing on stories and real lives more than big exposés.

Steeling my nerves, I explained who I was, trying to remember all I had to say.

The woman cut me off, the drone of traffic and the rhythmic clumping of her footsteps sounding like she was striding somewhere with a purpose.

"Yes, yes. Henry mentioned you. I'm not sure what you think I can do for you, and I have a full day ahead of me."

"I appreciate that." I tapped on my phone and sent her the couple of minutes of the video I recorded this morning. "Do me a favour. As you're heading to wherever you're going, watch my video. I'm posting it online today. Call me back if this interests you."

I hung up, my only strategy to make myself look interesting to her. It was risky. For all I knew, she could be best buddies with the police and jumping to quash my story. If that was so, I'd lost nothing. I'd still upload it.

Around the kitchen table, my sister, Thea, and Lottie waited with me. When I'd come downstairs, the women had been sorting through the photographs from McInver's wall, discussing in low tones how we'd ever identify them.

Someone had found Post-it notes to cover the nudity on each shot. I loved that tiny show of care.

The men were missing. I sighted them through the window, out in the sea, cresting waves on their surfboards and diving in. A tight pack, each with a tiny light that sparkled every now and again. Orange for Jamieson, purple for Camden, green for Sin, and blue for Struan. Even if they hadn't known each other growing up, they were so obviously brothers.

Lottie slid a plate of chocolate chip muffins my way. She'd baked this morning, and I was in awe of her skills.

I grabbed one and grinned at her. "You're the best."

"Facts," my sister said. "One day, I'm going to have you teach me how to cook."

I squinted at Breeze. "You went to catering college."

She pulled a face. "And how are my cooking skills? I only took that course for the business units. How are your skills working out for you?"

I stuck my tongue out, suddenly five years old again.

Lottie giggled. "What did you study, Summer?"

I wrinkled my nose. "A two-year course in hair and beauty. We were given very little choice as the government was supporting us. I can cut hair, so if I need to, I can get a job in a salon, but it's pretty far from the anarchist rebel I see myself as."

She tilted her head. "I can't imagine ye doing that. Not unless it's all undercuts and neon dye jobs."

I snickered. "Oh, do you know the best thing we did? Kids face paint. We practised on each other, not children, and I spent the day as a Viking shield maiden, bold patterns on my skin and my hair braided into an intricate style. It was badass."

Lottie widened her eyes. She always wore a braid, from what I'd seen. "Oh my God, that sounds amazing. My father never let me wear makeup of any kind, I never even experimented. I want to be a shield maiden."

"Can I as well? We're basically going to war," Thea added.

"Hell yes," was my sister's contribution.

I sat a little taller, liking the easy conversation. Jamieson had his tribe with his brothers, and maybe I had the start of the same with these women.

"If we had any makeup, I'd do it now," I chirped. "Battle-ready angry women."

My phone rang.

Our conversation abruptly stopped, everyone staring at the phone like it was a snake about to strike.

"It's her," I breathed and answered the call on loudspeaker. "Hello?"

"Is this some kind of joke?" Tricia snapped down the line.

"Not at all."

"Then you plan to blackmail the chief of police in Scotland and you're using me to twist the thumbscrews."

"Still no. It's an open and frank account of what happened to me. Every word is truthful."

"Are you an acting student? Or did someone pay you to make these claims?"

"Not at all. I never even heard of the man until he bought me. You can research my background. I am who I say I am."

My clip included my full name and how I'd come to be sold off. If Tricia wanted, she could delve into my past, and she'd only find things that strengthened my story.

"Listen," I said. "I don't expect much to happen from it. I know how it looks. I'm going to post them anyway because I have no other course of action and it's the right thing to do."

Her tone changed. "What do you mean 'them'?"

I held my breath. "My video is the first of four."

As I spoke, a text message landed on my screen.

Divine: Here you go, sis. I'm wearing a mask and I'll lie low for a week, but you've got me. I couldn't say no, and once you've watched it, you'll see why. Do your worst.

An attachment arrived right after.

She'd done it. She'd sent her video.

I had no idea what it contained, but it could only help us.

"I mean five videos," I spluttered. "All of them accounts from women who've been trafficked, raped, forced into prostitution, or dumped and left to pick up the pieces of their lives. One is a prisoner. One was kidnapped from another country. More recently, two went through virginity auctions in Scotland and were sold to prominent men."

"How recently?"

"Within the last six weeks."

The journalist went quiet.

I resisted the urge to rattle on. To try to persuade her.

"There are five of these accounts, and you name names. Are you implying there's a connection between the cases? Some kind of network? Do you have any evidence beyond the videos?"

I hesitated. I hadn't seen Divine's recording to know what she'd said, but hard evidence only existed in the form of the photos we'd found on McInver's wall.

A dawning realisation hit me, derailing my thoughts. I'd been so caught up in coming back to life, in Jamieson, and in pushing forward my revenge plot, that I'd missed something glaringly obvious.

We identified McInver in the videos.

The brothers relied on some kind of reconciliation with their father to get their little sister back. If we handed over the photos and the video of finding them, it connected my mother's account directly to McInver, making the implications against him far greater.

He deserved it, but the old man would never see past that slight.

I'd ruin Jamieson's chances.

"Possibly," I said, but it was weak.

The background sounds on Tricia's end of the line changed, a door swishing like she'd entered a building.

"Tell me what you expect from me," the journalist stated.

"All I'm asking you to do is watch them. I'm going to post these videos regardless of anything or anyone. Write a piece on them, if you want. Share them to others. I'd love there to be a change that came from this, but my expectations are low. In the past, nothing has ever happened, but if one girl or woman is helped, it's worth it. The only gratification I'll get is to feel I've done everything I can."

"You're attacking this full-on without hiding. I wish I knew why."

"I've told you it all. The videos say the rest. No woman could look at those and decide it was okay for the perpetrators to continue unchecked."

"Send me the others. I'm not promising anything, and I won't offer you any advice, because I don't think you'll listen, but I will watch them."

She hung up on me. I dropped back in my seat and exhaled.

Breeze rubbed my arm. Lottie and Thea congratulated me.

I felt only numbness.

In a quiet corner, I tapped out a reply to a picture Mum had sent. She was doing a painting with Jean, her new housemate, and said she just needed to know that I was okay and that she'd helped. I was forbidden from worrying about her, which I told her I'd try not to do.

Next, I opened Divine's message, and her face appeared on the screen. She'd removed her wig and the lavish make-up and hidden her mouth and nose behind a medical mask. At first glance, I wouldn't have known who she was, but her voice, the warm tones of my rescuer, were so familiar.

"My cousin sold me at auction the first time when I was fifteen years old," she started, launching straight into things. "He told me that rich old men like to buy up pretty young virgins, and between us, we'd make bank selling me over and over. I was smaller than I should've been at that age, probably from malnutrition, and I was scared of him. I only had my dad, and he was a drunk and always sick. No female role model to turn to. The money would mean I could eat. Buy the trainers I kept getting in trouble for not having for school sports. Steve, my cousin, had a friend called Vanessa who fucked men for money. She was kind. She told me what to expect from my first sale. Call me naïve, but I knew almost nothing about sex. I was so worried I'd mess it up, and then the second time my cousin brought me to her to sell again, she told me I'd done good. I was so happy."

She took a short breath. "Looking back, it's hard to decide which part of that was worse. The fact I was relieved that I hadn't disappointed the dirty old man who fucked me in his bed without even asking my name, or how to him, it would've been so obvious I didn't want him to touch me cos he had to hold me down, or that I came away with bruises in the shape of his fingerprints in multiple places on my body. I was sold as a virgin eight times before Vanessa deemed me too used to make the big bucks. I was still only fifteen, and let's add another item to my fucked-up list. How sad I was that my earnings dropped by half."

She continued on, giving her age as thirty-three, and

the fact that Vanessa had opened the nightclub Baby Girl as a front for her prostitution racket. Chief Daniels had been an early customer, and the nightclub never had any problems with raids or licensing.

Divine's shocking video brought names and dates.

"You know, sis, I have a photographic memory," she disclosed. "I never forget a face. If I check my phone and see the time and date and then meet a new person, it lodges in my mind. Who, when, where. My recall is perfect, not that it ever served me any use apart from remembering what tricks the johns liked. There was one in particular who had a fetish for blowing his load in my hair. Another who's a judge. He liked us to act out scenes from a book he was writing. I'd be the scared student in a school uniform, and he'd be the villain. No kink shaming here, but considering he made decisions on families and kids all day long, that one was a conflict of interest, if you ask me."

Divine looked down her hands and then back at the camera. "Women should have the right to choose if they want to sell their bodies. I don't want that taken away from me. I have no qualifications and I've never done any other job than this. I'm good at it, and most of my clients are kind and lonely. What I hate is seeing girls pushed into it in the way I was. Or women having kids taken away from them when instead they should be given support. My son was raised by his father—the man who bought my time and who considered my baby as his property. I had no hope. No one to turn to. I never got to take care of my little boy, was never permitted to tell him I was his mum for fear that I'd never see him again, and that cut me up. If anything should change, women need to have a voice. That's why I made this video today. I never had one, and at last, I got the words out."

The video ended, and I took a minute to feel her loss before I tapped out a reply.

Summer: I'm so sorry about your son. Are you sure you're okay to go through with this? There will be consequences.

Divine: I get it. I said what I have to say.

Summer: Thank you. I'm going to upload them all today. I'll keep you posted.

She didn't reply.

In a few clicks, I sent all five videos to the journalist. Step one, complete.

"Summer?" Jamieson hollered for me.

I jumped up and padded out to find him at the kitchen door, a sudden panic hitting me at the conversation we needed to have.

And the decision I knew I had to make.

35

Summer

Still in his wetsuit, Jamieson beckoned for me to follow him outside. He was barefoot, the bright neon light at his wrist still flashing.

I needed to speak first. "I spoke to the journalist and sent her the videos. I realised something that hadn't occurred to me before. Your father is named in the videos. He's going to be angry. It could make things harder for you to get help from him for Cassie."

Jamieson took my hand in his and led me onto the sands. I kicked my shoes off, the beach already warm, no storm or wind today.

"It's fine," he replied.

"No, it isn't. Remember yesterday behind the garage? This is my equivalent of growing the hell up and stopping being impulsive. There are consequences to my actions. I need everyone to be aware."

He squeezed my hand, no sign of concern in his sunny features. "We know exactly how McInver will take this. We talked it out in the sea. After they all gave me their reactions to my video yesterday. Sin said it was a far reach from the Daniels-bait sighting he expected. Cam threatened to tattoo a bullseye on my forehead."

I allowed a small smile. "What was said about the Mc-Inver thing?"

"It'll bounce off him. At worst, it might piss him off, but he wants an heir, and nothing about that changes how he thinks he can get one. The man's arrogant. Look at that wall he had. He stared my pregnant ma in the eye and told her where to go. My brothers' mothers, too. He thinks he's invincible."

I stared at the white-golden sands under my feet, the wave pattern that rippled over them. "I'll take his name out if you want. The only person to have seen them is the journalist, and she isn't authorised to share them until they're public."

"No need. I don't intend to hold back in any way from now on. None of us should."

He stopped, stepping in front of me so he could see my face. "Struan wants to marry Thea. Right now, he's upstairs telling her, and we're going have a beach wedding this evening. It won't be legal, but it still counts. It's a celebration of them, and we'll throw a fucking party. One last chance to relax before shite gets real."

He focused hard on me, like he was trying to read something in my eyes. "What will it take for ye to forgive me for how I treated ye? When we were on Torlum together, I asked for your understanding, but that was bullshit. In the same circumstances, you'd never have given up on me."

Except I had. One message after silence, and I'd crumpled.

"Don't answer my question now. Just listen to the message I'm about to send ye. It's from a couple of years ago, and it went into the archive from my unsent messages. I was too much of a coward then but I'm not now."

He ducked and kissed me, the taste of seawater and him taking over my senses.

Then he was gone, jogging back to the house. I watched him go inside, and seconds later, a message landed on my phone.

It had been so long since I'd seen his name appear with a voice message attached. My heart squeezed. I'd come full circle. From what had been a daily occurrence to an echoing nothingness, here he was, all up in my inbox again.

I'd never felt so happy.

"*So,*" a much younger Jamieson said as the message played. "*This is going to sound weird. I recorded this then deleted it and recorded it again. Who knows, maybe I'll never send this to ye and it's just me talking to myself again.*" He gave a kind of laugh then swore at himself. "*Okay, hyena laugh says I'm never sending this to ye, so I'm carrying on unfiltered. I'm in love with ye. You're perfect. One day, I'm going to marry ye, and we can live together. I'll get a job, or sell stolen cars, whatever. I'd look after ye and be your man. We'd have a bed, and we can hide in it together. The world won't find us there. It'll be just ye and me, and everything will be better because we'll never be apart. I love ye, Summer.*"

Then he shouted the same, laughing with it.

The message ended, and I held my phone to my chest.

If only he'd sent this.

I'd been so hard in love with him. More than a crush. The most real thing in my life, aside from the love for my family. My feelings for him had become my whole world.

Whatever barrier I'd had in my mind and heart crumbled. It was all still there. The space carved out for Jamieson. Nothing had changed.

I turned back the house. As I walked, I recorded my own message into our app.

Jamieson was right. No living in fear and no hiding. I told him how I felt. He deserved nothing less.

In the kitchen, I embraced a jubilant Thea. She did a lap of the rooms, telling everyone what we already knew, before disappearing upstairs to where her fiancé waited. Lottie and Breeze huddled together, talking about a wedding feast, Sin and Camden joining them.

It was time for me to post the videos.

In the living room, I found Jamieson by himself, and curled up on the sofa beside him. He instantly switched position to wrap around me and closed his eyes.

"Do your thing," he quietly instructed.

I stared at my phone. A quick check of our app showed me he hadn't yet listened to my message, but that was okay. He would. And until then, I had work to do.

Systematically, I set about creating fresh social media accounts in a private browser, then I researched all the tags and handles I needed from the various places of authority. Official police accounts, members of parliament, anyone I could think of. Then I added each video as a series. Mine first, followed by Breeze, our mother, Struan's mother, and lastly, Divine's.

I'd done all the thinking. Considered what we were putting out there. It could either catch people's attention or it would fizzle out to nothing. Just another minor scandal in the world where worse happened every day. But in tagging the official accounts, I hoped that someone would see them and decide an investigation was due. That the journalist would come good and do her thing. Or that the chief would spontaneously combust in rage, taking McInver with him.

A girl could hope.

When I was finally done, I sent links from the biggest site to all who'd contributed. Mum sent thumbs-up, Breeze and Thea clapped from their positions in the house. I closed my eyes and rested back against Jamieson. He squeezed my hip. Until now, he'd been my silent rock of support, just like he had last night.

"Listen to your message," I asked him.

"Not yet." He unfurled himself and jumped up. "Things to do, places to be."

"Such as?"

"We're surfing. I said I wanted ye on my board."

I opened my mouth to protest, but he grabbed my hand and towed me from the room.

"Camden, Struan, Sin, how about that surf lesson we agreed on? It's gorgeous out there," he called from the hall-way.

He was right, the warm morning had heated up even more, and there wasn't a cloud in the sky. For Scotland, it was a heatwave.

In the kitchen, Camden looked up from the big dining table. He had a stack of yellow papers in his hand, lines of holes down the edges. It was wider than normal printer paper, and had faint typing and lines on the top page.

"What's that?" I asked.

"I was going to ask ye. It was in the bottom of the box ye brought back from McInver's."

"Surf now, talk later," Jamieson demanded.

He veered us towards my sister and Lottie, pointing Breeze to the direction of the back door.

"Yes! Let's get out there," she agreed.

Sin entered through the kitchen door. "Struan and Thea will be a minute. Lottie, do ye want to come out with me? I won't make ye stand up."

She pointed at the oven timer. "Two minutes, and the cake will be done. It can sit there and cool while we play."

Something inside me released. A tight knot of fear, worry, and everything that had been burdening me lifted. I'd done all I could do to face off to the terrible things that had happened to me. It was healing, a release, even if it went nowhere.

Taking my sister's hand in mine, I skipped upstairs with her and we got into wetsuits.

Half an hour later, everyone was in the sea.

The sun shone, and we adjusted to the icy water with splashes and yells.

True to his word, Jamieson lined us up for a surf lesson. "The first rule of surf club is that this has to be fun. I want to see all of ye enjoying yourself. Anyone who doesn't gets dunked. Second rule of surf club is don't pop up too soon. Middle of the surfboard, right on the wave, nose up, don't let it submerge."

I waved at him. "My nose or the board's?"

He raised his eyebrows, a sly, sexy-as-fuck look on his handsome face. "Daft questions will also earn a dunking."

I snickered and gestured for him to continue.

My feeling of weightlessness grew.

All I knew for certain was right now, in this moment, I was the happiest I'd ever been. We got to play in the sea, then later, watch our friends marry, and just be young and in love.

Jamieson had us all lie out on our boards and paddle.

"Lie centred, legs together, arched back," he ordered, swimming closer to slap my wetsuit-clad backside. "Long strokes with your hands," he added with a wink at me that was decidedly sexual. "Then when the wave comes, point at the beach, press up on the board to get one foot under ye, then the other, find your balance, and go."

Easier said than done.

We practiced for an hour, Breeze getting it before I did. Lottie happily sat on her board being floated around by Sin. Thea and I took longer, but eventually, we all managed to ride a wave.

It was such a rush. I got why he loved it so much. As a prisoner, he'd had this, and I was so grateful for that.

"How was it?" Jamieson asked quietly when we dragged the boards out of the sea.

"Magical." I smiled at him.

Backlit by the lowering sun, he bent in and kissed me. This time, we both tasted of seawater. He'd taken me into his world, and I never wanted to leave.

What I wanted more than anything now was to take him to bed, to ignore the world, any notifications on my phone, not that I planned to check it for a while, but we had a wedding to carry out.

Our time together wasn't up yet. Whatever terrible things were going to come to us had to wait.

36

Arran

My father's rage took a couple of forms. Minor, day-to-day troubles would see him snap in temper or shout. Bigger problems had the opposite effect. They sent him cold. More calculating.

In a rising fury, only apparent in his solitary focus, my father strode into McInver's suite, a hospital orderly pursuing us. The man wasn't brave enough to try to stop the chief of police, but he apologised to McInver.

Dad turned to him. "Out."

The man ducked his head and left.

Yesterday, we'd been here for hours. Mostly, my father had me wait in the corridor while he tried to negotiate with the ancient Scotsman.

McInver hadn't given him what he wanted. I knew that from the way he treated me and the staff.

From what I could tell, there was some big bill to be paid. A sum in the millions that was required upfront.

My father didn't yet trust me to tell me the full picture.

but I'd worked out enough. Through the closed hospital doors, I picked up a conversation about ports and high numbers. The money was going into something illegal. Dad couldn't have anything to do with it because of his standing and his role. McInver, on the other hand, was an entirely private individual. Ancient, too. In his white sheets, and with a drip attached to his hand, he looked like a skeleton. If anyone had long held practices that had operated through the years and never been interrupted, it was this guy.

The one thing the men had in common was the women they used. Sometimes argued over. Which meant the money was associated with that.

For the whole night, I couldn't sleep, the same thoughts passing through my mind. Dad paid for the women who came to our house. Vanessa, his fixer, sometimes hosted auctions which he and McInver plus a few other men would compete in. They loved the game.

So why did they need to fund such a huge amount of money now? Dad had called it *extending their operations*.

For a while, I'd thought he meant drugs.

Then I remembered something one of the women had said in my earshot in our house. She'd asked a much younger woman, probably a girl, if she was okay. She tried again, then switched to another language. The girl burst into tears and replied to her, jabbering away with words I didn't understand. I'd been maybe twelve or thirteen, and I hadn't questioned what I'd heard.

I felt like such an ignorant child.

Lying in my bed, my realisation had come quickly.

Dad bought and sold women. The port reference made me think he was bringing them in by ship. How the fuck could that work?

I already despised his lack of respect for women. The casual references he made to my mother, whoever she was, grinding salt into that unhealing wound.

After we'd left the hospital, as we drove home again, my father had taken a call from Kenney, one of his detectives. I'd only heard one side of the call but got the impression someone had challenged Dad.

A fire had been set on an island somewhere with a video calling out my father.

Dad had iced over. He'd locked me away the moment we got home. Without my phone, which had been confiscated, I couldn't clue myself in on what had happened.

But I liked it.

Change was happening. Things couldn't continue like this, and I wanted a part of it.

Finally, this afternoon, Dad had released me from my room. Without a word, he'd marched me to the car and driven us to the private hospital again. White-knuckled, he drove too fast, taking corners precisely.

Now, I waited with bated breath to hear what he had to say.

In his bed, McInver was propped up, Golding, his lawyer, ever present at his elbow.

Dad sat calmly in a chair, perfectly still. "I'm sure you've seen the news."

The corner of McInver's mouth tweaked. "Golding mentioned something regarding a series of videos. What of it?"

I stood taller. A series of videos was bigger than the single one posted last night. I still had no clue what was in that, besides a fire.

Dad thinned his lips. "I am named. You are, too. I'd think it very clear why we should be concerned."

Ancient McInver shrugged. "Who's going to listen to the whining and crying of a bunch of women like that? Today's gossip is tomorrow's chip paper. You've been on edge ever since I woke. Calm down or you'll be the one having a stroke."

The lawyer straightened McInver's bedclothes then offered him a drink with a straw. "Quite right. No need to trouble yourself over such unnecessary fuss. Your throat sounds a little hoarse. A sip of water will help."

My father smiled. A crocodile wishing it could strike. "It is more than just a fuss. I have a reputation. Already, this has drawn attention. The time has come to bring in your boys."

McInver thrust away the plastic beaker, spilling it. He narrowed his gaze at my father. "What is it to do with them?"

Dad remained quiet for a moment. "Tell me the names of your children."

I already knew there was Camden and Jamieson.

But Dad was trying to paint a picture. He didn't know all of them. That had to be driving him insane.

McInver raised an eyebrow. "Why?"

"The girl in the first video is the little bitch who raided my police station."

McInver's superior expression dropped, and a tiny blip of rage crossed his features. He smothered it with a smirk, but I hadn't missed it. "Ye mean where my son was freed from your custody?"

"Your son," my father said, carefully, icily making the connection. "The man I was holding who set fire to your house."

"Ha," McInver exclaimed. "You're jealous. Ye wish ye had offspring half as interesting as mine."

My father's smile tightened. "No disrespect was meant. I was merely looking out for my business partner's best interests. In the past, you never showed any leniency to those who got in our way. Tell me the names of the others."

"Give me your reasons first."

My father gave a sharp nod. "One of the other girls who names you was up for auction recently. Your son, Camden, bought her. Another is named Theadora Stewart. She gives the story of a prisoner who is the mother of Struan Gallagher. I pulled his mug shot, and he bears a striking resemblance to Jamieson. The only boy you mentioned to me was named Sinclair, after yourself. By my count, that makes four."

McInver interlaced his fingers over his skeletal frame, his gaze distancing. "Ye believe these boys and those girls are colluding against me."

Four brothers, I fixed in my mind.

McInver was clearly proud of them.

From my father's stillness, he was digging four graves.

"This is your legacy," my father placed each word carefully. "And they are aiming to bring you down. They name Vanessa at the club. One woman claims she was trafficked from abroad. Don't you see how damaging this is? It's long past a game. This tell-all has been picked up by a journalist who shared the videos with a commentary on modern slavery in Scotland. Without correction or some serious effort from me, this is likely to lead to some form of investigation. It falls at my door. Your sons did this. All the while, you are refusing to progress our business matters."

Though Dad hadn't raised his voice, the lawyer took to his feet, like he was leaping to the defence of the sick man.

"Considering the accusations," Golding interjected, "it could be prudent to postpone your deal."

Dark light gleamed in Dad's eyes. "We've come too far for that. Money is owed. Call your children in."

McInver glowered at my father, then switched his gaze to his lawyer. "Have my sons responded to my deadline?"

Golding gave a single shake of his head. "Unfortunately not, sir. They have, however, visited your mansion. I had alerts from the cameras we installed."

"Ye see? They want to be part of my life. I won't have ye interfere with that." McInver wheezed and clutched his chest.

His skin purpled.

A heart monitor beeped, the regular sound getting louder and faster.

The lawyer gasped and pressed the red button hidden discreetly behind his bed. Nurses burst in, tending to the elderly man.

Dad retreated to a corner, paying no attention to his business partner's plight.

He placed a call, turning away to talk to whoever was on the line. "Those four names are confirmed. Progress the case by whatever means necessary." He listened for a moment, then produced a chilling smile. "You've outdone yourself, Kenney. Bring her in."

He hung up and turned to me.

"It is important to maintain your direction in life, by not only having a primary strategy but also a backup plan. Learn from this, Arran. I will need greater support ongoing, and you have the chance to prove yourself to me."

My brain did a kind of rapid summary of all I'd seen. McInver was playing games with Dad. He was in danger of backing out of their deal, or dying before it could be concluded.

My father had anticipated this.

He was going to use the old man's sons against him.

I wanted to watch the videos. I needed to see the claims against him so I could understand exactly what he was.

Maybe I was the only person who could stop this.

Dad's phone rang, and he stepped out into the hall to answer, leaving me alone.

At McInver's bedside, the nurses did something with his oxygen, settling the man.

I approached the lawyer. "I need to borrow your phone."

Golding opened and closed his mouth.

"I need to see those videos. Show me," I demanded.

He peeked at the door but handed it over, finding the first for me.

I watched them all, the sickening feeling in my stomach intensifying. But at the last video, my body registered a kind of shock.

The masked woman took me a moment to place. I thought her a stranger, then something registered. Her eyes.

Divine.

Sometimes Dad's favourite, often kind to me. I'd never seen her without a wig and makeup.

She'd had a baby boy taken from her by a client.

I'd never known my mother.

Truth stole over me in an icy wave.

Though I looked like my dad in almost every way, in one distinct area, I was different. The honesty in her expression was all mine.

Dad returned into the room, and I shut down the device and slipped it back to Golding unseen.

Now, I had no doubt. My father was a women trafficker, abusing his position as the police chief. More than once, he'd hurt my mother.

He'd definitely kill her for this.

37

Thea

"Women, move your arses," Burn hollered from his position out on the sands.

From the kitchen, I giggled, drawing on the last black line in the centre of Summer's cheek. Using the scant make-up we'd scrounged between us, she'd readied us all as a tribe, something between Viking shield maidens and Celts, ready for my and Struan's wedding. In turn, I'd done her makeup.

God. I was getting married.

Pure happiness filled me.

It felt like so little time had passed since I'd been alone and lost. My mother had left me for her new family abroad, my dad had vanished, and the people I considered friends had betrayed me. In the middle of all that, I'd found Struan. From the first sight of him on the ferry going to Torlum, I'd got caught in his dark gravity. It pulled me in. Linked me to him in a way I never wanted to escape.

In the same way, he'd considered himself mine, though

actually getting him to ask me to be his girlfriend had been a challenge. He'd always said it hadn't felt like enough. Too temporary a word when everything he felt for me had otherwise altered him completely.

He'd asked me to marry him while between my legs and ready to fuck me into acceptance. He'd been scared, I'd realised. Ready to convince me by way of orgasms that he wouldn't ever let me down. My rejection was never going to happen, but he feared it.

Now the two of us were making our commitment.

Our wedding wasn't legal, but that could be worked out later. The words were all that mattered. How we tied ourselves together at a time when the world seemed determined to try to break us apart.

My warrior get-up only made that feel more right.

I finished Summer's makeup and grinned. "Looking good."

On her forehead, I'd drawn a star design, bringing the lines out over her eyebrows then slicing down onto her cheeks.

"Good? We're badass." The newest member of our group, though one of the most vital and awe-inspiring people I'd ever met, tweaked the braid that weaved my dark wavy hair fully on one side, giving the impression of an undercut. It left the rest loose as my bridal style.

Bisecting each eye and down to my cheeks, I had a line of black dots, my eyes heavily outlined in dark pencil. Breeze had smudged black eye makeup across her eyes like a bandit.

Lottie gave a squeak of happiness and squeezed my

hands. "We look amazing."

My sister had opted for a design over one eye, and her hair up in a complicated twist, interlaced with tiny braids. All she needed was a battleaxe to play the part of a fierce warrior.

I peeked in the mirror and heaved a steadying breath. "Got to say, this is the best wedding I could ever imagine, and we haven't even got to the main deal yet. Thank you, everyone."

We'd all done our parts, and Lottie, Breeze, and their boys had cooked and baked. Sin had made a run to the shops for beer, then he, Scar, and Burn had all rounded on Struan, capturing him and carrying him outside.

That was fifteen minutes ago, and a lot of yelling had followed that had us all grinning and dying to get out there.

"Ready?" my sister asked me.

I took another deep breath and nodded.

We left the kitchen for the sunset beach.

As we emerged, Struan marched back from the surf to his brothers, sopping wet and fully dressed.

They'd clearly thrown him in the sea as some kind of bachelor ritual.

Around me, my bridal party cracked up.

My heart only thumped harder.

He flicked back his wet hair and spotted us, a grin following. Then he stripped his shirt and threw it in Burn's face. Next, his jeans came off, and he stood beside his brothers in just his damp underwear.

"Groom's party, ready," Burn quipped.

My ladies stood with me, Lottie on my arm to give me away in lieu of a dad I didn't miss, and Breeze and Summer walked ahead of us down an imaginary aisle the thirty yards to the men.

Tiny tealights had been nestled into the sand, the little flames flickering. With the orange-streaked sky behind, I'd never seen anything so pretty or romantic. Struan smiled at me, and my heart thudded.

I didn't have a wedding dress. No veil, licence, or any of the frills that came with getting married. None of that mattered as all I needed was him.

I stopped opposite Struan, and Lottie took my hands and put them in his.

His warm grasp enclosed mine.

Butterflies trembled in my stomach.

The men hadn't seen our makeup until now. Each of Struan's brothers stared at his woman as if seeing past the warrior to all that was perfect and precious. I could barely spare them a look. All my focus was on Struan and the almost painful way I craved him.

"I was going to make a joke about treating her right," Lottie said. "But all I care about is how happy ye make her. This is the perfect wedding for my perfect sister. No matter what happens next, for once, we got to live in the moment."

She pushed up on her toes and kissed my cheek then joined the line of women, opposite the men.

Burn stepped forward, and to my surprise, with no notes, began the vows.

"Struan and Theadora, from the start, ye were destined for each other. Your first meeting was with my brother in chains, to which Thea wound up having the key. Shocker, but also the start of something beautiful. The world brought your lives together, and even as it tried to separate ye, neither allowed it. I consider myself lucky to have witnessed how hard ye both fell because it proves to me that against all the odds, love always wins."

Struan kept his gaze on mine. I swallowed, hopelessly lost in his blue eyes. In the love that shone from them.

His brother continued with a smile in his tone. "Struan, may ye always have the strength to be what your woman needs, both in your heart, your head, and obviously in your bed. Thea, may ye always have the patience to tolerate his nonsense." He paused for effect. "And be able to support him, because God knows how this fucker will ever get a job. Now repeat after me."

Struan rolled his eyes, but with tolerance bordering amusement. He repeated Burn's words.

"I, Struan Gallagher, take ye, Theadora Stewart, to be my unlawfully wedded wife. To keep and cherish and love." Then he added his own words, ones his brother hadn't prompted. "I always said that your love graced me with a favour I didn't deserve. God knows I'm not good enough for ye but I'm selfish enough not to care what any other fucker thinks. Consider these vows my promise to earn that love. I'll never stop finding ways to prove myself to ye." He cut a short glance at his brother. "Including getting a good fucking job so you're free to do anything ye want. So long as I'm with ye, Theadora, I'm the luckiest man alive. I love ye. I need everyone to know, but most of all, ye. My life started the day we met, and it's complete now I'm your husband."

Around us, everyone smiled.

If I'd had any words of my own to say, they escaped my brain. He'd surprised me with a wedding and then with his words of love.

Stumbling, I repeated the simple vows, claiming Struan as my husband, adding, "I'm yours for always," at the end.

Dark light gleamed in his eyes. My love accepted and understood.

Burn grinned big. "Now kiss each other because all that fighting to throw that heavy fucker into the sea has left me really needing a beer."

Struan leaned in and took my mouth in a fierce, emotionally charged kiss that nearly brought me to my knees.

Around us, everyone burst into a round of cheers and applause.

It had been the simplest wedding for the most complicated of love stories. After everything we'd been through, the commitment we'd made broke and rebuilt my heart in the best way. The good girl loved the bad boy forever more.

Struan kissed me again and dipped me backwards. But I was his warrior bride and had moves of my own. I yanked on his arm, swept his leg, and dropped him into the sandy ground.

"Fucking hell," he groaned, the breath knocked out of him. "I'm so in love with ye."

Astride him, I took over the kiss to raucous laughter from everyone else.

Struan let me own him for as long as he could tolerate then stood, taking me with him in his arms. His gaze held mine, and his blue eyes darkened.

He strode into the house and climbed the stairs.

In our bedroom, he kicked the door closed and pinned me to it, pressing me against the wood while he devoured me with a passionate kiss.

Abruptly, he turned and dropped me on the bed. "I said vows in front of people but don't think I won't let them hear ye scream."

I scooted back, excited.

My boyfriend—no, husband—had an obsession with my body.

More, he was obsessed with me in every way. And I was with him.

"Clothes off. Get on your knees," he ordered.

I obeyed, stripping fast to kneel at the edge of the mattress.

Struan pursed his lips in a smirk. "Suck your fucking husband's dick."

Heat burst through me, my body alive and my skin tingling. I grasped his damp waistband and removed his boxers. His already hard cock jutted out, precum glistening at the end. I took hold of him and kissed the end then licked his shaft, curving my tongue over the thick vein.

But lightly, keeping the pressure off.

Smiling as I did it.

Struan swore under his breath. "I can't handle being teased right now. Not after what we just did. After ye became mine."

I peeked up at him, so much braver than the girl I used to be. "You became mine as well. I can do with you what I like."

He gave me a look that sent shivers down my spine, and I relented, taking his dick in my mouth and sucking hard.

Struan groaned and drove his fingers into my hair, controlling the blow job for a moment by jacking into my mouth. Then he released my head to slide his fingers over my body, cupping my breasts then down my sides.

"Arse up," he commanded, his voice gravel.

I adjusted my position, on my elbows and with my backside in the air. He cupped the globes of my ass and felt me up, stretched over me so his dick hit the back of my throat.

I was desperate for his touch. For him to be inside me. Half mindless with need for release.

Still, I needed to drive him wild, too, so I focused on withdrawing enough so I could keep sucking him, knowing how crazy it made him.

Struan's fingertips skimmed my pussy. But he didn't enter me as I so desperately wanted; instead, he coated them in my wetness then glided them back to my rear entrance.

I blinked my eyes open, hyperaware of his every move.

He pressed down and inched a finger inside, giving me a second before adding another. Fresh thrills chased through my nervous system. He'd always threatened to claim me in every way, but this was as far as he'd taken ass play.

Struan curved his hand, playing, *stretching* me.

Warnings flittered through me that this time, on our wedding night, he intended more.

Oh fuck.

In this position, I was caught with his dick as far in my throat as it could go. I couldn't breathe. My eyes watered. Still, he kept up his action, teasing me until he was knuckles-deep.

I throbbed around his fingers, the burst of pleasure fast and insistent.

My husband gave a dark laugh.

He snapped back his hips, withdrawing from my mouth. In a flash, he'd boosted me up the bed.

Then he was braced over my back and stretching for a drawer.

"What are you doing?" I asked, my voice trembling.

"This properly," was his reply.

Struan pulled something from the drawer and forced my legs open wide from behind. Without warning, he slid his rigid dick straight into my pussy.

I moaned and grasped at the quilt.

The stretch of him always shocked me. He was so big. So solid inside me.

Relief followed swiftly that this was how he wanted to claim me tonight, not in another way.

Then he slowed, and something cool drizzled on my backside. Struan kept his strokes slow and steady, ignoring the liquid he'd splashed on me to brush his hand over my clit.

He was keeping me guessing, but I liked it. Loved the sense of danger he gave me. I got off on the mild threats of the man who loved me beyond sanity.

The combined action of him sliding in and out of me

and his fingers making hard circles on my clit quickly had me easing towards a spectacular orgasm. I was so close. Ready to launch over the edge.

Then Struan stopped completely.

Still filling me, he brought his fingers back to my ass again and pushed inside. I moaned, half mindless now. It had been some kind of lubrication he'd used, as his fingers slipped in more easily now.

He finger-fucked my ass while otherwise holding me immobile.

My orgasm was still so close. One touch of my clit, and I'd probably fall. But I didn't move to get myself there. I needed him to own me.

"I've half a mind to keep ye on the edge," he said, landing a hard kiss on my shoulder blade. "But my warrior bride needs to come multiple times before I'll be satisfied. Starting like this."

He sat up, pulling out of me, and brought the blunt end of his dick to my ass.

I opened my mouth to say something, what I wasn't sure, but I lost my words because he thrust inside me.

"Oh fuck," my husband swore. "You're so tight like this. How does it feel?"

He was only a couple of inches deep, and shock had clouded my brain.

I shifted, easing back a little, a spike of blissful feeling showing me how to chase this. I did it again, gasping with the pleasure of it, then Struan growled, grasped my hip, and took over. His strokes grew longer, and he stretched me more as we finally reached the base of his dick, flush against my backside.

Sweat coated me. Sparks fucking flew.

He swore again, pulsing inside my ass.

His fingers found my clit again, and he worked me hard.

I couldn't help my triumphant grin, even where I closed in on my own orgasm. He was so close. I needed to get him there when I did.

I knew exactly how to do it.

"Keep going," I urged. "I love ye, husband."

Struan groaned out a masculine sound of pleasure then doubled down, his head against mine, fingertips indenting my flesh. Inside, he hit into me over and over. Faster and faster.

My orgasm smacked into me at the same time as he stopped and jerked.

I cried out at my dynamite climax.

It barrelled through me, blitzing every sense.

My first orgasm as a married woman almost knocked me out. Then my husband collapsed down on me and banded his arms around me, his breathing as ragged as mine. He came silently and hard.

It took a minute before my head centred again, and I twisted to kiss his arm. Any part I could reach while still pinned down.

He made me so utterly, deliriously happy I wanted to laugh.

Struan hugged me to him, then rolled up, taking me with him in his arms. "Shower time, sweetheart. Then more.

I wasn't kidding that we're doing this all night. Married life is going to be insane."

With him, it was only ever going to be that. Complicated, addictive, and wildly joyful. I wouldn't change it for the world.

38

Summer

Our party meandered to the fire pit where beers waited along with a good blaze.

Jamieson came to me. "I've been thinking about vows all day." He pushed my hair behind my ear, taking in my savage makeup with a smile. "Remember how we used to promise each other that we'd stop the other if we went too far?"

That ship had long sailed. Both of us had crossed the line and kept going.

"Let's go too fucking far," he amended. "Always, and in all things. We'll go too far, because nothing less than that will ever do."

I tilted my head. "Did you listen to my message yet?"

His smile faded. "No."

"You should."

"I will when I'm ready."

He took my hand in his and led me to the warmth of the fire. Someone handed out drinks, and we raised our bottles in celebration of love.

An hour later, we'd devoured the feast and all the beers. The happy couple had long disappeared into the house to celebrate in private, but the rest of us committed to the party. No one intended to get drunk. That would be out of the question. But living in the now was all we had.

We'd lost so much. Risked everything. This night was being felt hard.

"What does your vision of the future look like?" Lottie stared at the flames. "The one where Struan and Thea can live together and have jobs, and everyone's at peace. I know what my perfect world is. A big house with space for our whole family. All of us. Sin, me, lots of kids. Most of all Cassie. It was her version of happiness and that stuck with me."

A minute passed of quiet contemplation.

Breeze answered next. "Cassie's vision sounds pretty sweet. Our mum settled would be my only addition."

Camden leaned in and kissed her. "Anything with ye and my family at peace, whatever the fuck that could be."

Jamieson had his arm curled around me, spread out on the sand at my back. "This," he said simply. "Plus Cassie and world peace."

Suddenly, Camden leapt from his seat by the fire. "Holy fuck," he snapped and disappeared into the house.

My sister stared after him.

"What was that about?" I asked.

"I'm not sure. He's been puzzling over something all evening."

Camden appeared at the door again and marched to us, brandishing a wedge of paper. I recognised it. It had been in the box we'd recovered at McInver's. With all the photos to be examined, I'd barely paid it any attention.

Camden searched through the sheets, connected by perforations. Then he slapped the paper with the back of his hand. "There. Got it."

Jamieson squinted at him. "Want to clue us in?"

"On the phone, Sebastian gave us the names of three local judges who were corrupt as fuck. He thought we could bribe them. Sin, do ye remember the name of the last?"

His older brother paused for a second. "Villin."

Camden's eyes gleamed, and he held up the page. "Why would McInver have a receipt for Villin thirty years old? I knew I recognised something in this, but I couldn't figure it out. It's obviously from some kind of finance system, but old school. All the pages are a record of payments across a year. At least I think so. The system uses codes I can't understand, but the page before has a number four against the name Williams. Villin has eleven."

I leaned in. "It has to be the number of times he used a service." My stomach tightened. "When he bought women. Unless McInver was selling something else, which feels unlikely. He's rich, right? He wouldn't keep receipts for no reason."

We all went quiet, bringing together the pieces of this discovery.

My sister took the page and stared at it. "That's a really uncommon name. We can look him up." She pulled out her phone and searched. "Victor Villin, age seventy. Wife and two sons, three young grandchildren. This is him."

She held up a picture of a man in a judge's garb, the

model of a responsible citizen. "If he bought women from McInver, nobody knows about it because he's still working as a judge. Which means he's got away with it."

I pulled the phone closer. "Then the paperwork is proof of payment. Can we use it to blackmail him? Oh shit. See this. He works on the family court."

"Yes," Camden cut in. "That's exactly right. That's what Sebastian said. He suggested we could bribe him to help us get custody of Cassie. Except our bribe is going to be a threat."

Lottie stood, emotion crossing her features. Of everyone here, she was the most affected by the missing little girl. I'd never met Cassie, only having seen a picture Jamieson showed me on his phone, and I was ready to throw down to get to her.

"We need to find out how to reach him. Call Sebastian. I don't care if this fails hard or it's a mistake. We have to try."

But as she spoke, her phone rang in her pocket. She extracted it, frowning at the screen.

"Who is it?" Sin asked.

"My mother." She answered it and listened. "Who came? What did they ask?"

At whatever her mum told her, Lottie paled.

Sin stood at her side and curved a protective arm around her.

She thanked her caller and hung up.

"The police came with a fire crew to Torlum after the hostel burned down but left soon after. Two more people arrived this evening. They flashed detective badges and asked about me by name." Slowly, her gaze touched on each of us in the group. "They didn't mention the arson attack but named everyone here."

"Did she get their names?" Breeze asked.

"No, my mother was too intimidated for that. Her instinct was that I'd done something terrible because of the company I keep. Still, she said she told them nothing about Sin."

"What did they want?" I said through a tight throat.

I'd expected trouble. Other than checking in with Mum, and sending another message to Divine, I'd stayed away from my phone, just to have one night of calm.

I should have known it wouldn't be that simple.

"I'm not sure. Mum said she hadn't heard from me and didn't expect to, which is pretty much true, and they moved on to another house. What does this mean?"

"Nothing good," my sister answered. "This is what we wanted, though, right? When I made my video, I knew it would bring the heat. That's okay. It's the only way to change a system."

"They're collecting evidence," I uttered. "Isn't that what we're doing? They know who we are and are circling."

Jamieson stood from behind me, holding his phone out in front of him like it had electrocuted him.

It buzzed with an incoming call, and he held it up.

"I changed the name for Cam's old phone. It took me forever, but I knew my brain. Didnae want to ever get confused over who was on the other end."

"Who is it?" multiple voices demanded.

"Cassie."

39

Jamieson

"Inside," I choked out.

I jumped up and jogged the short distance to the house, Summer with me and my family directly behind.

I swiped to answer the call, and Camden dashed past, taking on the stairs in long strides.

"Hello?" I said.

Silence followed. Upstairs, footsteps thudded, then my brother led a wide-eyed Struan and Thea back down.

"Burn?" Cassie finally replied.

My heart skipped a beat.

Her sweet little voice, I hadn't heard it in so long.

After she'd been delivered to Torlum, her sunny per-sonality had changed our world. We'd changed everything, that we could, to make her life there easier. Then we'd let her down by allowing the police to take her. McInver had ordered it, but it was on us, her family, to care for her.

We should've fought.

I'd spent a lot of time in jail thinking of how much I'd failed her.

"It's me, sweetheart. Can ye tell us where ye are?"

A scuffling sound followed.

Summer curled her arms around my rigid, tensed frame. We all stared at the phone.

"She's at Kendrick Manor," a second voice spoke.

The rising bolt of happiness fell like lead. The speaker was male. Older. I raised my gaze to Camden. His horrified expression told me everything.

"Chief Daniels," Camden gritted out.

"Correct. The game is up. Cassiopeia Archer, why don't you tell your brothers how much you miss them?"

Cassie gave up a squeal that chilled me to the bone.

The chief laughed, and a door slammed. "If you want to see her again, all four of you will report to me here by midnight. Come alone. If you call in help, bring support, or make any other form of attack, you can imagine what I'll do to her. She's a tad young, but that will probably work in her favour. Don't test me on that. You have two hours, gentlemen."

The call disconnected, leaving us in stunned, terrible silence.

Lottie burst into tears and turned to bury her face in Sin's chest.

Of all the places she could have been. Of all the people to have picked her up.

I stormed away from my family and burst out of the house onto the beach. Then I yelled my fury at the uncaring stars.

I hadn't seen this coming.

The police had held me in secret, but I was just another minor criminal. How could the chief have taken a child? *Easily.* He could do anything he wanted.

Well, he couldn't have her.

Back inside the kitchen, my family were in their own stages of grief.

"Do we go?" Struan was asking.

"Of course we do," Sin snapped back. "He has her."

"But alone and with no way to defend ourselves," Camden added.

We were going to die, he didn't need to add.

Summer watched me, her expression soaked in pain. "This is my fault."

"No, it isn't," I retorted.

"If I hadn't posted those videos naming him—"

"Ye think he wouldn't have retaliated? I taunted him first with that fire. I refused to lay down and die when he caught me. We had every chance to go to our father to get help for Cassie, but I was too proud to bow to a man who abused my mother."

Over Lottie's head, Sin glowered at me. "We all made that choice. Don't ye dare blame yourself."

"I don't," I snarled back. "All we've ever tried to do is the right thing. We're not the ones abusing power or hurting people. All of the blame is with that fucking arsehole. I'm glad he's called us in. This needs to end."

I pulled Summer to me and hugged her.

"He ordered the four of us men to go," Sin said. "I'm with Burn. He might have commanded us there, but I'm fucking gunning for him."

He looked at me then on to our brothers. We all shared the same realisation. All held our women in the same way.

Sin tipped his head at the kitchen clock. "That's a two-and-a-half-hour drive, which means we need to have left ten minutes ago. How the fuck do I walk away?"

Lottie stepped out of his grasp. Her heartbreak played out over her tear-strewn face, her warrior makeup smudged. "I don't matter. All that's important now is getting Cassie back."

Sin's expression crumpled and reformed. "I know. We'll get her. But I promised to protect ye." He dropped to his knees and hugged her, pressing a kiss to her belly.

It looked like goodbye.

There was urgency between us. We had to move.

Utter despair socked into me.

What chance did we have against the chief of police on his turf? There's no way we'd walk away from that fight. He'd have his minions there. We'd be outnumbered before we even stepped foot on the estate.

I brought my gaze to Summer. Brushed my thumb over her perfect cheek.

I was never going to see her again.

After all those years of being pen pals, of breaking up and finding each other again, I was going to lose her for good.

Not wanting to waste another second without saying how I felt, I opened my lips, but Summer slapped her hand to my mouth.

"Don't you dare. Don't any of you dare think this is over. And don't for a second think that we're going to be sitting here waiting to never hear from you again. I've done that once and learned a lesson."

I held her wrists. "You're not coming. He'll hurt ye."

"I know, but luckily I have a brain and I don't think with my fists."

She shook me off and walked a few steps away before reeling around. With the braided hair and black makeup, she was a warrior queen. I was just as crazy about her clever mind, and how right now, she was plotting in our favour.

"The first thing he'll do is take your phones and any weapons. We don't have time to come up with any better plan than something we can do on the fly. Which means we need to have ears in that room." She extended her hand to her sister. "Breeze, give me your phone. One of you men will have two phones on you. The first will be confiscated, the second, with any luck, will be overlooked. Try to hide it. If you have it as an open line, we'll be able to listen in."

A tiny kernel of excitement battled my bleak state.

"If we get away with that," I said, "you'll be able to listen in, but what good will it do? Promise me ye won't come onto the property. I don't want ye anywhere near the man."

The rest of the family watched her, too.

Sin furrowed his brow. "Where are ye going with this, Summer?"

She pursed her lips, radiant in anger and indignation. "I'm not sure yet. All I know is you have to go and we don't have time to prepare. Without any intelligence, we'll be blind. We can't help you if we're in the dark."

"He said we can't call anyone in. He'll hurt our sister," Sin said.

Summer gave him a rapid nod. "Then she's your objective. Forget everything else. Forget worrying about us, or any of the other shit he'll throw at you. Survive, and secure Cassie. Trust us to work out the rest. We've got your backs."

I wanted to believe this could work.

But there was no time to think.

I kissed her. Pouring meaning into that loving touch.

Then we had to go.

In two cars, we peeled away from the safe house. Yet again heading into a fight, and this time, with everything to lose.

Darkness swallowed us.

At long last, I found Summer's message on my phone. Pressed play.

And settled in for our last battle.

40

Summer's last message

"It's been such a long time since I recorded a message for you, and yet muscle memory has me wanting to lie on my bed. Or tuck myself away somewhere no one can hear. It used to be school corridors. Then we grew up, and finally it's real life.

"I can't stop smiling over you. How happy you make me.

"You asked me for forgiveness for breaking us up. How about I ask you to forgive me? You were going through the worst time, and I'd guessed something bad was happening. Yet one message, and I crumpled. Years of friendship—

"No. More than that.

"Years of a supernova love shouldn't have burned out for me like that. I couldn't reach you anymore. I let that part of me wither and went on a campaign of self-destruction.

"But the flame never extinguished.

"It always made perfect sense to me, how you were obsessed with fire and water. They both have waves and a ripple effect, just like you had on my life, taking over every piece of me.

"I love you.

"I loved you from the start, and all through my pain of losing you.

"Your laugh, your bravery, your attitude.

"Your face, after that first picture you sent.

"You were always perfect to me. Then we met, and I realised how weak my imagination had been. Perfect has levels. I fell for you even harder as you climbed to the top.

"You're worth more to me than I could ever fit in a message, but I know you'll listen to this over and over like I plan to do with our archive. The record of how hard in love I fell.

"Let me spend the rest of my life proving it to you.

"When you've heard this, find me and tell me you're waiting for me to show you.

"And I will.

"Your Summer."

41

Summer

The roar of the engines diminished in the night. Outside the front of the safe house, the four of us women stood together.

Lottie's tears had dried, and she stood resolute. Her expression reflecting the anger all of us shared.

Her eyes flashed with it as she looked at me. "I'm not sitting around like a useless doll. Don't tell me to sit this out."

"None of us will." I gave a single shake of my head and led them into the house.

My tribe.

At the kitchen table, I convened the meeting of our War Council.

"Riddle me this. I'm the one who named and shamed the chief. Breeze and Thea, you're both in the videos, too. He's obviously made the connection between us and the men, because he ordered them not to do anything else to attack him, yet he demanded they attend him."

Three pairs of intelligent eyes took that in.

Thea lifted her chin. "Because he doesn't respect women."

I pointed at her. "Exactly. He thinks he can control us via our boyfriends. He's completely rejected the idea that we're going to be part of his downfall, because women don't feature in his plans beyond our use as sex objects."

"Sucks to be him," Lottie uttered.

I let my lips form a devious smile. This was what we needed. Purpose and a plan.

"We have three forms of attack, as I see it," I started.

"Listening in to what happens is one," my sister said.

I inclined my head.

"The McRaes. The rescue team," Thea surmised. "They took the family from Torlum while the islanders tried to stop them. They're an asset."

"That's two," I agreed.

"The judge," Lottie breathed. "Victor Villin."

"Exactly. Now listen up. We're leaving here shortly. First, we need to secure our backup."

Thea held up her phone. "I have Gordain McRae's number. Struan and I talked about calling him in an emergency."

"Good. Ring the man," I ordered.

She placed the call, and I switched to Lottie and Breeze. "We need evidence compiled for the judge. We have to assume our men can get Cassie. Our job is to keep her. The printout. The photos. Whatever information you have."

The two climbed up and got to work.

Thea set her phone on loudspeaker. "Gordain is on the line."

I introduced myself, taking control in a way I was born to do.

Everything else in my life had been training for this. Once upon a time, I'd been manipulated and blinded by my impulses.

This time, nothing was going to stop me from doing what I needed to do.

42

Arran

My father's home was a hive of activity. Usually, if Kendrick Manor was busy at this hour, it was with the women my father brought in. Tonight was so different.

My father was readying a trap.

Outside the front of the house, the big floodlights lit the exterior. Eight police cars were parked out of sight around the back of the building, a small troop of officers in attendance.

Instead of locking me up, my father kept me close.

I'd heard his call to Camden and McInver's other sons. Surely they suspected something like this. A sting operation.

My father didn't say as much, but I was certain he didn't plan to let them walk away. At least not all of them.

He was in his element, striding around the manor and issuing orders.

The small girl he'd had brought here wore handcuffs and a furious scowl. She'd been secured to a small platform at the top of my father's entertainment room and had wrenched against the restraint.

As we entered the room, she let rip. "My brothers are coming for ye. They won't let ye hurt me."

Dad ignored her, sweeping a look at me. "I'm counting on that. Are you paying attention? I want you to comprehend this lesson in managing a business. Be aware of all aspects, every string you can pull on if a situation becomes untenable."

I grunted what sounded like agreement but was more acceptance of facts. My father had sought out the best job that could protect his real career. He had to be making a massive amount of money from trafficking. What better than to own the police force which was the only way he could be stopped.

He continued. "Even after thirty years of being in business together, I had an ever-present awareness of my business partner. McInver's weak spot is his progeny. That little gang of delinquent sons. Theirs is her. She lived with her brothers for a while, but McInver had her removed to punish them. My officers unknowingly filled in a gap in information for me. When they picked her up on McInver's request, they took the names of the men and linked it to her case, including the foster home she was placed in. I've been aware of that one but had no use for it until today. Do you understand?"

Dad was a spider in a web. I nodded to show that I understood that perfectly.

And I had to bring him down.

The certainty grew in me.

I had no phone, no weapon, but I'd be the only one

with the opportunity. The moment McInver's sons arrived, they'd be restrained like their sister.

At the big double doors to the entertainment room, Kenney entered. Dad's most trusted detective, a hulking beast of a man, bigger than me despite the fact I was over six foot, approached us.

"Incoming," he advised, no attention given to the chained-up child.

"Which?" my father asked.

Kenney slid a look my way.

I stiffened, trying to work out who that could be. I had no one. I'd been raised by my father, allowed to attend a local school until the age of eight when I'd been removed, no warning, no friendships permitted. I'd lost touch with any friends I had made. No cousins, no aunts or uncles, no grandparents.

"Now or later?" Kenney asked.

"Now, I think," my father casually decided. "Do we have an ETA on McInver?"

"Five minutes, sir. The hospital staff were...reluctant."

My father hadn't even pulled strings to get his failing business partner here. He'd simply sent two patrol cars with orders to remove the old man. I'd suspected that Mc-Inver would come anyway to see his sons, but Dad didn't give him the choice.

He and his crooked detective talked on about the preparations, but I had got stuck on something I could see. The gun on Kenney's belt. Few cops ever carried handguns that I'd ever seen.

Would it be loaded?

Had to be.

We had guns in the house. Rifles and shotguns for hunting. Dad's handgun which I'd taken to help Summer free Jamieson. My father rarely carried them, but I'd seen that one in his office, like he'd collected it from the floor of my car.

I furrowed my brow.

He hadn't called me on that. There was no way Summer could've guessed the code to his safe. Yet my father appeared to have accepted my innocence.

I sensed the weight of his stare boring into me.

"Arran is going to play a crucial part in the proceedings," my father told his detective. "The core of our problem today is disobedient sons. Mine knows better than to act against me."

Kenney smirked and gestured to a plainclothes cop at the door.

The man disappeared then seconds later returned.

He thrust a naked woman in front of him, her hands restrained at her back. Free of makeup and her wig, she crept in, terrified. Her gaze clung to mine.

I understood it all. My father's insurance policy against me, another string for him to pull.

I stared at my mother then back to my dad.

His cruel smile said he knew it all.

Then the bastard confirmed it with a cold line.

"One step out of line, Arran, a single act of disobedience, and your mother dies."

43

Jamieson

Our tyres thrummed, and we rolled down the road to Kendrick Manor. Here and there, men lurked in the dark grounds. Spying on us to make sure we obeyed the chief, no doubt.

Before we'd left the safe house, each of us had grabbed a weapon and concealed them on our persons. It was a distraction.

We wanted them to find our phones and the knives or hammer, as Camden had picked, and miss the phone I'd taped under my arm.

At the bright entranceway, we parked facing outwards, like we had a chance to run to our vehicles and get away quickly.

None of us felt that. None of us felt anything but the deadly seriousness of what we were facing.

Sin had spoken to Lottie before we'd arrived. She'd told us of their preparations.

I loved that they were out there, acting for us. I couldn't

help feeling that any help would come too late.

Uniformed officers approached our doors.

"Wind down your windows," one snapped like a sergeant major.

We obeyed, and they passed us handcuffs.

I knew this drill. I snapped myself into mine, Sin doing the same beside me. In the other car, my brothers held up their arms to show the restraints were in place. The cops opened our doors, cinched the handcuffs tighter, then wordlessly escorted us into the entranceway.

My heart thumped.

A bigger man came out of a set of double doors, his gaze fixing on me.

I let my grin spread. "Detective Dickhead. What a surprise to see ye here. Quiet day for corruption in Inverness, is it?"

His superior expression dropped, and he barked an order at the collection of cops in the lobby. "Search them."

Men stepped up to each of us. Mine, a younger lad not much more than my age, went instantly to my jeans pockets and the outline of my phone.

I held myself rigid, too aware of the block of plastic, metal, and glass on the underside of my arm.

His hands shook, and he extracted the phone, holding it aloft in triumph. Kenney snatched it from him and powered it down, doing the same with my brothers'.

We'd removed the SIM cards and deleted all content on the way here, a last-minute strategy, Lottie had told us Summer suggested.

Summer had told me she loved me.

No matter how bleak it felt, I'd fight tooth and nail to return to her.

My cop returned to patting me down. He discovered the short-bladed knife I'd concealed in my sock, and his cheeks reddened. "A deadly weapon, sir," he bit out in disgust.

I raised a shoulder. "Be idiotic to come here without it."

Kenney didn't answer. Instead, he gestured for us to be moved out.

Holy shite.

I'd got away with keeping the open line.

It took everything in me not to look at my brothers. Whatever we'd face, we weren't alone.

We were directed into a large room.

There were people scattered everywhere, but my gaze went straight to Cassie.

"Burn!" she squealed.

It had been so long since I'd seen her, and I catalogued every inch of the little girl. Her black curls were longer and tangled. Her dress and tights were grubby. But her attitude, her spark for life, was right there in her bright-blue eyes.

"We're here. You're safe," I called to her.

She gave a fast and desperate nod, jumping her gaze from me to my brothers. Each muttered something similar, promising her we'd see her right.

Finally, I took in the other people present.

For the sake of those listening in, I opened my mouth. "I see you've got a pet shop of officers watching us. Detective

Dickhead, I really should know your real name. Chief Daniels. How is it I've only seen ye in pictures until now after you so craftily held me in illegal custody for so long? Who's the blond kid? Your son?"

The younger version of him had to be Arran, the boy who'd helped Summer and Camden. He didn't look my way and instead, glared at a closed cupboard in the corner.

I moved on. McInver sat in a wheelchair with blankets, oxygen, and a drip attached to him. Fuck. Why was that old dog here? A man fussed over him. I guessed that to be Golding, his lawyer, from the description Camden had given.

Arran was our best bet for help, but still, he refused to turn our way.

"Nice to see ye brought our dear darling dad in with his lawyer buddy," I concluded.

Sin let me finish my chatter and faced the police chief. "That's my daughter," he bit out. "I'll raise her as such. State your piece, ye corrupt fuck, then let her go."

Chief Daniels stared him down, no emotion present in his cool exterior. He waited a moment for quiet to fall in the room. "Sinclair Stone. There is a warrant out for your arrest for the murder of Augustus Stewart." He skipped his gaze to the next in line. "Struan Gallagher, likewise for the murder of Lionel Charterman. Also for the theft of a motor vehicle and several highway offences."

I recoiled, though it wasn't unexpected for him to go on the offensive. My brothers hadn't killed the men who'd imprisoned us on Torlum. Stewart had killed Charterman, then McInver had pulled the trigger on the shotgun that killed Augustus Stewart.

I got the feeling that detail didn't matter.

The chief moved on to Camden. "Camden Marshall. You are charged with grievous bodily harm for the assault of Mr Jack Jones. Additionally, the murder and illegal interment of Judy Mellows."

Jack had been Summer's mother's boyfriend, the man who'd kidnapped Breeze and deserved everything that had happened to him. Who the fuck was Judy Mellows? Maybe it was Keep, if interment meant burial.

He rested his gaze on me. Hatred seeped through that cool façade. "Jamieson Buchanan. Your name has been known to us for far longer. You are charged with four counts of arson incorporating a vehicle at Inverness police station, endangering life and limb of our proud police force, a mechanic's garage, a disused hostel building on the Hebridean island of Torlum, and at the Great House, causing extensive damage. Additionally, you are charged with the murder of Jonas McCaffrey and Kayden Jobs."

At least with me, he got all my crimes right. McCaffrey was the paedophile I'd burned in his bed. Kayden had earned his fiery death by hurting numerous women.

I shrugged and switched my gaze to Detective Dickhead. "Fury descended over your face at that vehicle arson. Was the BMW yours?" I grinned at him, showing them all exactly how I felt about this clown court.

Sin ground his teeth. "What's the point of this?"

The chief regarded him. "I have witnesses to all of the charges, and more. Good people who will swear under oath of your involvement in these crimes."

"I claim bullshit," I said on a laugh for the sake of the onlookers. "You've paid off people to make us appear bad. Do ye see us shaking in our boots? My brother asked ye what the point of this was. Answer him and stop dicking around."

I couldn't be afraid. Couldn't let in the possibility none of us would be freed with our sister.

When I'd escaped from jail with Summer, I'd vowed not to bring down my world of pain on my family. But that's exactly what had happened.

Right now, I had the chance to take the fall I'd always planned to.

The chief straightened his smart suit jacket. "You understand that extensive prison time awaits you? Each of you will be jailed for the crimes you've committed. You'll never see your sister again or the women who had the misfortune to align themselves with you. Who knows how great their misfortunes will go on to be."

He let the threat settle then turned to his detective.

At a gesture, Kenney led the uniformed cops outside.

My stomach tightened. This was it. The real crunch point. The chief had played out his cards publicly. Every officer in attendance knew our faces and would hunt us down for one of the crimes, let alone the list.

When the doors were closed, Kenney smiled at us.

The chief lowered his gaze to his right-hand man. "Wait outside."

Kenney's smile dropped, and I waved to him, speaking for the sake of those listening in. "Bye, corrupt cop toady. Join the other pigs in the hallway and try not to make a mess."

His orders left just us with the chief, Arran, McInver, and Golding, and Cassie.

I winked at our sister, and she managed a smile. Otherwise, she'd shrunk in on herself more and more.

I gauged our chances. Even with our hands cuffed, we weren't helpless. But one shout would bring the troops back in.

Casually, the chief strolled to where Cassie had been chained. I watched him, though out the corner of my eye, caught the smallest movement from McInver. He lifted a finger and tapped it once on his wheelchair, earning the attention of his lawyer. Until now, the two had been entirely quiet. I'd thought McInver may even be dead.

But at a sound from my sister, I jumped my attention back to her, missing the rest of their exchange.

The chief had a finger under her chin, tipping her face up.

Sin took a step forward, his expression pure anger. "Get your fucking hands off her or I'll break every one of your fingers."

"Don't even think about threatening me," the chief retorted.

He reached inside his suit jacket and extracted a small metal object. Flicked it open.

A barber's blade.

Horror lurched in me. Sin froze.

The chief gave a cool smile. "Don't make another sound or movement. If you disobey me, her life is forfeit."

He straightened and palmed the knife, the metal flashing in the bright lights. Purposefully, he sauntered over to McInver and stood behind the old man's wheelchair.

"You've heard the list of charges against you, and you

are now aware of your likely future. This evening, you'll all be taken to the station and charged. The child will be sold, a fate I feel appropriate for a relative of such men. She will only end up like her whore of a mother eventually anyway. But," he paused for effect, "there is an alternative path. Naturally, I would enjoy cleaning up the crime record for Scotland so neatly. The officers convened outside in the hall are loyal to me, and if I order them, they'll do exactly as I ask. Observe, ignore, it's all the same to them. Yet it feels like a waste to have them march you away when all of you have such potential. I offer one, and one alone, of you an opportunity."

With a flick of his hand, he sliced through McInver's oxygen tube then his drip.

The old man slumped.

"Your father and I went into business together many decades ago. He was a friend of my father's before me, did you know that? We all shared the same love for women, just like you boys do. McInver provided the starting capital and an established system for bringing girls into the country, or taking them from the streets and putting them to better use. I was able to facilitate his process in my position with the police."

Golding fluttered his hands over McInver. "You're going to kill him. He needs the oxygen to breathe."

The chief ignored him. "McInver's death is inevitable, like it is for us all. I hadn't realised how soon that approached until his stroke and his increased senility. Now, I find I have a need for a replacement."

A replacement?

A chill slid down my spine.

He wanted one of us to become a trafficker.

He was delusional. It couldn't continue. No matter what he did to us, there was still Summer's public campaign against him. It wouldn't just go away.

The chief left our father's side and moved to stand in front of us. "Before I decide which of you I'll work with on-going, I wanted to thank you for the gift of understanding you gave me. The whores you're associating with made videos about me and McInver. I have a team working to remove those from the public sphere, but I have also found it prudent to debunk them, just in case."

He crossed to a side table and picked up a tablet, tapping on the screen. A video played with high-quality CCTV footage.

I recognised the scene. My heart sank. It was the rear of the garage at McInver's house. On the video, I chased Summer down and tore her shirt.

To anyone else, it was a violent assault.

Beside me, Camden swore.

I looked away, and the chief tutted.

"We released this video earlier this evening with the clear message that Miss Andrews was nothing more than the disgruntled prostitute she was rumoured to be. In the video, she's engaged in a paid activity. If people don't believe that, they will question whether this was consensual or not, and why it wasn't referenced in her tell-all video. Put simply, it discredits her. As does footage we have of her mother who has on more than one occasion fucked men in car parks and in full view of CCTV. My officers were easily able to find that. The whores do it as an insurance policy in case their buyers get too rough."

His gaze touched on Struan. "Meanwhile, a certain jailbird who sang her story is going to be found suffering an unfortunate overdose by morning."

Struan gave an enraged howl, but chief Daniels quickstepped back to Cassie.

"And you, Camden. Your bitch girlfriend. I bet her mother would be glad to know exactly which relative of hers I bought her from. I remember that face. I'd had to resist her hard because the little blonde ones are exactly my type. Lucky for her, her cunt was worth more in pristine condition. I wonder if she'd remember me. I wonder how far she'd fall if all the details came back to her. I'll have the daughters all the same. Once I've finished with you, it will be no trouble tracking them down."

Camden tipped his head back, his pain all too clear.

Fury rose in me hot and fast. Summer and Breeze loved their mother so much. Now we knew exactly what had happened to her.

It had been his doing.

No way could we let him leave this room to carry out his threat.

"I could go on, but I think I'm making myself clear." He stared at Sin.

In a heartbeat, I knew he'd already chosen. Sin was McInver's first pick, too.

Big, stubborn, and fiercely loyal, if he promised something, he'd deliver it.

It meant the rest of us were dead.

It meant whatever I did next couldn't change that.

I readied myself. The brotherly bond between us told

me Camden and Struan were doing the same.

The chief clapped a hand on his son's shoulder. "You'll work alongside my son, shoulder to shoulder, like your father and I have done for years. Continuing the family business. It's in your blood. There's no use denying this. Isn't that right, Arran?"

Finally, the lad moved. He wrenched away from his father and stormed out of the room, returning just a few moments later. Arran extended his arm in front of him.

He aimed a gun directly at his father.

"Enough. You're not doing this," he snapped.

If the chief's show of strength was over, his son's had just started.

The chief's cool expression rippled. Without hesitation, he made for the closed door I'd noticed Arran staring at when we'd arrived. The chief yanked it open, and a naked woman spilled out of the narrow space. Like us, she was handcuffed, her mouth gagged.

The chief dragged her by her hair to her feet and put his blade to her throat.

"Kick the gun to me or she dies," he ordered his son.

Arran shook. "Let her go. Just stop hurting people. You have me, that's enough."

"I told you to kick that gun to me now," his father roared.

"Let my mother go," Arran screamed back.

The woman's eyes crinkled at the edges, emotion plain, and she whimpered behind the gag.

"Do as I ordered, or it's not just her life that's forfeit, but her baby's, too."

The son gave up a horrible yell of outrage then tossed the gun to his father's feet. It skittered across the floor.

The chief planted his foot on it, claiming it, then dead cold, slit the woman's throat.

Red gushed.

Arran's mother fell to the floor, blood pumping from her wound, a horrible gurgling sound following.

Entirely calm, chief Daniels stepped over her, picked up the gun, and aimed it at his horrified, broken son. "Like McInver's boys, you have a chance. To follow your mother to the grave or beg forgiveness for your pathetic act of defiance. I wasn't bluffing. You should've known I could not permit her to live. Not only did she help that whore escape, but she took part in the video show as well. Don't you dare mourn her loss."

It was over. We should've rushed him when we had the chance. At least Cassie had closed her eyes in fear. I didn't want her to witness the woman dying on the floor.

The chief had us in every way.

No witnesses would stand against him. Unless the women had been recording this, no one would know what he was capable of and what he'd done. The years of trafficking women he'd confessed to, the pain he'd inflicted.

"Arran, Sinclair, it's time to choose," the chief commanded.

Like a spectre, McInver rose from his wheelchair. "Not so fast," he uttered.

Suddenly not so weak, his voice rang strong.

"First, ye will listen to me."

44

Summer

In the helicopter, we pierced the dark, heading south. Over the headphones, Gordain McRae gave us an arrival time of a few minutes.

We were facing off with the judge.

It felt good to take action, and I was so ready to make the threat, but it meant we missed out on what Lottie could hear over the phone Jamieson carried. She was listening with headphones and texting updates across the helicopter. All four of us were sticking together.

The helicopter swung right, then the pilot brought us down.

Alongside Gordain, we had Sebastian at the controls, and Max, who apparently was a friend of Struan's. I liked the family. Instinctively, I trusted them, because Jamieson and his brothers did.

I'd explained our problem to Gordain, and he'd jumped right into action.

First stop, the judge.

Second stop was yet to be agreed.

We touched down, and I linked gazes with Breeze then Thea, raring to go.

Lottie reached across the cab and put her hand on my arm. She was still listening to something and gasped. "The chief mentioned you. A video he's put online to discredit you."

I didn't care. He could do anything now.

I shrugged. "Look into it? We'll be as quick as we can."

The three of us, plus Max who insisted on acting as bodyguard, stormed the field then into the judge's fancy garden. At the mock Tudor house, the doors flung open, and an elderly man in pyjamas and dressing gown opened the door. An older woman peered out from behind him.

In the helicopter, I'd fixed my warrior makeup, wanting the visual to go with how I felt inside.

I marched straight up, with not a shit left to give.

"Judge Villin," I queried.

"What is the meaning of this?" he spluttered.

I clutched the paperwork Lottie had put together. The receipt for payment. Pictures of women behind it, and paperwork the police had given her when they'd taken Cassie into care. "We have an emergency court proceeding to discuss with you."

"This is highly irregular. You cannot just show up at my house. Contact the relevant authorities and follow the process," he snapped.

I brandished the receipt under his nose. Then I peeled it aside to show the photos of women.

Recognition dawned.

I'd relied on this. Back when he'd started buying from McInver, the Internet didn't exist. No one had phones with cameras or pictures at the ready. He would have chosen women from photographic prints.

And the evidence was right there in his owlish gaze.

"What is this?" he said, lower and less steady.

He shot a quick glance at his wife.

Behind in the hallway, a younger woman appeared, carrying a sleepy child.

We'd woken the household, it seemed.

"It's a case relating to Mr McInver," I replied. "I can give you all the details here on your doorstep."

"McInver... No. I will see you in my office. Follow me."

Judge Villin led us inside to a room full of expensive-looking books and furniture. He turned on a soft green lamp, fright still in his gaze. "I don't know what you think you have there," he started.

"You know exactly what we have. We also have a witness who will attest to your involvement in McInver's services," I cut in.

The witness was a stretch based on my remembering that Divine had mentioned a judge.

Judge Villin sat in a leather seat and paled. "You have some nerve coming here to blackmail me."

My blood surged, and I resisted the urge to grin at him. "We're not blackmailing you. We are giving you the opportunity to remove some inconvenient evidence from the record. You can keep the receipt, and I guarantee the camera evidence will vanish into thin air."

Easy promises to keep as no camera footage existed as far as I knew.

He steepled his hands on the table. "What do you want?"

"A very simple court order awarding custody of this child to her brother." I thrust over the paperwork which named Cassie. "Her family love her and would never hurt her. She's in an abusive situation in foster care because of the actions of a vindictive relative. All of this will be set right with one signature from you. Your family and the public need be none the wiser to what you get up to with consenting adults, and we'll leave."

The moment played out.

The judge was known to take bribes. Sebastian had confirmed it on the way here. What we couldn't be sure of was how he responded to threats.

At last, the man nodded. "I appreciate you bringing this to me and not selling it to a paper. Tomorrow, I will arrange a court order—"

"Right now. We need to take it with us," I interrupted again. "Oh, and make a report so that foster family don't ever get another child placed with them again."

The impulses that had got me in trouble so much in the past were now under my control and working for me. They were hard to contain when the judge gave another nod, turned on his computer, and got to work.

We returned to the helicopter lighter one piece of evidence but brandishing the legal, signed court order awarding Cassie's custody to her brother, Sinclair Stone.

Part one and two of my fast-thrown-together strategy had played out.

I jumped back inside and handed it to Lottie. She sagged in relief, then I picked up on the tension in the cab.

"What's happened?" I asked.

"Get in," Gordain ordered. "We're flying to Kendrick Manor."

45

Jamieson

The chief of police stared at his business partner. He opened his mouth, but the old man cut him off.

"When did the servant decide to become the master?" McInver demanded. "For thirty years, I've put up with your upstart nature. Yes, it was useful having someone with your energy travelling out, teaching others the ropes, all so we could feed our habits. I liked the girls ye found. I won't deny it, and I rewarded ye in turn. But that wasn't enough, was it?"

McInver's eyes darkened. "I ended the life of the last man who I discovered had kept my children from me. I pulled the trigger, ending Augustus Stewart's life. And Stewart himself killed Charterman. He confessed it in front of me, and I will provide a written statement to that effect. As for all the other claims you've laid at my sons' doors, I can refute each one. They are innocent. Of everything but being mine." He chuckled. "At least in that, they can't escape the guilt."

The police chief sighed. "Enough, old man."

"Is it?" McInver squawked.

He turned to Golding.

The lawyer nodded. "Quite enough, sir. I recommend you say nothing further yourself, but the chief of police has given the public more than sufficient proof of his guilt."

Chief Daniels sneered. "My guilt? Nobody would believe you. Any of you. My officers heard the list of charges, and each of them would be considered an expert witness. The second those boys set a foot out of this room, they'll be taken into custody."

McInver gave a shrug. "Sinclair, my namesake, do ye want to tell him or shall I?"

Sin squinted at the old man, clearly none the wiser.

Then Golding collected something from the back of McInver's wheelchair and carried it over to him. A phone.

"Tell him what you see, boy," McInver said with glee.

Sin stared at the device. "This is livestreaming."

"Yes!" McInver cackled. "Golding set it up. The girls gifted us the idea with those videos they made, and I think it's rather genius." He advanced on chief Daniels, the madness slipping from his expression. "Now the world knows what ye are."

The chief's mouth fell open. He swung his gaze from McInver to Golding. Then he charged the lawyer, snatching the phone.

Golding staggered back then straightened. "My apologies, sir. It's far too late for that. The whole scene from the moment you sent your officers out to now has been beamed to a watching audience. Your profile online has been raised in the past day, and tagging you meant this has gathered quite the viewing figures."

Daniels howled and tossed the phone, shattering it.

Outside, a helicopter thundered, rattling the windows.

My heart restarted.

Throughout McInver's reveal, I'd barely managed to breathe. I'd wanted to add my own accusations to the pile, but not for a second had I forgot the chief had a gun. He'd been exposed but was still dangerous to the extreme.

The doors burst open, and Detective Dickhead stepped inside, his small army of cops flanking him.

McInver raised his hands, beaming. "Arrest him. Arrest me. I've confessed for both of us. But the only thing for certain is ye will have to let my children go. Start with the bairn."

One of the officers peeled off in a hurry to undo Cassie's restraints.

The detective and the other officers approached the chief, all focused on him. They didn't look at us or the body on the floor. Their intention was obvious.

The chief brandished his gun. "Think about what you're doing."

"Surrender the weapon, sir."

From behind the detective, a cop raised a device. One familiar to us from Keep's devoted care on Torlum.

A stun gun, though this was the type that had prongs that shot out.

The officer held it up.

"Drop the gun," Kenney shouted.

With a snarl, the chief swung his aim my way.

And fired.

Sin roared and dove at me, knocking us both down. Struan and Camden fell in front of us, creating a human shield.

At the same second, a buzz sounded. The stun gun activating.

The chief dropped, convulsing, the gun and his knife scattering.

From under a pile of my brothers, I took quick stock of my body. He'd fired at me.

But nothing hurt. There was no blood.

"Ye bunch of idiots," I yelped at my brothers. "Ye could've been shot."

Camden patted me down, his moves frantic despite his still-restrained hands. He dragged up my shirt and yanked out the phone.

"I'm not hurt." I shouldered him away.

He grinned and cuffed my head. Then his smile dropped, and he pointed behind.

A hole pierced the wall.

A second later, Cassie scampered from the plinth, snatched the knife from the floor, and dove into our pile of bodies. I lifted my arms around her and hugged her to me.

"Should I stab him?" the tiny girl asked.

For half a second, I indulged the thought. The impulsive, crazy, hacking to death of the chief. Death by a thousand cuts. We could all have a go. I'd bet his son would slice the deepest.

But there was a chance, the smallest hope that we

might get away with this.

I hugged Cassie closer. "No, sweetheart. He's in for a world of pain as it is."

Through the commotion in the middle of the room, with the cops focused on the downed chief and on McInver who argued at them, Arran came to me.

He helped me up and undid my handcuffs, I guessed with some kind of master key, then moved on to my brothers, releasing each of us in turn.

When he was finished, I pulled him aside. "I'm so sorry about your ma."

Someone had covered her body, but the gurgling had long stopped. The cut was too deep. She'd died as he'd watched on.

Arran's gaze remained dull. "Thank you."

Beyond our group, McInver returned to his wheelchair, grinning like he'd won the war. Detective Dickhead secured the police chief and came to us.

"We're taking our sister and leaving," I told him.

The corrupt bastard shook his head. "You can't walk out of here. And definitely not with a child. She'll go back into foster care. In fact, all of you will have to come with me."

I pushed Cassie behind us.

"Over my fucking dead body," Sin replied.

"All of ours," I added. "You won't take her."

Two cops stood behind the detective.

I was wrong. We had another fight on our hands.

The four of us stood shoulder to shoulder, protecting our sister. We hadn't come this far to lose her again. I couldn't allow it.

Then Arran shoved in front of me.

He held Detective Dickhead's gaze.

"What makes you think you're walking out of here and not in chains, Kenney?" the son of the chief questioned. "Don't think my father kept me ignorant of everything you got up to. I have evidence to put you away for years. A gun upstairs with your prints on it and a safe with footage my father took."

The cops in earshot exchanged glances.

Arran tilted his head, no humour, no softness, no forgiveness there.

The detective swallowed and glanced around at his support crew. "Go and see what that racket is outside."

They left, and he came back to Arran, his confident swagger gone.

"Fine. The warrants were a lie. Your father was building a case, but nothing is set in stone."

"Then let them go."

The detective shrugged. "I can't let them take the girl. She'll need to return to a foster care placement. In time, they can apply to the courts for visitation."

I wheeled around, but Cassie backed away.

"No, I won't go," she cried.

"I won't let them take you," I promised her.

A commotion came from the hall, and a man appeared in the doorway. Dressed like a butler, he spotted the chief on the floor and sucked in a dramatic breath.

Arran's gaze darkened. "Campbell," he ground out like a curse.

But my attention glued to the warrior who strode in behind him, knocking into the man's shoulder and sending him stumbling.

Summer entered the room like she owned it.

She cast a look down her nose at Campbell, who I remembered from her story had got physical with her, then at the chief. Her mouth curved in a beautiful smile. "Police Chief Daniels, please take me," she crooned.

The man revived, moaning from the electric shock but conscious.

"I'm right here, begging you for it, just like you asked," Summer taunted. "No? Then the deal is off. Maybe this time, you'll listen."

With one final look, she turned her back on him and sighted me. In her hands, she brandished a piece of paper. Held it up.

"A court order, signed tonight. Sin, you are now the legal parent of Cassie." She tilted her head at the little girl, peeking around me. "You're going home with your family."

Sin swung around and picked up Cassie, holding her to him like he'd fight anyone who came near. Summer handed him the court order, and he grabbed it and stormed away. The detective eyed the paper, but if he thought to check it, he changed his mind and let my brother barge out of the room of horrors.

Fuck. Holy fuck.

I hugged Summer hard. "As much as I hate seeing ye in this place, I love that you're here. How did ye swing that?"

She sighed against me. "Long story. I'll tell you all about it once Gordain's flown us home."

"Summer?" Arran approached once more, Campbell trailing after him.

"Take down the video," he demanded of the butler.

Campbell made a show of taking down the video of Summer and me. If it had done damage, there was nothing we could do about that. Summer's tightened features told me she'd already seen it.

"It doesn't matter now," she whispered to me alone.

A rush of awareness came to me. She was right. It didn't matter. It was over.

"Now apologise," Arran added.

"My sincere apologies, miss," Campbell spluttered.

The chief's son bared his teeth. "Now get the fuck out of my house."

"Sir?"

"I mean it. You're not welcome here anymore."

"But, but, sir, I've lived here all my life. I was born in a cottage on the estate. My father served your grandfather. I have nowhere else to go."

"Count yourself lucky I let you pack a bag. You have thirty minutes. If I see you here after that, I'll shoot you with my father's gun." Arran stepped back and glowered at the room. "That applies to everyone here. Get off my property."

From the doorway, Camden hollered for me, hurrying us up.

I turned back to Arran fast. "Thank ye for the help. For getting Summer to the jail to rescue my arse."

He shrugged. "Too little, too late."

"If ye want, I'll help ye burn this place to the ground."

He watched me for a moment then produced the tiniest hint of a smile. "I'll bear that offer in mind."

Arran walked away, snapping at a cop who pulled back the sheet on his mother's body.

"Leave her. I'll bury her myself."

I couldn't stick around to see if they let him care for her in that one final act.

46

Jamieson

We beat a fast retreat from Kendrick Manor. Gordain bundled us into the helicopter with a quick check over of me.

"Are ye sure ye weren't shot?"

"No, he missed."

"Thank fuck for that. Ye have no idea how that sounded from outside. Your band of warriors nearly rioted to reach ye."

As he slid the door closed, another helicopter landed.

Sebastian squinted at it then filled us in over the headphones. "A different police force. They've flown in another chief."

All the more reason for us to get out of there.

We abandoned McInver's cars, but by this point, the only thought echoing round my head was the need to get far away from all we'd been caught up in.

We'd gone from boys raised on the streets, to prisoners, to fighting for our lives against yet another person who wanted us dead.

"I thought I was going to die there," I muttered to Summer.

Around the helicopter's cab, my brothers all nodded or grumbled their agreement, their arms around their lasses.

I huffed a laugh, cluing in to the fact that everything I said, they could hear, too. Summer relaxed into my hold.

In the middle of us all, Cassie clung to Lottie. She hadn't said a word since our escape, just launched at the woman she considered a mother and who looked like she'd never let the little girl go.

In no time at all, Sebastian touched down in a field next to our beach hideaway.

Gordain climbed out. "If ye need to, come and stay in my castle. We'll take care of ye."

"We'll come, but we need some time alone first," Sin answered for all of us. "Do ye think anyone will come after us?"

"Hard to say how this will fall out. Lie low until you're sure."

Sin thanked the men and left them to fly home.

Outside the safe house, the fire pit still glowed. In Sin's arms and holding Lottie's hand, Cassie peered at it.

"Pretty, isn't it?" I told her.

Sin threw me a glance. "Oh, no. You're not making her a pyro."

"Sorry, Da," I groused back.

Outside the kitchen door, Cassie finally opened her mouth. "Are we home, Ma?"

Lottie took a shuddering breath and smiled. "Yes, my sweet girl. It is until we find a forever place. But with ye back, we're all finally home."

Emotion shook me.

My brothers and the lasses all looked the same.

Shaken up. Fucking floating on air.

Inside, everyone headed upstairs. In the morning, we'd talk. There was a lot to say. To worry about, and to prepare for. But a collective exhaustion held across us all.

"Back in a sec," Summer said, taking her sister by the hand and leading her down to the lounge. The overtones of a phone call made it back to me.

Lottie put Cassie into the shower, dousing her in conditioner to comb out her tangles, both giggling with their splashes. Sin and I carried a small bed into his and Lottie's room. The little girl drooped in her soft towels then yawned when Sin carried her to each door to say good night to us all.

"Watch her for a moment?" Sin asked me.

I agreed and gave Lottie a second to get her changed into one of her T-shirts to act as a nightdress, then sat on the floor of their room by Cassie's bed.

My brother and his girlfriend headed downstairs. I could guess why. They needed to reunite in private, same as I needed to do with Summer, whenever she was finished with her call.

In the meantime, I was more than happy to sit and just stare at our sister.

Cassie blinked owlishly. "Will ye still be here in the morning?"

"All of us will."

"Promise?"

"Swear to dog."

She gave me a tired smile. "Do ye mean God?"

"Nope." I reached for the bag of Cassie's things that I'd taken from the foster carer's home. Lottie had kept it with her, and the stuffed toy dog was on top. I handed it over.

Instantly, my sister grabbed it and tucked it under her arm so the dog's wee head poked out of the blankets. Without another word, she closed her eyes and drifted off, trusting us to protect her in her sleep.

After a couple of minutes, slender arms curled around me from behind.

Summer hugged me, and I twisted to sweep her around onto my lap. Silently, we guarded Cassie.

"Whenever we went into foster care," Summer whispered, "I'd sleep a lot."

"I did, too. It was the only safe place."

We didn't voice the natural conclusion. Cassie was going to take a long time to heal from her experiences. Luckily, she had a loving family to give her whatever she needed.

"We told Mum what the chief said," Summer confided.

"Is she okay?"

"She says so. She even said she wants to give evidence if a case is brought against him. We'll go and see her soon."

Sin and Lottie returned, the lass with her hair a mess, and my brother appearing one percent less furious.

We wished them good night and returned to our own room.

On our bed, with the lamp on and the curtains pulled, Summer tilted her head at me.

"Waiting," she quipped.

She extended her hand, my silver Zippo on her palm.

I'd given it to her for safekeeping, but right now, I had no interest in flames or waves. Only her.

I gestured at the bedside table to tell her to put it there, then shed my jeans in a flash.

Summer straightened then tutted at me. She patted the bed. "Let me."

I crawled to her and sat back on my haunches.

The woman I was in love with took a shaky breath then leaned in and kissed me.

I kept as still as I could, fighting the urge to throw her onto her back and dominate her. Tonight, she'd gone to unknown lengths to help me and my family. She battled demons here as well, touching me. Leading me.

Her kiss grew bolder, seductive.

I groaned against her lips, and she reached for my T-shirt, separating us only for the amount of time it took to get it over my head.

Then we were kissing again. Mouths fused like we never wanted to separate. I rolled onto my back, taking her with me. Summer shed her shirt and bra, placing my hands on her incredible tits. I squeezed her, moulded her, toying with her nipples. Under her, my dick hardened, and she rubbed against the bulge, driving me insane.

Then Summer abruptly lifted off me.

I grumbled my complaint, then shut my mouth as she

stripped her remaining clothes and yanked on the waistband of my boxers. I'd tossed them across the room and guided her back to my lap. Summer rose on her knees, fitted me to her entrance, and slid down.

I sucked in a breath, trying to think of anything to stop from coming in five seconds flat. She was leading this. Taking what she needed from me.

Nothing was hotter than watching her ride me.

Mesmerised, I interlaced our fingers and held her hands to my chest so she could use me as leverage. Summer worked me, rising and falling, chasing her good feeling.

My own pleasure went on pause while I watched her. Obsessed over every sound she gave up.

Then her pussy clamped down on me in a tight hold.

Summer moaned and arched her back, losing her rhythm.

Something broke in me, and I grabbed her hips and jacked into her. Her sounds of pleasure became louder, and she pulsed around me, her orgasm hitting fast.

A frenzy came over me. I'd forced myself to hold off so she could have me however she chose, but that restraint fled. Rising, I set her on her back with her legs over my shoulders, then I set a punishing rhythm, loving the slide in and out of her tight heat.

More than obsessed.

Completely in love.

The last thought broke me. I stilled, coming so hard my brain blipped out. I spilled inside her, shuddering, forgetting to breathe.

Then I collapsed down onto her, still hard inside.

Summer hugged me. "I'm so in love with you."

"I listened to the message. I'll play it every day until I die. And for the record, I've loved ye forever and I'll never stop."

I reached between us and found her clit, pressing onto her in firm circles. She notched her head against me and gasped, bringing her fingers to join mine.

I made her come again, this time with my cum in her. Feeling every spasm on my dick.

We slept hard, holding on like we never intended to let go.

47

Jamieson

We woke late and to the smell of food cooking. In the kitchen, the rest of the family was already up, Cassie at the head of the table and beaming at us all.

"I'm going to be a big sister," she chirped.

"I just told her the news a second ago," Lottie explained.

I curved around and kissed Cassie on the forehead. "You'll be the best big sister ever."

Her blue eyes fixed on Summer at my back.

"Cassie, meet Summer," I introduced. "Breeze is her big sister, and she's my girlfriend."

First time of ever saying that, the realisation hit home.

Summer passed me and knelt next to Cassie's seat, resting her chin on her hands. "You have the prettiest hair. When I was little, my sister would try to style my hair for me, but Breeze was never very good. So I went to hairdressing school and learned how to do all kinds of clever things. But I haven't had anyone to try my skills out on for ages."

Though Lottie had managed to detangle the worst of

Cassie's hair, it still looked like a family of rats had nested in it.

Cassie slid a glance at Lottie who gave her a nod.

She came back to Summer. "Ye can practice on my hair, if you're gentle."

Summer clapped and grinned. "I can't wait."

"Why don't ye come out to the beach with us?" Lottie asked. "We're going to paddle in the sea. Later, the boys are going to take Cassie surfing, but she needs some girl time first."

I got what she was trying to do. We needed to have a conversation, and it was better for Cassie if she didn't hear talk of danger and all the things we needed to do next to keep us from whatever reprisals were to come.

After breakfast, Summer and Lottie took Cassie for their walk, and the rest of us remained at the table.

Camden was the first to speak. "I was lying in bed this morning trying to work out where the fuck we are now. I don't mean physically, because at last, we're back together again. But that last night, that fucking shitshow…"

He drifted off, but the rest of us nodded, understanding him perfectly.

"Chief Daniels and his list of crimes against us has stuck with me most," Sin slowly added. "That can't go away. Can it?"

I raised an uncomfortable shoulder. "All those cops heard that list. They were his witnesses. The guarantee that we couldn't just walk away."

"Yeah," Struan cut in, "but they were all paid off, either by him or the detective, Kenney. From the way Kenney marched in, they all saw the video stream. Which meant they saw his demise. If ye were corrupt and your corrupt boss fell, what would ye do?"

I squinted at him, trying to follow his train of thought.

"Ye pass the buck," Struan explained. "Kenney didn't even blink before ordering Daniels to be tasered. He read him his rights in a heartbeat. Then he backed right up when Arran made his threat."

I hadn't even noticed the rights being read, caught up on all the other things going on.

My brother continued. "Sebastian told us another cop chief had been brought in, which meant judging by the speed of it, they'd already started investigating him from the exposé videos. The live stream confession by him and McInver brought things to a head."

That made sense.

My brain moved slowly. "So if Kenney, who I know as Detective Dickhead, was ready to put all the blame on the chief to save his own skin, what does that mean for his minions?"

Camden pointed at me. "They'd do the same. No one will stand behind the man taking the heat."

Breeze nodded. "I hope you're right, but we can't assume anything. I'm going to call the police and ask if they need witness statements. They let us go last night, but God knows why. Maybe because they didn't have the manpower there. If I talk to someone about the case against the chief, perhaps that will help us understand where we stand."

She hopped up and crossed to the other side of the kitchen, making her call.

I switched my gaze to Camden. "Can ye give me Arran's number?"

Somehow, one of my brothers had reclaimed our phones last night.

Camden did as I asked, and I placed a call to the chief's son, strolling outside, my gaze on the happy scene of the three lasses running in and out of the waves.

The phone rang several times. I was just about to kill the call, when finally, Arran answered.

"Who is it?" he said, flat.

"Jamieson. How are ye?"

He took a second to consider my question. "Worse."

He lost his mother and his father in one evening. His world had imploded. No shite.

"Want to come hang with us?" I asked.

"Maybe another time. Thanks for asking."

"What happened there after we left?"

Arran recited the story of the other chief of police sweeping in to take over the scene, just as Sebastian suspected. Detective Dickhead had scurried to make a story, pulling Arran aside to corroborate his version of events.

"The new account is that my father fell out with his business partner over their trafficking business, kidnapped his daughter, and tried to blackmail him and his sons. McInver was interviewed before being taken back to hospital. He happily went along with the tale, giving lengthy accounts of women who had been taken and all the gory details. His lawyer offered up a laptop with digital records. Looks like it's game over for Dad."

I stood on the edge of the beach, the sun warming me. "That can't be it. Ye were there. That list he read out, arson, murder."

"Will be quietly swept under the table," Arran interrupted. "I wasn't joking when I said I had material on Kenney. He will close those cases faster than my father ever opened them."

"No way. We can't just walk away from this."

"Why not? Others will. A huge sting operation can be claimed by the police who as we speak are shutting down the trafficking network of their dreams. Watch the news. They raided a port at dawn this morning. Dad brought women in on ships. He'll be fighting for his life and blaming it all on McInver. Kenney and the other people who he paid off won't help him. If he casts blame other ways, he'd have to prove it, and guess who's in control of his private files now? The son and heir who hates his guts and wants to see him rot. I've already destroyed anything relating to you."

Arran went quiet for a second. "I've got another call coming in. The funeral home. They wouldn't let me keep my mother's body, but I'm allowed to bury her. Got to go."

"Let us know and we'll come to the funeral," I promised, but he hung up.

It seemed unreal that all the drama and pain from our pasts could have come to an end. I returned to the house and updated my family, hearing from Breeze how her evidence probably wouldn't be needed.

Only time could prove anything to us now.

I headed outside again to find Summer, the rest of my family joining.

Sin made the trip out to get food, this time going to a major supermarket. He walked the aisles expecting to be grabbed. He returned to us unscathed.

We ate, took Cassie surfing, as promised, then repeated the same the next day.

And the next.

We were happy. In our bubble of a quiet slice of beach and with no one hunting us, that we knew of, we got to simply spend time together as a family. Cassie woke up every day brimming over with her smiles. She often cried in the night, climbing into bed to hug on to Lottie, but if that was the worst of her trauma, we'd got away lucky.

Best of all was the little surf light Sin picked up for her. A brilliant gold, it went with her everywhere, not just when we were out with her on our boards.

At last, she had her own colour, just like her brothers.

By the end of the week, the sense of danger that haunted us had begun to dissolve.

It came roaring back with a phone call from McInver's lawyer.

At the dinner table, Camden took the call.

"Golding. How are ye?" Camden asked.

"So kind of you to ask. I'm in the best of health. I'm sorry to interrupt you, but I'm unable to say the same of your father. I'm afraid the trials of the interviews he's given have taken their toll. He's rather unwell."

We all swapped glances.

"Does he want to see us?" Camden asked.

"Very much so. He requested all of you attend him. I

suggest at your earliest convenience. His doctors advise he has little time left."

"Holy shite, the old goat is dying," I muttered.

"It would appear so," Golding answered, hearing me.

"I'll let ye know," Camden said and ended the call.

Lottie held Sin's hand. "For what it's worth, I think ye should go."

Sin switched his gaze to her, listening.

"Not because he's owed anything as your father. He's done nothing to earn that right. But for your own sakes. If Golding is being truthful, this could be your last chance to air any burning questions, or just hear what he has to say."

Hugging on to her arm, Cassie wrinkled her nose. "Do I have to go?"

Sin reached out and stroked her hair, the black curls pretty and well defined after treatment from Summer's magic hands. "Only if ye want to. I can take any questions ye have to our father."

She glanced down then took a breath. "Does he remember my birth mother? That's all I'd like to know."

"Do ye remember her?" Lottie asked softly.

Cassie shook her head and huddled in.

"I'll go," Struan said. "If only to prove to myself that the miserable old fucker is on his way out."

One by one, the four of us brothers made the choice to see McInver.

The next morning, we set out, taking one of the remaining two cars.

None of us liked leaving the women, or Cassie, but true

to Arran's word, life was still quiet.

Following Golding's directions, we found the hospital and were led to an opulent room.

In the bed, our father appeared even more shrunken, his skin yellowed and paper thin.

Golding smiled softly at us. "You've made it just in time."

Four seats had been placed around the bed, so we fell into them, silence heavy over the room.

With a gasp, McInver opened his eyes. He trained his beady gaze first on Struan.

"Ah, at last. My eldest. Listen closely and don't interrupt. If ye wish it, I can take your mother from that jail." He jerked his focus to Sin. "Sinclair, I'll give ye a home to raise your family. The girl. My little Cassiopeia."

Sin leaned forward. "Cassie would like to know if ye remember her mother?"

"Her mother? Of course I don't. Don't interrupt." He bounced on, rambling. "Camden. Your mother I unfortunately can't forget. She once begged me to pay for plastic surgery to fix your face. I even looked into it, so that's yours for the taking. Want it?"

Camden's lips tweaked. "No, thanks."

"Ingrate! Onto ye, Jamieson, my firefly. Golding here has done extensive work in covering up your crimes. Grow up and throw away the matches."

I held in a retort. He wasn't done with me.

"I caught a glimpse of the video of ye and the girl." He leered. "The one who turned up with the black makeup like some kind of avenging angel. I liked the look on your face and the way ye had at her. We have that in common, the need to take out our venom on soft bodies. I'm proud of ye for that. Driven as much by lust and love, no? I lost a woman once. No one compared to her. If I'd raised ye, I would've taught ye how to use other bitches for your rage. Treat your sweetheart better or she won't come back."

With a grumble, he struggled to sit up, wheezing with the effort. Golding jumped to help, but the old man batted him away.

"I'm dying. It doesn't hurt, you'll be glad to hear. When I'm gone, you'll receive my will. I had great things planned for my boys. I'll be watching ye from Heaven to make sure they are carried out."

He gave the ghost of a cackle, sinking back down. Then his eyes fixed on the point in the ceiling, and his chest hitched.

A rattle came as he exhaled, and a machine next to his bed chimed an alert.

The door swished open, and a doctor rushed in. She peered at the machine and at our father, taking a minute over what was obvious to the rest of us.

McInver had died.

Right there in front of us.

With his final breaths, he'd made yet more wild statements. I knew exactly how we all felt about that.

"Time of death, ten forty-seven AM," the doctor declared. "I will give you time with your father, then if you come to my office, we can talk about the next steps for his funeral."

Golding took McInver's hand and pressed it gently.

"Farewell, sir."

He stood and left the room, his eyes wet.

I narrowed my eyes at the body. "What the fuck are we supposed to do?"

Struan snorted out a surprised laugh. "Be respectful, motherfucker."

I glanced at him in outrage. "Ye be respectful. Would ye talk over your father's dead body with a mouth like that?"

Camden stuffed his fist in his mouth, cracking up. "Don't. Golding will hear us. At least he's upset."

Sin rolled his eyes then stood. "McInver. Ye claimed you'll watch us from Heaven, but I'm pretty sure it'll be warmer where ye end up. I only hope we can go on to live better lives despite having ye as a da. Rest in peace."

"Rest in peace," the rest of us chorused.

"Motherfucker," I added at the end.

Sin reached out and cuffed me behind the ear while Camden and Struan fought back laughter. We took a minute to collect ourselves, then left McInver behind.

In the hall, Golding waited, still tearful. From his briefcase, he collected a folder. "In due course, I'll arrange for the reading of the will. This is a summary for you to view and understand in advance. Your father wished it. Before he passed, he requested several amendments. I'm afraid I was unable to enact them all in time, but I hope those which are now in place will go some way to you forgiving the sins of the past."

He held the folder out, and Sin accepted it, giving quiet thanks. Whatever it contained made no difference to us. We'd earned a freedom that now seemed possible.

We left the hospital behind without another look.

Epilogue

Jamieson

McInver's funeral took place at a small chapel in the grounds of the Great House. Our father was buried alongside countless relatives on a sunny September morning.

Other than us nine, and Golding, few others came. Only a housekeeper and a representative from the hospital made the trip. Then right before the service began, a man about our age showed up and slipped into the chapel.

Thea narrowed her eyes at him. "Henry Charterman," she hissed. "Distant relative. Ruthless cretin. Vulture here for the scraps."

We all ignored him.

For the first time ever, I felt the smallest grain of pity for McInver. He'd hurt so many, spreading his cruel reach without any sympathy, and the weirdest thing?

I was glad he hadn't died alone.

The vicar finished his waffling, and the ceremony was done. As one, we turned and exited the chapel.

Golding skittered to catch us. "I haven't heard from you regarding the will, yet," he said. "The hearing is happening now. If I could waylay you for just a few minutes, I promise I'll be swift."

"I'm on my way," Henry Charterman yipped, his polished shoes clipping on the chapel flagstones as he hustled in the direction of McInver's house.

None of us had read the will. That folder of paper had never interested us.

It had been too raw to face.

We got an extension for our stay at the holiday home, our safe house, and had been happily ignoring the real world, still waiting for the other shoe to drop.

Lottie's ma had called her with the news that she'd had a baby scan and all was well. She also reported gossip from Torlum. Jenkins had confessed to moving Keep's body. He'd dug her a grave in Torlum's churchyard, just like I'd guessed. Some of the islanders had witnessed it and would've told us if we'd stopped to listen.

They'd informed the visiting cops she'd been found dead and had been buried in accordance with island tradition. Aside from a warning and some paperwork, no investigation had begun. With any luck, she'd been left where she rotted.

Another of the doors closed.

Golding waited on our word.

I looked to my brothers, and we all shrugged, changing our direction for the mansion.

Summer held my hand, her face tipped towards the sun.

In time, I was going to ask her to marry me, but we were in no rush. She was mine for good, and I was hers. Inked into my skin and owner of my heart. Nothing would ever change that.

In front of the house, I paused, taking in the work that had been done since I last saw the place. The rubble had been cleared on the ruined wing, the rebuild continuing. Golding led us inside to the hall. The throne still sat in its position, hiding the basement where God knows what McInver had done beyond host his catalogue.

Henry Charterman spun around, taking in the place. "I made quite the impression on Mr McInver on my last visit. I'm sure the elderly gentleman remembered me in his generous way. I am, of course, his nephew."

"Second cousin's son," Thea amended with an eye roll.

"I don't know why you're being like that. I helped you with the journalist," Henry bit back, his friendly act dropping.

Thea stilled. "Did you think that changed anything? Your sister stabbed my boyfriend."

"Well, his brother shot my dad!"

Sin slowly turned his heavy gaze on the blond man.

Henry's shoulders rose, and he jerked his gaze away, his cheeks reddening.

I squinted at Golding, standing at the front of the party. He caught my eye and raised a wry eyebrow.

Seemed like Henry was out of luck.

The lawyer commenced the legal explanation, keeping the rambling to a minimum as promised. "Now to the crux of it. The Great House, the estate, and extensive holdings, all contents, personal possessions, and funds in various accounts, are to be split five ways between the following. Struan Gallagher, Sinclair Stone, Camden Marshall, Jamieson Buchanan, and Cassiopeia Archer."

He closed the folder.

Cassie squeaked. "I get something, too?"

Lottie squeezed her. "Of course ye do."

Henry Charterman's jaw dropped. "That's it? That's all he had to say?"

Golding nodded.

"It's ours, all of this?" I asked.

"Precisely that. As I mentioned, your father had several other conditions, but we were unable to enter them into the will. One was a demand for you all to take his name. That kind of thing. The simple handing over of property was thankfully achieved in time."

He'd done that for us. Golding had simplified McInver's scheming at the last hurdle.

"Good man," I told him.

The lawyer ducked his head, smiling.

"New question," I said. "This place is ours to do with what we like, correct?"

"Precisely," Golding agreed.

"Even burn it down?"

Beside me, Summer gave a soft laugh.

"If you wish."

"You can't," Henry yelped.

"Why not?" I flicked my Zippo wheel, summoning

sparks. "Ye heard the man."

Henry whipped a look at the rest of us then sprinted to the side of the room, grabbed a vase from on top of a mantlepiece, and fled outside.

I burst out laughing, and Thea stormed to the door to watch him go.

"We should burn it down just to spite him," she said.

"I'll let you get on with enjoying your home. Call me whenever you need to," Golding said quietly, then slipped away.

I turned on the spot, taking the place in, and hugged Summer to me. "For the love of all that is holy. This place is ours. What do we do? I'm half serious about incinerating the lot."

"I'm down," Camden agreed. "Whatever it started as, under McInver's reign, it became a place of abuse."

Breeze nodded along, but her gaze flitted to the door. "There's a beautiful library upstairs. Can we save the books first?"

Sin flattened his lips. "There's an oil painting of a man who looks just like me. I'd happily see that burn after we've saved the library."

Struan shrugged. "I don't care what happens to the place."

Cassie took a short inhale, her eyes round, beseeching us. "We can't burn it. This is our forever home. Didn't ye hear? Our father left it to us. I want to live here. All of us together, like we promised. Then we can spend weekends at the beach house."

I wrinkled my nose. "This isn't a nice place."

"But it could be. He doesn't live here anymore. We will," she begged.

We stood there and let the thought soak in. All of a sudden, we'd been gifted a permanent home. Even if we only ever camped in the grounds, it was ours.

Then Camden broke away from the group. "Whether we do or don't commit grand arson on the place, that chair needs to be in flames on the lawn." He booted the throne, smacking into it over and over again until it came off its screws. Then he dragged the heavy-assed thing across the hall with screeches that echoed to the rafters.

I jogged to catch up with him and grasped the other side. Together, we carried it out the front and tossed it to the grass, cracking the wood.

A thought came to me. The best idea.

"Every bed," I called to my family, convening at the door. "Every chair. Every flipping curtain," I cautioned my language for Cassie's sake. "I don't care if it takes us a week, but those things are going up in flames."

Summer grinned. "That sounds fun."

My brothers, Thea, Lottie, and Breeze broke out amused expressions.

"Cassie," I asked. "Is that allowed?"

"A bonfire of old things? Yes!"

At last, we were united by McInver. "Everyone grab something."

It took us three days to remove every item that we judged McInver to have tainted. Benches, carved tables, elaborately decorated four posters. We didn't give a fuck if it was antique. If he'd had the chance to hurt a woman on it, that piece of furniture was dead to us.

The pile grew, stacked high.

Then on a mild evening, in the grounds of our house, we were finally ready to send it all to ash.

We made a party out of it.

Celebrated with beer and food.

We invited Gordain, Max, and Sebastian over, and they drank with us, eyebrows raised at what we'd done but easy acceptance, too.

"Glad to have ye as neighbours," Gordain said. "So long as this is the only fire I have to worry about. I have a nephew-in-law who's a carpenter. He can help ye decorate."

"Not like ye can't afford more furniture, now you're a rich arsehole," Max joked with Struan.

It was true. From information Golding sent after the reading of the will, we had money. More than seemed real. The lawyer had already separated out a huge sum that had to go to the court as the proceeds of crime. But with the rest, we asked Golding to halve it, sharing it anonymously with a women's shelter in Inverness.

It still left more than enough for us to rebuild the house however we wanted, then fund whatever education or jobs the rest of us chose to pursue. Lottie's baby would never know the dark situations we'd been raised in. He or she would have the perfect wee cot and grow up surrounded by the best family I ever could have asked for.

The fire lit.

I raised a beer to it, my first of the evening.

It grew, catching the soft furnishings easily. The gentle autumn wind fed it, and every mattress and padded seat burned.

I backed up, wishing I could have set the whole house ablaze, but I needed my family to be happy more.

From the mean streets to a fucking mansion.

We had a pretty good chance.

To the tune of Gordain trying to persuade my brothers to join the local mountain rescue service, my phone rang. I took it from my pocket to see Arran's name on the screen

"I'd appreciate the visit you mentioned," the chief's son told me.

I caught Summer's eye, and she came over. Next week, we'd empty out her bedsit in Leith. Breeze was doing the same with her flat in central Edinburgh. There was no going back for any of us.

"Want to disappear with me for an hour or two on a mission?"

"Always."

"Be there in thirty," I said to Arran and hung up.

In the Aston Martin that was now legally mine, holy fuck, I drove us through the Cairngorms to Kendrick Manor.

Last time we'd come to the ugly grey manor house, with its dour, imposing architecture, it was with the expectation we might never leave.

I grinned at how that had turned out. The chief carried off by his own officers, foaming at the mouth and with the world aware of all he and his list had done. Fuck that guy. Prison was too good for him.

Arran met us outside. He slung a backpack into his car.

"Going somewhere?" I asked.

He shrugged. "Anywhere other than here." Then his gaze jumped past the house.

I followed it to a small area surrounded by railings.

A graveyard.

"I buried my mother yesterday."

Ah, finally the new chief had released the body, held as evidence for a while.

"Shite. Sorry, man. We would've come," I said.

Summer hitched her breath. She'd cried for Divine, whose real name we'd discovered was Audrey. Though she'd seen a body on the floor when she'd run in, brandishing Cassie's custody papers, she'd had no clue who'd died.

I'd done a lot of reassurance that it wasn't her fault.

I knew she felt it was from the video.

"I'm so sorry you lost her," she said to Arran. "And for my part in it."

His grey eyes showed only pain. "You did nothing wrong. That's all on my dad. All those years, she was right here in front of me, and I had no clue. I learned more about her from the video she made than from all the times we met before."

Summer sniffed and stared at her feet. "I'll go sit with her for a while and say goodbye. Without her, I wouldn't be here. She was the best."

Arran watched her go, a muscle in his jaw ticking. When we were alone, he spoke again. "Audrey had another child. I'm a brother now, though I don't know to who. All I could find out is someone's taking care of him or her but nothing more."

"Congratulations. My family is my world. I hope you can find the kid."

But I got the strong sense that despite his discovery, Arran was reeling and lost. His father had been charged with multiple crimes and publicly trashed, the press having a field day over each revelation. Vanessa at the nightclub had done a runner, but a couple of high-profile names had been leaked, presumably by McInver, and they'd thrown all the shade at the chief. However Arran felt about him, his world was upside down.

"Are ye okay? Is anyone threatening ye?" I asked.

"Don't worry about me."

"I was serious about staying with us. I've been worrying about Kenney coming after ye."

His lip curled. "Don't worry about that fucktard. Want to know what I have on him?"

At my nod, he continued.

"He runs a group of cops who moonlight as security guards. They're worse than corrupt and regularly do the heavy lifting of disposing of bodies. Some worked for McInver. My father employed them and enabled them but kept evidence for his own purposes. Guess who owns that now."

Which was how Arran had power over Kenney. "Dangerous position to be in," I muttered.

"Maybe. But I don't want your worry. I called to ask for your help."

"Name it."

"Every week, my father brought women here. Mostly, they were paid. Sometimes, they weren't. Sometimes, like my mother, he abused them. I heard things, saw things." A shudder ran through him. "I can't allow this place to stand any longer."

I held his gaze.

This was exactly what I'd wanted to do at McInver's, and which I'd half managed at my first attempt. I'd felt better and better since the bonfire, like I could have a home I loved simply because my family were there. A cleansing in a different way.

I could explain that to him.

But I was breathless with the picture he painted.

All of that happening here. The house was tainted in every way.

I produced the orange lighter Summer had once given me and handed it over, wielding my Zippo in the other hand, then gave Arran my happiest, demonic smile. "Give me the order."

"Burn it down."

The End.

To read a bonus scene giving a glimpse into the family's future (and a tiny special delivery for Sin and Lottie), visit jolievines.com/extras

Interested in Sebastian's story? Go devour *Lion Heart*.

Max's twisted tale is told in *Betrayed*.

Want to hear what happens next with Arran? Tell me

you need his story, and I might just write it.

ACKNOWLEDGEMENTS

Dear reader,

We did it! The story of the *Dark Island Scots* boys has come to an end. This series and our found family rocked me to my core. You've probably already heard me talk about how powerful this became and how it took over my world. While I was busy working on another series, Struan derailed my thinking and forced me to write his story. Then Sinclair commanded every bit of my attention, Camden grabbed me by the heartstrings, and Jamieson...

This man.

His impulsiveness, his infectious grin, his love for life (and for burning things) – he really brought the series to a close in style.

I always knew he'd be trouble.

Summer was a surprise, particularly in how she matched his energy so perfectly. Even in the depths of a very dark place emotionally, she fought to own herself once again, then her actions at the end brought a final win for the family that cemented her place among them.

What a ride. What an all-out wild story with more twists and turns than a Scottish country lane.

Anyone for a circle surfer tattoo?

The more serious side to the plot around the trafficking and coercion of women is centred in reality. There are few happy endings for those who end up in this system. As always, my default view with any telling is to believe her.

As you'll see from the end, we've left off with an intriguing situation for Arran. At 17, he's alone, one parent jailed and the other dead. He's homeless but not without family, if he can discover the whereabouts of his lost sibling, and definitely not friendless as the DIS family would undoubtedly step up for him.

Want more of Arran? You're going to need to let me know. Email me at jolie at jolievines dot com to tell me, and I might add his story to my list of upcoming projects.

If you liked ex-con pilot Sebastian and were intrigued by his story, you can read it now in Lion Heart.

As always, my thanks go to Elle Thorpe and Zoe Ashwood, Sara Massery, Shellie M, and Liz Parker for being my core team and the very bestest.

Cleo Moran makes amazing graphics as well as beautifully formatted copies, Natasha Snow provides wonderful covers, Emmy Ellis is my expert editor, and Lori Parks proofreads to perfection.

My ARC and Street Team are a source of joy and keep me going with their kind words, posts, and encouragement.

Narrators Zara Hampton-Brown and Zachary Webber do an incredible job reading this series, and it was their voices I heard when writing these scenes.

Join my Facebook reader group if you like to talk books (Jolie's Fall Hard Fans). Or add yourself to my newsletter to never miss a new release announcement.

My final words go to my husband and son. Both gave me space to work late into the evening to bring this book in on time but waited with open arms when I needed a hug.

Jolie <3

ALSO BY JOLIE VINES

Marry the Scot series

1) Storm the Castle

2) Love Most, Say Least

3) Hero

4) Picture This

5) Oh Baby

Wild Scots series

1) Hard Nox

2) Perfect Storm

3) Lion Heart

4) Fallen Snow

5) Stubborn Spark

Wild Mountain Scots series

1) Obsessed

2) Hunted

3) Stolen

4) Betrayed

5) Tormented

Dark Island Scots series

1) Ruin

2) Sin

3) Scar

4) Burn

Standalones

Cocky Kilt:

a Cocky Hero Club Novel

Race You:

An Office-Based Enemies-to-Lovers Romance

Fight For Us:

a Second-Chance Military Romantic Suspense

Visit and follow my Amazon page for all new releases
https://amazon.com/author/jolievines

Add yourself to my insider list to make sure you don't miss
my publishing news

https://www.jolievines.com/newsletter

ABOUT THE AUTHOR

JOLIE VINES is a romance author who lives in the UK with her husband and son.

Jolie loves her heroes to be one-woman guys.

Whether they are a brooding pilot (Gordain in Hero), a wrongfully imprisoned rich boy (Sebastian in Lion Heart), or a tormented twin (Max in Betrayed), they will adore their heroine until the end of time.

Her favourite pastime is wrecking emotions, then making up for it by giving her imaginary friends deep and meaningful happily ever afters.

Have you found all of Jolie's Scots?

Visit her page on Amazon and join her ever active Fall Hard Facebook group.